DISPENSATION:
LATTER-DAY FICTION

DISPENSATION: LATTER-DAY FICTION

Edited by Angela Hallstrom

With an introduction by Margaret Blair Young

ZARAHEMLA BOOKS

Provo, Utah

Copyright © 2010 by Zarahemla Books. Individual stories used with permission of the copyright proprietors.

ISBN 978-0-9843603-0-7

Cover design by Jason Robinson.

All rights reserved.
Printed in the U.S.A.

Published by
Zarahemla Books
869 East 2680 North
Provo, UT 84604
info@zarahemlabooks.com
ZarahemlaBooks.com

For Eugene England
1933–2001

CONTENTS

PREFACE

I WAS A TWENTY-YEAR-OLD BYU English major in 1992, the year Eugene England's seminal collection of Mormon short fiction, *Bright Angels and Familiars*, was published. At the time I had very little knowledge of—and, frankly, very little interest in—stories written by, for, or about Latter-day Saints. I had some familiarity with Mormon novels: Nephi Anderson's 1898 classic *Added Upon*, Maureen Whipple's 1941 polygamy novel *The Giant Joshua*, Jack Weyland's adolescent romance *Charly* (required reading for Mormon teenage girls in the 1980s). But Mormon short stories? The only ones I'd ever read had been published in the church's magazine for teens, the *New Era*, and while occasionally I found those stories entertaining or even instructional, nobody pretended they were great literature. No, if I wanted literary short stories, I looked to Flannery O'Connor or John Updike or Raymond Carver. I had no idea that vibrant, compelling, literary Mormon short fiction even existed.

Eugene England was my professor when *Bright Angels* was published, and out of respect for him I found some wiggle room in my college-student budget and bought the anthology. I remember my skepticism: if great short fiction was being written by Mormons or about Mormonism, why hadn't I, an English major at Brigham Young University, heard about it? But as soon as I opened *Bright Angels* and started reading, my skepticism turned to excitement. These stories were *good*. And they were about my culture, my community, my belief system. They resonated in a way I'd never experienced before.

Although immersing oneself in a completely foreign place or time is one of the fundamental pleasures of reading good literature, recognizing oneself in a work of fiction is an exhilarating experience, too. Reading *Bright Angels* at that time in my life was a revelation to me. And, yes, "a revelation to me" is a hackneyed phrase, but I believe the term *revelation* contains a significance here beyond cliché. In the introduction to *Bright Angels*, England writes, "Mormonism insists that divinity continues to reveal [truths] to prophets and further understanding of [these truths] to all people. One crucial way such insight can come, I believe, is through the telling of stories, and the stories here are such revelations" (xix). As a Latter-day Saint, I believed then—and continue to believe today—in the revelation England describes, and my experience with *Bright Angels* expanded my understanding and opened up possibilities that hadn't existed before I read those stories about my own people.

It has been seventeen years since the publication of *Bright Angels and Familiars*, and in that time the quantity and quality of Mormon literature has continued to increase. The genre of the short story, in particular, has seen tremendous growth, and dozens of writers with connections to Mormonism are publishing excellent short fiction in critically acclaimed collections, prestigious national literary journals, and high-quality magazines specific to the Mormon market. Some of these stories are written with a mostly LDS audience in mind and some of them are not, but no matter the intended readership, there's no doubt that excellent fiction written by, for, or about Latter-day Saints is more available than ever before.

Unfortunately, most of this fiction hasn't received the attention it deserves because it's *short* fiction, and short fiction is often ignored. Of course, it's not just Latter-day Saints who tend to ignore the short story. The publishing industry as a whole is leery of the genre—understandably, I suppose, since the average reader isn't as inclined to pick up a short-fiction collection as he or she is to purchase a nice, fat novel. In a rejection I received for my own novel-in-stories, one potential publisher put it bluntly when he said, "Short stories are the kiss of death." Speaking in terms of pure economics, that publisher has a point. Writing short fiction—or selling short fiction—can be a terrible way to try and make a buck. But in terms of sheer artistic pleasure, I find few things more life-affirming, more vital, than a finely wrought short story. And some of the best short stories I've ever read appear in this anthology.

The fiction in *Dispensation* represents a sample of the best Mormon short stories published in literary journals or short-fiction collections since the late 1990s. Chris Bigelow at Zarahemla Books and I agreed we should focus on contemporary fiction: *Bright Angels* and other anthologies have done a good job familiarizing readers with Mormon fiction's past, but we wanted to emphasize the startling talent displayed by those currently writing. So, for almost a year, I immersed myself in LDS fiction. I filled my office with back issues of Mormon journals such as *Sunstone, Dialogue*, and *Irreantum*; I lined my personal bookshelves with award-winning short-story collections by authors I'd loved for years, as well as some I'd heard of but never read; I searched out the work of writers with established reputations, and dug around for lesser-known gems by young writers whose careers were just beginning. Although I ended up plowing through my fair share of mediocre fiction, I found so many stories that moved me or challenged me or thrilled me that my most difficult task became deciding which stories to include. I had to make some hard choices, and I wish we could have included every worthy story, but I believe *Dispensation* is representative of the best of the best in contemporary Mormon short fiction.

Every story in this anthology is Mormon in some way. Each writer, as well, has either religious or cultural ties to Mormonism, enabling him or her to write from personal experience about a theology and a people that remain mysterious to so many. Most stories feature overtly Mormon characters or Mormon settings, and every story, in my opinion, contains Mormon themes. What constitutes a "Mormon theme" is an open question, of course, and some readers might be surprised to find stories in this collection that deal frankly with doubt and sadness and sin. While many of the stories in *Dispensation* explore the conflict inherent in mortal life, I believe hope threads its way throughout the book, perhaps because so many stories acknowledge the influence of a world beyond the troubled one in which we live.

But even though a story's "Mormonness" influenced whether or not I felt it belonged in *Dispensation*, more than anything I wanted these stories to represent quality writing. As one who writes and edits fiction with Mormon elements, I'm keenly aware of the genre's lackluster reputation. LDS fiction is often maligned as trite or clumsy or lacking in sophistication, and sometimes with good reason. But I believe this anthology can stand as an emphatic example of the excellence—

brilliance, even—that is possible when writing with Mormonism in mind.

The stories in *Dispensation* deserve a wide readership, beyond the small cadre of loyal readers of Mormon literature. I hope these stories will reach Mormons who love good books but have steered clear of LDS fiction due to doubts about its quality. I also hope this anthology extends beyond the borders of Mormonism, and that those unfamiliar with the Latter-day Saints will come away from these stories convinced of the universality of human experience. Ultimately, though, I don't care too much about *why* these stories are read. I'm just glad they will continue to be. I hope you enjoy them as much as I do.

—Angela Hallstrom

INTRODUCTION

Margaret Blair Young

This is simply a splendid anthology of short fiction. The fact that it's written by Mormons or writers coming from the Mormon tradition makes it intriguing as a cultural representation, but it stands on its own as a collection of fine literature. It continues the vision and efforts initiated by Neal Lambert and Richard Cracroft, when they published *Twenty-Two Young Mormon Writers* (poetry and short stories) in 1975. *Greening Wheat*, edited by Levi Peterson, followed in 1983, featuring fifteen excellent Mormon-themed stories. Then, in 1992, Eugene England, the great champion of Mormon literature (and founder of courses on the subject at Brigham Young University and at Utah Valley University), edited the sweeping anthology *Bright Angels and Familiars*, which included stories spanning the distance from the "Lost Generation" (Maurine Whipple and Virginia Sorensen) to LDS writers just coming onto the scene, such as John Bennion and Phyllis Barber. Orson Scott Card and David Dollahite gathered good Mormon fiction on family life in their 1994 anthology, *Turning Hearts*. And now, in *Dispensation: Latter-day Fiction*, Angela Hallstrom has assembled twenty-eight gems—each a star in a brilliant constellation. This particular collection is a pinnacle. Metaphorically speaking, it represents the harvest of that greening wheat which Levi Peterson bundled twenty-five years ago.

The temptation for writers working within a religious framework is to let a dogmatic agenda form the story, rather than allowing fleshed-out characters to guide it to a conclusion which is rarely tidy and never preachy. Too often, Mormon writers resolve hard questions with a prayer and a paragraph, rather than allowing characters their inalienable right to grapple with their choices and their conflicts. Not one of these stories falls for such easy outs. In each, the language flows; the characters ring true; the plots pull us into the story's core; and the structure satisfies. We easily suspend our disbelief because we love the people who inhabit these stories, we believe what they say and enjoy how they say it, and we find that their circumstances are familiar—even if the fiction takes us beyond earth or includes episodes we haven't ourselves imagined. Thus disarmed of any resistance to cliché, predictability, or strained dialogue, we are led to contemplate new possibilities and to plumb our compassion. And we are constantly, delightfully surprised by the fresh touches in each story: a word we wouldn't have expected but which is simply the perfect choice; a plot point we wouldn't have anticipated but which makes sense and invites us to deeper examination of the story and of ourselves; dialogue so true to what we hear in our day-to-day lives that we must pay attention—not only to the story, but to the voices we think we already know. I am especially pleased that several of the stories take us beyond the center of Mormonism in the U.S. West and into distant lands.

Paul Rawlins, for example, takes us to South Africa during the turbulent years made inevitable by apartheid. A Mormon missionary, separated from his companion, finds himself in the garden of a black farmer. The farmer's own son has been killed by whites, and his grandson wants the missionary to suffer. The missionary looks at his surroundings. "*Streets and houses full of people whom he loved and feared, an alien world of stupefying want where he could labor but could not live, where some would kill him and some would call him angel, and he, with his imperfect heart, could not tell one from the other and probably could not love both.*" The quandary he faces suggests the most probing and intimate questions any person of faith must answer. And the climactic epiphany is among the most beautiful I've ever read.

Also set in South Africa is Todd Robert Petersen's "Quietly." Petersen gives us an intense, provocative piece about John, a Zimbabwean, who goes into South Africa to dedicate a grave. The violence and the possibility of violence provide an undercurrent throughout the story: "*Marie had found her husband hanging upside down in a tree three days earlier, fastened by his ankles to the limbs with yellow and black electrical wire. She told the branch president that Immanuel had been gone all night, that they were both newly baptized after having met two American missionaries in Pretoria.*" In

"Quietly," Petersen insists that we consider stories we might want to ignore—but which, in many ways, define our humanity and give us a pattern for hope. Laura McCune-Poplin's "Salvation" takes us to France, where sister missionaries (one a compulsive list maker) try to adjust to the country and to each other. Juxtaposed, a French woman deals with her husband—who is also a compulsive list maker. The little details of life—even troubled life—make the stories of both companionships compelling and convincing.

Several of the stories (including my own contribution, "Zoo Sounds") show us pieces of family life, often examining the relationships between mothers and their children, as well as women's choices—sometimes firmly placed within Mormonism and sometimes rubbing against it.

In "Out of the Woods," Karen Rosenbaum introduces us to Carma, a woman with rheumatoid arthritis, who ponders the ways her illness and decisions—including the decision to not participate in Mormonism—have impacted her family. She watches her gifted daughter perform in *Into the Woods* and thinks about her other daughter—who has chosen the faith Carma rejected and married in a ceremony Carma could not witness. The narrator invites us into Carma's world: "*Eight years ago now. That whole year the arthritis flared and nothing helped and nobody slept well. . . . Dan was shocked when Carma asked if he wanted to divorce her and find someone who could believe as he believed, who could join him in that hierarchical hereafter. And she was grateful that he protected her, as he must have done, from visits by those who wanted to persuade her that she was ruining her family's chances for salvation.*"

Lisa Madsen Rubilar's "Obbligato" is another tender piece about a woman's choices. A successful musician comes home to her mother and finds her life a lovely obbligato to the gifts her mother, a "lover of gardens," has given her. The narrative invites contemplation: "*And you realize that your kitchen's still spotless, despite all the cooking Mother's done in there, and you know she's keeping it that way, and she's doing it for you, out of love for you, like when she washed dishes at midnight because you were tired; because you were practicing; because you had a gift. And a gift takes precedence. But you have to pay. If your mother taught you anything, she taught you that.*"

Further exploring women's choices, Helen Walker Jones writes about an opera-loving teenager with an attractive but floundering mother in "Voluptuous." The voices in the story are pitch-perfect. "*I never want to be fifty-two years old, divorced, and bopping at the disco with my pathetic, face-lifted girlfriends*," says the daughter—and we can hear her easily. This is an initiation story, full of complex and beautifully explored relationships.

One of my favorites in this collection is "Clothing Esther" by Lisa Torcasso Downing. It is the moving tale of a woman (Mary) dressing her mother-in-law's dead body and reflecting on the journey the two of them have shared, from the time of Mary's unplanned pregnancy and quick wedding to the end of the mother-in-law's life. It is a story evocative of Ruth and Naomi and depicts a relationship as tender as the biblical one.

Following the theme of mother-child relationships, Eric Samuelsen (best known as a playwright but gifted in all literary genres) gives us "Miracle"—the often humorous and always intriguing story of an elderly woman and her forty-three-year-old daughter who invite a bum to dinner. Is it a miracle that circumstances have converged to let them feast together, or is this unusual Sunday meal the beginning of something cataclysmic? Samuelsen amuses his reader with wonderfully realized characters as he unfolds the story with dramatic irony: the reader can see beyond what the characters themselves are seeing.

Working within a similar circumstance but with very different characters, Darin Cozzens gives us "Light of the New Day," in which an aging mama's boy (Hewell) conducts a subtle courtship with a Mexican meter checker—covertly leaving her gifts and eventually exchanging notes. Hewell, vaguely reminiscent of Harper Lee's Boo Radley, invites not only the meter checker but the reader to fall in love with him. I found the invitation irresistible.

Other stories explore dimensions of marriage. Bruce Jorgensen's "Measures of Music" is, as the title promises, a lyrical composition, the measured story of a marriage, of growing comfort and strange discomfort. Jorgensen's writing is as musical as the title suggests: "*She watched the stream. She saw it toss small boulders into the air, heard it mumble. She thought of the empty houses under Thistle Lake and the stripped rooms with water gliding through windows and doors, secret along halls, up stairwells on obscure errands. . . . The voice of water and silt and stones fluttering on her skin, strum-*

ming her tendons, jarring the beat of her blood." The story lingers in the mind like the last chords of a cantata.

"Who Brought Forth This Christmas Demon" by Larry Menlove leads us into the despair of a seller of Christmas trees whose wife has left him at the height of tree-selling season. He hires a young man, Brick, and soon realizes that Brick has his own sins and heartbreak to negotiate. Surely speaking for both men, Brick says, *"I am in the process of forgiveness or of damnation. I often wonder which path I am on."* The story unfolds with perfect pacing toward a fully satisfying conclusion.

Mental illness, also a reality which demands acknowledgment, is Angela Hallstrom's subject in another work about marriage: "Thanksgiving." Through multiple points of view, Hallstrom masterfully crafts the story of Beth and her bipolar husband, Kyle. Beth agonizes over her choice to leave Kyle, and Kyle contemplates snowflakes as a Thanksgiving feast winds down and guests leave—or appear, uninvited. "Thanksgiving" is a devastatingly beautiful, heart-wrenching work.

Lewis Horne likewise talks about guests—invited by some, categorically uninvited by others. Horne, whose stories have been selected for *The Best American Short Stories* series, shows his skill in "Healthy Partners." The story is about Bruden, a down-on-his-luck panhandler who accepts an invitation for a home-cooked meal from a good Mormon man. At the home, he meets an apparently ideal family—unaware that his presence has ignited old conflicts about privacy versus the Christian call to compassion. Ultimately, Bruden himself will have to choose between opposing calls for loyalty. We have a sense that there's an entire novel within the tight prose of this piece.

Since this anthology is a Mormon one, the theme of polygamy must come up somewhere amidst the family stories. Thanks to Phyllis Barber, it does. In "Bread for Gunnar," Barber explores a plural marriage with her characteristic incisiveness and empathy. Anna, Gunnar's first wife, contemplates the upcoming change in their family, which insinuates itself into her dreams: "The Principle, *I said to myself all night as I tried to find a place in the bed where sleep would bless my churning mind. After a time, the words became a rhythm in my head:* prin-ci-ple, prin-ci-ple, *like the wheels on the train I could hear on clear nights. I finally dropped into a restless sleep where I saw a crowd of women keeping me from Heber. They pushed me away and held his hands in vise grips. He's ours now, they said. He's mine, I shouted back, he's mine! I shouted all night in my dreams."*

Dispensation also contains superb speculative fiction. Stephen Tuttle's "The Weather Here" is reminiscent of Cormac McCarthy, a sparely written masterpiece set in a post-apocalyptic world. The prose is stark: *"He said that we needed the rain to cleanse ourselves, that it was a metaphor for something, and that the fleas were also a metaphor but that he wasn't sure what they stood for."* Tuttle creates a world and a pervasive mood in this story.

Set in a far more distant place, Lee Nelson's "Hymnal" is a story which Ray Bradbury would surely be proud to include in any anthology he might edit. This work depicts the end of the universe, juxtaposed with redemptive words from Tennyson as the few remaining survivors take *"one last look."* One line from this story could well be the justification for the anthology as a whole: *"They're just words strung together. And yet, there's a power in them that could light up a night sky. Find some way to save the words."*

Certainly, the words in Darrell Spencer's "Blood Work" are worth saving and savoring. Spencer, a renowned wordsmith, provides pleasant verbal jolts and fresh takes on language—and especially Mormon language—throughout his story. On the surface, "Blood Work" is simply about a jogger, J. J., who is told by a faithful Mormon woman that she'll *"put his hamstring in the temple"* for healing (meaning that she'll put his hamstring on the prayer rolls). In fact, the story is about many kinds of running and compels the reader to run with the language, sentence by sentence. Spencer's stories always do.

Many writing instructors tell their students that there are really only two stories: A man goes on a journey; a stranger comes to town. Of course, both stories are really the same story—with the perspective switched. In Matthew James Babcock's "The Walker," the stranger and the man on the journey merge brilliantly. Babcock takes us into the mind of a man awaiting the results of his wife's biopsy and longing to repeat the many "firsts" he has lived (*"First once again, we want to kiss someone beautiful who loved us outside the high school Valentine Formal . . ."*), sometimes catching a glimpse of an evanescent figure who seems to have been observing him throughout his life.

Coke Newell gives us a classic, wonderfully crafted journey story in "Trusting Lilly," as a traveler meets and falls in love with a Mormon girl. She, too, is on a journey, and leaves him when "Sangre de Cristo"—a place named for the blood of Christ—beckons her home. *"At some point,"* says the protagonist, *"I realized I was digging in Mormon soil, planting a piece of my heart. I didn't know much else, but by then I'd had some time to look at life with a long lens, and so I sniffed the wind, threw a few pebbles in the creek, and headed back to the rail yard as lonely as I've ever been."* Other stories in this anthology have unusual takes on Mormon themes, issues, or settings. Jack Harrell's "Calling and Election" will undoubtedly start conversations about righteousness and deception. In it, a man is informed that his "calling and election" have been made sure—but he must sign a paper accepting everything such elevation entails. The consequences prove incalculable. *"Even your goodness is your enemy,"* he is told—and the reader is left to ponder, and almost certainly to discuss.

Arianne Cope's "White Shell" is important not just because of its quality, but because it addresses a time in recent Mormon history which is being quickly forgotten. Cope takes us to the beginnings of the Indian placement program, wherein white, Mormon families fostered Native American children, removing them entirely from their own culture. Mary, a seven-year-old Navajo, tries to adjust to a world in which she is a "Lamanite." The narrator describes the cultural conflicts felt even by one so young in passages like this: *"Mary does not understand why her new mother is acting uncomfortable for her. Mary's skin color is commonplace on the reservation. Of course there were certain places off the reservation that would not serve Navajos, but that was as much for fear of fleas as skin color."* For those of us old enough to remember the placement program, this story lets us better understand how "placement" felt to those coming from another world.

In "Christmas at Helaman's House," Orson Scott Card (the most commercially successful of Mormon authors) presents a conflict felt by many returned missionaries as they come home from poverty-stricken lands to almost unthinkable wealth in "Zion." In this story, the returned missionary who is visiting Helaman's house is also a potential suitor of Helaman's daughter. But the extravagance of the domain drives him away: *"I just don't belong here,"* he says. *"Enjoy your new house, really, it's beautiful. It's not your fault that I taught so many people whose whole house was smaller than your bathroom. But the Spirit dwelt there in their little houses, some of them, and they were filled with love. I guess I just miss them."* The homeowners are left to decide how they will justify their extravagance. Can they possibly keep the most sacred promises they've made and still live in a mansion?

Fans of Brian Evenson won't be surprised that his story opens with a tantalizing mystery. In "The Care of the State," a Mormon bishop (Prater) has apparently and secretly been institutionalized for years during his service, and has simply left "the care of the state" each week to cover his ecclesiastical responsibilities, ultimately taking his life after being released from the calling. Evenson's narrator describes the suicide: *"Prater apparently stepped out of this stand of aspens, knelt, and placed his head on one of the rails. None of the newspaper accounts I subsequently tracked down indicated whether Prater's head was positioned so as to look toward the oncoming train or away from it."* How has the bishop, while surely listening to others' confessions, managed to hide his own secret so well? This is Brian Evenson at his best.

Mary Clyde's "Jumping" takes us into the mind of a woman who can't quit thinking about an accident she witnessed in her youth, wondering about many what ifs and trying to make sense of the senseless. *"You know, some good came of it,"* says her distant friend years later, and the first-person narrator muses on the religious context from which the friend is speaking: *"She means something spiritual. Mormons hope tragedy improves the soul. But for me, what I'd like is for the accident not just to have mattered but to surrender some kind of meaning."* Clyde's details are characteristically rich, and the story's structure beautifully woven, spanning decades with ease. *"They fell to their deaths,"* says the narrator. *"We jumped to life. Instead of meaning, there is only that fact."* In this work, all of Clyde's characters "jump to life."

No Mormon short-fiction collection would be complete without stories by Levi Peterson and Douglas Thayer—who are both at the top of their game and show why we Mormon writers (and others who appreciate fine literature) revere them so much. Peterson's "Brothers" is a stunning piece about brothers recognizing where life and religion have divided them and at what points they are bound in an unearthly sealing. The story, set in mountain trails and peaks, suggests a fugue on the theme of brotherhood in all its meanings and layers. And though

Douglas Thayer's "Wolves" might surprise some readers by its subject and violence, he has, in this work, fulfilled the literary destiny started in his first collection, *Under the Cottonwoods* (1976). His writing is, as always, concise and precise; the dialogue spare and sometimes disturbingly believable—especially at moments we hate to acknowledge as possibilities, as when a young man is about to be violated. "Wolves" is a haunting story.

The last story in *Dispensation* is Brady Udall's "Buckeye the Elder"— a probing work full of compelling characters caught between their best and their worst selves. Buckeye, a Mormon convert, comes to town and courts a Baptist girl—and mostly hangs out with the girl's brother, whom he initiates into beer drinking. Buckeye the Elder doesn't know his own strength—or his own weakness. *"Over the past couple of weeks,"* says the story's narrator, *"I've begun to see the struggle that is going on with Buckeye, in which the Lord is surely involved. Buckeye never says anything about it, never lets on, but it's there. It's a battle that pits Buckeye the Badger against Buckeye the Mormon."*

There are many "battles" in this anthology—most internal. Some show us marriages at risk, minds in turmoil, faith in shreds. Most show redemption—or promises of it. All honor the characters, the plots, the language, and literature itself, presented under a Mormon sky—which holds both familiar and sometimes surprising lights, includes unexpected flashes, and suggests the promise of something amazing on the horizon.

DISPENSATION:
LATTER-DAY FICTION

THE GARDEN

Paul Rawlins

THE TASTE OF GRAPES WAS THE TASTE south of his grandmother's garage back home. Small as marbles, green and sour skinned—when you bit them, the skins split and squirted the globe of flesh into your mouth, smooth and soft; if there were any sweetness, this is where you would find it. He could not define the taste, the wildness, something shocking and undomesticated, that set the hard little fruits off from the sweet Thompson seedless in the grocery stores, which were oblong and swollen with watery pulp. He ate without thinking, plucking the fruit from the stems and pushing it through his lips, not hungry, but taking comfort from the automatic motion, something to do.

He had been in shock; he was sure of that, hadn't known exactly what he was doing, where he was running to. His companion, Elder Porter, had been with him, but not for very long; whether they had split up out of instinct, whether they had gotten separated or disagreed over a turn to the left or right, or if he had simply sprinted on ahead, he did not know. He had thrashed through yards of trash, flung himself over fences, run through weeds and over the hard-packed ground where children played, past doors where young men stood abruptly and shouted or stared, or sometimes they gave chase, but he weaved and scrambled. He had no plan, didn't know where he was going, so there was little advantage for those chasing him who might have known the alleys and footpaths, all the tricks and dangers of the township. All the sounds were shouts; all he felt was fear. Elder Porter might be dead. Unless the Lord had come down and plucked him up or parted the way for him, he was certainly dead, dead as Stephen, stoned under the hands of the incensed mob, a martyr sure of heaven.

While he had been the faster runner.

Maybe it was the Spirit that had brought him here, maybe those had been the wings that had lifted him over this wall, the top sown with jagged teeth of broken glass, and into this garden of well-kept rows. It was February, late summer, and there were the leafy tops of potato plants; tomato bushes hung with small red bulbs; two short rows of corn, dry leaved, mostly husk and stalk; grapes that dangled from the vine that had been trained along the wall; tiny water ditches scooped between the rows. His hands weren't shredded—weren't even cut—from the glass atop the wall. He must have thrown his satchel up first. He didn't know.

He had wet himself somewhere along the way, and he tugged his pants down his hips now, tried to peak them in the front to keep the damp cloth away from his skin. Somewhere, too, he had slipped and ripped the left leg of his pants, where a bloody rash showed through. He must stay here until dark at least. But even in the dark, how was he to find his safe way out? How was he supposed to make it home? He heard shouts from the street and pushed himself deeper into the vines.

For any chance he had, he might as well be on the moon.

They had turned a corner, he and Elder Porter. They had not heard any news that day; they had not been paying attention, missed the clues. They were coming from a good appointment; a family named Vis was going to be baptized. There were six of them, three of them over eight years old, the age of accountability required for the ordinance. The Vises had come to church, they called the elders *engeltjies*, little angels, who had brought them the truth from God. He had been excited, jabbering with his companion about the upcoming baptismal service, enjoying for the first time success in the work, the sheaves they were gathering in. The whites, among whom he had labored for his first eight months, seemed limp and apathetic, but amongst the blacks and the coloureds, they had found good ground, softened and thirsty for the refreshing of the latter rain.

They hadn't been paying attention. They turned down a side street and drove into a riot. And then they had done everything wrong.

He couldn't remember if the car had stopped, if they couldn't back up, how or why they had gotten out of the front seats. They had seen it, though. The necklace, the burning tire forced down around the arms of a black policeman. The man—the body—was tipped on its side, knees together, the flesh charred and crumpled, the skull laid against the road, the body smoldering. The mob was a pulsing, thick-muscled whip, coiling in on itself and stretching out. They had seen this, he and Elder Porter, and the people had seen them, two white boys on the edge of the crowd. There was pointing and shouting, and the elders had run.

He had run. He thought he remembered Elder Porter running.

He caught himself whimpering and grabbed his ankles, beating his head against his knees while he prayed to God until his heart stopped shuddering and he could distract himself with thoughts of home, re-membering the vines behind his grandmother's garage, the oxidized paint that came off the tin siding onto your hands, your shirt and pants, so he and his cousins couldn't play around the garage without someone knowing where they had been, out among the grapevines and the money plants, or farther back, into the weeds that grew up around the stump of what had once been a red maple tree, with a split trunk that made two seats, rotted a bit, favored by box elder bugs and spiders that spun webs in intricate octagons and tetrahedrons, patterns he had had no names for then. There was shade there, the long stalks of sunflowers, and the weeds and scrubby suckers that shielded the tree stump from the low back windows of the house.

It's where he and his cousin Peta would sit and tell each other dreams and remarkable things they had seen. When there was nothing remarkable, they made things up. He once said he had seen the ghost of their grandfather in the back hall standing near the pantry when he had been on his way to the bathroom. Peta once poked out her belly and told him she was going to have a baby. Until he was old enough to know better, and to like other girls, he had thought he would grow up to marry his cousin Peta.

She had written him once since he had been here. They had grown apart. She'd come to be a small, sort of stoop-shouldered girl who played the clarinet in the band and had no aspirations he knew of after high school. She was white haired, and when he had last seen her, at the farewell lunch held in his honor back home, she wore large, plastic glasses with translucent pink in the frames. Something about her made him think of a rabbit.

A low coop of some sort, empty, pieced together of scrap, shielded the far corner of the garden from the house. He shifted farther into the tiny wedge of shade created by the corner, folded his arms over the top of his head to deflect the searing heat from the top of his skull. Peta the rabbit. He was going crazy, that was all. Under the circumstances, it was to be expected.

He did not hear the old man soon enough even to get his feet beneath him. He started to move only after he saw him, unsure of whether he should go back over the wall or attack or perhaps just talk. The man looked to be sixty or more—gray dust in his hair, shirt hung open over his belly—carrying a hoe with a thin, worn blade and a broken handle. A black man, of course, the old man who kept this garden. He had come home from work or back from the riots. He had had himself a bottle of lager or a carton of beer, had eaten his dinner, probably *putu* and maybe some chicken, and now he had come out to work in the garden, where he found a white boy, nineteen years old, muddy white shirt and torn pants, amongst his grapevines. The elder held out a hand in front of him, as though he were signaling stop, opened his mouth to speak, but the man had only gaped at him—he had the beginnings of a grizzled beard, white brows above his eyes—then turned and walked away.

Now the elder's stomach began to shake. He did not follow the man toward the house. He shoved a fist into his mouth to keep from making noise, but he cried anyway because now he had been found, and now he was going to die. The mob would beat him, they would puncture and shred his body with makeshift *pangas*, they would burn him while he was still alive. The fear finally made him heave, and he knelt in the dirt on his hands and knees, retching up the sour grapes. He pulled his satchel to him, but he did not scale the wall. It was still light out; the streets around him rocked with chants and shouting, and he did not know where he was. Perhaps it was the voice Elijah heard, small and still, that told him to stay, but he could do nothing else. He squeezed his satchel between his knees while he prayed, his mortal need pressed into words. No one came. Not the old black man, not a crowd of hostile boys, not an angel or a vision. He prayed, and no one came.

Spent finally, he lay down on the earth, uncertain, as the night hours came, whether he had given up or he was safe. He was not sure. Beyond the wall, he did not know which way to go. Tomorrow, he would fast because his situation was perilous. But he would not leave the garden.

Simon Bob had been shocked near dead to find a white boy in his garden. There was a woman in the congregation where he went sometimes with his wife who claimed she saw the souls of the dead. They came to her in her house, standing by her stove or behind her where she could glimpse them in a window or a mirror. He had thought of what a fright that would give him; he had no interest in ghosts. But seeing the white boy in his garden, he thought that's what seeing a ghost would be like; in fact, he believed, or would have before, that he had a better chance of seeing a ghost at his bedside than he did a white man, other than the police or army, sitting in his garden. One was unlikely, the other impossible.

He wondered what the boy was doing there, and he thought many times during the night that he should go out and talk to him, to see where he had come from and what he was planning. But he did not. Only trouble could come from that. He stayed in the tiny house, worried the boy might knock on his door; then, when that did not happen, he knew that the boy had gone.

The next day he learned who the white boy had been, a young minister from America, lost, feared dead within the township that shook still with chants and songs and burning busses. People said the army was coming; they would drive the streets in armored cars, the boys would throw them with stones, and a few might be shot, but they would not find the boy they were looking for. They would never find him here, not if President Reagan and America declared war.

Others would. When they did, the young men would run him down in the streets like a frightened buck and kill him.

But that, anyway, was who the boy had been.

• • •

When Simon Bob came to his garden the next evening, the boy was still
there, huddled in the dirt amongst the leaves and stalks. This he had
not dreamed. Vines crackled as the boy pushed himself to his feet. Simon Bob stood looking a moment, then jabbed at him with his hoe.

"Go, you," he said. "*Voetsak.*"

The boy shook his head.

Simon Bob brandished the hoe in front of him like he might shake
it at a dog.

"Go."

"Help me," the boy said. The voice came out like old paper unfolding. The boy had been sitting here all day, scoured by the sun.
Simon Bob wrinkled his forehead.

"You have to help me," the boy said again. His hands bent like
claws toward his chest.

Simon Bob shook his head. "Go, before my grandson finds you
here." He pointed with his hoe. As if to mimic him, the boy shook his
head in turn.

Simon Bob struck him a light blow across the shoulder with the
hoe's handle. The boy curled his back, putting his arms above his head,
trying to tuck his whole self between his knees. Simon Bob poked and
hit, striking the boy across the back and arms, jabbing at his stomach,
legs. The boy started to cry, but he would not move. He burrowed
himself amongst the grapevines, pressed to the garden wall, until the
heat passed from Simon Bob, and he stopped striking with the hoe
and left him.

The elder waited, after the man left, for the sounds of feet, the grum-
ble of the mob. They did not come. The sun dipped lower in the west,
and a shadow grew from the wall at his back, covering his head, his
knees, and finally his feet. He felt safer at night, as though he were
invisible in the dark, though he could discern that the blocks outside
the garden grew restless, keen with sound: calls for children, hollering
between neighbors, greetings and farewells, profanity, threats, trouble,
violence. He wondered what had happened to Elder Porter, if he was
in the same mess somewhere, if he could be nearby, hearing the same
sounds, whether anybody even knew they were gone.

He was tired now, hurting from the old man's beating. He had not eaten that day nor drunk, though the air felt hot enough to burn if you struck a match, and he sat amongst the leaves and bushes and ripening fruit with a hat he had made of leaves to keep the sun off his scalp. He imagined that his proximity to temptation and his resistance would add power to his fasting. Much of the day, as best he could as he circled and squirmed to keep out of the sun, he had spent in prayer: an hour cataloging and begging forgiveness for his sins, ceaseless cries for deliverance. No thoughts had come to him, no answer, no way, and he thought now, if the situation did not change, he may do as Jesus had done, go forty days in the wilderness without the taste of bread. And when Satan came to sit him on the pillar of the temple, he would go with him as far as the edge of the location, to the first white streets of town, and then he would turn and run from the devil.

Matches for the lamp lay on the wood-topped table beside him, but Simon Bob sat in the growing darkness of his house, the hoe laid across his lap, drinking beer after beer brought to him from a *shebeen* by a young boy he had hollered at from his open door. He could be killed for hitting a white man. He could be killed by others for letting him go. He could be killed for many other things as well—or for nothing at all. It was best here to live without being seen. The police didn't see you and harass you about your papers. The *tsotsis* didn't see you and knife you in the street.

His son had been seen, and in detention the Afrikaans policemen had made him stand for hours on top of bricks; they beat the backs of his legs and the soles of his feet, touched the bare wires from the end of a lamp cord to his penis, shocked him until he shat on the floor, then cursed him and made him clean it up. His daughter, a man looked at her, and she had her first baby at fifteen. No, that was not the worst thing. She lived far away now, in Natal, but she was still with her man, who still promised to finish paying her bride price, the *lobola* Simon Bob knew he may never see.

But there was friction that came from living so close, every man rubbing against his neighbor. There was friction, and friction, he knew from the machines he worked on, generated heat, and with heat things expanded. That was what was happening in the world now, in the bristling streets of the township: friction, heat, a growing pressure—a new law, a new arrest, a new song, a new killing, a new baby, a new shack, all onto the little plot of land inside the fence where already there had been no room. Always, since the white man and the black man had come to live together, it had been like this. "They won't let me be a man." Simon Bob remembered him saying that, his son, before he was killed one night in the road. "They won't let me be a man."

Simon Bob set an empty bottle on the floor without looking down in the dark. Now there was a white boy in his garden—not just a white boy, an evangelist, a minister. What would God say about this? Love thy neighbor? Pray for the one who uses and who persecutes you? Give him your other cheek to strike you there as well?

Simon Bob did not know what the boy preached, but he had lived long enough with little to find the truth of small things: his papers were in order; he had a place for his garden, no trouble with his wife. The Christians told him that his son was alive somewhere with Jesus. That was good enough for Simon Bob. That was all.

Everyone—his friends, his brothers and cousins, the girls—was all excited when he told them what the letter from Salt Lake City had said: Africa. They all knew boys being sent as missionaries to Europe or South America, the Philippines. But Africa—he had pictured himself rumbling through the bush in a Land Rover. Ignorant. On the news, the place was on fire, Winnie Mandela telling the crowd that with their matchbooks and their necklaces they would set the country free. His mother was going to write the church, tell them they couldn't send her son into a war zone. There was always a war, his father had told her. Their son was enlisting in the army of God; he was already at war with the world.

He had come, bleary-eyed and dry-mouthed after the long flight across the Atlantic. The jet lag, the difference of a dozen time zones dogged him for a week. His companion bent the rules, let him sleep late, find his feet. For nine months, he saw no war here. He tracted, knocked on doors in the white cities and the suburbs, asked the black maids who answered for glasses of water, promising to come back when the missus was at home. The people weren't interested in their message. The people had their own church. The people didn't care, and sometimes his companions didn't care much either. He talked very little about the gospel in those first months. He was homesick. He grew despondent, then indifferent himself and lazy. He learned about surfboards, diamonds, politics: The blacks fought amongst themselves. They were superstitious. They had no education. They stole. *Ja*, apartheid; there would be hell to pay someday. *Ja*, the Americans didn't understand it, didn't know their blacks. It was going to take time, that's all, time to bring them along.

There were riots—but they happened in the townships, the locations, the growths that attached themselves by asphalt veins and a ceaseless string of PUTCO busses to the cities. There were killings there, necklacings; there was danger. The townships, that's where the war was.

And that's where the elders wanted to go, where he had been transferred after nine months. They could not live there, but the township was their field of labor, a field black and ready to harvest. He had not been sent as a reward for faithful service, but perhaps as a project for reclamation. Here the world was different. Here his companion was Elder Porter, nervous and willing. Here they did not knock on endless doors like salesmen; here they served, struggling to look after the needs of their people. They taught in homes where one convert invited a half-dozen friends to share what he had found. Their car served as taxi, supply wagon, ambulance. Here he had begun to find a sweet taste to the work. He had begun to hurry, had making up to do, lost time. They had first met with the Vis family only three weeks ago. This was what it was supposed to be like, that's what he was getting ready to say to Elder Porter when they had turned that corner. This, a family brought to God—brought to God, whom he, for perhaps the first time in his life, was coming to know himself.

He leaned against the garden wall. He had been waiting on God. He had been waiting for the old man in the house to come back with a policeman or an army sergeant. He had been waiting for God to pluck him up and spirit him away. To sleep, wake, and find himself miraculously somewhere else. To feel the assurance that he could rise up and walk unnoticed through the streets, the eyes of his enemies holden, and pass through the crowds like Jesus did through the Pharisees at the temple. Every shout on the street, every passing footstep on the other side of the wall brought him to a crouch or to huddle closer in the cornstalks or the vines. He had thought of going to the house; he had crept up last night, to the door, knocking, whispering as loudly as he dared, but no one came. Then he had heard voices on the street, a light flared up in the house next door, and he scrabbled back to the garden plot, where he tried again to clear his mind, to sift through anxious thought for reason or inspiration amongst the pounding worry.

He did not sleep. He examined his faith, weighed his doubts, found himself somewhere in the middle, the fulcrum on which the scale balanced. It seemed pointless to give up on his faith now, for then he would both be alone and know it. He decided that if his enemies came, he would stand before them and declare the word of God as though he had been sent for that very purpose. Perhaps he had. Maybe all of this would yet be turned to good. He opened the scriptures and read stories of deliverance: Daniel from the den of lions; Meshach, Shadrach, and Abed-Nego from the fiery furnace; Alma and Amulek from death and prison; David from the hand of Saul.

The New Testament, though, he found full of martyrs: James, Stephen, the saints who were stoned or sawn asunder, even Peter and Paul in time. His legs cramped from sitting, so he stood to stretch them, though he could not stand straight or his head would appear above the wall. His stomach grumbled, and his bowels were loose. A martyr to the cause was assured his place in heaven.

The thought gave him no comfort.

"You have to help me," the elder said.

Simon Bob had hoped, though he had not been so certain this time, that the boy would creep off during the night, and then it would never have happened. But the boy did not go. He had peeked early in the morning and had seen him there still, and the thought of this troubled him that day. His wife would not come until the weekend. Daniel, son of his own dead son, did not come around home much. If he did and found the boy, that would be the end of the trouble.

"I did not put you here," Simon Bob said. "You climbed my wall to get in—climb it tonight and get away."

"I'll never get away. I don't even know where I am."

"I can't help you."

"Why not?"

"What am I going to do?"

"Call the police. They'll come get me."

"No." Simon Bob shook his head. "I want nothing to do with police."

"The army, then. There's somebody you can tell."

"You do not want to be on the wrong side here," the old man said. The worst thing was to be thought a traitor, and there were so many sides, so many to be offended.

"Nobody will know if you just call the police."

"Everyone will know. It is two miles to the police station, and then I must bring them back here, to my house, and then I must bring them to you in my garden, and all the neighbors will say, 'What are you growing back there, Simon?' " The old man rubbed at his scalp. The boy's face was dirty, and his hands. His eyes were tired and red. "What are you doing here?" he said.

"I was running."

"You're an American. What are you doing in South Africa? Won't they make all the Americans go home soon?"

"I'm a missionary," the elder explained. "We come here to tell people about the church of Jesus Christ."

"You're a Christian," Simon Bob said.

"Yes," he nodded. "Yes. The name of the church is The Church of Jesus Christ of Latter-day Saints."

The old man said nothing.

"Do you believe in God?" the elder said. Automatically, he reached for his bag.

Still Simon Bob stared down at the elder. He did not look as though he had heard a word.

"Don't you think God would want you to help me? Maybe God brought me here because you're the only one who could help."

"Is your God in that book?" Simon Bob said. He pointed to the binder the boy had drug from his satchel.

The elder tipped up the cover, then thumbed through the pages. Simon Bob waited. Finally, the boy turned a page toward him. There were three people in the picture: two men, with white hair and white beards, floating in the air with a glow around them, and beneath them another on the ground, his arm tipped up as though to shield his face.

"Your God is white," Simon Bob said.

"Jesus was an Arab, I think. Something like that," the elder said, fudging.

Simon Bob smiled.

"Then he must stay over in the Indian township. We need many gods here. The Afrikaner's god says we are the cursed children of Ham. The Englishman's god—he says many different things. The Indians, they need many gods, too, because theirs is a land like ours of many people."

"We believe there's one God, and one Jesus."

"I think so, too," Simon Bob said. "Who is this?" He pointed to the third man in the picture.

"Joseph Smith," the elder said. "God's prophet."

"Do you have any black prophets in that book?" Simon Bob said. The boy was not from here, and Simon Bob enjoyed cheeking him, giving him grief. What could the boy do?

The elder closed his book.

"Why don't you get the police?"

The old man wrung his hands around the handle of his hoe, scraping at his top lip with his bottom teeth.

"They'll kill me," the elder said.

"They might kill me, too," Simon Bob said. "There is no leaving for me."

"I wish you could," the elder said.

Simon Bob looked at him. "That way is east," he said, pointing behind the elder's shoulder and past the wall. "You must go that way."

This time, the boy followed toward the house. Simon Bob did not go inside, but walked through the narrow gap between his house and the one to the west, toward the street, where the boy would not go. He reached the street himself and stopped. There were few people out on the block. Tomorrow, that would change. The busses would be running again. The mood was calming, people would be going back to work, the flow of bodies that pulsed like a wave, flooding into the white city, where the boy in his garden belonged, sucking back out again to fill the black one. What was he supposed to do? Fly? Carry the boy back to the city in a sack? He leaned the hoe against the wall of the house, feeling the heat stored up from the day radiating from the blocks.

His grandson, his grandson's friends, they would kill the boy. They would run him in the street for sport, maybe. They would necklace him, maybe. They would do worse, worse than the policemen had done to his own son—though that was bad enough, and in the end, Simon knew in his heart, it had killed him, not the drink, not the car. This boy seemed very young, young in a manner his own son, his grandson, had not been for very long. He was taller than Simon Bob, with a narrow waist, sloping shoulders, blonde hair matted and greasy from three days in his garden. He was not from here.

The boy was a Christian. Simon would give him over to the Christians. God, then, could do with him what he would. He set off walking toward the church. It would be out of his hands.

"The lost boy, the white boy, he is in my garden." Simon Bob explained it to his pastor.

"Does anyone know he is there?"

"If anyone knew, he would be dead. He was alive when I left him, and if he is alive there still, then nobody knows."

"Is he safe there? Does your grandson know?"

"He has been there three days. My grandson is not at home. And when he is, he is not in the garden where there is work to be done."

"I can't imagine that he will be safe in your garden. Can you hide him in your house?"

"No," said Simon Bob.

The pastor pursed his lips to think, bearing down on Simon Bob without speaking a word. He was a man, Simon Bob knew, who loved a mountain set before him. When there had been a church to build from nothing more than promises and empty pockets, he had gone house to house like a crafty beggar, supplicating in the name of the Lord, with a heavy hand on your shoulder. He looked down on Simon Bob now with an aspect of great thought, bulging eyes with hardly any brows, lips parted as if he were about to whistle.

"You couldn't bring him here?"

"No."

"No, of course not," the pastor said. "We need a car."

"I have no car."

"We need a car." The pastor was waving a finger. "Go and see that he is still there."

Simon Bob nodded and turned back home.

Simon Bob picked up his hoe from where he had left it alongside the house. The boy was still in his garden, on his knees in the brick-colored dirt, surrounded by the vines. He was praying, whispering to himself, hands clasped in his lap. The boy's white shirt was filthy with grime, his arms and face, the crown of his head burned red from the sun. He wore a little black name badge on his shirt pocket, scuffed black shoes with thick soles run down at the heel. He would tell the boy to wait, someone would come. Then he would go down to the *shebeen* himself. When he came home, the boy would be gone.

The boy jerked away from him, eyes wide, once he sensed someone standing there. He stood in a crouch, brushing off the knees of his pants.

"I'll give you everything I have," he said. "My watch. I have thirty rand in my wallet." He stopped, maybe realizing it wasn't much to offer. Then Simon Bob saw that the boy was looking over his shoulder. He turned to see his grandson.

"Daniel," he said.

"What is that?" his grandson pointed at the elder.

"Daniel," Simon Bob said again. His grandson moved to come closer, but Simon Bob barred his way. Daniel Bob was older than the boy in the garden, twenty-four, but still young and full of smoke. To his grandfather's eye he was not a revolutionary, but a hood. His friends were arrested for stealing and assault, not sedition. He did not work often and spent most of his nights down the road in one of the *shebeens*, drinking, listening to tapes of music from America, stealing out sometimes to huddle with a group that assembled for a moment to share a cigarette, then disbanded again in three or four different directions with nods of the head and short shouts of reminder or insult.

Daniel looked at the old man with his head cocked and chin raised, as though he might say something wise.

"What are you going to do with him?" Daniel said.

"Nothing. I am doing nothing with him, and you are doing nothing with him," Simon Bob answered. "He can go out the way he came."

"No," Daniel said. He shook his bowed head as if he were haggling over a price in the market.

"He is not from here," Simon Bob said.

"I know he is not from here."

"He is an American."

Daniel shrugged. "I don't care where he comes from."

"Daniel," the old man said. "Go now."

"No, no," Daniel said, shaking his head. "We'll give him a chance. Let him run. Run, boy." He bent and put his hands on his knees, while he called to the elder. The elder stood with his hands at his sides. Daniel Bob's head was shaved; he wore a slick nylon jacket, the sleeves pushed up toward his elbows, baggy chinos. There was menace about him, in the cocky way he stood, the fashion of his clothes.

"Get away," Simon Bob said. A change came over Daniel's face, a transformation settling like a cloud front down a mountain.

"No," he said.

Simon Bob swung with the hoe's handle, striking his grandson across the cheek. Behind him, the boy would be waiting for Daniel to strike back, to wrestle the hoe from his grandfather's hands, beat the old man with it himself. But he did not. He stood, half-turned from his grandfather, a hand to his face. He started to walk toward the house, then broke into a jog.

Simon Bob stood, trembling, watching where his grandson had gone, the world finally come apart.

"He'll come back," the elder said.

Simon Bob, his back still turned, nodded.

"He'll bring his friends."

"Yes," the old man said.

Simon Bob stood there, still watching where his grandson had gone, twisting the wooden handle of the hoe in his hands.

Finally, he turned to the boy behind him, whose legs had given out. He had sunk down against the garden wall, where the grit of the bricks scraped at his back where his shirt rode up. It was done now.

"Come," he said.

• • •

The elder heard them first, the harsh shouts from the knot of young men down the dirt street and kitty-corner to the house. They stood looking at one another: the white elder and Simon Bob, who had hold of him by the shoulder, and the young black men down the street. The street was like dozens the elder had seen: packed dirt, water tap with a skid of mud the shape of a pennant in front of it. Houses of blown block and adobe with corrugated zinc roofs, dust on everything, giving the whole world here the texture of sandpaper. Streets and houses full of people whom he loved and feared, an alien world of stupefying want where he could labor but could not live, where some would kill him and some would call him angel, and he, with his imperfect heart, could not tell one from the other and probably could not love both.

From the corner, Daniel whistled and pointed.

The elder wrenched himself from the old man's grip. It was too late, but he would run now, now that he had a direction—away from the crowd of men on the corner. He took a few hopping steps to the side, putting the old man between them, putting him on their side, as though the old man had brought him not for deliverance, but to be delivered. He was hopping, edging sideways toward the opposite corner, trying to pick a road, as if he were testing the young men to make sure of their intentions, taunting them, egging them on to race. They stood smiling and talking amongst themselves, looking his way. They would bait him longer. They weren't ready to run yet.

He would run. He did not think about his martyr's death. The fear in his body had turned to fuel.

There was another sound, a coming cloud of unison and heft. He had not noticed it until the crowd came spilling around the corner closest to him, from the direction he was prancing toward. It was the sound of the crowd again: rhythmic, raised voices, clapping hands. People were stepping out of doors to see. Some joined in, women clapping and starting to sing, children, little ones, coming out in the dirt yards to dance.

A choir dressed in purple robes filled the street from side to side, singing in Zulu or Xhosa. The elder didn't know the tune; the words came to him only as sound, harmonious but inexplicable. Some in the choir clapped, some raised their hands. He could see their faces, some with smiles, some with eyes half-closed in concentration, as if they

would praise their hearts right out through their pores. Some faces
were squirrel-cheeked and fat, some heads smooth-pated with a ring
of tight gray hair like moss, some with glossy braids or stiff, curled
coifs. All the faces dark, blue-black and brown, all of them singing, all
looking beyond him as if there were no white boy gaping at them from
the side of the meager road as they came marching, no pack of wolves
on the next corner waiting to do murder.

They came on, flocking around him in their purple vestments,
folding him into their undulating sea as they moved down the street
with hands raised high above him so the wide hems of their garments
hid his face and shoulders as they bore him away. He was in the midst
of the song now, that sound, as though it came out of him in all directions, robed in their purple, urged on by the touch of a hundred
hands, feet that pressed his own to move. There were other shouts,
but the choir pulsed forward, flowing around and past the obstacle,
undaunted, unperturbed.

He did not see if the old man had been swept up with them. He
barely had the wit to follow as the wave took him forward off his own
feet. There was a car, the boot gaping open, and then he lay shut inside
the lightless trunk, body bent, the hard-worn road beating him at the
hip and shoulder as they drove, feeling invisible in the darkness as the
sounds of traffic fought around him, praying only not to stop. The old
man was not in the car when it pulled off the road outside the township, not among the circle of faces that peered in on him as the lid
raised or the hands that lifted him out of the boot. The strangers asked
if he would be all right from here, gave their soft handshakes and good
wishes, then climbed back into the lopsided Toyota and made their
U-turn while he stood beside the road in his soiled clothes at the edge
of town.

The streetlights were still cut off in the township. He could see
the flicker of fires here and there in the dusk, a white haze like some
fallen star that marked the police station. Two miles, the old man had
said, from the garden and the wall. He thought—maybe in that moment when he had broken away, when everybody saw him do it, maybe
that had been enough to save the old man. He closed his eyes, trying
to see a picture, to assemble words into prayer, lips cracked, his head
light from hunger. Then the bones went from his legs, and he scissored

down into the dirt along the road outside the city, his body leaching out the poisons of adrenaline and fear, replacing them with mystery and grief.

Simon Bob turned away as the choir passed, going back to the garden, where he bent to work among the rows. Nothing grew in the thin dust of the township except around the privies, where it fed on human waste. It had taken years to build this soil. He had nursed the ground with scraps of vegetables, chicken dung, blood and bonemeal; turned each year's vines and husks and tops back into the plot; built the wall during better days. It was strange luck that had brought the boy here— good or bad, he could not tell. He would have to wait to hear.

In the corner was a pile of grape stems, a flimsy cap fashioned out of leaves. Simon Bob spread the bits about, then chopped at them with his hoe, working them into the earth around the base of the vines. He worked as shadows bloomed along the ground, thinking of a boy, until he heard footsteps coming up behind him. Then he propped his hoe against the garden wall and turned around to meet them.

OBBLIGATO

Lisa   Madsen   Rubilar

A HALF-GALLON OF MILK DOESN'T SPOIL as fast as you might think. It can
sit out on the kitchen counter all morning in August heat, and if you
shove it into the freezer for half an hour, it'll be cold enough to drink
for lunch. A half-plucked chicken, left in the sink for seven hours with
a couple of cereal bowls rimmed in mummified Cheerios, will do fine
if you leave tap water trickling over one thigh. Sometimes my mother
left clothes on the line for three days at a stretch, as other duties took
precedence (harvesting tomatoes, making raspberry jam). My jeans
would dry stiff, drink in an Idaho rainstorm, dry out again, absorb the
pollens and dusts of the cottonwood trees, shake them free with another pelting rain and dry once more, hopping in the breeze of a new
morning. When I'd wear a pair of jeans cured by this method, the smell
of sap and dew walked with me through the day. Now you pay good
money for the sun-bleached look. We got it for free.

But my mother taught me you have to pay for everything, one
way or another, mostly with the hours of your life. So if you have
to choose between raspberries for dinner and promptly washing the
breakfast bowls in which you'll eventually eat them, you'll choose the
raspberries, of course. You'll be out there in the raspberry patch, hat
brim bobbing as you search out the exquisitely ripe fruit—leaving the
almost-ripe to swell another day because you'll be out there again tomorrow, and there'll be enough spare berries for the blackbirds to steal
their quota—because the bowls will, one way or another, get washed
in time for dinner, probably by your daughter (me) mumbling under
her breath, who's also the person who'll finish plucking the chicken
while you say, "Open, Lovey," and pop a raspberry in her mouth so

she'll feel your cool finger on her lip before the burst of flavor hits her tongue. I paid for *that* moment with the chicken grease and blood on my hands.

My mother was a terrific cook. Our family would polish off every last crumb of the fried chicken (one piece each); fill up on mashed potatoes; then gorge on raspberries and cream for dessert. My father sat at the head of the table, shoulders slumped from carrying the mail bag, spoon in his fist, saying something like, "What a treat, my Sweetie-Sweet!" At one point there had been ten of us at the table, with Ted in the high chair, but by the time I was plucking chickens, there were eight of us. Mel was married and disappointing my parents by working at the sugar factory; Bradley was in Boise at the university. That left six of us awash in the mayhem of home, five boys and me, who'd be the next to leave. I couldn't wait, since I didn't know yet it wasn't every day you eat sun-warm raspberries from your mother's hand; and I didn't know there'd be so many dire warnings in years to come printed on the packaging of chickens about how you had to defrost them in the refrigerator and get the leftovers back to forty degrees as soon as humanly possible.

What I wanted most, at that time, was to know what was humanly possible. I'd sworn not to repeat my mother's life.

When you pluck a chicken, the feathers resist extraction. Your fingers get greasy and coated with invisible fluff and the smallest of the feathers stick to the backs of your hands. This is when you ask yourself why—when most people can drive to the supermarket and pick up a bare bird and pop it in the oven in half an hour—you have to spend your time like *this*? Because it wasn't like you had an actual farm. The chickens scratched around a yard out back that otherwise might have been a grassy place for sunbathing or maybe even for tossing a Frisbee with friends (not that you'd ever learned to toss a Frisbee straight or had friends who liked to do that kind of thing). But your mother felt redeemed somehow by those chickens, and believed in the law of the harvest: that you'd darn well better get some fruit and vegetables, flowers and edible chicken flesh off your two acres of earth or you'd be a blind steward, ungrateful for your allotment on God's green planet.

• • •

My first memory is of riding in a car seat, forearms at rest on a metal rim, the fervid bodies of my brothers struggling on either side, a hot wind through the windows, a sticky residue of tears on my face, the plump curve of my mother's cheek as she half-turned to call out to us, her hands on the steering wheel.

My mother, the lover of gardens, the craver of loam and greening shoots, lived a great deal in the gasoline-smelling Chevy station wagon, driving us to piano lessons, wrestling practice, Primary children's parades, 4-H expositions and drama classes. We—all of us—had gifts, and Mother spent her days facing us toward the sun. Our job was to blossom and grow. We built blanket caves in the living room and played in them for days; we painted in watercolor and acrylic and she papered the walls with our work; we recreated Rome with generations of wooden blocks, and sidled for weeks around coliseums and waterways; we staged Punch-and-Judy puppet shows that consisted mostly of punching, and her laughter was our only audience. Just one thing made her angry: to see us wasting time. Sloth was the least forgivable sin. Five minutes before the school bus came, we'd be reciting *Hamlet* aloud, and if the bus honked mid-soliloquy, beware if you ran for the door. She'd grab a coat collar and give a shake and say, "You'd trade Shakespeare for five extra seconds on the bus?"

And yet she was never harsh. Home from school, I'd sit on her lap and rest my ear on the soft shelf of her breast. She smelled of lavender and bread. I wonder now how she held me so long, amid my brothers' clamor.

Such questions present themselves at unexpected moments. Like when it's January in Chicago, and you're starting up the stoop to your dreary third-floor apartment when you spy a discarded poinsettia in a garbage can next to the curb, and for a moment the spidery, leafless thing cries out to you like a child; so you lug the plant upstairs where it sheds the last of its green and red leaves into the sink before you lug it back down again. And you say to yourself Mother would have done better. Then you recall she paid the price for her green thumb; she paid with greenish cottage cheese in the fridge and dust-clots under the beds and an untrained contralto voice that could have put her on the stage. She herself had a gift. Her voice could have been operatic.

Instead she was digging earthworms ("Look at the size of this fellow"), tucking them back into the soil like flailing toddlers into their cribs; fashioning crutches for the limbs of the tomato plants; shoring up the raised potato beds; sacrificing nascent carrots so others would have space to grow. In my mother's book, when you give life room, you assume a sacred trust to bring it to fruition. Therefore your outdoor duties—performed where nothing but a few miles of air lie between you and God—take precedence over those inside the house, which is safeguarded by a roof built of someone else's strivings. My father's. Day after day, he bore up under the weight of the world's messages in order to keep us from rain and snow.

He'd sit at the head of the table, hunched from the burden of all those letters, and he'd be licking the chicken grease from his fingers while I watched him with abject love and disgust, and my mother would be saying something like, "My ring came off in the garden today. I think it was in the pole beans." This wasn't the first or the last time she lost her wedding ring out there. While most people accumulate weight over the years, she gradually discarded it. Now her ring was slipping. She was looking old, and I resented her for it.

"We'll send the kids out to look after dinner," Dad said. I wasn't considered one of *the kids* by that time, since my job was the kitchen—where chicken feathers still coated the sink; where a gray sludge still murked at the bottom of this morning's oatmeal pot—*unless* I had to practice my horn, which I almost always did, because it was my gift, and one's gift took precedence over everything, including dishes. (From time to time, surfacing from dreams in the middle of the night, I'd hear Mother clattering in the kitchen. I don't recall ever getting out of bed to help.) So the hours after dinner and after breakfast too, during the summer, would find me on the French horn, the most difficult of the brass instruments, with intervals so close that the undisciplined lip yawls among the notes; the instrument with the richest sound. I chose it because my junior high band instructor, Miss Wirthin, advised me not to, advised me, in fact, to go with a "more feminine" and a "less costly" instrument ("considering your family situation," she said), such as a clarinet or a flute, of which the school had plenty of student models to rent for ten dollars or so a month. Instead, my father drove me to Pocatello to buy a horn on installment from Moe's Music and More, and for years (even after I left home, I think) he sent in the twenty-five-dollar-a-month payments. Meanwhile I was saving whatever I could from babysitting or dog-tending to buy a silver-plated Alexander, because I knew even then that my life would depend on its voice. That kind of knowledge makes you self-protective. You don't want to end up in a patch of weeds when you could be on stage. So when push comes to shove, you're probably the one doing the shoving, of others, right out of the lifeboat. It's as though you weren't raised by someone who took each moment, each seedling, each child by the collar and said *Live!*

So there I was in my bedroom upstairs perspiring in the August heat and practicing the horn (I was good by then; I was very good: the best horn player Bridger High School had ever had, Mr. Carlyle, the orchestra director, had told me; so good he was choosing pieces now he'd never dared in his whole career, like *The New World Symphony*, because there was a horn player, for once, who could hit the darn notes, that *vivacissimo* flourish near the end)—there I was practicing while Ted, Matt, Pete, Jimmy, Sam and Dad were crawling among the beans. And because I didn't join the search, I was the one who found Mother's wedding ring.

I was thirsty. I went into the upstairs bathroom to get a drink. I had my horn under my arm as I leaned over the sink. As I said, it was a hot August evening, the air heavy, the sun still blazing away outside. But while I was slurping out of my hand, a gust of wind—a strangely cool morning-like breeze—blew the toilet paper roll, which had been standing on the sill, right into the toilet bowl. (Toilet paper rolls never made it onto the dispenser at our house; they got used up too fast to make it worth the effort.) I grabbed for the roll and dinged my horn on the edge of the sink and I swore, and swore again when I saw that one of the boys had urinated without flushing and I knew they'd be flushing without looking next, which would clog the plumbing. So I placed my horn on the mildewed bath mat in the tub and grabbed a rubber glove. I'd never put on one of those gloves in my life: cleaning the bathroom was something my mother did; when you least expected it, there would be the bathroom, sparkling clean. Now I pulled the glove on so I could fish the toilet paper out of the toilet. And there in the finger of the glove was my mother's ring.

My father declared it a miracle. For me, the miracle was the look on his face and the way he threw his shoulders back and grabbed my mother and scattered the chickens as he danced her around in the dust while the boys whooped and slapped me on the back.

"But it wasn't a miracle, really," I said to my mother. We were standing side by side at the sink again, hemmed in by tilting monuments to breakfast, lunch and last night's dinner; I was snapping the ends off green beans with bursty little pops. I said: "Do you honestly think God made the day hot? Made me thirsty? Made the wind blow? Made the toilet paper fall into the toilet? Made someone forget to flush so I'd put on the glove? Not to mention that you would've found the ring yourself the next time you cleaned. Plus now I have a ding in my horn. Did God make that happen, too?"

"I was going to throw those gloves out," my mother said. She kissed me on the cheek. I felt the warmth of her breath. "They were making my hands itch," she said. "I had fleece-lined gloves on my shopping list."

She pulled the list off the refrigerator door to show me. *Fleece gloves*, it read.

I got a scholarship to Western Michigan University, where Clive Russet was teaching. I auditioned there just so I could study under him. My parents never suggested I apply to an in-state college. In fact, they seemed to agree that success was directly proportional to distance from home, boasting to neighbors that Bradley was living in Lubbock now, which alone seemed to prove him an exceptional engineer.

The first time I played for Clive Russet he leaned back and folded his hands over a neat paunch that sat under his ribcage like a pregnancy. After I finished playing, he just sat there for a few seconds rubbing his belly. He looked me up and down. He told me I had what it took. He told me not to look back, that the sky was the limit. "Astounding," he said. "Astounding. I wouldn't recommend you get those teeth fixed, either. Not on your life. Don't mess with that embouchure." After that I bought on credit the silver-plated Alexander with a fifth valve for E sharp and A sharp, and when I graduated with a master of fine arts in music performance, I told my parents not to come to the ceremony because there was a vacancy in the Chicago Symphony and Clive had

gotten me an audition. I was the underdog, the unknown from Kala-
mazoo, but Barenboim called me "another Helen Kotas," shaking his
head in wonder, then shaking my hand.

I moved to that city in the middle of a snowstorm. I thought the
plane would crash on landing and I worried most about my horn;
I imagined it tumbling end over end, smashing into a cornfield, a
brief sunburst of silver fragments among the desiccated stalks.

When you choose music as your life, you tend to focus on the sounds
your horn contains, not what contains *you*. In other words, you rent a
third-floor studio apartment in a cinder-block building as grimy on the
outside as it is gloomy on the inside because it perfectly meets your
needs: you can practice any hour, day or night, without angering the
neighbors. That means you can't hear *them*, either, of course, except
for vague thumps or murmurs, through closed doors, as you walk up
or down the crumbling stairs. You live in perfect silence, except for
when you play.

In Chicago, I cooked frozen potpies or packaged burritos and
washed the dishes after each meal. I dried them and stacked them
in the cupboard instead of leaving them in the drainer. I stowed the
drainer under the sink after every washing, so I had this vast expanse
of countertop to set out the unstained cookie sheet on which I placed
side by side, in the center of the Teflon surface, two machine-folded
flour tortillas containing beans and chili-cheese. (I was living life as my
mother never imagined it.)

I paid for that store-bought precision with the silence, which, I
discovered, was never quite that. There was always the sense of a met-
ronome ticking just at the edge of soundlessness. Sometimes I could
even sense the tempo, the measures clicking past, and I discovered
that silence, like music, was a way to measure time. That's what music
is made of: measure after measure of time. But when I played, it was
the silence I noticed most—the rests, welling into the cracks in the
sound.

My parents visited Chicago once a year to hear me play, usually in February, the bleakest season (after Mother's marathon Christmas baking and before her massive spring planting of tomato seeds in Dixie

cups). I offered to pay their airfare, but they always said no. Mother filled her carry-on with jars of raspberries she'd canned the summer before, each wrapped in a colorful dishtowel or stuffed inside an oven mitt the shape of a rooster. Her bag was so heavy, I don't know how she lifted it onto the x-ray belt at the airport. Once I'd exclaimed over these presents, my parents let me give them concert tickets: center seats in row five, where the music could wash over their heads, although Mother always said she'd rather sit where she could see at least the top of *my* head.

"You don't need to see me, Mother," I said. "The whole orchestra is me. When I'm sitting back there, the violin part runs in my veins; the timpani's my own heart. It's like Paul said, 'Should the foot wish to be the hand or the hand the head?' "

"What're you, the big toe?" said my brother Pete, who'd come along this trip, having nothing better to do since he graduated from high school than, according to my father's bemused chagrin, "bum around." After dinner he and Father trudged off in the wind to the corner market because I'd forgotten to get cream for the raspberries. I told them the rusty mesh over the windows and the graffiti on the walls were deceiving; it was very safe, the Korean owner very friendly. From the kitchen window, I watched them walk past the stunted trees out front, heads hunkered to one side, my father shorter now than Pete, his coat open in front, his gait a jarring limp. The streetlights had just come on. They walked in and out of the light.

I had scrubbed the pots and pans as Mother cooked, so there weren't many dishes to wash. Mother had prepared a pot roast recommended to me by the Venezuelan butcher two blocks down: I'd thought about buying a chicken but couldn't stand the sight of its squashed featherless skin under the plastic. I didn't admit this to Mother as she whipped real potatoes into clouds; as she rolled out biscuits, her fingers deft in the dough as a potter at the wheel. I told her how I'd shaken Yo-Yo Ma's hand, the very hand insured for who-knew-how-many millions of dollars. I wished later I'd let the dishes stack up, for old time's sake. Instead we stood by the empty sink watching my father and brother recede through broken oblongs of light toward the barred windows of the corner store. My hands felt dry. Restless. Like they needed something to hold. They itched for my horn (I hadn't had a chance to practice), but that wasn't it either. I rinsed my hands a second time and dried them on a paper towel.

"Don't worry about Father," Mother said. "He finally asked for a transfer to the sorting facility; he can sit on a stool there most of the time."

I hadn't been worried. Now I was. "What, are his knees worse? His arthritis?"

"Well, that's not what concerns me," Mother said, having just told me there was no need for concern. "It's his blood pressure."

"I thought he was on medication."

"It has side effects. He can't sleep. Gets the shakes. And that makes him upset." She took from the cupboard a glass tumbler, which I'd just put away, and her own hand was shaking as she filled it from the tap. She'd been fighting the tremors for years, even way back when I found her ring in the rubber glove. Graves' disease had winnowed the woman I'd known as a child, the one who bustled from the garden to the sink, apron weighted with plum tomatoes and muscadines. Now she wore her wedding ring on a chain around her neck.

"Mother," I said. "Why didn't you try to stop me from coming here?"

She pressed her hands against edge of the sink.

"Did you want me to?"

"No," I said. "But I've wondered why you let me go so easy."

"How can you say that?" Tears came to her eyes. "Who said it was easy? But how can we keep our children from happiness?"

She looked out the window at the runt trees, at the parking meters, the cinderblock building across the street, a soundproof, weatherproof replica of my own. I wished she'd say *Please come home*. When she didn't, I said, "Thank you for letting me go."

In one sense, my mother was right. When you're a musician, you're a midwife to joy. That's your mission: to bring joy into the world. These were the things I told myself as I settled my horn in its velvet case late at night. The cinderblock walls absorbed perfectly the snores and sobs of my neighbors as I curled into the silence of my bed. Yes, Mother was right: I was happy. At least sometimes. When you live for music, you have happiness for the asking, at least at odd moments, at least when you're inside the notes, a place you can arrive any time you want just by picking up your horn. This is the *real* gift: the doorway into a world that has nothing to do with pole beans or the roof over your head. You come to realize, so slowly you hardly notice (just as I hardly noticed, over the years, how Mother was losing weight), that the world beyond the doorway—the shiver at the heart of the music—isn't anything you have a hand in, except as raw material: the coal shoveled into the boiler, the oil poured onto the altar. You come to see yourself—the way I think my mother saw herself—as a vessel of time; as an hourglass, and the sand is flitting grain by grain through your narrow throat, and each grain is a seed, a seed that sprouts and flowers as it falls.

Why did Pete come with my parents that year? Later I realized it would have been easier for him to stay home, to take a break from my mother's wrath. She was furious with him for not applying to college; she'd never admit it, but she was giving him the silent treatment. He'd gotten in a few wisecracks at dinner, but other than that he'd been quiet, so quiet I hadn't gotten used to the bass of his voice. Whenever he spoke, my insides lurched.

After my parents went to bed, he made up for that silence. "Let's get out of here!" he said, interrupting me when I tried to say good night. "Let's go someplace!" He stood blocking the narrow hallway, loose-jointed, rubbing the bristles newly sprouted on his chin.

"Where do you want to go, Pete? Everything's closed." I meant the galleries, the museums. We had a trip to the Art Institute planned for the next morning, then my concert at night. We had a full day ahead, and I wanted to get to sleep.

"*Everything's* not closed," he said. "It's only ten-oh-five."

"I don't have a car." The words came out as a five-note melody, the sing-song reminder of stupidity we kids had used among ourselves, even after I wasn't one of *the kids*. Had he forgotten we'd taken a taxi home from the airport? Maybe he wasn't aware how much that cost.

"So how do you get places?" he asked. "You walk everywhere?"

"I usually take the bus. But they only run on the hour this late."

"Well, call a cab." Pete opened his wallet and waved some bills in the air. This was Pete, my little brother, the one who'd used a similar gesture to surrender a block fortress to himself before kicking it to smithereens. There he was with a beard on his chin and an Adam's apple at his throat waving a fistful of twenties. "Call a cab!" he said again, even louder.

I was afraid he'd wake Mother and Father, so I agreed. We left our parents sleeping and walked down to the street. It was miserably cold. Ancient piles of snow pitted with soot sat along the curbs like blackened molars. A white-haired cabdriver pulled up, looking as hang-dog and weary as I felt; but when I opened the door he said with a lively grin, "Where to, folks?" I asked him to take us along the shore.

The city was almost deserted. Who wanted to be out on such a night? Even the streetlights seemed frozen, as though reflecting instead of producing their light. A deformed trash can rolled across the street in front of us and lodged against the curb, jouncing slightly, as if to free itself. A backhoe sat at a construction site, its toothed bucket embedded in congealed soil; a *No Trespassing* sign on the fence had been vandalized. But none of this put a dent in Pete's enthusiasm. As we drove past North Avenue Beach, he yelled, "Hey, pull over! Let's stop a minute." The driver stepped hard on the brake and my shoulder hit the back of the seat as I turned to argue with my brother.

"The meter's running," I said. "I don't know—" But Pete had already leapt from the car, his slouched body unfolding in sudden athletic grace.

"Ah, go have fun," the driver said. He turned on the dome light and pulled a ratty paperback from under the seat. I got out and followed Pete across the trucked-in sand down to the water. We had the beach to ourselves. The wind off the lake carried ice in its teeth.

"It looks like the sea!" Pete shouted as I came up to him, my face tilted toward my shoulder, eyes slitted against the blast.

I yelled, "In the daytime there are seagulls."

"It's like it never ends. Like it just keeps going!" He walked along the beach, picking up a beer bottle, then a stone, and throwing them with fierce abandon so far out I didn't see where the dim turbulence swallowed them. But even Pete couldn't stand the cold long on that lonely shore. We forged back to the cab, which felt warm and cozy inside, like our living room back home when the fireplace was alight, gloves and hats steaming on the grate, Mother on the couch reading

Whitman out loud. The cabdriver put down his book and greeted us with a thumbs-up, like he was in on some family joke, some family memory. His white eyebrows were so long they almost touched the white hairs wisping from under his black wool cap.

"Onward or backward?" he asked jovially, and Pete answered by singing words from a rousing hymn: "Onward! Ever onward!" Then Pete looked at me. "Hey! That's the first real smile I've seen since I got here. Lookin' good, Sis." He'd never called me "Sis" before, and I felt like he was playing a part; but then he leaned across the seat and said quietly, "Do you *like* it here in Chicago, Nan?"

"Well, I'm here, aren't I?"

"You got friends?" Pete and I had never had a heart-to-heart, and a cab in Chicago seemed a strange place to start. I was six years older. Pete was one of *the kids*.

"Sure," I said. "Mostly people in the orchestra. And a lady upstairs."

"What's her name?"

"Rae Ann Ladd."

"She from Chicago?"

"South Carolina. She was walking upstairs one night and heard me playing the *obbligato* from Mahler's Fifth. You can't hear anything through the walls, if you noticed, but you can hear a little through the doors if you're out in the hall. She knocked on the door, and when I opened it, she clapped."

"Cool," Pete said. He chafed his hands against his jeans. "I never clapped."

"You can do it tomorrow night."

"So what'd you do, play her the whole symphony?"

"Who?"

"Your friend. After she clapped."

"No. We just talked awhile. Rae Ann sings with the Lyric Opera. But her parents aren't like ours. They told her not to come up here, and now whenever she calls home they just go on about her biological clock running out; she's about ten years older than me. I have to hand it to Mother and Dad; they've never bugged me about stuff like that. They know I made my choice."

"Your choice?"

"I mean I chose my music, over, you know, getting married, having kids."

"I didn't know you chose. I thought that's just the way things turned out. You've still got plenty of time to—"

"I *chose*," I said.

That silenced Pete for a moment; then he said, "Well *I* chose not to go to college, and no one's got respect for *that!*" He sounded again like the whiny kid I remembered. "Mother won't even talk to me."

"So what's the deal?" I asked. "What're your plans?"

"Why can't I just *not* have plans for a while?"

I felt like giving him a slap. I said to the driver, "Let's head back."

"Not yet!" Pete said. The driver nodded and kept going. Pete leaned forward, giving me the cold shoulder since I wasn't sympathetic to his nonplans. "You from Chicago?" he asked the driver.

"Nah. Farm boy. Grew up in the sticks about a hundred miles from here, no place you ever heard of."

"You can tell we're tourists, huh?" Pete laughed. "Well, at least, *I'm* a tourist. She lives here. She's a musician. She plays with the Chicago Symphony."

The driver whistled. He drove with his mouth still pursed for a few seconds, then he said, "I heard about this five-year-old girl whose mother played the cello. And this girl suddenly starts singing something, and nobody knows what she's singing until her mom figures out it's the music she was practicing before the kid was born. So this kid learns the song when she's a fetus, and one day out of nowhere she starts singing it!"

"See what I mean?" Pete said, not to the driver but to me, and his voice was that unfamiliar bass again. "Did you hear that? Who says you have to choose between music and kids?"

This didn't seem exactly the point of the cabdriver's story, but the man chimed in: "Yeah, what they think? That you got to choose between music and life? You play music, you get married, you have a kid, the kid sings, life goes on."

I felt like the two of them were ganging up on me. "I think we'd better get back," I said again.

Pete shrugged and hunkered down in the seat, his knees levered into the one in front. "You can choose all you want, but sometimes things just happen," he muttered. "They just happen." He looked through the window, where everything was stripped to concrete and glass yet seemed jittery, almost ephemeral, out there in the cold.

I found myself thinking of my mother, her garden. I thought of her singing as she knelt among the green beans or hollyhocks, her voice pure and thin, stretched to a single gold thread. With proper lessons she could have opened her vocal cords, she could have developed a real voice, like Rae Ann's, which was in the same register, and which set the air of concert halls trembling with love or terror or grief. Rae Ann's voice hadn't just happened. Neither had Mother's. They'd each made a choice.

The driver found a place to turn around and started back the way we'd come. "Pretty soon I won't be out on cold nights like this," he said a little too loudly over his shoulder, as if forcing some cheer back into the atmosphere. "I'm retiring in three weeks and five days."

"Wow!" Pete's posture didn't change, but his tone of voice had, once again. "I guess *you'll* be sleeping in."

"Nah. I'll be up all right. I milked cows for thirty-two years, so I'll be up."

"Still got cows?"

"You kidding? No room for the little guy in the dairy business no more. The government paid me to slaughter the herd. But I still got a few acres. I told my wife I need to get out of the cab, get back to the dirt. I'm thinking about planting hollyhocks, gladiolas, and selling them at the farmers' market. They say the best business is cut flowers."

The crash happened the instant after he said those words: *cut flowers*. The cabdriver had just enough time to swerve; if he hadn't, the guy who ran the red light would've struck the door on my side. Instead, the blow was glancing, although my face went straight into the front seat. I broke my nose, and my teeth went through my lower lip. The way Pete was hunkered must have saved him from anything worse than bruises. The driver got out of the car and started yelling, glass glittering in his wool cap and red drops gleaming on the white strands of his eyebrows like Christmas lights.

When you bite right through your lip, you don't play with the Chicago Symphony the next day. What you do is sit around your apartment with an ice pack on your fourteen stitches feeling sorry for yourself, but unable to fully wallow in self-pity because your father keeps saying, "It's a miracle it wasn't any worse, Sweetie"; and your mother is making chicken noodle soup in the kitchen; and your brother's limping a little but nothing's broken; and you think, "Thank you, Heavenly Father." Then you think, but I wouldn't be sitting here with an ice pack on my face if my brother hadn't told me to call a cab, and he wouldn't have been here if he'd gone to college, and Mother and Dad wouldn't be here if I weren't here. And you think, Why am I here? And you wonder if you made the right choice. And you wonder if, like the cabdriver said, you don't have to choose between music and life: it isn't like that. And you think, no matter which choice Pete makes, he'll never again be what he is right now. And neither will you. And you realize that your kitchen's still spotless, despite all the cooking Mother's done in there, and you know she's keeping it that way, and she's doing it for you, out of love for you, like when she washed dishes at midnight because you were tired; because you were practicing; because you had a gift. And a gift takes precedence. But you have to pay. If your mother taught you anything, she taught you that. You pay for your gifts—for good or ill—with the minutes, with the hours of your life. Hadn't your mother's kitchen testified of that? And the blue jeans that hung on the line for three days? And the raspberry she placed on your lips while your hands were sticky with gore? And the chicken carcass and cereal bowls she left in the sink while the brim of her sun hat wavered out there in the garden, where she loved to kneel in the sun?

Brothers

Levi Peterson

ABOUT A YEAR AND A HALF AFTER Mitch fell, he decided on a come-back climb. Understandably, his wife was less than enthusiastic about it. Everyone agreed the fall should have killed Mitch or, worse, made a quadriplegic of him. It happened on an easy cliff in the Sandia Mountains. He had three pieces of protection placed, but they zippered out. He had broken his neck, a shoulder blade, an ankle, and a dozen ribs. He wore a halo brace with screws anchored in his skull for months. At night he couldn't sleep more than two hours before the brace woke him up.

His wife, Jan, had to bathe him and wipe his bottom when he used the toilet. Actually, Jan wasn't his wife. He had needed a reason for being excommunicated from his church, which was Mormon, and living with Jan without the benefit of matrimony sufficed. However, they both counted on getting married sooner or later. So she gave him his baths and wiped his bottom.

He tried to assure Jan that the come-back climb wouldn't be technical. Someone had told him that you could get to the top of the highest peak in Wyoming by a scramble if you knew the route. That was what he had in mind. He wanted to get on with his ambition to climb the highest summit in each of the fifty states. The problem was that none of his Albuquerque friends were interested in driving so far for a scramble. He told Jan he would be okay going solo. In fact, he needed a solo outing of some sort. He needed to see where his life was headed, what with technical climbing being out of the question. But Jan said someone had to go with him. If nobody else went with him, she would have to, an impossible eventuality because her idea of a vigorous workout was a half-hour in a gym.

Against his better judgment he let her phone his stepbrother Bernie in Salt Lake City, whom he hadn't seen in twenty years. Bernie, who was a total Mormon, was properly skeptical of getting involved in this little adventure. He said he was afraid of heights. Jan said the point of a scramble was that you didn't expose yourself to dangerous falls. Bernie then said he didn't have the stamina for it. However, his wife Carol got on the other phone while this conversation was going on and said he did too have the stamina; he was a Scoutmaster and just last summer had taken thirteen boys to King's Peak, the highest point in Utah. Bernie briefly considered raising yet another objection, which was that he was afraid of being alone, and as far as he could see, a five-day trek in the Wind River Mountains with a stepbrother from whom he had been estranged for decades wouldn't be much different from being there alone. However, he was ashamed of this phobia, which seemed not just juvenile but downright infantile, and he couldn't mention it to Carol. So her assertion that he had been to King's Peak with thirteen Scouts just last summer clenched the matter, and he reluctantly agreed to go along with Mitch.

Mitch and Jan drove to Salt Lake on a Sunday. He told her she didn't need to go to the trouble. She said she didn't trust him enough to let him go alone; once on the road, he could very well change his mind and head for the Wind River Mountains without Bernie. Mitch protested her suspicion, but not with much vigor because the thought had occurred to him more than once during the preceding week.

Bernie and Carol took them in, Carol with more enthusiasm than Bernie. Obviously, Jan and Carol had already struck up a warm friendship over the phone. Jan left Mitch to unpack in the guest room while she went out to the kitchen to help Carol get dinner. During their after-dinner talk Jan pressed it on Bernie over and over that he had to keep a close eye on Mitch and not let him do something foolish, given the fact that he was still so stove up from the accident that he couldn't raise his hands much higher than his head. Bernie promised to do as requested, falling into a sullen resignation because, being a total Mormon, he knew he'd have to honor his promise. As for Carol, she had been on a spiritual high for days, marveling over the prospect of Bernie being the instrumentality by which his lapsed brother might be induced to rejoin the church and marry his gentile girlfriend and of course convert her and then take her to the temple and be sealed to her for time and eternity. Glowing with good will, she had let Bernie have sex every night during the past week, a frequency unheard of since the early years of their marriage. She was worried that it might sap his strength for the climb, but he said, no, it would actually make him stronger. According to an article he had read in a chiropractor's office, a man who was emptied of his regenerative fluids had an improved ability of arms, legs, and lungs.

In bed that night in the guest room, Mitch grumbled about how complicated a simple climb had become. Having been raised a Mormon, he could see clear as day which direction Bernie and Carol were headed. He warned Jan to be on her guard during the coming week. She would see that Carol would tow her around to Temple Square and also undoubtedly to that building that used to be Hotel Utah where he had heard that a film on the history of Mormonism was pumped without cost and at high pressure to unsuspecting gentile tourists.

"You need to check yourself over pretty carefully every night," he said, "to see if you are becoming infected with her testimony. It's contagious as small pox."

"What's a testimony?" she asked.

"It's a witness that you have had a message from the other world. Mark my word. Carol has had a big one."

"They both seem like awfully decent people," Jan said. "I can't figure out why you've been hiding them from me all this time."

Well before dawn, Mitch and Bernie loaded their gear into Mitch's car and headed for Wyoming. Neither of them found it comfortable to be locked up in a car with the other. The last thing either of them wanted to talk about was their years spent together in rural Idaho. Eventually, the silence got to Bernie, and he began giving minor details about his eleven grandchildren, whose photographs Mitch was already familiar with because they covered a lot of wall and table space in Bernie's house. Mitch didn't reciprocate, though he did have a couple of kids by his first marriage, a son and a daughter, both respectful and affectionate toward Mitch, married with growing families, both doing the Mormon thing full time, thanks mostly to their mother and also to their stepfather, who had turned out to be a pretty decent fellow.

When they had got onto the high plains of Wyoming, still heading east into the early sun, they could see the Uinta Mountains off to the south just across the border in Utah. Bernie said he had been taking Boy Scouts to the Uintas every summer for twelve years. He admitted it was a scary business to be a Scoutmaster. Boys of that age didn't think; they operated on impulse, the more unintelligent the better as far as they were concerned. You never knew when one of them might try scaling a cliff or swimming across an ice-cold lake. Some Scoutmasters weren't so smart either. He knew one who had carried a dozen hymnbooks in his pack on a ten-mile trek so his Scouts could sing at the campfire. Another allowed himself to be tied to a tree by his scouts in what was supposed to be a game; the boys then hiked into a nearby town to hang out all evening with girls at a drive-in.

East of Fort Bridger they left the freeway and took a state highway headed north. In time their road began to follow the Green River. The river was slow moving and of a brown, muddy color that made people ask why it was called the Green River. Cottonwood trees lined its banks, and grazing cattle dotted its wide grassy bottom. To the east rose the wild, rugged wall of the Wind River range. An hour later, they stopped in Pinedale and bought some freeze-dried dinners at a small sporting goods store. While they were paying, Bernie told the cashier, a young woman who looked like a granola cruncher from Yosemite or the Cascades, that they were brothers.

"That depends on what you mean by brothers," Mitch said to her. "His dad and my mom got married. So we spent some time on the same farm. That was a long time ago."

On the way out they passed by a display of rock-climbing gear. Mitch pointed out a spring-loaded cam, a device with tiny cogs and looped cable. "That's the kind that pulled out and let me fall," he said.

The cashier was still watching. "My fall is the reason this fellow is with me," Mitch explained to her, jerking a thumb toward Bernie. "My wife figures somebody ought to be along to keep an eye on me even if he can't climb."

"I don't apologize for being afraid of heights," Bernie said.

They got into Mitch's car and continued driving north along the river, which paralleled the mountain range closely. Mitch pointed out that somewhere on its barren, jagged crest was an indistinguishable prominence called Gannett Peak, their ultimate destination.

They were both thinking about what Mitch had said to the cashier. Mitch was thinking he had been unnecessarily blunt. He granted it showed insecurity on his part. It had something to do with Jan and Carol warming up to each other. As for Bernie, he was feeling snubbed and angry. A backpack trip with the Scouts was an ordeal. He looked forward only to its end. This trek promised to be worse—five days of brutal labor, entirely unrewarding in and of itself, to escort a man who didn't want escorting to an elevation so nondescript that you had to take the word of the geologists that it was sixty or eighty or a hundred feet higher than the elevations around it.

After a while Bernie said, "My dad adopted you. Your mom adopted me. We have two sisters in common. It seems like to me that makes us brothers."

"I never regarded your dad as my dad," Mitch said.

"Yes, I know," Bernie said. "You called him Jim."

"I went to a lawyer six or seven years ago and said, I want to repudiate an adoption. I don't want it down on the records that I am the legal son of Jim Lindmuller. The lawyer said, We can change your name easy enough. What do you want to change it to? I said, To Taylor, which is my real dad's name."

"I knew about that," Bernie said.

"So now my name is Mitch Taylor again," Mitch went on. "No disrespect meant to you."

"No, of course not."

About an hour later they got to a trailhead at the end of the road. They strapped on their packs and headed into the mountains along the wide, deep canyon of the Green River. They crossed meadows and went through stands of lodgepole pines and aspens. There were moose and elk droppings in the trail—also a good deal of horse dung. Sometimes the trail came close to the wide, rushing river, which did seem green here, a milky greenish color probably derived from the grinding of boulder fields and glaciers. Bernie complained about his aching back. He said he knew his shoulders wouldn't stop hurting till he took off the pack. He said he had never started a backpack trip without wondering why he was doing it. Mitch for his part was trying hard to recapture the old euphoria of a climb. It ought to be turning on almost any moment, he kept telling himself. In the meantime, his shoulders were hurting so much that he considered turning back. No pain, no gain, he began to tell himself, repeating the mantra of weight lifters. It stood to reason his back would hurt less on his next trip. This trip would condition him. Furthermore, you shouldn't expect to make a summit without some cost. That was what climbing was about.

Early evening they made camp on a bench above the river. They heated a couple of the freeze-dried dinners over Mitch's tiny camp stove. Mitch scowled while he ate. Camp food was all pretty much tasteless. However, you had to eat to keep up your strength. He watched while Bernie opened the pop-top lid on a small can of diced fruit. Bernie offered him half. Mitch shook his head. "You hauled it; you eat it," he said. There was an issue here. He had disapproved when he saw Bernie putting the cans in his pack on Sunday night. "Too much weight," he had said. "It isn't worth the expenditure of energy required to carry it."

They both had a miserable night, lying in a narrow tent with a half-inch of cellulose foam between their sleeping bags and the ground. Mitch groaned sometimes when he turned over. "Let me just ask you," Bernie said on one of these occasions. "What's so important about getting to the top of a mountain?"

"That's a good question," Mitch said. He admitted climbing was a strange business. If you couldn't make the top, you might just as well stay home. He talked about the first ascent of Denali, attributed to an Episcopal minister named Hudson Stuck. In 1913 Stuck and three partners arrived on the south summit of Denali, from which they could clearly see a fir pole planted on the lower north summit three years earlier by the most improbable climbers in the history of mountaineering, the so-called Mt. McKinley sourdoughs. Four miners, spurred on by a bet made in a Fairbanks saloon, had toiled across the Muldrow glacier and established a camp around 11,000 feet. From that camp, in a single epic day, three of the miners climbed more than 9,000 feet to the north summit, unfurled a flag on a fir pole they had carried, and returned. But it didn't count. They hadn't made the true summit.

The next morning, Mitch and Bernie shouldered their packs and, without the benefit of a trail, turned up a lateral canyon named Tourist Creek, which proved to be seriously misnamed. Its steep slopes consisted of gigantic boulders fallen from sheer granite cliffs. Angular and multifaceted, the boulders overlaid one another in utter confusion, leaving no shred of soil anywhere visible. Many were as large as a car. Some were as big as a dump truck. Weighted by their full packs, Mitch and Bernie levered themselves upward over the boulders with aching muscles and gasping breath. Footing was at best precarious—on sharp edges or tiny projections that accommodated only the toe of a boot. Mitch, mumbling "No pain, no gain," moaned every time he stretched for a hold above his head. Bernie was panting hoarsely. This was, he saw, no hike but an exhausting climb only a little short of technical. Certainly it gave a new meaning to the word *scramble*. He found it helpful to watch Mitch's foot and hand moves. Every few minutes he was faced by a wide gap between boulders, requiring either that he consume five or ten laborious minutes climbing off one boulder and onto another or that he accept the exposure—the empty space between himself and the rocks fifteen or twenty or thirty feet below—and leap heedlessly across the gap. It gave him no pleasure to realize that more and more he was resorting to this last measure. It seemed a gesture of desperation, a serious compromise of good sense.

Noon found them perhaps two-thirds the way up the canyon. They sat with their feet dangling over a small boulder and ate a lunch consisting of cheese, crackers, and lemonade made from powder.

"Going back to this thing about us not being brothers," Bernie said, "Jan seems to think we are."

"Yes, and she thinks Scoutmasters are mountaineers, which they aren't. So she just might be mistaken on this other matter too. No disrespect meant."

"No, of course not."

"On this thing about your dad," Mitch said. "I was nine when Mom married Jim. I already had a dad, and he had walked out on me. I had very complicated feelings. On the one hand, I needed a dad; on the other hand, I felt like Mom had given up on my dad too soon. I kept hoping he would come back. He had been a nice guy. I can remember a lot of nice things he did for me. He took me places, did things with me. So when Mom said Jim was going to adopt me, I protested. Then Mom took out her twelve-gauge shotgun, so to speak, and fired both barrels. She said my dad had signed off on Jim adopting me in return for being free of child support. I was young, but I wasn't stupid. I knew

I had been sold. I'm not claiming I have been a good daddy myself. But at least I paid child support, and my kids saw me at vacation time."

They got up, shouldered their packs, and began clambering over the boulders again.

"I think my dad actually did love you," Bernie said.

Mitch turned to face Bernie. "Get real!" he said. "Do you remember that year you and I were supposed to stay on the homestead all summer and not come into town except on Sunday? I was fourteen, and you were ten or eleven."

"I remember."

"Jim said, 'Mitch is in charge. Bernie, you mind him.' About the third or fourth day we were out there, we went into the pasture to catch the work horses so I could hitch them up and mow alfalfa. I asked you to carry one of the bridles. Just on principle. You refused. I thrust one of the bridles into your hands. You dropped it. I picked it up and hung it over your shoulder. You pushed it off. I tied the reins to your wrists. You collapsed and lay on the ground. I dragged you a few yards. You were howling and cursing. So I gave up and took the bridles and somehow cornered the horses without your help and went to work, mowing hay. When I got back to the shack at noon, you were gone. You had walked into town even though Jim had said we weren't to do that. Nobody showed up to tell me anything about it till Sunday morning when Jim drove out to take me into town for church. I said, 'Is Bernie coming back out with me tonight?' Jim said, 'No, and by the way, it isn't your privilege to discipline Bernie. That's my job.' And I was out there the whole summer by myself."

"I was in the wrong," Bernie said.

"I don't blame you," Mitch said. "Jim is the one who was in the wrong for putting us out there in the first place. And my mother, for letting him do it."

"No," Bernie insisted, "from start to finish, my behavior was inexcusable."

Inexcusable yet inevitable, Bernie admitted to himself. He remembered all too clearly the aloneness of the homestead. During his waking hours he had had this strange impulse to run. There was something terrifying, something imminently lethal, about isolation. He hadn't walked back into town the day he had abandoned Mitch. He had run.

But it wasn't something he could tell Mitch about, or anyone else for that matter. It seemed too shameful, too infantile.

Late in the afternoon they turned southeastward out of Tourist Creek, taking a side gorge that was a little less steep and offered stretches where grass alternated with boulders. Toward evening they arrived at a crescent-shaped lake perhaps an eighth of a mile wide and a half-mile long, which stood, according to Mitch's altimeter, at 11,000 feet. They made camp with difficulty, there being only sparse spots of grass in a terrain composed mostly of rock. As they heated water for supper, the clouds that had covered the sky most of the day parted and a late sun came out. To the southeast stood high final peaks on the Continental Divide with snowfields and glaciers, Gannett itself being still out of sight. For supper they shared an unpalatable freeze-dried meal of potatoes, beef, and gravy. Bernie opened another can of diced fruit and offered half of it to Mitch.

"No way," said Mitch. "What are you trying to do? Break down my morals? You don't bring canned goods on a climb. It's a matter of principle."

"You have a strange sense of principle," Bernie said. "Considering that you got yourself excommunicated from the church."

"That was a matter of principle too," Mitch said. "As you know, I was sealed to Jim and my mother for time and eternity when they got married in the temple. So after I changed my name back to Taylor, I began inquiring how you go about getting unsealed from someone. It turned out the easiest way was to get excommunicated from the church. That undoes all your ordinances and sealings. So I did it. I began shacking up with Jan, and my bishop obliged by holding a church court, which I didn't show up at."

"I would think you'd at least want to be sealed to your kids," said Bernie.

"I never was sealed to them. I don't belong to anybody. That's the way I feel. I'm out there all alone."

By the time they had finished supper, Mitch was starting to feel good. He was pleased with the hard scramble up Tourist Creek. If your body hurt as much as his did, it had to be good for you. This wasn't a trek for couch potatoes. He could see he wasn't finished, not by a long shot. He wasn't sixty yet, way too young to give up real climbing. He was starting to feel that Bernie's presence was irrelevant. If he couldn't add anything to the climb, at least he couldn't detract much from it either. Mitch looked out on the lake, a purple mirror beneath a darkening sky. A single planet burned in the cloudless west. Talus slopes of jumbled boulders, fallen from looming cliffs, edged the lake on either side. Sparse patches of grass showed here and there. The only sign of animal life was a few flies—no birds, no mosquitoes, no fish circles spreading on the breathless lake. You couldn't be depressed in a place like this. Things were uncomplicated here. Simple gestures, clear and unambiguous, kept you alive.

Unlike Mitch, Bernie hadn't cheered up. The stark, unadorned landscape depressed him. He longed for Carol. About now he should have been helping clear the dinner table, carrying the dishes to her while she loaded the dishwasher. He was feeling little twinges of the old hysteria over being alone. It didn't help much to be in the presence of a morose, uncommunicative fugitive from righteous living like Mitch. It struck Bernie that this must be a foretaste of the telestial kingdom, that unhappy place where the unvaliant among the Mormons and the wicked among the gentiles will dwell throughout all eternity. He saw clearly now how it would be there: barren, unfurnished, sterile, populated by souls who took no comfort in one another's presence, who lived, that is, in effectual isolation forever and ever.

"I don't understand why you would deliberately get yourself unsealed from your family," Bernie said while they were preparing to get into their sleeping bags. "Especially from your mother and our sisters. You share their blood."

"If I didn't feel like part of the family on earth, why should I feel like part of it in eternity?" Mitch said.

"Well, what about Jan?" Bernie insisted. "Don't you want to be with her in eternity?"

"You bet. I plan on it. I lucked out when I ran into Jan. I'm whopped on her. She's whopped on me. We've agreed after we die we'll look each other up."

"You can't just look each other up."

"What do you mean we can't?" Mitch said. "What's to stop us?"

"Because you're not married in the temple. You're not sealed for time and eternity."

Mitch rustled about in his bag, turning this way and that, groaning a little as he sought a comfortable position. "I hope you don't know what you're talking about," he muttered. "Because if you do, the Big Fellow upstairs is a whole lot meaner than I had any idea."

Somewhere late in the night they both got out of the tent to urinate. There had been spatters of rain on the tent earlier. Now the sky was broken, with vast patches of luminous, star-studded sky showing.

While they were settling into their bags again, Mitch said, "I looked up my dad—my real dad—a couple of times before he died, which was about fifteen years ago. I knew his name of course, but I didn't have an address. I didn't even know what state he lived in. So any time I traveled, I'd check the local phone book, in airports, gas stations, motels. One night in a Motel 6 in Rapid City, South Dakota, I looked in the phone book and there he was. I phoned him right then. It was eleven o'clock. 'It's you!' he said. 'Well, come on over.' So I went. Didn't get to bed till two or three in the morning. He wasn't living with anybody. He had run through four or five wives. Last time I saw him, he was dying of kidney failure from diabetes. A nurse phoned me from the hospital, and I flew in from Albuquerque. He held my hand and cried, and when I said, 'I'll look you up on the other side,' he said, 'I'd like that.' 'Yeah,' I said, 'we'll get to know each other.' 'Let's do it,' he said. 'I'll count on it.' "

Mitch was weighing the odds. Could God be so mean, so punctilious and worried about protocol, that he wouldn't let people associate with each other in eternity even if they wanted to unless they had knuckled under to the church and gone through all the ceremonies and made all the vows and kept all the commandments, all four or five thousand of them?

After a while he said, "I guess I don't believe you on that business of being sealed for time and eternity. It's a bunch of hocus-pocus. God wouldn't be that malicious."

Bernie squirmed about, trying unsuccessfully to fit his body around a couple of rocks located in just the wrong places. Mitch was the one who was in the wrong, of course. It wasn't a matter of God being unforgiving; it was a matter of God giving some simple rules. Obey and you get the blessings; disobey and you don't. Nonetheless, things did seem unreal to Bernie just at this moment—the dark tent, Mitch's occasional moaning, the vast rocky wilderness outside, indifferent to human plans and human desires. Sometimes Bernie believed God's emanations filled the entire universe. You couldn't go anywhere God wasn't. But this place made him wonder. Maybe God let the universe tend itself, ruled by natural law, and when it was time to save you, he'd send out a search and find you and bring you home.

About an hour later they got up and fixed breakfast in the dark. Soon after dawn they left camp with emergency gear in their packs in case they had to bivouac. They trudged past the lake and up another narrow, winding valley filled with jumbled rock and an occasional patch of grass. From the end of that valley they could at last see Gannett. They went on, laboring over a half-dozen old moraines and across a tundra littered by boulders from a long-departed glacier. Midmorning, they started up the final crest, traversing a snowfield which differed from a glacier, as Mitch informed Bernie, in that it didn't migrate and therefore presumably harbored no crevasses. Beyond the snowfield, they angled across a talus slope toward a cliff towering just under the final peak. Mitch was convinced he could see an easy way up the cliff.

"Right over there to the left," he kept saying. "Not bad at all. A pretty good scramble, actually. Thirty, forty yards of touchy stuff, and then we're free for the top."

Bernie eyed it over—a kind of fractured, rocky staircase that deepened while it rose through the cliff. "That doesn't look like a scramble to me," he said. "That looks dangerous."

He sat on a big rock while Mitch looked for a better route. When he came back, Mitch said there wasn't a better one. "It's this or nothing," he said. "I admit it's tricky. However, no mountaineer would rope up for this chimney. It's just a scramble. Just do exactly what I do, and you'll be okay."

He started up the staircase, placing his hands and feet carefully. There were plenty of good holds, but of course if you happened to slip, you'd tumble all the way to the bottom of the staircase.

"I can't do it," Bernie called up to him. "I told you I was afraid of heights."

Mitch backed down and sat on a rock beside Bernie. "Guess it's turn-around time," he said morosely. "It's pretty painful anyhow, reaching up for those handholds. Though I was doing it, as you just saw."

They sat for maybe fifteen minutes, eating lunch. The sun was very hot, and they both slathered on another layer of sun block.

"What if I went on alone?" Mitch said. "You'd wait here. I could do it up and back in about two hours."

Bernie didn't answer. He thought about the homestead in Idaho. It had been six miles from town. He didn't know how many miles this place was from a town. He did know it wasn't a place for breaking into a mindless run, which was what he felt like doing just now.

"So what about it?" Mitch repeated. "Are you okay with me making a go for it alone?"

"That'd worry me," Bernie said.

"Nothing to it," Mitch said. "I keep telling you, it's just a scramble."

"What'll I tell Jan?"

"No need to tell her. What she doesn't know won't hurt her."

"It'd really worry me," Bernie said.

They sat another ten minutes or so. Mitch was again inclined to concede. It wasn't just a matter of pain when he had to stretch his arms for a handhold. His muscles were only about half as strong as formerly. He wasn't sure he could rely on them in a pinch. But then he began thinking about how close the summit was and how he would go on for the rest of his life wanting to kick himself in the butt for not having the grit to give it a real try. He got up and shouldered his pack. "I'm going to do it," he said. "Sorry, Bernie. You wait right here. Have yourself a nice nap."

He started up the staircase, whistling cheerfully. About a hundred feet up, he shouted, "See you in a couple of hours." Then he disappeared.

Bernie sat in the shade at the base of the cliff, wondering whether climbers climb because they want to escape their social obligations. Mitch had got what he wanted, which was to be alone. As for himself, he had wasted three days and was fated to waste two more just to find out the fellow he had always thought of as a brother was as distant and alien from him as a man who had been picked out at random from the general population.

Below him stretched a jumbled slope of boulders and beyond that a vast gleaming snowfield and beyond that a narrow, rocky valley with

a couple of small lakes and barren cliffs on either side, topped by a
skyline of jagged, irregular rock. No trees, no shrubs, no meadows. No
butterflies, no bees, no birds. Just lichens. It was true, he now noticed
for the first time. On all hands, the rock, close and distant, was covered
by a gray-green scale of lichens. A strange despair came over him. How
could you identify with lichens? How could you take any comfort, find
any shred of fellow feeling, in such a dry, thin veneer of textured color
upon otherwise bare rock? He noted, with a touch of curiosity, that the
old fear was accelerating inside him, like a vehicle getting up to speed.
Solitude exerted a pressure like an atmosphere. He could feel it on his
skin. He wanted to run. Just where was unclear.

It occurred to Bernie that, if he hurried, he still had time to catch
up with Mitch. He got to his feet and shouldered his pack. He studied the staircase a moment. He decided he could manage it. The trick
would be to place his hands and feet on those convenient ledges without looking down, because if he looked down, he would be finished.
He'd do something like go rigid or have spasms.

Once he was at it, the climbing seemed easy. He went up and up.
Euphoria came over him. But pretty soon he realized that holds for
his hands and feet were becoming harder to find because the stairway
was fusing with a band of vertical rock. He had apparently got past the
point where Mitch had left the staircase. He decided to retreat. Looking down, he was dizzied by the empty air. He kept climbing, reasoning
that he would top the cliff at any moment and there would be Mitch
heading toward Gannett.

After four or five advances, he saw that the granite was bulging
into an overhang. He could see that he was done for. He clung in a
stupor of terror, the toes of his boots resting on a four-inch lip, his left
hand cupping a doughnut-shaped knob, the fingers of his right hand
bending into an inch-wide crack. Warmth spread around his crotch,
and he realized he had lost bladder control.

About an hour later Mitch made the summit. The summit itself wasn't much to look at, something of a round table of rock rising
above the jagged, serrated ridge that stretched away in either direction.
The full circle view was spectacular: rugged mountain ranges and vast
shimmering plains rimmed by a horizon mysteriously vague in its indication of where earth ended and sky began. On the summit was a

gallon can covered by a flat rock, inside of which were a pencil and a register of persons who had recently been here. Mitch added his name to the list. He wasn't ecstatic. He was too tired, too full of aches and pains, for that. But he was satisfied. The old man wasn't down and out yet. He just might make it back to technical climbing. He'd try for it; that was for sure.

He sat on an edge, dangling his feet over empty space and mulling possibilities while he ate an energy bar and took a drink of water. There was a saying: if you keep climbing long enough, you die on the mountain. If only it were guaranteed, he wouldn't give the matter a second thought. You couldn't ask for a better way to die. But what if it put you in a wheelchair? What if it sentenced you to ten years in a quadriplegic's bed?

All of which got him to thinking how Jan had so patiently given him baths and wiped his butt for three months, and that brought him around to thinking about the next life and the possibility that God would say the following to him on Judgment Day: *You had plenty of warning; you knew you had to get sealed to Jan in the temple in order to have her here; as it is, you have to go off with that bunch of strangers over there and spend eternity milling around among them, and don't try anything funny like trying to form some new friendships and love relationships, because if I get word you're up to that, I'll send in the immigration officers and transfer you to a new location.*

The climb down proved slower and more risky than the ascent. Mitch dropped off the main ridge through the rubble of a declivity. At the bottom of that, he got onto a precarious, foot-wide ledge, along which he sidestepped, gratefully seizing handholds if they were available. There was about a hundred-foot drop here. The trickiest part was the transition off the ledge into the staircase. He had to admit it was a technical situation. No question of it, he'd have welcomed a belay here. It was lucky Bernie hadn't come along. But, sure enough, he made it safe and sound into the staircase, which left him feeling much more euphoric than he had on top. It was true; the old fellow still had some grit in him.

About then he happened to look upward and was stunned by what he saw. In fact, he had to ask himself whether he was hallucinating. It was Bernie, maybe forty feet above, hung on sheer rock.

"What are you doing up there?" he shouted.

Bernie tried to answer. The sound wasn't much more than a whimper. He longed to let go and get it over with. His hands seemed to be of another mind. They gripped ferociously. They seemed frozen into position. They had long since turned numb. He heard Mitch say, "I'm coming up. Hang on." What seemed a complete thought broke the blank paralysis of his mind. It was that he had to tell Mitch about the file marked *Important* in his desk at work. It would inform Carol about the insurance and retirement. Mitch was saying something more, but Bernie couldn't focus on what it signified. He was being enticed, seduced, by that longing to let go and get it over with. It seemed a sensible, peaceful solution to his dilemma. He marveled that his hands couldn't grasp that fact. It was as if someone else controlled them.

He could hear Mitch again, clearly now, saying, "I can see a good hold for your left foot. Get your weight onto your right leg and let your left foot down easy. I'll tell you when to plant it. Then I'll tell you where to place your hands."

"It's no good," Bernie said. "I'm finished. There's a file in my desk at work. Bottom drawer, way to the back. Tell Carol about it. It'll tell her about the insurance and retirement."

"Don't be stupid," Mitch said. "Get your weight on your right leg, then lower that left foot. Just take it easy. Keep your toe in contact with the rock."

Bernie didn't move, and Mitch repeated the directions. He still didn't move. "Can't you get into motion?" Mitch said. "It's only a couple of hours till dark."

"I keep wanting to," Bernie said. "But my body won't cooperate."

Mitch began to rethink this attempt at a rescue. He wasn't sure how long he himself could cling to his present hold, which wasn't as secure as Bernie's position. His upper back was a throbbing mass of pain. They were on epic rock, the kind only zealots and suicidal heroes attempt without protection—and climbers of that sort, having made it up, would rappel down or find a safer route elsewhere, there being few things more certain to produce disaster in the entire sport of mountaineering than downclimbing sheer rock.

He considered the ethics of the situation. No one could fault him now for climbing down. He had made an honest—and highly risky— effort to save Bernie. The longer he waited the more likely Bernie was to fall and take Mitch down with him. It didn't make sense for both of them to die.

Strangely, Mitch himself now seemed in a kind of paralysis. Instead of starting down, he studied the granite about four inches from his eyes. If you looked close, you saw that granite was composed of crystal-like particles tending toward a hue of bluish gray. Some climbers spoke of intimacy with the rock, as if rock loved to be climbed. They talked that way at parties and in bars. Thinking about that kind of vain, pretentious, and unknowing talk emptied Mitch of emotion. He wondered what some of those armchair mountaineers would recommend in the present crisis. How would they feel abandoning a brother who had gone catatonic on a cliff? How would they feel about waiting in the dark near the base of the staircase for the inevitable rattle of rock announcing that Bernie had at last lost his hold, followed by the sickening thump of his body at the bottom?

It seemed that, as a bare minimum, he should say some kind of formal good-bye to Bernie before he started down—tell him, for example, that, yes, he would convey his message to Carol and also that—and this was a surprise to Mitch, something he had had no premonition of before this instant—he did appreciate those years they had lived together in the same house and actually did regard him as a brother despite his hostile talk in that sporting goods store in Pinedale.

"Where I went wrong," Mitch said, abstractly and to no purpose, since he assumed Bernie had shut off his hearing, "was by splitting up our party when I decided to make a try for the peak. The rule is you don't split up a party in the mountains."

"Things went wrong," Bernie said, "because I didn't know we weren't brothers. I should have stayed home. I thought maybe we would get to know each other again."

"Well, you are my brother," Mitch said. "If I didn't know it before, I know it now."

He could hear a strange sound. He realized it was Bernie sobbing.

"Do you want to try lowering that left foot?" Mitch said. "Get your weight on your right leg. Keep your toe in contact with the rock. I'll tell you when it's reached the new hold. Then I'll tell you where to place your hands and your other foot."

It took ten minutes to talk Bernie into completing the move.

"You wouldn't be able to speed things up a little, would you?" Mitch asked after he had given directions for the next move.

"Maybe I can," Bernie said. "I'll try."

JUMPING

Mary Clyde

THIS IS WHAT NEVER HAPPENED.

Kelly and Veronica and I are standing in front of the church waiting for rides home. The boys are chasing each other with their jackets open, even though their faces are red and roughened by the cold. Then childhood's most exuberant exclamation: "You're going to die!" One boy to another, completely true and completely not.

"Yeah, yeah," Kelly says, with a mittened shooing motion, feigning magnificent indifference to hide the awful excitement of girls turning thirteen.

"I think he likes you," I say to Veronica. (Notice, please, my generous compliment. What is more kind than a recognition of someone else's love?)

"Who? Brent?" she says, acting surprised, but I see she's already thought it.

The mothers' car tires slurp through wet snow.

Kelly says, "You'll make a cute couple." Coming from Kelly, this means something. Coming from Kelly, it means you're in.

Veronica's smile always made her look stupid, so when I invent this scene, I can't let her mess it up by smiling. I allow her a contented nod. I want everything to be perfect. When Veronica climbs in her mother's car, cold but happy, I know that it is.

It would have happened thirty-three years ago. It would have helped if it—or something like it—had. *If only.* I see it all the time in my work, how small events can change history. I study names, nomenclature: place names, given names, family names, ethnic names, nicknames. A time or two I've been an expert witness. Once I was interviewed on network news. I turn up forgotten information about why baby girls were named Artemisia; why some place was called Maybe. I know the name Wendy first appeared in *Peter Pan*, and the most common name in the world is Mohammed. I've learned the flukiness of names and name-giving. I've seen how a name's viability can be lost because of a bad-apple Judas or Benedict.

I think of Veronica, the ski lift accident, and the time that came after as I've thought of names and naming—a freakish thing that has made all the difference, though I'm still trying to identify what that difference is.

Recently the accident's details started coming back to me—a return like comets or geese. A reentry, an insistent one, like a birth. Parts of what happened then interrupt my day now, insisting I think about it, somehow respect it, understand it matters—I don't know all what. I find myself explaining to my husband Dave a particularity of the ambulance ride—that the sirens were off—or recalling the sky, how the air was truly clear.

"Joan?" he says, curious but patient. "Joan, why are you talking about it now?"

They fell from ski lift chairs, and we thought it was just someone throwing garbage.

"What the heck?" Kelly said. We had been taught littering was a crime.

But then we saw: too big, too heavy. They were actually being thrown themselves, launched from their seats, bucked like rodeo riders, tumbled like dice. They fell gracefully downward. Floated on a summer day in tragedy's own slow time.

I said, "Kelly, what should we do?" I rubbed my eyes behind my eyeglasses, a pantomime of disbelief, but how could this be true?

We had been camping with our church group lower on the mountain, and this afternoon we were riding the ski lift to enjoy the view. But now beneath us, ahead and thirty yards farther down the hill, we could see our companions, three girls and our camp leader, lying on the ground. They moved, but it was only a leg or two, lethargic, ineffectual efforts, as if they had all stumbled while drunk.

"Jump," Kelly commanded, "before they start it up again, before it throws us out."

One of the ski lift chairs was wrapped crazily around a huge support beam. The ski lift was disabled. It wouldn't have started, couldn't. I saw that, knew it exactly.

Kelly jumped first, landed in a crouch, steady as a gymnast.

I hung from the footrest twenty-five feet above the ground, looking at aspen trees. Their leaves fluttered encouragingly. The beauty of the day would be remarked on—how it was shattered by tragedy—when our story was reported later on the ten o'clock news. But, of course, nothing was shattered. It was an "America-the-Beautiful" sky: noble and particularly blue.

I later said how I felt it in my stomach, the wind that blew my body slightly just before I let go, but I have no confidence in that now. It may be just part of the story and not part of the truth. I know I counted to five, twice. I remember the hurt and relief of landing.

I called to Kelly. "Wait for me. I'm bleeding." I had fallen forward and scraped my face and bent my glasses. I was desperately afraid of what might happen next—what *did* happen—that she would run down the hill for help. That would leave me to follow doing . . . but what *would* I do when I got to our companions? I might have counted again before I ran, but I didn't hesitate long. This impresses me, that as a child I faced this, went forward into the mayhem, recognizing there was no way out.

I felt the hot and cold sting of the scrapes on my face. Rocks made the path uneven. I recall stubby milkweed pods and fragile Queen Anne's lace. There was a Utah summer's own dusty, bitter, green smell. But then as I got to where they lay, there was no picture and only one sound. It came when one of them called my name. Linda spoke to me, but I was too frightened to understand her.

Later, in the hospital, I asked her what she'd said. She was in an immense cast, traction like a cartoon strip. She had disappeared and become someone new. Her eyes were blackened, and she sucked water from an accordion-hinged straw. She said, "I guess I told you to get help." Her jaw was wired shut, but that wasn't why what she'd said hadn't sounded true. I felt that on the mountain she'd asked me something important, but also not obvious. Some secret available only to someone surprised and crushed after falling through the summer sky.

But besides the empty sound of her question, I recall nothing. In those moments on the hill there was shifting color; there was shape; but it tumbled without form or meaning, kaleidoscopic, as if I too were falling. The victims seemed dismantled by the plunge, not just injured but unformed. I ran again after Linda spoke to me, blindly following Kelly. Down, down, down. A flight over a quiet ski run, pursued by demons I would have years to get to know. Stopping to check my bleeding, I looked up at the bottom of another girl's shoes. We were spaced irregularly on the lift. Hers was probably the next occupied chair.

"What's going on?" she said. She was peevish. She swung her legs and chomped her gum. "Why aren't we going?"

It strikes me even now, as it did then, that what I was about to tell her would change her life. I felt the messenger's importance, a power I wouldn't feel again for many years until I was the one who had to tell my father his sister had died.

"They're hurt," I said. "It's bad."

She chewed her gum slowly, readjusted her headband, and tried to look back.

Then I heard a voice behind me say, "Lie down." I recognized a woman from the church camp. "Look, see," she said, "you're bleeding." She thought I was why Kelly had been so excited.

My glasses were sitting crookedly on my face. I feared they might cause her not to take me seriously, and I had something important to say. "It's not me who's hurt." Appearing worried then, she handed me a wrinkled tissue and trotted up the hill.

I realized my glasses' lenses were scratched. I'm extremely nearsighted, and damaged glasses pose a frightening threat. "Kelly," I whispered below the ski lift, willing her return and my rescue, wishing I had gone with her, thinking how she'd escaped.

"Shh," the girl above me said. "I think I can hear them bawling."

I could hear the abrupt *tda-tda-tda* of winged grasshoppers and the purr of a few clover-seeking bees. The aspen trees seemed to tremble, and I wanted Kelly—and the old life she represented—more than I've ever wanted anyone in my life.

• • •

Three years before, on the way to see the school nurse in fifth grade, Kelly had said, "I have a secret." Though Kelly called herself a tomboy, Kelly and her mother bought her dresses at J.C. Penney. They had attached petticoats that made a stiff elegant sound. While the rest of us worse saddle shoes, Kelly wore black patent-leather slip-ons, which she rubbed with Vaseline.

That day I suspected she loved Stephen Edison, and I presumed she was about to confess, maybe even tell me what it was like to be kissed. Instead she confided, "I have to wear deodorant."

"Deodorant?" This was excruciating, because I'd already started wearing deodorant and I hadn't thought to tell her first.

Kelly said, "You're so lucky not to have to." She combed her hair with her fingers and tossed it over her shoulders in the cold, world-weary way that girls with long hair learn. "What are you going to be when you grow up?"

"Teacher," I said, feeling doomed and lowly.

"I'm going to be a nurse in an operating room because my mom says I can think on my feet. Possibly I'll marry a doctor." Then, pitying me, she turned me toward her. "You'll be a great teacher because you remember all those things no one else cares about."

When I told my sister that Kelly was my best friend, she said, "Yeah, but are you hers?"

My mother and our neighbor took me home from the hospital, where I hadn't needed treatment. My father had been called to the ski resort because he was the Mormon bishop. He found me on a stretcher in the back of the ambulance but stayed when it left because Sister Bennett, our camp leader, was being given blood and was not transportable. Everyone realized she was dying.

My mother had a car, but we rode home from the hospital in the neighbor's. I believe my mother accepted his offer because it seemed her part in what was expected: that she must be too distressed to trust herself to drive. Tragedy is about playing roles. I was already suffering the guilt of survival when she saw me in the emergency room and said, "Oh, Joan!" What was probably an expression of concern seemed to me an accusation.

The neighbor turned the car radio knob and the red needle glided through the numbers. He didn't say a word. Finally I asked, because no one volunteered it, "Who died?" My voice sounded strange and empty. Maybe this is why my mother took the ride, so she wouldn't have to be alone with me and the question. She touched her throat. "Veronica," she said. "And Sister Bennett is very badly hurt."

The burden I'd assumed in asking was not what I'd expected, not the pain of loss but the difficulty of an appropriate response. The fact was, I didn't feel like crying. I felt raw as my scraped face, but also stoppered. As my mother looked at me, most of all I wanted to be alone.

That night in my dreams white sheets hung from a clothesline. They floated, then dropped suddenly and became the humps of ghosts who chased me.

My mother's idea of comfort was to say, "Shh, shh, shh."

The year I was born the top five names for girls were: K(C)atherine, Susan, Deborah, Karen, and Mary. Her name was Veronica Fuke. She never had a chance, you see. The first name was too exotic, the second blunt or angry or obscene. She licked her lips tentatively just before she spoke, and when she talked you noticed moist breathing. Asthma, I now guess. Her nose wasn't so much fat as flabby.

She was in 4-H. She grew vegetables with ignoble shapes or names: banana squash and rutabaga. Her family ate dehydrated fruit and were glad to show you their dehydrator—proud as though it were a new car. The boys at church teased her, which she took with such a diffuse lack of interest they were forced to stop. She had a blue mole by her eye; her little finger curved slightly inward.

I can't recall a single unkind, impatient, or angry thing she ever did. And I didn't like her. Worse, I didn't care about her. I don't know if I smiled at her, ever. There are bonds stronger than love. And what I know is that, if she'd lived, I'd have completely forgotten her. My behavior toward her then would not seem to matter now. So this is it: in her death I was caught, frozen in my indifference, an indifference nothing will ever help.

Her mother was pudding—soft with small, swollen feet. Later, she died of a tumor so big the whole congregation would watch it grow. It tugged at the shape of her formless dresses. She did not seek medical intervention and was patient in her suffering. Apparently the alternative—survival—seemed too perplexing or complicated to undertake. The elders gave her blessings and prayed for her return to health. But her daughter had been thrown from a ski lift. That might have proved something to her, or left her less susceptible to religion, more available to fate.

I want to believe Veronica died as calmly as her mother. If patience in death isn't courage, it's certainly the next best thing. I imagine Veronica surprised and then done with it, done with living on a day too beautiful to have given any warning. Perhaps she slipped out of life with simple grace.

The newspaper caption under her picture said, *Fell to her death.* I remember when I first read it, for some reason I thought it was *fell through* her death. And it seemed for a moment—though I knew better—as if she'd miraculously survived.

The morning after the accident my mother made me go with her to see Veronica's mother. It didn't occur to me to protest.

"Sister Fuke," my mother said, "we want you to have this." She shoved something draped by a dishcloth. It takes on a bread shape as I see myself standing on that narrow porch, but it also reminds me of Veronica's own covered form beneath the ski lift. Veronica's mother wrapped her arms around it, hugged it. She had other children: a boy who later grew a scraggly black beard to cover acne scars when he was only fifteen, a young daughter who would take to her stepmother with tenacious goodwill. But they were not around that day.

Veronica's mother bent toward me; her face was a haggard wilderness of suffering. I was young, still thought the worst pain was physical. Fascinated, I didn't know enough to look away. I wondered if this was what had turned Lot's wife into the pillar of salt.

Then I realized Veronica's mother was speaking to me. Too late, I saw her need. She said, "Honey, did Veronica say anything before she died?"

Grief, I saw, is shameless.

I looked to my mother, but she had slipped into her survival mode, become something firm and carefully closed. Behind Veronica's mother, I could see the clutter, newspapers scattered by the broken-down sofa. I knew where they kept some of their belongings: that there was a picture of Jesus ascending to glory in the living room, that a large yellow cat balanced on the edge of the kitchen sink and swatted at a spider plant. I saw how knowing those things hadn't stopped anything from happening, any more than the horseshoe that hung by the back-door.

"Dear?" Veronica's mother whispered.

"She just cried," I said. I spoke the lie humbly, knowing I'd failed her. Veronica's mother moved back into the room and suddenly she blurred, seemed to expand. It scared me until I realized that she'd moved into line with the scratched part of my lenses. She put the bread on the sofa and then slumped down herself.

When I called Kelly on the phone she said, "We must shut our eyes and promise to never even walk down their street again."

My father spoke to the families with radiant conviction about life being eternal, which is, after all, a paltry comfort when there is the whole of mortality to be somehow gotten through. At the funeral, he read Veronica's poem because her young cousin broke down, and he handed Sister Bennett's daughter his handkerchief. Then, right there, he raised money for a flagpole. Something had to be done, something to help us all sleep and eat and live. The flagpole was tangible, a solution. Its erection was an action, a counteraction to the falling. Something of an exchange.

It stood in front of the church with a stone wall behind it. *In memory of,* a plaque said. It gave the impression Sister Bennett had died for something, giving service to her camper girls. But of Veronica Fuke, what might be said? How do you make her noble? How do you make it feel as sad as it should when she wasn't particularly likable?

By Thanksgiving I was washing my hands between thirty and forty times a day. First my knuckles, then my fingertips became fiery and etched like Martian canals. They bled in the tender crusty valleys between my fingers. My mother took me to the doctor, who held them gently, as if touch could injure them more. "How are you sleeping?" he said, turning them over, and I knew he'd guessed.

Sometimes leaves blew off aspen trees in my dreams. Or news-papers fluttered from wire cages and then turned vicious as they flew toward me. *Shh, shh, shh,* I'd tell myself.

"Fine," I said. "I sleep okay." I knew better than to be found out. On the remaining Fourths of July of my youth, we raised the flag at the church in a sunrise service. Then the deaths seemed patriotic.

Can you believe it? the invitation crows, under a picture of a geriatric bulldog. *We've been out of high school twenty-five years!* I show it to Dave the way you show people your driver's license—hoping they won't laugh, but ready to join them when they do.

"You going?" he asks, pinching cilantro into Mexican salsa—his own recipe, of which he's overly proud. He's got a baseball cap on backward, which proves the seriousness of his chore.

"High school," I say, "is like a party where you drank too much. You hope you didn't embarrass yourself in ways you can't entirely recall."

"That, you see, just might be the fun of it—the amnesia factor, the wait-and-see." He plugs his mouth with a finger dipped in salsa.

"Needs more onion," I say of his recipe.

He wipes a hand on his apron. "You should go. They'll be glad to see you." He angles the knife in my direction in an unintentionally dangerous way. "Though they won't know you without your cat's-eye glasses." He growls and tries to nip at my ear.

I'm indignant. "In high school I wore contact lenses." We reserve our tenderest vanity for the least significant things.

Two weeks later I'm waiting my turn in Optical Boutique. Suddenly this pops into my head: They bounced when they landed. No floating, none at all. Why is this revelation so amazing to me? Why does it seem so relevant?

The spectacles for sale are lined up in lighted glass cases. They look like Hollywood or synchronized swimming. I'll feel intrusive and clumsy when I take one from its place.

This: I have fallen from innocence. Fallen in love. On my face. Also into line. But this must be said: I *jumped* from the ski lift.

Two other girls were hurt, injuries that changed their bodies as well as their minds, bones crushed in uncompromising ways. Linda would wear forever the appearance of an invalid—a shriveled arm, one leg shorter. But she also wore an expansive calmness, as if the accident had freed her of the worry of too much good fortune. I've heard she is an excellent mother, that she teaches business ethics and even plays the guitar.

The other girl, Kathy, became obese. She was addicted to pain medication, but also apparently to pain. She spoke about both with authority as well as awe, like a serious art collector. She'd been adopted as a baby, and in late adolescence went on a quest to find her birth father. When she found him in a big Eastern city, she slept with him, in what must have seemed a brilliant, definitive revenge.

It was called The Accident, as if there was or would only be one. There was occasional need for clarification about what exactly had happened, and so I was asked. It amazed me how I'd become an expert on this: the how of how people died.

The summer before I started high school, I gave up washing my hands. I weaned myself slowly, using Jergens hand lotion as a crutch (its smell still makes me feel vulnerable). Then I painted my nails the color the seniors were wearing, a pearly white—drama and sophistication both. My disgraceful hands became my glory. Isn't it so often so? I was known for having beautiful nails. Confidence is built on such small things.

Kelly and I went to the same high school, but she became dramatically out of date. Her rebellions were quaint and naïve. She put cold cream and cornflakes on the math teacher's windows. She wrote toothless letters to the school newspaper's editor. Her popularity plummeted, and—I confess—I wasn't sorry. I had moved on. I had the stuff of high school success: nice legs, a smart mouth. Teenagers are merciless, a bit sadistic. What did I care that her petticoats no longer rustled? What did it matter when the world was exploding, blooming with forbidden pleasures—sinewy boys and smudgy-edged sins.

Kelly still had that sense of purpose. When the rest of us were painting on thick eyeliner and conscientiously cursing our parents, Kelly had school spirit and a quiet, too-tall boyfriend. You would see them on the school lawn, laughing or walking hand in hand into the dance. She had no need for subversion. She simply lacked outrage.

When my mother said, "I haven't seen Kelly in so long," I shrugged. "Yeah?"

My mother narrowed her eyes and said what she often did: "Is that any way to talk?"

"We don't have anything in common," I whined, because what can you have in common with someone after you've watched people die? We passed in school halls with only a "Hi there." Embarrassed like former lovers. Knowing we shared a guilty knowledge—the how of how people died. Or maybe she was shy because we were no longer friends. But our past connection was an impossible attachment, severed by an event of unbearable significance and terrible discovery. Mortality is not a subject a teenager should dwell on. And how can you be friends with someone who knows a secret as big as all that?

Only once do I remember us talking. I was at a church dance, sending a confused message to my nonmember boyfriend. She approached me while her boyfriend was outside to tell me her brother had received his mission call to Australia that her mother had been praying for. I thought how Kelly could do more with her appearance. For one thing, she should cut her hair. And I wondered how the accident had changed her. Had it taught her to be good or just to be unaware? Then suddenly I feared she'd talk about it, and I had no idea what I would say. But instead, she said, "You know, you have really pretty eyes," and I remember thinking how I wished she'd said that back when it would have counted, back when it would have done me some good.

In the yearbook under her picture, it said, "Girl most likely to stay out of jail."

Years ago, at the end of trying to have a baby and getting to where it stopped hurting so much, Dave floated on our water bed and diagnosed me. "Obsessive-compulsive disorder," he said in an accent he claimed was Viennese.

"Getting up in the morning?"

"*Having* to get up in the morning. Stay," he said. "Let's eat brie and crackers and make crumbs and love. We'll send Queenie for the newspaper. We won't get up until we've renamed all the major cities in America."

The bed rocked as if he were keeping time. The clock radio was regrettably still. I said, "Is that any way to face life?"

"Aha!" he said, as if he'd caught me. "You don't *face* life. You *live* it." He was prone to mottoes of treacly optimism.

"I could stay in bed if I wanted." But I had to grip the blankets when I said it to keep from throwing them off.

"Couldn't," he said.

"Could." It seemed hard to breathe, though the blankets weren't at all close to my face. Concentrating, I counted but only got to five. "Long enough," I said. The cold air and being upright made it feel as if I'd won.

"Admit it," he yelled. He leapt to his feet on the bed, causing waves that he convincingly surfed in plaid boxers. "You *do* things. You fold every towel long, then short. You wipe off the table left to right. You floss!"

"To clean my teeth," I said, too primly, but then remembered suddenly the long-ago pleasure of washing my hands, knowing how important it was to keep moving. How could I explain it? The awful phrase: like a sitting duck.

Sometimes I dream of snowfalls that are sucked back up into the sky. Once I dreamed of four water birds diving toward the earth, then suddenly swooping upward, sunlight glittering from the sequined eyeglasses they wore.

Sister Bennett had a nasally laugh I can no longer quite remember. She once told us, "For Pete's sake, drop the 'Sister Bennett.' You girls can call me Louise"—which we did, but only until she died. We loved her. Maybe that's why I don't speak of her. Maybe in loving her I've more successfully put her to rest. Or perhaps she doesn't haunt me because she was not my age and even though she died, she couldn't have been me.

Veronica means "true likeness."

I wish I'd been friendly to Veronica Fuke.

I wish Kelly had come back for me, so that I wouldn't have had to go back up the hill and hear Sister Bennett moan or ride down the canyon alone in an ambulance.

Kelly sang "The Impossible Dream" in a chorus at graduation. Kelly didn't die.

• • •

Quickly, before I can think what I'm doing, I get on a plane to go to my high school reunion. "Obsessive-compulsive disorder," I explain to Dave, who smiles in agreeable acceptance as he kisses me good-bye.

The reunion is at a water-slide park I didn't know existed, situated next to what we used to call the State Mental Hospital. Surely they've let all those folks go.

Can any place look as foreign as the place where you were born?

A man barks my name and embraces me. I have no idea who he is.

"Look at you," people keep demanding. "Will you just look at who's here?"

There's a man on the fringe of the group, left out of the hugs and squeals of enchantment, missing front teeth—old, surely not our age. Then someone places him. A boy who was left out back then or laughed at, still not included. But here he is, present, because it is *his* class, too.

Dependables of a high school reunion: only the people who were too skinny in high school are skinny at all. But also: the nice kids all became nice adults.

"Kelly's looking for you," my classmates tell me, as if we were best friends, as if I should even be here.

They show pictures of their children, who look more like themselves than they do. A classmate has died of an ominously initialed disease. "Didn't you know?" the others say to me. It occurs to me I did, but I've forgotten. Forgotten too how his widow married his best friend and for many that eased the pain.

Then Kelly's arms are around me. She holds me like—of course, a long-lost friend—but also possessively. For a moment I think she holds me like her own child.

She whispers in my ear, "I'm sorry I made you jump."

"You didn't," I say.

"We *had* to jump," she says, looking for something in my face.

"Yes." It's an insignificant enough concession—and suddenly, possibly even true.

She has small blue eyes. When I notice the beak of her nose, I realize she resembles some kind of waterfowl. She is a handshaker, a woman who refers to herself by her last name. She doesn't put up with

regrets or last chances or grudges. Before she tells me about how she
became a school principal, or asks me how my father is, we have to talk
about the accident. This is what reunion means, I think: the effort to
make something whole.

She says they screamed as they fell.

"Yes," I say, "now I remember."

She says she lowered the footrest.

"You told me to roll when I landed," I say.

She shakes her head. "I must have gotten that from movies."

She tells me she spoke to each of them. Linda asked for help.
Veronica didn't answer. And I feel a sick confirmation, all these years
later, of how she'd already died. Kelly says she slept with her mother
that night and dreamed she would raise a retarded child. She awoke
knowing that would be her life. "It has been," she says simply, explaining her brain-damaged daughter.

I slap at a mosquito, wondering what causes what. Kelly tugs rest-
lessly at her bangs, a mannerism so startlingly familiar I can't believe
I'd forgotten it. She tells me her husband fell off scaffolding when they
were dating, was impaled on rebar from two stories up.

"No—*fell*?" Are lives prone to motifs?

Her smile is rueful, as if the joke's on her. "But really, now he's
fine."

When I don't say anything, she says, "Look. We jumped to save
them." And I can see her going down the path below the ski lift, sure-
footed, even wise. I think, though I do not tell her, that in jumping
we saved ourselves. In the action, we exercised an option; we made an
exclamation. We said, *We have survived.*

I can ask my classmates about Linda and Kathy, but I don't. It just
feels like too much to know. Kelly sips the drink she's holding as she
stands in front of the illuminated contortions of a water slide. I tell her
about how lately I keep thinking about it.

She says, "That happens. What else would you expect?" Then,
"You know, some good came of it." She means something spiritual.
Mormons hope tragedy improves the soul. For me, what I'd like is
for the accident not just to have mattered but to surrender some kind
of meaning. But it merely teases. The only thing that *feels* as if it's significant is that Sister Bennett was the same age that we are now.

The park lights flicker.

I imagine the four of them, a grotesque sculpture garden in the moonlight, still lying beneath the ski lift, ten miles up the canyon at a ski resort a movie star now owns. They are stone blocks of ancient ruins, worn and weary of their work. And if we hadn't jumped? Would I then imagine us sitting there as well? Still? Action won't always save you, but it at least allows you to imagine you can be saved.

Here is the difference, I think suddenly: They fell to their deaths. We jumped to life. Instead of meaning, there is only that fact.

When the management locks us out of the water park, we stand under the unsteady lights of the parking lot and continue to tell our stories. "Fun as a blue M&M," I hear someone say. Kelly looks at me fondly. She bends to tie her Reeboks—now she's the one wearing sensible shoes. Then there are only a few of us remaining. Rhonda, still well-groomed and placid, talks about her book about monster trucks. Patty touches my arm, says, "You always had beautiful fingernails."

Suddenly it's just the two of us. Kelly puts her hands on my shoulders and turns me toward her. What I see in her face is not the child she was but, like a ghost, the grandmother she will shortly be.

I know what she'll say before she says it. "I'm sorry I didn't come back for you."

My grandmother said, "Dreams are better than real—they're true." In mine, Dave and I go to a redwood forest. In a gift-shop cabin we buy a packet of seeds. On the back is this earnest plea: *The mighty sequoia is endangered. Please, kind traveler, germinate these seeds. Help us save our trees.*

I plant them in the backyard. First one, then thirty or forty. Oh, the pleasure of planting those trees! The delight of giving them names: Larkin (from the songbird), Ulysses (the cunning hero), Gabriel (with his Judgment Day horn). Names for the children we never had. But they grow like Jack's magic beans into shocking and unkempt adolescents. I tend them and try to talk them out of such unruly heights, but they slump and act disrespectful. They do forest wheelies, wear mirrored sunglasses, and smoke cigarettes.

I say, "I think I'll call California, see if they want them back."

Dave, of course, smiles and sings, "Let them be."

But in the backyard they're shoving each other. They've begun to leave messy fingerprints as they scrape the bottoms of clouds. Then suddenly I see a pattern. My trees are thick as a logjam, plugging up the summer air. You could step securely from one to another, like Towers of Babel. Everywhere you could walk up and down in the summer sky.

CHRISTMAS AT HELAMAN'S HOUSE

Orson Scott Card

THERE WERE TIMES WHEN HE WANTED to give up and live in a tent rather than fight with the contractors one more time, but in the end Helaman Willkie got the new house built and the family moved in before Christmas. Three days before Christmas, in fact, which meant that, exhausted as they all were from the move, they *still* had to search madly through the piles of boxes in the new basement to find all the Christmas decorations and get them in place before Santa showed up to inaugurate their new heat-trapping triple-flue chimney.

So they were all tired, weary to the bone, and yet they walked around the house with these silly smiles on their faces, saying and doing the strangest things. Like Joni, Helaman's sixteen-year-old daughter, who every now and then would burst into whatever room Helaman was in, do a pirouette, and say, "Daddy, Daddy, I have my own room!" To which he would reply, "So I heard." To which she would say, hugging him in a way calculated to muss his hair, "You really do love me, now I *know* it."

Helaman's old joke was that none of his children had ever been impossible, but they had all been improbable more than once. Twelve-year-old Ryan had already been caught twice trying to ride his skateboard down the front staircase. Why couldn't he slide down the banister like any normal boy? Then at least he'd be polishing it with his backside, instead of putting dings in the solid oak treads of the stair. Fourteen-year-old Steven had spent every waking moment in the game room, hooking the computers together and then trying out all the software, as if to make sure that it would still work in the new house. Helaman had no evidence that Steven had yet seen the inside of his own bedroom.

And then there was Lucille, Helaman's sensible, organized, dependable, previously sane wife, kissing all the appliances in the kitchen. But the truth was that Lucille's delight at the kitchen came as a great relief to Helaman. Till then he had been worried that she was still having doubts about the house. When the movers left, she had stood there in the main-floor family room, staring at the queen-size hide-a-bed looking so forlorn and small on the vast carpet. Helaman reassured her that in no time they'd have plenty of furniture to fill up the room, but she refused to be reassured. "We're going to buy a truckload of furniture? When our mortgage is bigger than the one on our first store back in 1970?"

He started to explain to her that those were 1970 dollars, but she just gave him that how-stupid-do-you-think-I-am look and said, "I took economics in college, Helaman. I was talking about how I *felt*."

So Helaman said nothing. He had long since learned that when Lucille was talking about how she *felt*, none of the things he could think of to say would be very helpful. He couldn't even begin to put into words what *he* felt—how proud he had been of this house he had caused to exist for her, how much he needed to know that it made her happy. After all their years of struggling and worrying to try to keep the business afloat, and then struggling and worrying about the huge debts involved in starting up the branch stores, he knew that Lucille deserved to have a fine house, the *finest* house, and that he deserved to be the man who could give it to her. Now all she could think about was the huge amount of money the house had cost, and Helaman felt as though someone had taken the very breath out of him.

Until she came into the kitchen and squealed in delight. It was exactly the sound his daughters made—an ear-piercing yelp that gave him headaches whenever Trudy and Joni got excited for more than a minute at a time. He had almost forgotten that it was hereditary, that they got that glass-shattering high note from Lucille. She hadn't been surprised and happy enough to make that sound in years. But she made it now, and said, "Oh, Helaman, it's beautiful, it's perfect, it's the perfect kitchen!" It made up for her reaction to the family room.

If it hadn't, he would have despaired—because he had worked hard to make sure that the kitchen was irresistible. He had kept careful track of everything she had ever admired in magazines or home shows; he had bought all new appliances, from the can opener and toaster to the microwave and the bread maker; he had brought those all into the house himself and had his best crew install everything and test it so it ran perfectly. He had inventoried every utensil in her old kitchen and bought a brand-new replacement; they had chosen new silverware and pans and dishes for daily use, and he had arranged it as close to the way she had her old kitchen arranged as possible, even when the arrangement made no sense whatever. And he had kept her out of the kitchen—with tape across the door—all the time he was doing it, and all during the move itself, until that moment when he told her she could tear away the ribbon and walk through the door. And she squealed and kissed all the appliances and opened all the drawers and said, "Just where I would have put it!" and "I can't believe there's room for everything and there's *still* counter space!" and "How did you get them all out of the old kitchen without my seeing you do it?"

"I didn't," Helaman told her. "I bought all new ones."

"Oh, you're such a tease," she said. "I mean, here's the old garlic press. I've never even used it."

"Now you have two of them."

And when she realized that he meant it, that he had really duplicated all her utensils and put them away exactly as she had always had them, she started to cry, which was a sign of happiness even more certain than the squealing.

So yes, they loved the house, all of them. Wasn't that what he built it for? For them to feel exactly this way about it? But what he hadn't expected was his own feeling of disappointment. He couldn't match their enthusiasm; on the contrary, he felt sad and uncertain as he walked through the house. As if after all his struggling to cause this house to exist, to be perfect, now that it was done he had no reason to be here. No, that wasn't quite the feeling. It was as if he had no *right* to be here. He strode through the house with all the rights of ownership, and yet he felt like an interloper, as if he had evicted the rightful occupants and stolen the place.

Am I so used to struggling for money all my life that when I finally have visible proof that the struggle is over, I can't believe it? No, he thought. What I can't believe is *me*. I don't belong in a place like this. In my heart, I think of myself in that miserable three-bedroom tract house in Orem with the four makeshift bedrooms Dad built in the basement so all his six kids could have rooms of our own. Well, I'm not a wage man like Dad, and my kids will not be ashamed of where they live, and my wife will be able to invite any woman in the ward into her home without that look of apology that Mother always had when she had to bring chairs from the dining room just so there'd be enough places for her visitors to sit.

Yet even when he had told himself all these things, reminded himself of the fire that had burned inside him all during the building of the house, he still felt empty and disappointed and vaguely ashamed, and he just didn't understand it. It wasn't fair that he should feel like this. He had *earned* this house.

Well, what did he expect, anyway? It was like Christmas itself: The gifts were never as good as the preparations—the shopping and hiding and wrapping. He felt as he did because he was tired, that's all. Tired and ready for it to be the day after Christmas when he could get back to running his little empire of five Willkie's stores, which sprawled on their parking lots in choice locations up and down the Wasatch Front, beaming their cheery fluorescent lights to welcome people in to the wonderful world of discount housewares. This had been a record Christmas, and maybe getting the accountants' year-end reports would make him feel better.

Then again maybe it wouldn't. Maybe this is what it is, he thought, that makes all those lonely women come to see the bishop and complain about how they're so depressed. Maybe I'm just having the equivalent of postpartum blues. I have given birth to a house with the finest view in the Darlington Heights Ward, I'm sitting here looking out of a window larger than any of the bathrooms, the twinkling lights of Salt Lake Valley on Christmas Eve spread out before me, with Christmas carols from the CD player being pumped through twenty-two speakers in nine rooms, and I can't enjoy it because I keep getting the postpartum blues.

"They're *hee*-eere!" sang out Trudy. So the new love of her life (the second in December alone) must be at the door. At eighteen she was their eldest child and therefore the one nearest to achieving full human status. Unlike Joni, Trudy still spelled her name with a *y*, and it had been more than a year since she stopped drawing the little eyes over the *u* to make it look like a smile in the middle of her signature. At church yesterday she had fallen in love with the newly returned missionary who bore his testimony in a distinctly Spanish accent. "Can I invite him to come over for the hanging of the stockings?" she pleaded. In vain did Helaman tell her that it would be no use—his *own* family would want to have him all night, it was his first Christmas with them in two years, for heaven's sake! But she said, "I can at least ask, can't I?" and Lucille nodded and so Helaman said yes, and to his surprise the young elder had said yes. Helaman took a mental note: Never underestimate the ability of your own daughters to attract boys, no matter how weird you think your girls have grown up to be.

And now the young elder was here, no doubt with so many hormones flowing through him that he could cause items of furniture to mate with each other just by touching them. Helaman had to get up out of the couch and play father and host for a couple of hours, all the time watching to make sure the young man kept his hands to himself.

It wasn't till he got to the door and saw *two* young men standing there that he realized that Trudy had said *they're* here. He recognized the elder, of course, looking missionary-like and vaguely lost, but the other was apparently from another planet. He was dressed normally, but one side of his head was mostly shaved, and the other side was partly permed and partly straight. Joni immediately attached herself to him, which at least told Helaman what had brought him to their door on Christmas Eve—another case of raging hormones. As to *who* he was, Helaman deduced that he was either a high school hoodlum she had invited over to horrify them or one of the bodacious new boys from the Darlington Heights Ward that she had been babbling about all day. In fact, if Helaman tried very hard he could almost remember the boy as he looked yesterday at church, in a lounge-lizard jacket and loosened tie, kneeling at the sacrament table, gripping the microphone as if he were about to do a rap version of the sacrament prayer. Helaman had shuddered at the time, but apparently Joni was capable of looking at such a sight and thinking, "Wow, I'd like to bring that home."

By default Helaman turned to Trudy's newly returned missionary and stuck out his hand. "Feliz Navidad," said Helaman.

"Feliz Navidad," said the missionary. "Thanks for inviting me over."

"I didn't," said Helaman.

"*I* did, silly," said Trudy. "And you're supposed to notice that Father said Merry Christmas in Spanish."

"Oh, sorry," said the missionary. "I've only been home a week and everybody was saying Feliz Navidad all the time. Your accent must be good enough that I didn't think twice."

"What mission were you in?"

"Colombia Medellín."

"Do I just call you Elder or what?" asked Helaman.

"I've been released," said the missionary. "So I guess my name is Tom Boke again."

Joni, of course, could hardly bear the fact that Trudy's beau had received more than a full minute of everyone's attention. "And this is *my* first visitor to the new house," said Joni.

Helaman offered his hand to Joni's boy and said, "I know a good lawyer if you want to sue your barber."

Joni glared at him but since the boy showed no sign of understanding Helaman's little jest, she quickly stopped glaring.

"I'm Spencer Raymond Varley," said the boy, "but you can call me Var."

"And you can call me Brother Willkie," said Helaman. "Come on in to family room A and we'll tell you which cookies Joni baked so you can avoid them and live."

"Daddy, *stop* it," said Joni in her cute-whiny voice. She used this voice whenever she wanted to pretend to be pretending to be mad. In this case it meant that she really *was* mad and wanted Helaman to stop goading young Var.

Helaman was too tired to banter with her now, so he pried her off his arm, where she had been clinging, and promised that he'd be good from now on. "I was only teasing the spunky young lad out of habit."

"His father is *the* Spence Varley," Joni whispered. "He drives a Jag."

Well, *your* father is *the* Helaman Willkie, he answered silently. And

I'll be able to get you great prices on crock pots for the rest of your natural life.

The family gathered. They munched for a while on the vegetables and the vegetable dip, the fruits and the fruit dip, and the chips and the chip dip. Helaman felt like a cow chewing its cud as he listened to the conversation drone on around him. Lucille was carrying the conversation, but Helaman knew she loved being hostess and besides, she was even worse than the girls, waiting to pounce on Helaman and hush him up if he started to say anything that might embarrass a daughter in front of her male companion for the evening. Usually Helaman enjoyed the sport of baiting them, but tonight he didn't even care.

I don't like having these strangers in our home on Christmas Eve, he thought. But then, I'm as much a stranger in *this* house as they are.

By the time Helaman connected back to the conversation, Joni was regaling her fashion-victim boyfriend with the story of the marble floor in the entryway. "Father *told* the contractor to lower the floor in the entryway or the marble would stand an inch above the living room carpet and people would be falling down or stubbing their toes forever. And the contractor said he wouldn't do it unless Father accepted the fact that this would make them three days late and add a thousand dollars to the cost of the house. And so Father gets up in the middle of the night—"

"You've got to know that I warned them while they were putting in the entryway floor that they needed to drop it an inch lower to hold the marble, and they completely ignored me," said Helaman. "And now it had the staircase sitting on it and it really would have been a lot easier to just install a parquet floor instead, but I had promised Lucille a marble entryway and the contractor had promised *me* a marble entryway and—"

"Father," said Joni, "I was going to tell the *short* version."

"And now he said he wouldn't do it," said Helaman, and then fell silent.

"*So*," said Joni, "as *somebody* was saying, Father got up in the middle of the night—"

"Six in the morning," said Helaman.

"Let her tell the story, Helaman," said Lucille.

"And he got the chainsaw out of the garage," said Joni, "and he cut this big gaping hole in the middle of the entry floor and you know what? They realized that Daddy *really meant it.*"

They laughed, and then laughed all the harder when Helaman said, "Remember the chainsaw if you're ever thinking of keeping my daughter out after her curfew."

Even as he laughed, though, Helaman felt a sour taste in his mouth from the chainsaw story. It really *had* cost the contractor money and slowed down the house, and when Helaman had stood there, chainsaw in hand, looking in the first light of morning down into the hole he had just made, he had felt stupid and ashamed, when he had *meant* to feel vindicated and clever and powerful. It took a few minutes for him to realize that his bad feelings were really just because he was worried about somebody walking in without looking where they were going and falling down into the basement, so he wrestled a big sheet of plywood over and laid it *mostly* over the hole, leaving just enough of a corner that the contractor couldn't help but know that the hole was there. And then it turned out that *that* wasn't the reason he felt stupid and ashamed after all, because when he'd finished he *still* had to come home and take a shower just to feel clean.

Of course, while he was thinking of this, they had gone on with the second marble story, only now it was Trudy telling it. "So this lady from across the street comes over and Mom thinks she's going to welcome us into the neighborhood, and so she holds the door open and invites the woman inside, and the first thing she says is, 'I hear you're going to have marble in the foyer of your new house,' and Mom says yes, and then the woman—"

"Sister Braincase, I'll bet," said Var.

"Who?" asked Lucille.

"Sister Barnacuse," said Var. "We call her Braincase because she's going bonkers."

"How compassionate of you," murmured Lucille.

"*Any*way," said Trudy, "whoever she was—Mrs. Barnacuse—said, 'Well, I hope it isn't that miserable fox marble.' And Mother just stands there and she's trying to think of what fox marble might mean. Was it a sort of russet shade of brown or something? She'd never heard of a color called *fox*. And then all of a sudden it dawns on her that the woman means *faux* marble, and even though the marble in the entry *is*

real, Mother says to her, 'No, the marble *we* have is *faux*.' As if it was
something to be proud of. And the woman says, 'Oh, well that's different,' and she goes away."

Var laughed uproariously, but Tom Boke only sat there with a polite missionary grin, which Helaman supposed he probably perfected
back before he really knew the language, when he had to sit and listen to whole conversations he didn't understand. Finally the young
man shared with them the reason for his failure to laugh. "What's foe
marble?" he asked.

"Faux," said Lucille. "French for false."

"It means fake," Ryan said, in one of the brief moments when
his mouth wasn't full of chips. "But ours is real. And our toilets flush
silently."

"Ryan," said Lucille in her I'm-still-acting-sweet-but-you'd-better-
do-this voice, "why don't you go down and pry your brother away
from the computer and ask him to come up and meet our guests?"

Ryan went.

"Old Braincase is such a snob," said Var, "but the truth is all the
marble in *her* house really *is* faux, but we think the contractor sort
of misled her about it and she's the only one who doesn't know that
there's not an ounce of real marble in her whole house." Var cackled
uproariously.

"How sweet of you not to break her heart by telling her," said
Lucille. "We'll keep the secret, too."

"Guided tour time!" cried Joni. "Please, before we hang the stockings or anything? I want Var to see my room."

"This is the best time to do it," Helaman said to Var. "It'll be the
last time her floor is visible till she goes away to college."

Var smiled feebly at Helaman's joke, but Tom Boke actually managed to laugh out loud. I'll count that as my first Christmas present,
Helaman said silently. In fact, if you do that again I'll ask you to marry
my daughter, just so I can have somebody to laugh at my jokes around
this house.

This house this house this house. He was tired of saying it, tired
of thinking it. Six thousand square feet not counting the garage or the
basement, and he had to take yet another tour group to see every single
square foot of it. The living room, the parlor, the dining room, the

kitchen, the pantry so large you could lose children in it, the breakfast room, the library, and back to the main-floor family room—giving the tour was almost aerobic.

Then downstairs to family room B, the big storage room, and the game room with the new pool table and two elaborate computer set-ups so the boys wouldn't fight over who got to play videogames. Not to mention the complete guest apartment with a separate entrance, a kitchenette, two bedrooms, and a bathroom, just in case one of their parents came to live with them someday in the future.

Then all the way up two flights of stairs to see the bedrooms—eight of them, even though they only used five right now. "Who knows how many more we'll need?" said Helaman, joking. "We're still young, we'll have more to fill 'em up."

But Lucille looked just the tiniest bit hurt and Helaman regretted saying it immediately; it was just a dumb joke and for *that* he had caused her to think about the fact that she'd blown out a fallopian tube in an ectopic pregnancy two years after Ryan was born and even though the doctors said there shouldn't be a problem they hadn't conceived a child since. Not that their present crop of children gave them any particular incentive to keep trying.

No, thought Helaman, I must never come to believe my own jokes about my family. Most of the time they're great kids, I've just got the blues tonight and so everything they do or say or *think* is going to irritate me.

"*Will* you have more children?" asked Tom.

It was an appalling question, even from a recently returned missionary who had gone so native that he was barely speaking English.

"I think that's for the Lord to decide," said Lucille.

They were all standing in the master bathroom now, with Ryan dribbling an imaginary basketball and then slam-dunking it in the toilet. Tom Boke stood there after Lucille's words as if he were still trying to understand them. And then, abruptly, he turned to Trudy. "I'm sorry," he said, "but I've got to go."

"Where?" asked Trudy. "We haven't even done the stockings yet."

"I didn't know it would take so long to see the house," said Tom. "I'm sorry."

"*See*, Dad?" said Trudy. "If you'd just learn how to give shorter tours, I might actually someday get to . . ."

But before she could finish affixing blame on Helaman, even though it was Lucille who had insisted on the tour for her daughters' gentlemen callers, Tom Boke had already left the master bathroom and was heading out the master bedroom door.

"Get him, Father," said Trudy. "Don't let him go!"

"If *you* can't keep him," said Helaman, "what makes you think he'll stay for *me?*" But he followed Tom all the same, because the young man had looked quite strange when he left, as if he were sick or upset, and Helaman didn't feel right about just letting him go back out into the cold.

He caught up with him at the front door—Helaman assumed that the only thing that slowed Tom down was the fact that it was so easy to get lost when you came down the back stairs. "Tom," said Helaman. "What's wrong?"

"Nothing, sir."

But the expression on Tom's face declared his "nothing" to be a lie. "Are you going to be sick? Do you need to lie down?"

Tom shook his head. "I'm sorry," he said. "It's just . . . I just . . ."

"Just what?"

"I just don't belong here."

"You're welcome under our roof, I hope you know that."

"I meant America. I don't know if I can live in America anymore."

To Helaman's surprise the young man's eyes had filled with tears. "I don't know what you're talking about," Helaman said.

"Everybody here has so *much*." Tom's gaze took in the entryway with its marble floor, opening onto the living room, the dining room, the library. "And you keep it all for yourselves." The tears spilled out of his eyes.

Helaman felt it like a slap in the face. "Oh, and people don't keep things for themselves down in Colombia?"

"The poor people scratch for food while the drug lords keep everything they can get their hands on. Only the mafia have houses as large . . ."

The comparison was so insulting and unfair that Helaman was filled with rage. He had never hit anyone in anger in his life, not even as a child, but at this moment he wanted to lash out at this boy and make him take it back.

But he didn't, because Tom took it back before he even finished saying it.

"I'm sorry," Tom said. "I didn't mean to compare . . ."

"I earned every penny of the price of this house," said Helaman. "I built my business up from nothing."

"It's not your fault," said Tom. "Why should you think twice about living in a house like this? I grew up in this ward, I never saw anything wrong with it until I went to Colombia."

"I *didn't* grow up in this ward," said Helaman. "I *earned* my way here."

"The Book of Moses says that in Zion they had no poor among them. Well, Darlington Heights has achieved *that* part of building Zion, because no poor people will ever show their faces here."

"Why aren't you home telling your own parents this, instead of troubling *my* house?"

"I didn't mean to trouble you," said Tom. "I wanted to meet your daughter."

"So why don't you just stay and meet her, instead of judging me?"

"I told you," said Tom. "It's *me*, not you. I just don't belong here. Enjoy your new house, really, it's beautiful. It's not your fault that I taught so many people whose whole house was smaller than your bathroom. But the Spirit dwelt there in their little houses, some of them, and they were filled with love. I guess I just miss them." The tears were flowing down his cheeks now, and he looked really embarrassed about it. "Merry Christmas," he said, and he ducked out the door.

Helaman had no sooner closed the door behind him than Trudy was down the stairs railing at him. "I always knew that you'd drive one of my boyfriends away with all your teasing and the horrible things you say, Daddy, but I never thought you'd send one away in *tears*."

"What did you *say* to him, Helaman?" asked Lucille.

"It wasn't anything I said," Helaman answered. "It was our bathroom."

"He *cried* because of your *bathroom*?" asked Trudy. "Well thank heaven you didn't show him your cedar closet, he might have killed himself!"

Helaman thought of explaining, but then he looked at Trudy and didn't want to talk to her. He couldn't think of anything to say to that face, anyway. She had never whined and demanded and blamed like this when she was little. Only since the money. Only since the money started happening.

What am I turning my daughter into? What will she become in this house?

Helaman wasn't feeling the blues anymore. No, it was much worse. He was suffocating. It was desolation.

Helaman's hand was still on the door latch. He looked at Lucille. "Do the stockings without me," he said.

"No, please, Helaman," said Lucille.

"Oh, good job, Trudy," said Joni. "Now everybody's going to be mad at each other on our first Christmas in the new house."

"I think I'd better go home now," said Var.

"*I* can't help it if my father and my sister both went insane to-night," said Joni. "Don't go, Var!"

Everyone's attention had shifted to Joni's pleading with Var; Hela-man used the break to slip out the front door, Lucille's remonstrance trailing him out into the cold night air until at last he heard her close the door and Helaman could walk along the sidewalk in the silence.

The houses rose up like shining palaces on either side of him. Mrs. Braincase's pillared mansion across the street. The huge oversized bi-level two doors down. All the houses inflated as if somebody had been pumping air into them up and down the street. Christmas lights in ever-so-tasteful color-coordinated displays on the trees and along the rooflines. Every house saying, I have succeeded. I have arrived. I am somebody, because I have money.

He imagined that it wasn't him walking along this sidewalk tonight, but a Colombian family. Maybe a father and mother and their two daughters and two sons. Big as these houses were, would any of them have room for them tonight?

Not one. These houses were all too small for that sort of thing. Oh, somebody might slip them a twenty, if anybody wasn't too terrified of robbers to open the door in the first place. But there'd be no room for them to sleep. After all, they might have fleas or lice. They might steal.

Helaman stopped and turned around, looking back at his house from a distance. I can't live here, he thought. That's why I've been so depressed. Like the day I cut out the entry floor and forced them to redo it—I was powerful and strong, wasn't I! And yet all I had the power to do was get my own way by bullying people. I built this house to prove that I had what it takes to get a house in Darlington Heights. And now I'll never see this house without imagining that poor Colombian family, standing outside in the cold, praying for somebody to open the door and let them come inside somewhere that was warm.

What am I doing here, living in one of these houses? I hated these people when I was a kid. I hated the way they looked down on my family. The way they could never quite imagine Dad or Mom in a leadership calling, even though they were always there helping, at every ward activity, every service project, bringing food, making repairs, giving rides. Mom in the nursery, Dad as permanent assistant to four scoutmasters, and all the time Helaman knew that it was because they weren't educated, they talked like farm people because that's where *they* grew up, they didn't have money and their car was ugly and their house was small, while people with nowhere near the kindness and love and goodness and testimony got called to all the visible, prominent callings.

Helaman remembered one time when he was thirteen, sitting there in the office of his bishop, who told him how he needed to set goals in his life. "You can't separate the Church from your career," he said. "When Sterling W. Sill had the top insurance agency in the state of Utah, he got called to the First Council of the Seventy. My goal is to have the top agency by the time I'm forty, and then serve wherever the Lord calls me from then on." The unspoken message was, I'm already bishop and I'm already rich—see how far I've come.

Helaman had come out of that interview seething with rage. I don't believe you, he had insisted silently. The Lord doesn't work that way. The Lord doesn't value people by how much money they make, the two things have nothing to do with each other. And then Helaman had gone home and for the first time in his life, at age thirteen, he saw his father the way that bishop must have seen him—as a failure, a man with no money and no ambition, a man with no *goals*. A man you couldn't possibly respect. Helaman's prayers that night had been filled with rage. He stayed up finding scriptures: It's as hard for a camel to pass through the eye of a needle as for a rich man to get into heaven; let him who would be the greatest among you first be the servant of all; he who would find his life must lose it; sell all you have and give it to the poor and come follow me; they were not rich and poor, bond and free, but all were partakers of the heavenly gift. All those ideas still glowed in Helaman's memory as they had that night, and when he finally slept it was with the sure knowledge that it was his father, the quiet servant without ambition for himself, who was more honorable in the sight of God than any number of rich and educated men in the Church. It was the beginning of his testimony, that peaceful certainty that came that night.

What Helaman had never realized until right now, on this cold Christmas Eve, standing on this street of mansions, was that he had also believed the other story as well, the one the bishop told him. Maybe it was because he still had to see that bishop there on the stand, week after week, and then watch him become stake president and then go off as a mission president; maybe it was because Helaman was naturally ambitious, and so his heart had seized on the bishop's words. Whatever the reason, Helaman had not modeled his life on his father's life, despite that testimony he had received that night when he was thirteen. Instead he had followed the path of the people who had looked down on his father. He had built a house in their neighborhood. He had brought his children to dwell among them. He had proved to them that he was exactly as good as they were.

And that was why he felt so empty, there in his new house, even though his whole family loved the place, even though he had worked so hard to build it. Because the fact that he lived there meant that he was exactly as good as those people who had despised his father, and he knew that it was his father who was good, not them.

Not me.

Lucille even tried to stop me, he thought. She knew. That was why she kept saying, We don't need such a big house. We don't need all those rooms. I don't have to have a separate sewing room—I *like* sewing in the family room with everybody around me.

Helaman had been deaf to all she said; he had taken it for granted that she was only saying these things because she always worried about money and because she was too unselfish to ever ask for anything for herself; he knew that secretly she really wanted all these fine things, these big rooms, these well-earned luxuries.

Only once had she put her foot down. The architect had specced out gold fixtures everywhere, and Lucille had rejected it immediately. "I'd feel like I had to wash my hands before I could touch the faucet to turn it on," she said. Helaman was all set to go ahead anyway, on the assumption that she really wanted them after all, until she looked him in the eye and said, "I will never use a bathroom with gold fixtures, Helaman, so if you put them in, you'd better build me an outhouse in the backyard."

Even then, what had finally convinced him was when she said that chrome fixtures went better with all the towels because they didn't have a color of their own to clash with.

I wasn't listening, thought Helaman. She was telling me exactly what the Spirit told me that night in my childhood, showing me in the scriptures what my goals should be and what I should think about money. And I knew she was right, yet I still went ahead and built this house and now I can't bear to live in it because every room, every bit of wainscoting, every polished oak molding, every oversized room is a slap in the face of my father. I was so angry at those snobs that I had to get even with them by becoming just like them. I don't belong here, I don't want to live among people who would build and live in houses like these, and yet here I am.

Tom Boke stood in my house and wept because I had so much, and I kept it all for myself. I am the opposite of my father. I had the money to do good in the world, and I used it to build a monument to Helaman Willkie, to win the respect of people whose respect isn't worth having.

He was trembling with the cold. He had to go inside, and yet he couldn't bring himself to take another step toward that house.

It's a beautiful house, said a voice inside him. You earned it.

No, he answered silently. I earned the right to live in a house big enough for my family, to meet our needs, to keep us warm and dry. There is no work in the world that a person can do that can earn him the right to live in a house like *this*, when so many others are in want. I sinned in building it, and I will sin every time I put a key in the lock on that door as if it were my right to take this much of the bounty of God's Earth and keep it for just my family to use.

The door to the house opened and light spilled out onto the porch, onto the bare trampled ground that didn't yet have a lawn. It was Lucille, coming outside to find him. Lucille, wearing a coat and carrying another, looking for her husband to keep him warm. Lucille, who had understood the truth about this house all along, and then loved him enough to let him build it anyway. Would she love him enough to let him abandon it now?

He could not walk back to the house, but he could always walk to his wife, and so he called out to her and strode on trembling, uncertain legs toward where she waited for him.

"Here's a coat," she said. "If you don't have the brains to stay indoors, at least wear the coat. I don't want to have to bury you in the backyard, not till the landscapers come in the spring, anyway."

He took her teasing with good cheer, as he always did, but all he could really think about was the impossibility of telling her what he needed to tell her. It was so hard to think of the words. So hard to know how to begin.

"So can I stay out here and talk to you?" said Lucille.

He nodded.

"The house is too big, isn't it," she said. "That missionary has told you about poverty and you took the news as if you'd never heard of it before and now you feel guilty about living here."

As so often before, she had guessed enough about what was in his heart that he could say the rest himself. "It wasn't the boy, what he said. I was already unhappy here, I just didn't know it."

"So what do we do, Helaman? Sell it?"

"Everybody will think we built a house bigger than we could afford and *had* to sell it."

"Do you care?"

"There'll be rumors that Willkie Housewares is in financial trouble."

"It's not a corporation. The stock won't drop in value because of a rumor."

"The kids will never forgive me."

"*That* is possible."

"And I don't know if I could ever look myself in the eye, if I gave you a kitchen like that and then took it away because of some crazy idea that living here means I'm ashamed of my father."

"Your father loves this house, Helaman. He's been over here a dozen times during the building of it, and if he hadn't promised your sister Alma that he'd spend Christmas with *her* family in Dallas he'd be here with us tonight."

"What about you?"

"Moving is a pain and I won't like doing it twice," she said. "But you already know that I never wanted a house this big."

"But I wanted you to have it. I wanted you never to be like my mother, living in a ward where all the other women looked down on her, raising a family with no money in a tiny house."

"*Our* old house wasn't tiny, it was just small."

"You love the new kitchen. I don't want you to give up the new kitchen."

"You sweet, foolish man, I love the kitchen because you took so much care to make it perfect for me."

"I'll give it all up," said Helaman. "Because I can't live with myself if I stay in a place like this. But how can I take it away from you and the kids? Even if you didn't really want it, even if you never asked for it, I gave it to you anyway and I can't take it back."

"So, will you rent an apartment near the main store and come visit us on weekends? Helaman, I couldn't bear it if this house came between us. Why do you think I didn't try to stop you from building it? Because I knew you wanted it so much, you were so hungry for it—not for yourself, but to give it to us. You needed so much to give this to us. Well, you *have* given it to us, and the kids and I love it. You meant to build it for the best motives, and as soon you realized that maybe it wasn't such a good idea, you were filled with remorse. The Lord doesn't expect you to sell it and live in a tent."

"Sell all you have and give it to the poor and come follow me," Helaman quoted.

"That was what he said to a rich *young* man. You're middle-aged."

"And you're just saying whatever you think will get me back into the house where it's warm."

"Well, what *are* you going to do, then? Never come back inside again?"

To Helaman's surprise, he found tears running down his cheeks, his face twisting into a grimace of weeping. "I can't," he said. "If I go back inside then it means I'm just like *them*."

"So don't *be* just like them," said Lucille, putting her arms around him. "You never *have* been just like them, anyway. You've never run your business the way they do—you've been fair and even generous with everybody, even your competitors, and everybody knows it. There's nobody in the world who resents your having this house— your employees love you because they know you've paid them more than you had to and made less profit than you could have and you work harder than any of them and you forgive them for mistakes, and every one of them is glad for you to finally move out of that house that we've stayed in since 1975. Most of them don't understand why it took us so long to move. You can live in this house with a clear conscience. You're *not* like the rest of these people." She looked up and down the street. "For all we know, half of *them* might not be like the rest of these people."

"It's not about them or what anybody else thinks," said Helaman. "I just can't be happy there. It's like what that missionary said. Tom, right? He said, I just can't live in America anymore. Well, I just can't live in that house."

Lucille stood there in silence, still holding him, but not speaking. Helaman was still full of things to say, but it was always hard for him to talk about things inside himself, and he was worn out with talking, and even though he had stopped weeping now, he was afraid of feelings so strong that they could make him cry. So the silence lasted until Lucille spoke again.

"You can't sell the house," said Lucille. "It won't be a poor person who buys it, anyway."

"You mean I should give it away?"

"I mean we should give it away in our hearts."

He laughed. He remembered the testimony meeting where Sister Mooller, who had more money than General Motors, had gotten up and said that thirty years ago she and her husband had decided to consecrate all they had to the Lord, and so they gave away "in their hearts," which was why the Lord had blessed them with so much more in the years since then. Whereupon Lucille had leaned over to him and whispered, "I guess the Lord really needed that new Winnebago they bought last month."

"Don't laugh," said Lucille. "I know you're thinking about Sister

Mooller, but we could *really* do it. Live in the house as if it weren't our own."

"What, never unpack?"

"Listen to me, I'm being serious. I'm really trying to find a way for you to have all the things that you want—to give this house to us, and yet not be the kind of man who lives in a big fancy house, and still keep the family living under one roof."

"That *is* the problem, isn't it." He felt so foolish to have gotten himself into such a twisted, impossible set of circumstances. No matter what he chose, he'd feel guilty and ashamed and unhappy. It was as if he had deliberately set out to feel unrighteous and unhappy no matter how things turned out.

"Let's consecrate this house to the Lord," said Lucille. "We were going to dedicate it tomorrow, anyway, as part of Christmas. Well let's do it tonight, instead, and when we dedicate it let's make a covenant with the Lord, that we will always treat this house as if others have as much right to use it as we do."

Helaman tried to think of how that would work. "You mean have people over?"

"I mean keep watching, constantly, for anybody who needs a roof over their heads. Newcomers who need a place to stay while they're getting settled. People in trouble who have nowhere else to turn."

"Bums from the street?"

She looked him in the eye. "If that's what it takes for you to feel right about this house, and you'll be here at night to make sure that the family is safe, then yes, bums from the street."

The idea was so strange and audacious that he would have laughed, except that as she spoke there was so much fire in her eyes that he felt himself fill with light as well, a light so hot and sweet that tears came to his eyes again, only this time not tears of despair and remorse but rather tears of love—for Lucille, yes, but more than for her. There were words ringing in his ears, words that no one had said tonight, but still he heard them like the memory of a dear old friend's voice, whispering to him, Whatever you do to help these little ones, these humble, helpless, lonely, frightened children, you're doing it for me.

And yet even as he knew that this was what the Savior wanted him to do, a new objection popped into his mind. "There are zoning laws," he said. "This is a single-family dwelling."

"The zoning laws don't stop us from having visitors, do they?" said Lucille.

"No," said Helaman.

"And if somebody stays very long we can always tell Sister Barnacuse that they're faux relatives."

Helaman laughed. "Right. We can tell her that we've got a lot of brothers and sisters who come and visit."

"And it'll be the truth," said Lucille.

"This can't be one of those resolutions that we make and then forget," he said.

"A solemn covenant with the Lord," she said.

"It isn't fair to you," said Helaman. "Most of the extra work of having visitors in the house would fall to you."

"And to the kids," she said. "And you'll help me."

"It has to be like a contract," said Helaman. "There have to be terms. So we'll know if we're living up to the covenant. We can't just wait for people in need to just happen along."

"So we'll look for them," said Lucille. "We can talk to the bishop to see who's in need."

"As if anybody in *this* ward is going to need a place to stay!"

"Then we'll ask him to talk to the stake president. There are other wards in this stake. And people you'll hear about at work."

"Someone new every month, unless the house is already full," said Helaman.

"Every month?" said Lucille.

"Yes."

"Like home teaching?" she asked.

It was a sly jab indeed, for she well knew how many times Helaman had come to the end of the month and then would grab one of his sons and run around the ward, trying to catch their home teaching families and teach them his famous end-of-the-month procrastination lesson. "Even when I'm late, I *do* my home teaching."

"If you think you can find somebody every month, then that's the covenant," said Lucille. "But you're the one who'll have to take the responsibility for finding somebody every month, because I don't get out enough."

"That's fine," said Helaman.

"And if we find that we can't do it," said Lucille, "that it's too hard or it's hurting our family, what then?"

"Then we sell all we have and give the money to the poor," said Helaman.

"In other words," said Lucille, "if we can't make this work, then we move."

"Yes."

It was agreed, and it felt right. It was a good thing to do. Hadn't his own parents always had room on the floor for somebody to lay out a sleeping bag if they had no other place to stay? Hadn't there always been a place at his parents' table for the lonely, the hungry, the stranger? With this covenant that he and Lucille were making with the Lord, Helaman could truly go home.

And then, suddenly, he felt fear plunge into his heart like a cold knife. What in the world was he promising to do? Destroy his privacy, risk his family's safety, keep their lives in constant turmoil, and for what—because some missionary cried over the poverty in Colombia? What, would there be a single person in Colombia who'd sleep better tonight because Helaman Willkie was planning to allow squatters to use his spare bedrooms?

"What's wrong?" asked Lucille.

"Nothing," said Helaman. "Let's get inside and tell the kids before we freeze." Before my heart freezes, he said silently. Before I talk myself out of trying to become a true son of my father and mother.

They opened the door, and for the first time, as he followed Lucille onto the marble floor, he didn't feel ashamed to enter. Because it wasn't his own house anymore.

Joni was all for having Var stay through the whole rest of the Christmas Eve festivities, but Helaman politely told Var that this was a good time for him to go home to be with his family. It only took two repetitions of the hint to get him out the door.

They gathered in the living room and, as was their tradition on Christmas Eve, Helaman read from the scriptures about the birth of the Savior. But then he skipped ahead to the part about "even as ye have done it unto the least of these," and then he and Lucille explained the covenant to their children. None of them was overjoyed.

"Do I have to let them use my computer?" asked Steven.

"They're *family* computers," said Helaman. "But if it becomes a problem, maybe you can keep one computer in your room."

"It sounds like this is going to be a motel," said Trudy. "But I'm going to college after this year and so I don't really care."

"Does this mean I can't ever have my friends over?" asked Ryan.

"Of course you can," said Lucille.

Joni had said nothing so far, but Helaman knew from the stony look on her face that she was taking it worst of all. So he asked her what she was thinking.

"I'm thinking that somehow this is all going to work around so I have to share my bedroom again."

"We have spare bedrooms coming out of our ears, not to mention a whole mother-in-law apartment in the basement," said Helaman. "You will *not* have to share your room with anybody."

"Good," said Joni. "Because if you ever ask me to share my room, I'm moving out."

"We don't make threats to you," said Lucille, "and I'd appreciate it if you'd refrain from making threats to us."

"I mean it," said Joni. "It's not a threat, I'm just telling you what *will* happen. I waited a long time to have a room of my own, and I'll never share my bedroom again."

"We'll be sure to warn your boyfriends that your husband is going to have to sleep in another room," said Trudy.

"You aren't helping, Trudy," said Lucille.

"Joni," said Helaman, "I promise that I'll never ask you to share your room with anybody."

"Then it's OK with me if you want to turn the rest of the house into a circus."

For a moment Helaman hesitated, wondering if this *was*, after all, such a good idea. Then he remembered that Joni had brought home tonight a boy who was attractive to her only because his father was famous and he drove a Jaguar. And he realized that if he let Joni live in this house, in this neighborhood, without doing *something* to teach her better values, he was surely going to lose her. Maybe opening up the house to strangers in need would give her a chance to learn that there was more to people than how much fame and wealth they had. Maybe that's what this was all about in the first place. He had wanted this house to be a blessing to his family—maybe the Lord had shown him and Lucille the way to make that happen.

Or maybe this would cause so much turmoil and contention that the family would fall apart.

No, thought Helaman. Trying to live the gospel might cause some pain from time to time, but it's a sure thing that *not* trying to live the gospel for fear that it *might* hurt my family will *certainly* hurt them, and such an injury would be deep and slow to heal.

As he hesitated, Lucille caught his eye. "The stockings seem to be hanging in front of the fireplace," she said. "All we need to do now is have our family prayer and bring presents downstairs to put them under the tree."

"You aren't going to make us give away our *presents*, are you, Dad?" asked Ryan.

"In fact, that's why we all got lousy presents for you this year, Ryan," said Helaman. "So that when it's time to give them away, you won't mind."

"Da-ad!" said Ryan impatiently. But he was smiling.

Instead of their normal Christmas family prayer, Helaman dedicated the house. In his prayer he consecrated it as the Lord's property, equally open to anyone that the Lord might bring to take shelter there. He set out the terms of the covenant in his prayer, and when he was done, the children all said amen.

"It's not our house anymore," said Helaman. "It's the Lord's house now."

"Yeah," said Steven. "But I'll bet he sticks you with the mortgage payments anyway, Dad."

That night, when the children were asleep and Helaman and Lucille had finished the last-minute wrapping and had laid out all the gifts for the morning, only a few hours away, they climbed into bed together and Lucille held his hand and kissed him and said, "Merry Christmas and welcome home."

"Same to you and doubled," he said, and she smiled at the old joke.

Then she touched his cheek and said, "All the years that I've been praying for another child, and all the years that the Lord has told us no, maybe it was all leading to this night. So that our lives would have room for what we've promised."

"Maybe," said Helaman. He watched as she closed her eyes and fell asleep almost at once. And in the few minutes before he, too, slept, he thought of that Colombian family he had imagined earlier. He pictured them standing at his door, all their possessions in a bag slung over the father's shoulder, the children clinging to their mother's skirts, the youngest sleepy and fussing in her arms. And he imagined himself holding the door wide open and saying, "Come in, come in, the table's set and we've been waiting for you." And Helaman saw his wife and children gather at the table with their visitors, and there was food enough for all, and all were satisfied.

THE WEATHER HERE

Stephen Tuttle

1

WHEN MANDELBAUM DOESN'T COME back for what must be days, we assume the worst for him; and although we haven't come to any consensus on what the worst might be, we are collectively relieved that for the first time in recent memory no one is saying anything about the Doppler radar. It was Mandelbaum who was most likely to disagree on any given subject, and so his absence gives us some relief. We have considered that he may have left by choice because he kept saying he was going to; but he said all sorts of things, and we see no good reason to start taking him at his word now. What we know for sure is that he is gone and that we do not miss his complaints.

2

It is because we have become so good at prediction that we feel such confidence in our conclusions about Mandelbaum. We have become expert prognosticators in our time, and we like to congratulate one another for our talents; it is our unique ability, we are sure, to be so good at anticipating the future. We have successfully predicted many things and continue to do so with an ease that does not surprise us. We will not have food again tomorrow, we say, and we are right. We will not sleep and can only vaguely remember ever having done so; again we are unanimous. It will rain again tomorrow, we are sure. We have no precise means of measuring days, but we are in agreement that the fleas come at intervals that feel, roughly, day-like. And when the fleas do come, we have no recourse but to lie in the mud and wait for them to tire of us and move on.

3

It is hopeless for us to waste our energies, and so we return to what we know best. Tanner removes himself and begins pounding away again at the slabs of concrete that are slowly revealing themselves to be the letters H and L. With these letters and a host of cumulonimbus rocks, he is preparing to explain to us, in graphic form, why it is possible though not likely that the rain will subside within five to seven days. It will rain again tomorrow, Tanner tells us, but there is a ten percent chance that change is on the horizon, see. He has found a stick somewhere and uses it to point at the detritus all around his feet. Perhaps this is too much for us to make sense out of just yet, Tanner says. He sits down in an enormous puddle and sets to work on a High Pressure Zone that will, he assures us, make everything clear.

4

We cannot see the sun, but we are not convinced that it is absent. We admit that we cannot see much at all and that the darkness here is something we are still struggling with. We would like to believe that whatever rain clouds are above us are so thick as to block the sunlight from reaching us. But some of us have begun to question whether or not we ever had a sun to begin with. When Villagran mentions the sun, he has started using his fingers to suggest quotation marks to remind us that he was the first to theorize that the sun we are so determined to remember may never have existed in the first place. Is it not possible, Villagran has asked us, that the sun is just a myth we have so fully embraced that we have forgotten that we have never had a sun? I mean, really, Villagran has said to us.

5

We have walls but nothing above us. Mandelbaum called this place a ruin. He said that the broken stones around us were evidence enough that something better had once been here but that now things had all gone to pieces. We did not share his surety that the presence of crumbling walls necessitated the history of something better. We hypothesized that this had been the site of good intentions never completed, or that these walls were all that this place was ever meant to show for itself. Like Mandelbaum we also wished for a roof over our heads, for some protection from the elements, but we did not share his opinions on most other things. These walls are all we know, and they were enough to send Mandelbaum searching for something more. We know, of course, that our best efforts should involve more than aimless wandering and that we must wait things out. Once the rain has gone we will be in a better position to think clearly, to assess our situation, and to make plans for our future. We agree completely that Mandelbaum was an impetuous and impatient man.

6

Orton and Halston are standing shoulder to shoulder, faces turned at the sky while the rain pours over them. Does Orton know the difference between Partly Cloudy and Partly Sunny, Halston wants to know. The rain hits his body with a force, and he takes it, eyes open but blinking frequently. Orton's eyes are closed, and he smiles. Of course Orton knows the difference, what does Halston take him for? Halston happens to take him for a fool, Halston says, because he knows, as Orton obviously does not, that there is no difference between Partly Cloudy and Partly Sunny. Semantics, Halston says, that is your difference. Ah, Orton says, ah. But have you forgotten that it can be Partly Cloudy at night whereas it is unlikely that it will ever be Partly Sunny when the sun is nowhere to be found. And here, Halston says, what would you say we have here? Orton does not open his eyes to say that we have rain. You see my point then, Halston says, you see that I am right and that you have simply been misleading yourself? No, Orton says, I see no such thing. All Orton sees is rain. And all Orton wants to know is if Halston really believes that his semantics matter in a situation like this, in a situation where it is obviously Fully Cloudy and not sunny at all.

7

It was Mandelbaum's contention that all of us here are dead. He was wrong, of course, and we proved it to him a dozen different ways. Will a dead man complain about the fleas that will not stop biting him? Will a dead man talk to other dead men? Will a dead man make predictions about the weather? He would hear none of our arguments. He could not remember eating or sleeping or whether he had a family, and these things were proof enough, he told us. We took it as our task to convince him that he was wrong, and that his failing memory was certainly not reason for such skepticism. He was alive, we told him, because his hair was still growing. He was alive because he had the energy to conjecture in the first place. Because dead men do not wonder if they are dead; dead men know as much. He was quick to tell us that he knew a thing or two about life and death and that this was like no life he knew anything about. He was a nervous man, Mandelbaum.

8

Fitzpatrick is convinced that the rain is coming to its end. He cites, as his evidence, the lack of foliage and ground cover. This much rain can exist only in an ecosystem that is lush and tropical, he tells us, and the lack of greenery suggests that it has rained too long, that the ecosystem has lost its balance. These things correct themselves, Fitzpatrick says, these things most certainly correct themselves. Villagran calls Fitzpatrick a buffoon and tells him that not one of us has ever said so much about something he knows so little about. You are absolutely and exactly wrong, Villagran says. He says that this rain will create an environment in which the flora will thrive and bloom. Hollinger agrees with Fitzpatrick and Villagran enough to say that he too anticipates an end to the rain. But Hollinger fears that the rain will be followed by a drought, a period as dry as this one is wet. How long has it been raining? Hollinger asks us. How long? We have no concrete answer, but we agree on certain things. We agree that it has been raining for a long time, a very long time, longer than any of us can remember. And how long, Hollinger wants us to tell him, can we remember? And what can we say to this but that we cannot remember a time before this time, that we have no memories that do not include rain. Exactly, Hollinger says, and soon enough, we will have no memories that do not include a dryness so extreme that we will curse the lack of moisture then as much as we curse the overabundance of it now. We admit to ourselves that Hollinger's logic is not so convincing as we had hoped it might be. But we are less concerned with his logic than we are with his conviction. We tell Hollinger that we see his point, and that it is a good one. Except Fitzpatrick. Fitzpatrick says no, no, no. Fitzpatrick says he cannot agree with Hollinger's hollow and obviously flimsy argument, which is based on nothing but unscientific hypotheses. It is useless,

Fitzpatrick says, to assume that this rain has come to us without some cause. And that cause, he says, is the plow. The plow? Hollinger says, I see no plow; can you please show me a plow? My point, Fitzpatrick says, is that this ground has been plowed, that it has been made ready for this moisture, and that this rain is a natural response to the plow. There is a circularity you must admit to, Fitzpatrick says to us, and we say that yes, we would like to admit to a circularity. But wait, Hollinger says, why must we admit to anything so vague as that? Why must we agree with you before you have proven anything? But that's just the point, Fitzpatrick says, I have already proven everything. And so we applaud Fitzpatrick, we admire his resolve and his cunning, we cheer his name, in the rain, waiting for the ecosystem to correct itself. Except for Villagran, who is sulking.

9

We find it odd that while the rain seems to maintain a certain consistency we are sometimes able to speak at conversational levels, but just as often, we must yell in order to be heard. Tanner is most disturbed by these changes because his voice is so soft. He tells us, when he can, that the problem is one of focused attention, and that we would be able to hear him quite clearly if we would make half an effort. The rain is louder, Tanner says, when we allow it to be. This sort of explanation is exactly the sort of thing that gets Halston all worked up. It is Halston's opinion that we are not in a position to enact much change and that we can do little more than accept the rain. The rain, Halston argues, is constant, and it does us no good to look for minute distinctions between one moment and the next. Our position, he says, is unchangeable, and the sooner we accept that the better. But what Tanner wants to know is why it is, if our position is so helpless, that Halston is always the last one running around when the fleas come, and why he refuses to simply let them do what they will do.

10

Mandelbaum spoke so often of the Doppler radar that we began to fear for his sanity. While it is true, as he often said, that a little technology can go a very long way, we were not prepared to spend our days waiting for a radar system that could only tell us what we already know.

What we know is rain, and what good is technology that simply re-states that which is clear to us? Rain is rain, we told Mandelbaum, and we need no technology that will tell us nothing more than that. Mandelbaum said that there was something more than rain and that he was going to find it. He said that he could not stand the fleas any longer.

11

The fleas come in enormous waves that cover the ground completely. They come by the millions and cover every inch of our bodies until we are so thoroughly bitten that nothing remains for the fleas to bite. We have tried to hide ourselves from the fleas, to run from them or cover ourselves; but they move more quickly than we can hope to, and they are more patient than we ever gave them credit for being. We have come to respect the fleas for their incredible sense of timing. They are capable, these miniscule little beasts, of avoiding the rain that so thoroughly drenches us, and they know just how often to return to us, just when our itching blisters have begun to recede. Villagran suggests that we take a lesson from the fleas, that we find a means by which we can avoid the rain by keeping on the move. We have made attempts at Villagran's plan but have only made ourselves tired and hot, soaked through by rain and sweat. Fitzpatrick and Tanner were never convinced that such a plan could work in the first place because we are, they thought, too large and too slow as men. What we need, they both said, is a roof. Villagran has not stopped running, though, and although he looks more tired than ever, we have come to admit that he does look faster than ever before.

12

Tanner suggests that it is perhaps our lack of historical context that is making things so difficult for us. He proposes that we make a list of the things we can remember and that we all agree on. Tanner is convinced that it is only through consensus that we will ever achieve anything worthwhile, and he speaks so loudly that we find it hard to disagree. And so we begin. We have no means of writing since the mud at our feet will not maintain its shape, but we feel confident that we can create a verbal consensus among ourselves. Orton remembers the last wave of fleas, and how they have made it difficult for him to walk. Hal-

ston remembers rain and nothing else. Hollinger remembers Mandelbaum and his constant longings for technology. Villagran remembers
the words Low Pressure Zone but admits that he cannot now make
sense of them. Tanner remembers his clothing when it was more than
the torn and ragged cloth that it is now. Fitzpatrick remembers a time
when he thought the end of rain was near. We agree that we have the
sense of a time before the rain, but not one of us can conjure an image
from that time or a sense of whether it was any better than this time.
We agree that Mandelbaum has been gone for quite a while now and
that his return, which once seemed imminent, seems less likely now
than ever. We agree on a lot of things, but then Orton wants to know
if he's the only one who remembers making this list before.

13

Fitzpatrick says that his knee no longer hurts and that he had given up
on his hope for an end to the rain but that this is something to really
believe in. His knee, he says, is never wrong. Halston finds it odd that
Fitzpatrick would not have mentioned his knee before if Fitzpatrick
is willing to invest so much in its ability to predict the future. For his
part, Fitzpatrick cannot remember mentioning his knee either, but he
is sure he must have because it has bothered him so much. His knee,
he tells us, hurts when the rain is coming, and the fact that it has hurt
for so long has always meant that more rain, in addition to whatever
downpour we were in the middle of at that moment, was on its way.
But now, he says, now. Now that his knee is pain free he has something
concrete to deal with. The rain is coming to an end, Fitzpatrick says,
and the proof is in my joints. But wait a minute, Halston says, wait
a minute, are you sure it ever didn't hurt before? Are you even sure
which knee it was? And Fitzpatrick is sure, so very sure, so completely
sure that the pain was in his left knee, and so what if his right knee
hurts a little bit now, if it causes him to limp a little more than any
of us can remember, so what if there's a new pain in a different joint,
his left knee is pain free and that should count for something.

14

Mandelbaum liked to use the term Higher Power. He said that we
should at least consider the possibility of punishment, that we should

give some thought to things we had done before we got to this point. He said that we had all said and done things for which we could not be forgiven and that he needed no more explanation than that. He said that we needed the rain to cleanse ourselves, that it was a metaphor for something, and that the fleas were also a metaphor but that he wasn't sure what they stood for. He said that we needed to find some answers to some questions and that the Doppler radar was going to provide those answers because when had it ever done us wrong, when had technology ever been less than what we needed? He said that we were being punished for misdeeds and that our pasts were catching up to us. He said that this place was the opposite of a resting place, that it was a restless place where we would never know peace again, because we had hurt people, and done them wrong, and presented as truth things which we knew were not.

15

We agree, when we set our minds to agreeing, that certain things are not so bad, that the fleas are fine if they get what they want, and that the rain is not so hot or so cold as it might be, and that the mud feels good between our toes and in our hands. We agree that our skin is never dry or cracked and that we are never thirsty and that we cannot remember exhaustion that was not quickly relieved. We agree that things are not so bad as Mandelbaum would have had us believe. But we cannot help wishing he were here. We cannot help feeling that his contrariness was important to us and that we are somehow diminished by his absence. We cannot help but hope that even now he is returning to tell us more firmly than ever that we are receiving our just rewards. We want Mandelbaum to correct us and remind us that the rain is not to be enjoyed. And we want him to long for technology that he cannot have. We can see him there, just beyond our field of vision. We can see that he is coming back to us and that he is bringing with him the first clear skies we have ever seen. We can see that Mandelbaum has found some means by which to call an end to our problems, to rid us of our infestations, to allow us, for once, something better than this.

CALLING AND ELECTION

Jack Harrell

JERRY SANGOOD STEPPED OUT OF HIS car and into the darkness of the church parking lot. The sky above was black, without a moon. A thick cloud cover hid the stars from view, and Jerry felt the darkness like a hardened pit growing inside his brain. He shut the car door and stood for a moment in the far corner of the parking lot, near a row of Lombardy poplars as old as the town itself. The Mormon pioneers who had founded this part of Idaho had favored these narrow trees that grew tall and hearty in the sandy soil. They planted hundreds of them in long rows to break the relentless winds. Standing against the darkness of the trees, Jerry watched Bishop Gordon of the Third Ward switch off the lights inside the church. The bishop walked out through the darkened entryway and locked the glass doors, stopping a moment to look behind him into the stillness of the building before he turned and went toward his pickup.

As Bishop Gordon started his truck and pulled away, Jerry Sangood knew he had a choice. He could shake off this moment. He could go home and pray for the safe return of his good wife, who had flown to California to help their daughter and her new baby. He could pray for a way to tell his wife what the doctor had found that afternoon in the X-ray. But even if he did, even if he turned and went home to pray in his secret chambers, God would still be waiting, patient as the Wasatch Mountains, for Jerry to return to this moment. In a week or a month or a year, God would send someone to ask Jerry to put his hand to the plow without looking back.

As the taillights of the bishop's pickup disappeared in the darkness, a dull pain coursed its way up the back of Jerry's neck. At least now it made sense—the headaches, the mood swings, the memory lapses. For weeks he had thought he was losing his mind. Hiding the pain had only made him more irritable, had only made his behavior more erratic. Now he walked toward the building's double doors, pushing back the pain by sheer will.

"Don't be late," the man on the phone had said.

"This shouldn't be hard," he told himself as he looked at his watch; he was right on time. *What shall it profit a man,* he thought, *if he shall gain the whole world?*

Waiting in the church parking lot with a tumor in his brain, Jerry knew that God had given him so much. He and Camille had paid off the house. They had money in the bank, enough for a mission and more. They had Jerry's job as a seminary teacher. They had their daughter, Gwen, and her husband and children. They had their friends and their good reputations. Above all, they had the gospel, which had taught them to work hard and save and steer clear of the world's counterfeit joys. And still God desired to give them more, always more. Even this knot growing in his brain was an invitation, Jerry believed.

"God dwells in eternal burnings," the Prophet Joseph Smith had taught. The burnings were glories that mortals could not yet endure. Everything that had happened was part of God's plan. Their daughter and her baby in the hospital—it was a test. Jerry's headaches, and now this invitation to meet a representative of the prophet—it was all part of his own inching closer to redemption.

Jerry paused at the church doors. He had been passing through these doors for thirty years, since the day of the building's dedication. The plainness of the dark, empty ward house impressed him anew. The structure and design were both functional and austere—brick and metal and glass and carpet. Jerry was like this building, he realized: practical, artless, a means to an end. The scripture said, "There is no beauty that we should desire him."

He had watched Bishop Gordon lock the door a few moments ago, but with a believing heart, with the same heart that had moved him to act all his life in the face of doubt, Jerry reached out. When the tips of his fingers touched the metal door handle, the hallway lights came on. An elderly man appeared in the hall, next to the stake president's office, his hand on the light switch. He wore a black, three-piece suit and carried a small silver briefcase. When he waved Jerry inside, Jerry pulled on the door handle. It opened with ease.

Jerry stepped inside, and the man approached him. He had wire-rimmed glasses and a stony smile that showed a row of crooked teeth. He was bald, and his eyebrows were bare. "I'm Brother Lucy," he said, shaking Jerry's hand. His grip was bony and firm. "Thank you for coming."

Jerry sensed that they were the only two in the building.

"I apologize for making an appointment so late," Brother Lucy said, leading him toward the stake president's office. "This will take only a few minutes."

Jerry didn't recognize Brother Lucy from the pictures in the church magazines. "Did you travel alone?" he asked. "I thought the Brethren always traveled in pairs."

"The Brethren often do," Brother Lucy said. "Please," he added, offering Jerry a seat. They both sat down at the desk, opposite the stake president's empty chair. Brother Lucy opened his briefcase. "I'm not one of the Brethren." He looked at Jerry with bright eyes that appeared younger than the rest of his face. "I'm just a messenger. I do a lot of traveling for the Brethren, though. 'Going to and fro in the earth,' as the saying goes. Shall we begin?" he asked.

Jerry nodded, shuddering a bit at the pain in his neck.

"Are you all right?" Brother Lucy asked.

"Just a headache," Jerry said. "I'll be fine."

Brother Lucy considered him for a moment. "Well, let's get right to business," he said. "Get you home so you can rest." He took two sheets of paper from his briefcase. Then, speaking in a scripted voice, he said. "Brother Jerry Sangood, we are here at the promptings of the Holy Spirit. Our Heavenly Father knows your faithfulness. He has heard your secret prayers and whispered counsel to you in your extremities. You have magnified yourself according to the oath and covenant of the priesthood. Your life has been one of exemplary service, and your brethren in the priesthood have confirmed your worthiness."

The man stopped for a moment, adjusting his glasses. "Brother Sangood, I have here two letters. One is from the prophet, electing you to the higher blessings of the priesthood. The second letter is addressed to the prophet. In order to receive this election, you must sign the second letter, which states that you accept the weighty charge that comes with this high and holy calling. If you sign the second letter, I will then deliver it to the prophet. Brother Sangood, do you understand the calling and election I am extending to you?"

"It's the Second Anointing," Jerry said.

"That's right," Brother Lucy said. "This is the Second Comforter." Then he paused for a moment, leveling his gaze on Jerry. "Brother Sangood," he said, "a new dispensation awaits you, if you are willing to receive it."

"A new dispensation," Jerry repeated, thinking about the tumor growing in his brain.

"A literal *pouring out* upon your head," the man said.

Jerry winced as a sharp pain erupted and subsided in the back of his neck.

The man put the letters on the desk before Jerry. "Read them carefully," he said, "before you sign."

Jerry recognized the letterhead, the prophet's signature, the familiar and reserved tone of church correspondence. *Dear Brother Sangood,* the first letter read. *The Lord has looked upon your heart and desires now to magnify your inheritance.*

The pain in Jerry's head reasserted itself. Earlier that day, Jerry had gone to see Dr. Slater, complaining of headaches and mood swings, loss of memory. When the doctor came into the examination room with the X-ray, he put it on the screen and said, "There's the culprit." He circled the air above the image with a silver pen. In the black and gray figure of Jerry's skull was a small white stone the size of a quarter. Jerry stared at it for a long time, like a man having a revelation. Dr. Slater scheduled a biopsy for Monday, in Pocatello. He said they wouldn't know anything until then.

A few minutes after leaving the doctor's office, Jerry came home to an empty house. He picked up the cordless phone and sat on the couch. Camille had been in California for nearly a week, having left the day before their daughter Gwen was scheduled to deliver. Camille had been on the plane when Gwen's uterine wall broke. When she called Gwen's cell phone from the airport, Neal, their son-in-law, answered: Gwen and the baby were in intensive care. The doctors had performed an emergency C-section. They found the baby's leg outside the womb, pressing against Gwen's internal organs.

Jerry didn't know when Camille would be coming back, and Dr. Slater had said they wouldn't know anything until after the biopsy on Monday. Jerry put the cordless back on its cradle. He wouldn't worry her until he knew more, until after the biopsy. A moment later, Brother Lucy had called. Now Jerry was looking at two letters—and a new dispensation.

On the second letter, which was addressed to the prophet, there was a space at the bottom for Jerry's signature. Jerry read the words *Second Comforter* and *serve with all my heart, might, mind, and strength.* He looked at Brother Lucy. "What happens if I sign?"

"Each case is different," Brother Lucy answered, taking a pen from his coat pocket and handing it to Jerry.

Jerry took the pen. He would hold back nothing from the Lord. When he taught his students in seminary, he often quoted the Primary song: "Keep the commandments! In this there is safety; in this there is peace." He signed the letter and handed it back to Brother Lucy, trusting in the hand of God.

Standing in the parking lot with the man a few minutes later, Jerry asked, "Will there be an ordination? Will my wife be called?"

"Each case is different," Brother Lucy said once again. Then, he lowered his head for a moment, scowling, like a man arguing with himself.

"What is it?" Jerry asked.

Brother Lucy looked out at the darkness of the parking lot. "I feel impressed to tell you something, Brother Sangood," he said. "I feel impressed to caution you."

Jerry felt an odd tingling in the back of his head.

"A lot of people have lived on this earth." Brother Lucy looked up in contemplation at the dark sky. "And a lot of people will yet live on this earth."

In the black and overcast sky above them, three stars had become visible: Vega, the falling eagle; Cassiopeia, placed in the sky to learn humility; and Aldebaran, the follower.

"Not all of God's premortal children were faithful," Brother Lucy said.

"There was war in heaven." Jerry said, inspired.

Brother Lucy smiled wryly. "Billions of people have lived on this earth," he said. "Billions will yet be sent. But a third of the hosts were cast down to earth for rebellion—unembodied spirits roaming the earth, seeking their brothers' and sisters' destruction."

In Jerry's eyes, Brother Lucy suddenly looked like a small, needle-toothed mammal, like a predator. "How many of them are there?" he asked. "How many spirits roam the earth, combined against each one of us?"

Jerry felt a gloom that seemed to emerge from the hardened pit in the back of his own skull. He felt it in the air around him, in his ears, in his nose and mouth, like a living, cancerous smoke. He clenched his eyes shut, unable to resist the vision of dozens of devilish fiends encircling him, entering his thoughts, taunting and tempting, blaspheming his faith. He fell to his knees, the sound of Brother Lucy's voice swirling amid the devilish air. Writhing on the pavement of the LDS church parking lot, Jerry struggled against the hosts that beset him. He felt the cold blacktop against his face and teeth as they tugged at his soul, as the very pavement seemed to heave and pitch beneath him, becoming a hard, black sea of evil, ready to swallow him whole.

When Jerry pulled into the parking lot of the LDS seminary the next morning, he felt tired and agitated, barely himself. He got out of his car and walked stiffly toward the building, his muscles aching. He remembered meeting with Brother Lucy the night before and signing the letter. He remembered Brother Lucy talking about the hosts who fell from heaven. Then he remembered waking up in his own backyard, soaking wet, in a morning rainstorm. Cold and confused, he had ducked through the basement door, which stood open, the knees of his suit pants shredded and soiled, one sleeve of his suit coat torn, his tie gone, his hands and shirt filthy.

He put his ruined suit in a trash bag and took it out to the garbage. Whatever had beset him the night before, he knew he must faithfully accept God's vision of his own future. He showered and put on another suit. He had just enough time to open the seminary building for the students who would soon be coming in for their first classes.

Reaching the seminary building, his limbs stiff and aching, he remembered the predatory look on Brother Lucy's face, like a small, menacing animal. He remembered the words, *Each case is different.* He put his key to the lock. Then he saw that the door stood open, just an inch. Perhaps Brother Severe, the director, had already arrived, he thought. But the lights were off, and no one responded when he stepped inside and called out a greeting. He walked down the hall, switching on lights and checking rooms. Everything seemed to be in order, until he got to his own classroom.

He sensed the darkness even before he switched on the light, even before he saw the pictures, hundreds of them, printed on ordinary computer printer paper. Images from the Internet—grainy, explicit, hardcore—covered the walls and cabinets of his classroom. More pictures were scattered on the floor and on the students' desks. For an instant Jerry stood paralyzed, confounded in his acknowledgment of God's hand in all things.

A frantic, irrational spirit burst upon him as he realized that the students would be coming in at any moment. Fearing all that he had to lose, he began tearing pictures from the walls, gathering them in a flurry. Despite the ache in his limbs, despite the sharp pains in the back of his skull, he tore images of women and men from the walls, grabbed them up from the floor, peeled them off the cabinets. Like a madman he stuffed pictures in the crook of one arm as he moved through the room. For every picture he tore at, others fell from his grasp, crumpled and torn in his wake. Dozens of other pictures still hung on the walls, untouched. He rushed to his desk, vainly believing he could stuff the obscene pictures in the drawers and hide this unreasonable, unbelievable thing that had happened. But the drawers of his desk already had pictures in them, dozens of pictures, neatly stacked—Christ at the well, knocking at the door, showing himself to the Nephites; Joseph Smith, Noah, and Isaiah; family prayer and baptism. Jerry thought then that he must be losing his mind. These pictures had been on the walls just the day before, which now seemed a lifetime away. Throwing open the last desk drawer, he saw a picture of Adam and Eve in the garden. The image of the couple holding hands in Eden seemed more real than ever as Jerry stood in his seminary classroom, an armload of torn and crumpled pornographic images clutched to his chest.

His goodness stripped naked and mocked, Jerry saw three ninth-

grade girls standing in the doorway. They stood frozen in their innocence, holding their books and backpacks, their eyes wide and their
mouths agape. Jerry knew these girls. He knew their parents. He'd attended their brothers' mission farewells and homecomings. An un-
characteristic curse fell from his lips as he lunged toward the girls, the
pictures still clutched in his arms. The girls fled into the hallway, crying
out in shock to the other students. Just as Jerry reached the doorway,
calling incoherently to the girls, Adam Birch and Greg Hill appeared.
The two boys, strong, tall seniors raised on potato farms, looked past
Jerry and into the room, their faces drawn with astonishment.

Jerry tried to move beyond the boys. "Girls, girls!" he called out
in a vulgar cough, his legs nearly giving way beneath him. "Please!" he
cried, reaching after them. Several students had gathered in the doorway now, having heard the commotion. As Jerry fell forward, Adam
Birch caught him by the arm. "Go get Brother Severe," Adam said to
someone behind him.

Jerry tried to slough off Adam Birch's hold on his arm. He called
the girls' names: "Terra, Isabel." But they were already out of sight,
lost behind the crowd of students straining to see inside the classroom.
Jerry tried to push through, but he was too weak. The boys drove him
back into the room, wrestled him to the floor.

"No," Jerry managed to say as he reached out, trying to cover the
eyes of the boys holding him down.

"You frickin' pervert," Adam Birch said, holding down Jerry's
arms. "You're not getting to those girls."

The weight of five or six boys was on him now. The gathered students spun on their heels, eyes wide with dread as they saw the pictures
on the wall, as they saw their teacher being held to the floor by their
friends.

"Brother Lucy! God, Brother Lucy!" Jerry called out. He was trying to break free of the boys' grasp, trying to cover their eyes. He felt
so weak. He wanted to get the students out of this room. He wanted
to wake up and find that he was out of his mind, that he wasn't in this
room at all.

When his seminary brethren burst into the room, they stopped
short, as though they'd hit an invisible wall. Brother Severe came
through the doorway first, followed by Brothers Blaine and Parker.

The room fell silent as the three men took in the scene—their fellow teacher held to the floor, the classroom covered with pornography. The students looked at the three men expectantly. Resting for a moment, Jerry uttered a single pathetic moan as he let out his breath.

Brother Parker groaned, "Dear Father." Brother Blaine turned absently, eyes down, as if he might simply walk away, until Brother Severe touched his sleeve, halting his exit.

"Okay, everybody," Brother Severe said, "okay." He reached down, touching each of the boys on the shoulder or sleeve. One by one, the boys released Jerry and wordlessly moved aside. Brother Severe glanced up at the walls only once, as if to make sure it was still real. He lifted Jerry to his feet. Jerry stepped toward the wall, toward a row of pictures hanging there. He looked at the pictures, seeing the eyes and faces of women and men, the room so silent that he might have been alone. He turned, and then, as if there had been some kind of explosion, the boys were on Jerry again. Jerry hurled himself toward the wall, sobbing now, pulling down a dozen or more pictures at a handful. Imbued with indignation, the boys pinned Jerry to the wall. Coughing, sobbing, Jerry barked out an incoherent curse: "Hell if I ever!" he shouted, swinging random fists full of pornography. "Hell on you all!" he spat.

Brother Severe moved toward Jerry, but Jerry tackled him, pushing a fistful of pornography at his face. When Brother Severe fell against Blaine and Parker, the three men toppled into a wall of students as Jerry rushed past them and darted down the hall. The stunned students cowered and gave way as Jerry raced down the hall, shouting and cursing, until he finally burst from the building like a madman.

The county jail was housed in a new annex of the historic, sandstone-faced courthouse building on Main Street. The interior of the new jail was hard and smooth—concrete floors and walls painted white, metal cell doors a deep blue. The cells were small concrete boxes with bunk beds, stainless steel toilet/sink units, and small, barred windows. Outside the six cells was a sky-lit enclosed area with two steel picnic tables, the legs embedded in the concrete floor. As the sheriff led Jerry into the enclosure in handcuffs, Jerry showed signs of recognition. He had been there before, as a stake officer conducting Sunday services for the prisoners. When the sheriff took off the handcuffs, Jerry held up his hands lamely, showing his palms. He bowed his head and, in a whispered chant, said "Amen, amen."

The sheriff had found Jerry in a sheep shed on Glade Raines's farm on the edge of town. Glade had called saying Jerry was wandering his property, chasing sheep and shouting questions about the prophets. Raines held Jerry at bay with a shovel until the sheriff got there, saying he'd hit Jerry only a couple of times, and only when he tried to get away. During the ride to the jailhouse, Jerry had sat in the backseat, handcuffed, muttering the lyrics to Elvis songs, mingled with scripture.

Sheriff Fisher sat Jerry down at one of the tables. He snapped his fingers in front of Jerry's face to get his attention. Then, pointing to an open cell door, he said, "That's your cell, Brother Sangood. There's a bunk and a toilet. If you don't cause any trouble, you can sit out here as long as you want." He put his hand on Jerry's shoulder. "Understand?"

Jerry bowed his head. "O, God, the Eternal Father," he said, nodding.

"I've got a couple of deputies cleaning up your classroom," Sheriff Fisher said. "We're looking at property damage charges for sure, and probably a public decency violation. I'll have you arraigned before Judge Hill in the morning."

Jerry stared at the metal table. Something was stuck there in front of him—an old sticker from a banana.

"You know Judge Hill, don't you?" Sheriff Fisher asked.

Jerry picked at the sticker, pulling part of it away, leaving behind an outline in dirt. "Don Hill," Jerry said without looking up.

The sheriff squatted on one knee to catch Jerry's eye. "There's something else," he said. He paused a moment. "A couple of the girls said you sexually harassed them."

Jerry stared hard at the metal table. If he raised his eyes too long, he might see those combined against him. Like mincing shadows with claws for eyes, they'd assailed him in the parking lot with Brother Lucy, buffeted him as he wandered Glade Raines's sheepfold.

"One of the Peterson girls says you made sexual comments," the sheriff said.

Jerry nodded. The Peterson girl had talked to him after school and told him her boyfriend had dumped her for someone prettier. "She was crying," Jerry said, still picking at the banana sticker. "Such a beautiful girl." He remembered telling her how pretty she was and promising her the other boys would see that, too. "Yes," Jerry said to the sheriff, nodding, smiling a little.

"And the Compton girl," the sheriff said. "She claims you got out of line with her, too."

Jerry looked up at the sheriff. He shook his head back and forth, saying, "No, no." He started to get up, as if he might walk away. The sheriff simply sat him back down.

"The Compton girl," the sheriff repeated.

Jerry counted on his fingers, grasping for something like logic. "The revealing tops, the short skirts, the high heels." He'd prayed for the girl and her parents, recently divorced. He'd cautioned her about her appearance. Jerry looked at the sheriff pleadingly. "Her body's a temple," he said. He returned his attention to the sticker, picking at it studiously.

"Do you realize what's happening here?" the sheriff asked. "You're in pretty deep."

Jerry looked up, abruptly confident. He smiled and patted the sheriff's arm. "I was in prison, and ye came unto me."

"I'll call your wife," Sheriff Fisher said.

Jerry looked back at the table. The ache from the blows of Glade Raines's shovel spoke to him like an old regret. Jerry had grown up a long time ago, it seemed, in a small house near the railroad tracks in Pocatello. An old man lived down the street when he was a boy. The man had a knife and he said he could cut off Jerry's ear. A sunny afternoon, and Jerry's father was there. The man showed his knife. Jerry didn't understand that the man was teasing him. Then Jerry remembered something else. He'd been a young husband. He and Camille drove a Thunderbird convertible he'd borrowed from his friend Raymond Hayes. They'd driven to Las Vegas to see Elvis. He remembered the feeling of Camille's beautiful, delicate hand on his arm as he drove. And he remembered standing in front of his students, the familiar sensation of his leather-bound Book of Mormon in his hand, testifying in one of those rare moments when all of the students were silent, truly listening, listening not just to him, but to the Spirit testifying. He remembered that morning, carrying his tattered, soiled suit to the garbage, like a man hiding a shameful sin.

When Sheriff Fisher came in next, leaving the door open to the office, the outside light from the small, barred window was growing dim. The sheriff sat down across from Jerry at the metal table, looking at him for a long time before he spoke. "We've been to your house," he said. "The pictures you put up in the classroom were probable cause. The back door to the house was wide open. All those pictures—they were printed from your computer. All we had to do was check the computer history. It was all right there."

Jerry remembered seeing Sheriff Fisher as a boy, riding a silver bicycle all over town. He could ride with no hands from one end of town to the other, his arms folded over his chest. As the sheriff spoke, Jerry reached out and patted his sleeve.

"We found something else," Sheriff Fisher said. "When we sat down at your computer, it was already on. It was open to your bank's website. All your accounts have been zeroed out, all the funds were transferred. We talked to the bank. Did you plan on skipping town, Jerry? Is that why you empted the accounts? Is that why you did it while Camille was gone?"

"Who needs money?" Jerry said, quoting an Elvis tune.

The telephone rang, and Sheriff Fisher stood up, heading for the office. "If that little trick down at the seminary was your way of getting back at this town for something," he said, "then it was a hell of a way to go."

Jerry sat at the metal table, his hands before him, his fingers outstretched. Too many things were happening, too many things to think about at once. The sheriff had told him there was a room with a bunk. He realized that now. He could go to sleep. He looked up at the cell, the door standing open. The sheriff had found his house that way, with the door standing open. He could go to sleep. He had awakened in the rain that morning, in the backyard, with the door of the house standing open. He got up and went to the open door of the cell. He stepped into the cell, thinking he might shut the door behind him, but he didn't want to disturb the evidence. He lay on the bed, facing the wall. He was glad it wasn't raining. He didn't know if those combined against him were in the cell with him, though he knew they were in prison. He didn't want to turn and see. He heard the sheriff talking on the phone in the office. He heard the sheriff say the words, "That's what it looks like."

Then the sheriff was in the cell, tapping him on the shoulder. "It's your wife," he said, handing him a cordless phone. "She doesn't sound too good."

Jerry sat on the edge of the bed and took the phone.

"The baby isn't breathing right," Camille said, her voice like light.

Jerry opened his eyes, emerging from a spell. "Camille," he said.

"I can't talk long. They put Gwen back in intensive care. She's bleeding again."

"We can say a prayer," Jerry said. "We can give her a blessing."

"What's happening to us?" Camille asked.

"Heavenly Father . . ." Jerry said, unable to finish.

A long silence stretched between them. Jerry could hear her muffled sobs. He knew the rhythm of her breathing, like the pulse of his own blood. He imagined being with her, kissing the tears on her cheek, smelling her soft skin. He closed his eyes, hoping it might simply come true.

Then he heard her voice. "Jerry," she said.

He opened his eyes. He was still in the jail cell.

"This is my fault," she said. "You don't understand what's happening. This is a test. We just have to get through it."

"I'm in trouble," Jerry said. "I'm in jail." He looked up at the walls of the cell, at the metal tables outside the cells where he'd taught gospel lessons to the prisoners when he'd served here as a stake officer. The words came to his lips: "I was in prison, and ye came unto me," he whispered.

"I'll try to come home," Camille said. "I have to see to Gwen, too, and the baby—he's so precious," Camille said. "This is a test, Jerry," she said. "Heavenly Father . . ." she said, her own voice trailing off.

A moment later, when she said good-bye, Jerry didn't switch off the phone. He lay there with the receiver to his ear until the sheriff came in and held out his hand. "I need the line free," Sheriff Fisher said.

That evening Jerry Sangood had three visitors who came to him like messengers in a dream. Brother Severe asked Jerry about his headaches.

"Dr. Slater found something in my head," Jerry said.

"I bet he did," Brother Severe answered, talking there in the darkness of the cell, sitting on a metal folding chair. "Maybe that thing in your head drove you crazy," he added.

But Jerry knew it was more than that. He knew God was standing above them all, greater even than the earth upon which all their lives rested. Despite the rattle and thrash of all their ambitions for exaltation, despite the hiss of all the devils combined against them, despite the cars and the songs and the empty hearts, God moved through their lives like a giant flaming sun rolling through space, quiet and sure, like the very blood coursing through their veins.

"I contacted Salt Lake," Brother Severe said. "You're through teaching, of course. The sheriff said there's no question, the evidence is all there." He stared at his clasped hands in the darkness. "Maybe if they decide you're crazy, no one will judge you. I don't know," he said, letting out a halting laugh. "I guess I was crazy there for a while, too. Do you remember that, that first year we worked together? You saved my life, Jerry." He paused for a moment, putting his face in his hands. "I'd never had that kind of attention from a girl," he said, looking up at Jerry, "especially one who looked like that." He laughed a small desperate laugh, shaking his head. "I thought I was beyond temptation. I would have lost everything, Jerry, if you hadn't been there that night. I hope they decide you're crazy, for your own sake."

Brent Blaine came next. "I was standing in the doorway," he said. "I had the tithing deposit in my hand, over twenty thousand dollars. I could just borrow a little, I thought, pay it back. I knew no one was supposed to be alone with the money. You saw me, and it was like you knew. 'Headed to the bank?' you asked. 'I'll go along.' You had to know. And now it's you. I don't get it."

Then it was David Parker, who was still in his twenties, with a wife and two small children. He sat in the folding chair, just as others had, talking into the darkness. "Except for my bishop back home," he said, "and that therapist in Utah, you're the only one who knows. What am I supposed to do, tell Brother Severe? Mr. Righteous? 'Oh, by the way, I used to have an eating disorder. But it's okay. I force myself to eat, and I stuff my anxieties. No one suspects it because I'm a man.' " He choked a laugh. "You have to be crazy, Jerry, to do what you did. Who am I going to talk to now?"

Jerry didn't speak. Unseen others clamored in the air, some combined against Jerry, some against Brother Parker. Jerry reached out across the darkness, taking the young man's hand.

"I'm sorry it had to be you," Brother Parker said.

At dawn, Brother Lucy came. He stood over Jerry, shaking him awake.

"It's time to go," he said. "Get up." Jerry put on his shoes, his head cloudy and thick. Brother Lucy took him by the arm, standing him up. Then Brother Lucy simply walked Jerry past the only deputy on duty, who was sitting with his back to the door, watching TV. They walked out of the building like two angels stepping away from a fallen prison. Outside it was a chilly, overcast morning as they walked north on Main Street, past Heritage Mortgage and Belknap Chiropractic, past the empty storefront where J.C. Penney had once been. The stores were closed, and the only cars on the road were still driving with their lights on.

When the dryness in Jerry's throat cleared enough that he could speak, Jerry simply asked, "Why did they let me go?"

"Just walk," Brother Lucy said.

Jerry could feel the tumor in his head, could feel it growing. He could taste it like metal in his mouth. Maybe the spirits who had attacked him in the church parking lot had grown out of the pit in his head. Or maybe they were waiting to enter in through it, like a portal. "Whatever God wants," Jerry said, "he can have."

"Keep walking," Brother Lucy said, taking him by the arm and walking faster.

They turned the corner and went down Heath Street, heading east. Jerry looked ahead, staring into the sun. He stared at the white-hot ball on the horizon as long as he could stand it, burning his eyes with the sight of it. Everything began to burn in on him—the life he was losing. He looked at the sun for a long while and then looked down, unable to see for a moment. "Why do I need my eyes?" he said.

When he looked away from the sun, he only saw a pink whiteness. He walked ahead, blind for a moment, until the vision returned. He saw his necktie hanging loosely from his neck. "I don't need this," he

said, taking it off and dropping it to the ground. He took off his suit
coat and absently let it fall to the sidewalk as well.

"You're littering," Brother Lucy said. "The sheriff will get you."

"What's happening to my daughter?" Jerry asked. "Why does she
have to be a part of this? And the baby—why isn't the baby breathing
right? What did he do wrong?"

"He was born," Brother Lucy said. "That's enough."

"It's not right. God can have him, but it's not right."

They continued down Heath Street, walking out of town toward
the grain fields and the purple mountains in the distance. At the edge
of town, where the sidewalk ended, they took to the blacktop street,
walking parallel with the railroad tracks and East Canal, headed toward
the old sugar factory.

"Where are we going?" Jerry asked.

"When you drained your bank account," Brother Lucy said, "that
account number I gave you was for the Catholic Relief Fund. They'll
be very grateful, I'm sure."

"Why did I do it?" Jerry asked.

"The thing which I greatly feared is come upon me," Brother Lucy
said, quoting scripture.

Jerry looked at the sun again, walking into it. He didn't want to see
anymore.

"We author our own hell," Brother Lucy said.

They were walking the middle of the blacktop road, along the canal, a row of litter and gangly weeds beside them. "I've lost my life,"
Jerry said.

"You've lost nothing that matters."

"Then nothing matters," Jerry said.

They were at the old sugar factory now, a building that hadn't been
used in years. The windows were broken out; a moat of high weeds
grew up around the walls. The stories of hard-working Mormon farmers carrying in loads of sugar beets in big, horse-drawn wagons were
all gone, too. East Canal, a major artery of the local irrigation system,
ran between the dilapidated building and the blacktop road where Jerry
and Brother Lucy stood. In the distance, beyond acres of potato and
grain fields, the Wasatch mountain range lay between them and the
distant sunrise.

"Certain people in Salt Lake City were up all night talking about you, Jerry," Brother Lucy said. "You're going to be on the news this morning, all over Utah and Idaho. Someone took pictures of your classroom. They have pictures of you, too. It was good of you to leave the house unlocked. One of the General Authorities wants you excommunicated. He'll probably get his way."

Jerry looked up at the old abandoned building. He had played here as a boy, riding his bike around the place at night, throwing rocks into the canal. "Take me home," he said absently. "I want to go home."

"Your old life is gone, Jerry. You signed the letter. Besides that, you just escaped from the county jail. You're a fugitive. Add that to the other charges against you."

"Why are we here?" Jerry asked. The pain in the back of his head was growing warm, like something seductive and wicked.

Brother Lucy took Jerry's arm and walked him a few feet down the road. They stood at the edge of the canal. "Look," he said, pointing to a dirt-and-gravel parking lot behind the sugar factory. Camille was there, standing a hundred yards away, pacing in front of her car. She wore blue slacks and a white blouse, the same clothes she had on when she flew out to California. Spotting them, she began walking in their direction, head down, arms folded over her chest.

"She loves you, Jerry," Brother Lucy said, "more than her whole life in this town. More than her grandchild, more than her daughter. More than she loves herself."

Jerry fell to his knees. The pain in his head was blinding. It was too much to think that he had brought her to all this, their lives shattered. He tried to stand. He stumbled, moving toward Camille, toward the canal. Looking only at his wife as she made her way toward them, he stepped into the canal, the water deeper than he expected. His feet slipped on the muddy bottom. He went completely under the cold mountain water before coming up out of the current, coughing and splashing.

Brother Lucy eased down the incline and stepped carefully into the water. "Take my hand," he said.

Jerry reached for Brother Lucy's hand, and in a moment he landed on his back, prostrate in the water, thrashing and gasping in a panic as Brother Lucy held him under, his knee on Jerry's chest, his hand shoving Jerry deeper and deeper under the current. The pain in his head,

like a black cloud of devils, disoriented him. Then, just as quickly as
he had pushed him under, Brother Lucy pulled Jerry to his feet and
shouted, "Are you giving up? If you're going to give up, spare us all
and do it now."

"No," Jerry said, gasping and spitting water. "No, I'm not giving
up." He was struggling to stand on his own, grasping at Brother Lucy's
body to steady himself.

Camille stood at the edge of the canal now, reaching for her husband. "Let go of him!" she demanded. "Get away from him! Let him
go!"

Jerry wiped at his eyes and looked up at her, standing on the bank.
Her hair was disheveled, and her clothes were wrinkled. Her face was
red, and her eyes were puffy from crying. She was the most beautiful
person he'd ever seen.

Taking courage from the sight of his wife, Jerry pushed Brother Lucy away and stood back a pace, toward the bank where Camille
stood. "I'm not giving up my life," Jerry said. "I didn't give it up. You
took it from me, from both of us."

"I didn't take anything," Brother Lucy answered. "God holds your
life in his hands. He always did."

"If he wants my life," Jerry said, "he can have it. He's already put
a tumor in my head."

"You don't understand," Camille said to Jerry. She stepped down
the embankment and into the water behind Jerry. "This is all my fault,"
she said. "He came to me with a paper." She pointed to Brother Lucy.
"I signed it, and that's why Gwen and the baby are in the hospital.
That's why all these things are happening."

Jerry looked at Brother Lucy, enraged, the pain in his head like
an angry stinger. He was ready to move toward him, angry enough
to kill him.

"Don't, Jerry," Camille begged, clutching at him. "Please don't."

Jerry roared at Brother Lucy, his fists hitting the water. "I didn't
want this!"

"Your life is gone," Brother Lucy said. "Don't you see that? You
can't have it back. Right now, someone in Salt Lake is calling your
priesthood leaders in Idaho. There's going to be a church court. You
won't even have your church membership!"

"It's not right," Jerry said in a low, angry voice. He swayed, chest deep in the water, ready to explode. His white shirt clung to his chest. His face twisted with pain and anger. "Nothing about this is right!" he roared as he sprang at Brother Lucy, putting his hands around the old man's neck. "I worked all my life," he said, shaking the man. "All my life!"

Brother Lucy gripped Jerry's hands, attempting to pull them from his neck. Camille pulled at Jerry's arms, crying out, calling Jerry's name, and begging him to let go.

"I've kept the commandments," Jerry cried.

The three thrashed in the water, struggling to stay upright on the muddy bottom of the canal. Brother Lucy managed to get his own hands between Jerry's grip and his neck. Camille had managed to get herself partly between the men.

"I've cared for my neighbors," Jerry said in self-defense. "I put up with them, and with their children's silliness, and all of their blind obedience to this stupid, stupid world." Then, giving up his hold on Brother Lucy's neck, he said, "And I've loved them, too!" He stopped fighting for a moment. "I have loved them! Doesn't that count for anything? I've spent hours and hours on my knees, begging God to teach me how to love them. Good God," he said, "I built a reputation in this town as a good man!" Jerry shouted, "And now I've lost everything!"

He turned away, stumbling back a pace, his energy spent. The three of them stood there in the water.

After a moment, Brother Lucy spoke. "What have you lost?" he asked.

"Everything!" Jerry said in a broken voice.

"You've lost your reputation?" Brother Lucy asked.

"Yes!"

"The collective opinion of fools?"

"I've lost my good name!" Jerry said.

"There is none good but God!"

"What about our money? The money's gone!"

"Filthy lucre," Brother Lucy answered.

"We could lose our daughter," Camille said.

Brother Lucy turned to her. "Dear mother, you know that child's soul. In all the eternities, you'll never lose her. How could you doubt it?"

Camille dropped her face into her hands and began to weep.

Jerry went to her, put his arms around her. Her clothes and her skin felt so cold. She cried into his chest, embracing him. He didn't care about himself. She was the only one on this earth that mattered. He'd exhausted all his words, all his defenses. He had nothing but her, nothing but his life and hers.

Brother Lucy stood off a pace. His face softened into a smile as he looked at Jerry standing there, holding his wife. "Brother," he said, his hands outstretched. He stepped toward them, reaching out, smiling assuredly. "Let go, Brother," he said, touching Jerry's sleeve. "Just let go."

Jerry shook his head. "No," he whispered, rocking Camille gently in his arms, moving from side to side as she wiped her tears and composed herself.

"Your Heavenly Father loves you," Brother Lucy said. He put his hand at the base of Jerry's neck. "Just let go of this world," he said. "You'll see his love, just like the scripture says: 'Stronger than the cords of death.' "

Jerry looked into the old man's fading blue eyes, as light and blue as a summer sky. Jerry knew his own heart. He was ready to believe, ready to accept. He couldn't do anything else, even if it damned him. He trusted in his Father's love. He trusted in the goodness of the earth, the goodness of his wife, the goodness of most of God's children. He knew that God had his blessings in store. He knew his daughter Gwen would be just fine, even if there was trouble for a little season. He was ready to let go of whatever it was that he held back from God.

Brother Lucy stood beside them, his touch tender at the base of Jerry's neck, just below the spot where a stone was growing in Jerry's skull. Then Jerry saw a change in Brother Lucy's face. The menacing look of a predator returned.

"Dear Brother," the old man said in a voice, strong and hollow, "let go."

Jerry felt himself slipping under the water, being pushed under the water as easily as a child might dip a toy in the bathtub. He still held on to Camille, too shocked to let her go. The water was murky and cold. Camille, still in his arms, didn't struggle. She only held on to Jerry as Brother Lucy pushed them both down, one hand on Jerry's neck, the other hand and one knee on their bodies.

Hungry for breath, for the light of day, for life itself, Jerry resisted the force of Brother Lucy's body on theirs. He pushed at the old man's limbs, kicked until his feet slipped on the muddy canal bottom. He thrashed until he felt his back hit the mucky bottom. He needed a breath. He needed to save Camille. He needed to save them both.

Then he felt it. Camille reached around his body, embracing him fully. She was not resisting. She was holding on to him, holding him closer, like a lover in bed, holding fast to her love. Beneath the water, in the blackness, at the end of his life, he returned his love to her. He held her close, and finding her face under the murky water, he put his lips to her. He stopped fighting.

He let go.

They drove all day and all night, unable to speak. They simply got in the car in their wet clothes and drove until the car's engine died on the edge of a rural two-lane highway in North Dakota, near the Canadian border. After looking under the hood for a moment and not recognizing anything there, they walked toward the nearest town. At the city limits of Wicapiwakan, North Dakota, Pop. 8,271, a sign read, WHERE HELL FREEZES OVER. They rented a kitchenette in a rundown motel and soon got jobs—Camille as a lunch lady at the junior high, and Jerry as a janitor in the town's only nursing home. Jerry didn't say anything about the pain in his head, though it rang in his skull like a hammer. For weeks they only worked and slept, barely talking, both of them fighting a profound sense of loss.

"It's the buffetings of Satan," Jerry said one night as they lay awake, their darkened faces red in the glow of the vacancy sign outside their window.

After cashing her first check from the school district, Camille called Gwen. She stood at a pay phone outside a convenience store, next to the ice machine at the side of the building. The noisy traffic passed on the highway just a few yards away.

Gwen said she was fine. She said the baby was fine. She wanted to know where they were, why they hadn't called. She asked Camille if Jerry was holding her hostage.

Camille refused to tell her where they were. "Your dad and I can take care of ourselves," she said. She watched the highway as a semi-truck pulling a load of logs passed. She heard the truck move through its gears as it slowed to enter the city limits.

"I understand about Dad," Gwen said on the phone. "Some men can keep that sort of thing a secret for years."

Camille stood there, her hand on the cold metal phone cord, while a short, dirty man in a cowboy hat eyed her as he got into his pickup. "You don't understand what's happened," Camille said to her daughter.

"It's okay, Mom," Gwen said. "It doesn't mean the church isn't true. Some of those people Dad taught, they're blogging about leaving the church. I bet they never had testimonies in the first place. And half the stuff they're saying isn't even true," she added.

"I need to go, Sweetie," Camille said. She felt sick inside.

Gwen's voice came back in a maternal tone. "Mom, if you need to leave him, you can stay with me and Neil. We'll pay for the plane flight. I can come and get you. Whatever you need."

Camille stood there in silence for a moment. "I'll call in a few days," she finally said, and hung up the phone.

A small branch of the LDS Church met on the other side of town. When Jerry and Camille's church records came in from Salt Lake, they listed Jerry as excommunicated. But with only twenty-five members in regular attendance, President Lewis gladly gave Jerry a job as the branch janitor.

Every Monday afternoon, after he got off work at the nursing home, Jerry let himself into the building to clean. He vacuumed the carpet in the entryway and the four classrooms. He moved the folding chairs in the room where sacrament meeting and Sunday school were held and vacuumed the carpet there. In the offices of the branch president and the clerk, he vacuumed the carpets and dusted the desks. He washed all the windows, and he swept the floor in the little kitchen, where priesthood meeting was held on Sunday. After that, he cleaned the bathrooms.

One winter afternoon, while he was on his hands and knees wiping the floor around the urinal, a simple thought came to him: he was cleaning bathrooms for Jesus, wiping up urine for God's true church. Someone had to do it. Jerry paused for a moment, wringing out his cleaning rag in a bucket of soapy water. If God's kingdom was destined to fill the whole earth, someone would have to wipe up the piss. Kneeling there in the small bathroom in the empty building, Jerry felt as whole and happy as a child. Only then did he realize what he had lost and why it didn't matter. Only then did he realize that the pain in his head had left him.

That weekend, the Relief Society president asked Camille and Jerry to go down to Bismarck to pick up the welfare order at the bishop's storehouse. It was a two-hour trip down Highway 83, through a light snow and haze. After the backseat and the trunk of their car were filled with canned goods, dry cereals, and boxed dinners, they stopped at the Bismarck temple to walk the snowy grounds in the evening light. The temple itself was small compared to the other temples they'd seen, oblong and blockish with only one level above the ground. It was beautiful, though, with the lights illuminating the walls and the angel Moroni statue, and the plaque above the door that said THE HOUSE OF THE LORD in gold letters on white marble.

As Jerry and Camille walked the grounds, a few patrons came and went, carrying their small suitcases of temple clothes and walking briskly in the light snowfall and the chilly winds. Jerry and Camille walked until they reached the back corner of the building, past a white brick fence, and beyond that, to a driveway that led alongside the air-conditioning units and the garbage dumpster. They stopped at the edge of the driveway, seeing three aged men a dozen or so yards away, standing next to the loading dock, talking and laughing. The man standing closest to the service door was dressed in a white temple suit. The other two men were wearing dark suits, white shirts, and ties.

One of them was Brother Lucy.

When the men saw Jerry and Camille, their laughter subsided. The other man in the dark suit dropped a cigarette to the pavement and crushed it out. Then the man in the white suit handed Brother Lucy an envelope before disappearing into the temple through the metal door. Brother Lucy nodded to his companion, who got inside a black Chrysler parked near the loading dock.

"I've been wondering when you'd turn up," Brother Lucy said. "Still having those headaches?"

Jerry looked at him narrowly. "Let's go," he said to Camille.

"You'll be back, you know," Brother Lucy said, holding his attention, "inside of a year, I predict. I've seen it before: excommunicated from the Lord's church, and sweeping his floors." Then, taking the envelope in his hand and touching it dramatically to his forehead, he said, "I prophesy! In a year from now you'll be in this temple, doing ordinances and serving potatoes in the cafeteria."

Jerry took Camille's arm. They turned and began to walk away.

"Just one thing," Brother Lucy said, calling after them.

Jerry and Camille stopped, their backs to the bald man in his dark suit. Looking down at the sidewalk brushed with snow, Jerry imagined Brother Lucy staring at the back of his neck, seeing into his skull where a stone the size of a quarter slept, would continue to sleep, for at least a year. Jerry stood motionless, braced for whatever icy truth waited in Brother Lucy's words.

"Remember this," Brother Lucy said. "Think on this," he said. "Even your goodness is your enemy."

It was the truth, and Jerry knew it.

"Remember that," Brother Lucy said, calling after them as they walked away. "And tell all your friends."

Jerry and Camille went to the car. They got on Highway 83 and drove north through the snow. The truth of Brother Lucy's words waited like a cancer with them in the car. It was in the snow and in the icy pavement on the road. It was in the very sky. But Jerry didn't mind it. He could already feel himself in the temple, dressed in white, wearing a hair net and a paper apron, dishing potatoes and feeling the Spirit of God.

SALVATION

Laura McCune-Poplin

3

SHE HELD THE UMBRELLA CLOSE TO her head, limiting her vision to the circle of stones at her feet. Anna watched her companion's hemline bounce in time to the click of her heels against the cobblestone. Water from Soeur Buckley's shoes flicked upward, soaking the back of her skirt. They walked past a pharmacy. A neon cross flashed above the closed doors, intermittently tainting the wet sidewalk green. Nearby, somebody was burning cedar in a fireplace and Anna inhaled, holding the smell of smoke and rain in her lungs.

Soeur Buckley stopped walking. "Let's go down this street," she said. She checked the name on the blue sign against the one on the map. "Then we can cut across the park."

Soeur Buckley was always trying to find a new route home. At night she would take a yellow highlighter and color the streets she had walked on a map, which hung on the wall above her bed. Her goal was to have colored every street in the city before she was transferred.

Today's street was narrow and crooked; uninterrupted walls of four-story buildings lined both sides. Water pooled in the road where cobblestones were missing or worn down. In one of the puddles sat a dog, licking raindrops off the face of an old man.

"Is he dead?" Soeur Buckley asked.

Anna looked for someone who could help, but the street was silent except for the sound of raindrops drumming the nylon above her head. She closed the umbrella. Soeur Buckley held out her hand to the dog and petted his head while Anna knelt next to the body. When Anna put her cheek next to the man's mouth she could smell his breath before she felt it.

"He's just drunk."

Anna rolled him onto his back while Soeur Buckley held the dog's leash. The puddle had soaked through the clothes on the left side of his body. His raincoat fell to the side, and Anna could see a dark patch of urine staining the front of his trousers. Gently, she shook the man's shoulders. Then less gently.

"Monsieur."

The dog growled, and Anna looked up at the leash in Soeur Buckley's hand.

"Try again," Soeur Buckley said.

"Pardon, Monsieur."

He moaned softly and touched his forehead, water dripping off the tip of his elbow. Anna helped him sit up, her grasp squeezing the water out of his sleeve.

"My papers? Where are my papers?" He fumbled with his hands, checking the pockets of his raincoat. He felt a bulge in his chest pocket and pulled out a sopping envelope stuffed with folded squares of paper. He put it back.

"Where is Ilka?"

Soeur Buckley handed him the leash. She helped Anna lift the old man to his feet. He was short and frail-looking. His wet clothes clung to his skinny limbs. Rain rolled down the front of his bald head and pooled at the tip of his nose. Anna held his hand and supported his back while Soeur Buckley took his elbow and the leash. He nodded to the left. They started walking.

"Who are you?" the old man asked, squinting through the rain at the black nametag on Anna's coat.

"Soeur Adams," she said.

"You're nuns?" He looked over at Soeur Buckley, mouthing the name on her plaque.

Soeur Buckley smiled. "Missionaries. Les Mormons."

"I don't want anything to do with your church," he said after a moment. The man wrinkled his eyebrows together. They were full of captured raindrops.

Soeur Buckley laughed, looking at Anna over the top of his head. "Even drunk men don't like us," she said in English.

"I'm Catholic, nonpracticing."

"We know," she said. "The whole country is Catholic, nonpracticing."

"So what are you doing here?" he asked, turning his head to look at Anna.

She frowned. "Helping you."

They arrived at a red door at the bottom of a four-story building. Pulling his hand away from Anna's, the old man reached into his pocket and handed her the wet envelope.

"Take one."

She pulled out a piece of paper.

"Take one for her too," he said solemnly, pointing to Soeur Buckley.

Anna took another paper and put them in her pocket. Suddenly, the old man leaned back and cupped his hands to his mouth.

"Mireille," he shouted. The loud rasping noise made Soeur Buckley jump. The old man started to fall over, and Anna reached out to steady him. He kept yelling.

"Mireille," Soeur Buckley shouted with him.

The door opened.

"Michel. Where have you been?" A woman with white hair pulled into a bun took his arm and helped him inside. "How did you get so wet?" she asked, wiping her hand on her apron.

"I fell." He glanced at the missionaries to see if they would contradict him. They didn't. Soeur Buckley held the leash out to the woman.

"Here's your dog," she said.

The woman took the leash and looked at Michel, waiting for an explanation.

"They're Mormon missionaries," he whispered into her ear.

The woman's eyes narrowed. "We're not interested."

She shook a crooked index finger at Anna and Soeur Buckley and quickly shut the door. The missionaries remained on the doorstep, standing side by side. Anna leaned in closer to examine the cracks in the red paint. The door used to be painted white.

After a minute, Anna stepped back from the door and held out

her hand. She looked over at Soeur Buckley and smiled. "It stopped
raining."

1

He looked past his reflection in the mirror that lined the wall of the
booth. The details of his face disappeared as he focused on the stacks
of paper covering his table. He leaned toward the mirror, trying to
make out a single word from the rivers of backward letters. Instead, he
saw a dark red stain spreading through the stacks. He glanced down at
his overturned glass and watched the red wine dissolve columns upon
columns of neatly penned words.

Michel stood up and clumsily blotted the folded papers with the
cloth napkin from his lap. He left the soiled napkin on top of his ruined work, gathered the rest of his piles, and shoved them into an
envelope, which he placed in the pocket of his raincoat. He moved to
another table.

"Another glass of wine, please."

The garçon brought over a glass and a small silver ashtray. Michel
took the bill from the tray and replaced it with a ten-franc coin. He
began to write on the back. *Places I've spilled my drink: Café de l'Art, La
Fete de Bombage, Brasserie de la Poste, Tonton's Birthday Party – 1956, Gare
de Lyon . . .*

Michel covered the paper lengthwise. He turned it sideways. He
wrote carefully, like a first-grade student learning cursive for the first
time, making sure to cross all his t's and connecting his a's low so they
wouldn't be mistaken for o's. When he finished, he took another paper
from the envelope in his pocket and wrote, *Drinks I've spilled: red wine,
hot chocolate, cognac, coffee, warm milk, whiskey, mint syrup . . .*

He stopped writing at the bottom of the third column and asked for
more wine. He carefully refolded the paper into three equal portions and
placed it on the table. Michel leaned back against the booth and wiped
the white residue from the corners of his mouth. His fingers smelled like
tobacco. He felt the tightness return to his chest like a hand grabbing his
heart, as it always did when he stopped writing. One day the hand would
squeeze so tight Michel would die, but Michel had almost finished.

"We close early on Sundays," the garçon said, filling his glass halfway while glancing at the clock above the bar.

Michel motioned for him to keep pouring. "My last drink."

The garçon started stacking chairs on the tables in the center of the room. The metal gate in front of the glass door hovered like an eyelid half closed. Michel stood up to leave. He noticed a piece of paper on the floor and stooped to pick it up, his knees cracking like broken twigs. A shoe print covered half the paper. Michel turned it over, *People I've met in cafés*, and put it with the others in the envelope.

The garçon raised the metal gate and handed Michel a piece of beef. "For the dog," he said, motioning toward the door.

Michel shuffled out the door while patting his pockets, looking for his pen. *Names of dogs I've owned.* The gate creaked closed behind him as he fed the meat to Ilka.

Ilka, Chipie, Beni, Chiot, Bilou . . .

Ilka's wet nose sniffed his hand looking for more. Michel untied her leash, and they stood together under the awning, watching the rain rebound off the cobblestones.

2

The letter slipped out of the Bible while she was dusting. Holding her back, she bent down to retrieve the paper folded in thirds.

Another list, she thought. Michel usually hid his lists in a wooden box under the bed. He always waited until she was in the bath. Through the hollow door she would hear the box sliding against the linoleum, the rustle of papers as he emptied his coat pockets. Mireille could see the scratches the rusted nail heads carved into the floor. He never mentioned his box crammed with bulging envelopes. Perhaps he thought she didn't know. Perhaps it was just a game, a contrived intrigue to make life interesting, as though life could be prolonged in the recording of it.

She unfolded the paper in her hand and saw her name in the top left corner, *Chere Mireille.* For a second, she was tempted to read it, but obviously Michel did not intend for her to find the letter until after he died. Mireille never opened the Bible except to enter the names and dates of important family events. For the last fifteen years, the only entries had been deaths. Her husband's would be next. Quickly, she folded the paper and replaced it between the fragile, yellowed pages. She glanced at the clock. Michel would be home soon. She turned the Bible over and stroked the cracked leather cover with the smooth skin of her palms—only the outsides of her hands were wrinkled. Mireille looked inside the front cover and traced four generations of death with her finger. She stopped at the bottom of the page. Here she would write Michel's name. Michel as ancestor. No more drinking. No more lists. Just venerated memories half-forgotten.

She replaced the Bible on the bookshelf and continued dusting. She would read the letter when he died. After she cleaned out his clothes, threw away his lists. She would give everything to the Croix Rouge. The older she got the more she threw away, disgusted by the waste of leaving things behind. When she died she hoped her existence would fade to nothing more than the ink used to write her name in the Bible next to Michel's.

Mireille pulled back the lace curtain and looked out the window. Rain pattered against the glass trying to get in and succeeding in the corners where the window frame had warped with age. She took the washcloth out of her apron pocket to wipe up the puddle of water pooling on the windowsill. The street below her was empty. She looked as far left as she could without opening the window. No Michel.

In the kitchen, the duck had started to boil over. Perfumed steam permeated the apartment. Mireille turned the heat down on the gas stove and covered the bird to let it simmer. Dinner would be ready.

Mireille shook the crumbs off the tablecloth and set the table for two. The thick vapor of boiled duck filled the kitchen, covering the walls with a thin film of grease and moisture. She opened the window to let out the steam and sat down to wait.

4

The candle flame flickered in the draft from the window, bouncing lilac-scented shadows off the walls. Anna lit a candle every night before going to bed. Its glow colored the insides of her eyelids orange when she said her prayers.

Soeur Buckley stopped reading and slammed the Book of Mormon shut.

"You're keeping that?" she asked, looking at Anna, who sat cross-legged on her bed, surrounded by books and small scraps of paper.

Anna nodded. She put down the scissors and started painting

circles of rubber cement on the back of the old man's paper. *Animals I have seen in zoos.* She smoothed the list into her journal, rubbing the corners to make sure they stayed down. *Brown bear, dromedary, boa constrictor.*

Soeur Buckley laughed to herself and pulled the blanket up under her arms.

"Did you see the look on that lady's face when she found out we were missionaries?" she asked. "If I had a picture of her, that's what I'd glue in my journal." Soeur Buckley leaned back on her pillow and closed her eyes, still smiling.

Anna checked the journal to make sure the glue had dried. *Lion, orangutan, gazelle.* She inclined her head toward the open pages and could see the indentations Michel's pen had pressed into the paper. His handwriting looked deliberate, as though every word had been written to last forever. Anna closed her journal and watched the flame's reflection dancing in the windowpane. *Rhino, giraffe, elephant.* She turned off the lamp and knelt next to her bed, placing her folded hands on top of the blanket as she bowed her head to pray.

HEALTHY PARTNERS

Lewis Horne

BRUDEN HAD NO TROUBLE SLEEPING at night, however hot and airless the house in August. Which some people might find strange since they wouldn't think he hustled enough during the day to tire. But they couldn't know how tiring his days were. Still, at night, the traffic on Circle Drive, two blocks away, and the noise from the bar around the corner, however rackety, didn't jostle his steady, naked doze.

Even so, whenever Ian John came in, however quietly he moved in his stocking feet, as irregular as his dark hours were, Bruden's eyes snapped open. The kitchen door would barely scrape the worn linoleum. The soles of Ian John's feet would whisper by Bruden's door, slip inaudibly past Wolfgang's across the way. Scarcely a sound from the large bedroom Ian John had claimed—the only room in the house with a mattress on a bed frame, a queen-size at that. Then, assured that Ian John had settled, sleep fell on Bruden again.

At first, Wolfgang had slept in the big room—after all, the house was his—but within a week of moving in, Ian John had suckered him out of it.

Tonight, Ian John stopped at Bruden's door.

No word from the full boyish lips.

In the street light from outside, Bruden could see how spruce he looked. Like he'd stepped out of the Bessborough Hotel.

"What you want, man?" Bruden finally asked.

"I want some help. It's heavy."

Most of the stuff Ian John brought in was light—fishing equipment, leather clothing, air compressors, tools—or else for something like a big TV or filing cabinet, there was a dolly.

"A love seat. It's awkward."

As Bruden pulled on his faded trousers, Ian John said, "We could be partners, you know. I told you before."

Bruden didn't answer. Though he'd heard it before, he didn't want to huddle too close to Ian John and his trespasses—his girls and loot and secrets. You'd never learn all Ian John's secrets, and unless you did, you could never stand up to him, never be a full-fledged partner.

In the dark, Bruden made himself look into Ian John's pale eyes. He shrugged his bare shoulders—no comment—at the renewed proposition and grinned what he knew was a sheepish grin. The less you said to Ian John, the less you committed.

Ian John wanted the love seat in the house instead of the garage with the padlocked double doors. They bumped the wall of the hallway twice on the way to the living room, almost upset a pile of wooden picture frames outside Wolfgang's door.

"He won't wake," said Ian John. "He takes pills."

They placed the love seat in a corner of the living room. Now he could watch TV in comfort, Ian John said. Though Bruden seldom saw him watching, seldom saw him in the house.

As Bruden turned, Ian John said, "Partners, man. Healthy ones. I could give you thirty percent."

"I do okay," said Bruden.

"Two is stronger than one. You think about it."

Next day. His regular spot.

What should he think?

"No, I won't give you money," the man said, though he spoke in a pleasant manner with a pleasant smile in a pleasant healthy face.

Bruden watched a street-corner breeze lace thin hair. Usually, "Any change?" was all he could get out before the person crossed the street to enter the mall. But often enough, often enough to make it worth his hours out here, two or three times in the day, someone would slip him coins. Now, with a loonie—a one-dollar coin—in circulation, sums increased. Pretty soon the two-dollar coin would be out.

(*Think of that, Ian John.*)

"But," continued the man with his smile, "I'll take you home and give you a meal. My wife cooks well. I don't do bad either, for that matter."

Bruden didn't blink. "You think I'm asking for a handout."

"Aren't you?"

"Some people don't approve of handouts. They say people should help themselves."

"I'm willing to help you," the man said.

"But no handout."

"Not from me."

Bruden—a thin-faced man with pale disheveled hair, straight and loose, some of it hanging over his forehead—said, "I guess I'll take you up on it."

"My car's in the lot," said the man. "I got off work early today. I work in furniture at Sears. Salary and commission. I worked late last night so I can take off early today." He pointed up an alley. "My car's in this lot."

The car was an old-style luxury model. A Buick maybe. A crack ran across the passenger side of the windshield. But Bruden knew the man had never bought the car new. First of all, he wasn't old enough to have afforded it when it was new. Second, his twisted tie and wrinkled white shirt didn't go with a new car such as this one would have been. The tie and shirt went with the way it was now—used, unwashed.

"Dog hairs on the back seat," said the man. "The dog's dead, but we haven't gotten rid of the dog hairs yet. My wife's car is cleaner. You can toss those empty bags on the back seat."

His wife's car might be cleaner, Bruden decided, gathering up the garbage, but it wouldn't hold any more promise than the four-door Buick. Hers would be an economy model more than likely, maybe foreign compact. Something for her to zip to work in. Probably in just as big a need of a wash. Bruden was the sort who knew these things, what other people couldn't see. He wasn't psychic, but he had enough of the eye to get glimpses. Like he couldn't see the man's wife, but he knew her car. Bruden considered himself half-psychic. Where else did his pictures of Ian John come from?

"Incidentally, I'm Horace," said the man as he turned the ignition.

"Bruden."

Bruden spoke louder. He spelled the name. "Like it sounds."

"Good to meet you, Mr. Bruden. If you wouldn't mind fastening the seatbelt."

Like they were buddies.

Bruden had been standing at the corner for three hours, though much of the time he'd been leaning against the wall, saving himself wear on his back. Thinking sometimes of Ian John, sometimes of other things. He'd been about to go into the mall for a rest when Horace approached. He couldn't see ahead what kind of meal he'd be getting. With money—a handout—he could measure the coins. Not a fancy eater, a hamburger would do as well as Chinese food. Then the rest of the coins he would tuck away in his hiding spot in the house.

Wolfgang and Ian John—in the house, they had their hiding spots, too. He knew where Ian John's was, behind a stone in the basement wall, but he'd never checked it out. Ian John had his mean streak. Bruden wished Wolfgang would send Ian John traveling, but Wolfgang was afraid, even if the house was his. Since his mother died a year ago. How long he'd have it Bruden didn't know, since Wolfgang refused to pay property taxes. "I'm not paying the city to live in my own house." Bruden asked him where they'd be if the city took the house from him. "With Ian John," said Wolfgang. "But not without a fight."

Wolfgang, a dim little butterball of a man, was hard to persuade.

Ian John had been in prison. This was a fact Bruden had seen first thing that Wolfgang hadn't. Ian John wouldn't mention prison, a closed-mouth sort like him.

"You passing through?" asked Horace behind the steering wheel, proving that Horace himself hadn't an ounce of the energy, not a bit of the eye, wasn't a quarter—or an eighth—psychic.

Bruden started to say he lived with a couple of friends. But he said, "Yeah. Just passing through."

"A bit down on your luck," said Horace.

"You could say that."

"It happens to us all. But in different ways, I guess."

Horace's seatbelt was tight across his belly. He'd have a pot belly if he wasn't already heavy enough that the belly—to the front, to the sides—seemed like a part of his general roundness. A kind of robust look it was. Almost.

"Good Samaritan," said Horace.

"What's that?"

"You know the story."

As Horace began to tell it, Bruden said, "Yeah, I know it."

"Sometimes you might be walking the road, healthy as can be. Other times, you might be in the ditch. So you do what you can when you can."

"I guess I'm in the ditch."

"Not trying to offend," said Horace.

Bruden stared through the windshield at the traffic. He felt no offense, but he didn't say so. He hoped Wolfgang would pay his taxes. Life's a ten-cent magazine, and if you've got only a nickel, you go with the nickel.

"Got any music?" he said.

"Sorry," said Horace and turned the knob on the car radio.

"Where you passing through from?"

"Edmonton."

"I have a sister there," said Horace.

"Me, too."

"That right?"

"Another one in San Diego—and one in Thunder Bay. Then there's one that lives outside Toronto—" The pictures kept flashing in Bruden's head. But he stopped. They weren't real pictures. They were games. He had no sisters. He didn't mind games. But you had to be credible with people. He added, "The last one lives in northern Idaho the last I heard. Haven't seen her since I was a kid, not after she run away from home. She stays in touch with the sister in Edmonton— off and on."

That was enough. He rubbed his fingers on his jeans, then the palms of his hands.

Horace had turned the car into a residential area, older frame houses with some large Manchurian elm trees. Some of the houses were narrow and two stories. Most were one story.

It looked to Bruden like Horace's neighborhood as much as the old Buick looked like Horace's car.

"Woozie and I have three children—"

"Woozie?"

"Her name's Claire. But people call her Woozie."

"What does she call you?"

"Horace."

"Oh."

Horace laughed. "It's just Woozie—what her father and mother called her. I was always Horace."

"That is good, isn't it," said Bruden as Horace came to a stop before one of the two-story houses.

"What is?"

"I don't know. That you got Woozie. That her name is Woozie. That you got three kids."

"Sid is the only one at home."

"Sid and Woozie."

Horace unbuckled his seatbelt. "His sisters have their own families. Sid was our accident. An afterthought. He's in high school."

The street was narrow, the houses across the way seeming close-up, as close-up as the two-story house with the glassed-in porch and the lawn that needed mowing.

Bruden said, "Maybe you should show me where the lawn mower is."

Horace took him seriously. "No, no. I invited you to supper—"

"Don't want any handout."

"An invitation to supper," said Horace. "Fair and square."

At the top of the front steps, Bruden found the glassed-in porch warm from the sun. A folded newspaper lay on one of the wicker chairs. A bag of fertilizer and a bag of peat moss, both opened, stood in one corner. Bruden left his shoes beside Horace's outside the door. Horace's shoes must smell, too. For sure, Bruden's wingtips weren't giving off all the stink.

As he followed Horace into the living room, stairs on the right next to a coat closet, he saw a room that matched the picture he'd already made in his head. What Ian John might notice. The couch, the chair that went with it, were possibly second-hand, maybe gotten from a relative, and had held up under a lot of butts, all shapes and sizes. The cushions' dark floral pattern had faded too deep to show much anymore. The throw rugs on the floor, throw rugs on top of an oatmeal-colored wall-to-wall, were dark, too. Bruden could tell from

the feel of the place—like the doors had been closed since morning—
that no one else had been home all day.

"Woozie at work?"

"At the school board," said Horace. "Something to drink?"

Bruden would have liked a beer, but he shook his head when Horace said, "I could mix up some lemonade. No problem." Then he said, "I better call Woozie."

Bruden couldn't get a picture of Woozie, not even when he heard Horace saying, "Yeah, it's like the last time, Woozie. It will all work out." Silence on Woozie's behalf. "Well, hon, it's better than a handout. He even offered to mow the lawn."

Horace appeared around the door. "Woozie told me to put potatoes in the oven. Why don't you relax?"

Looking about from the chair he eased himself into, Bruden decided this was how the house of his sister in Edmonton would look. Over the fireplace was a colored photograph of a church-looking building. A big one. To its side was a framed photograph of three men. No surprise that Woozie and Horace were churchgoers.

Someone close at hand had drawn the framed picture above the couch, he decided, crouched figures with faces distorted like those in a cartoon except the faces were frightened, not funny. It was the Tower of Babel, he thought, and language was being confounded. His sister in Edmonton would have had mountains, maybe the Swiss Alps, from a furniture store where she bought her couch. By the front window that had lace curtains, Woozie had a table with a bowl of dried flowers on it, a big bowl with stiff blossoms.

Horace was humming in the kitchen as he scrubbed potatoes under running water.

Better than coins in the street? Ian John would say so. Wolfgang wanted to clear out his garage, but he couldn't do it without Ian John taking care of the stuff he'd stacked there. Whenever Ian John took something out, he'd bring in something else to take its place. Computer, radio, bicycle, speakers. Best to know nothing of Ian John with his sweet smile.

Horace handed Bruden the folded newspaper. "Haven't had a chance to read it myself. Sometimes I don't care to know what's going on. Woozie thinks I'm too free and easy, not caring what's going on. A free spirit, she calls me."

"Because you don't care what goes on?"

Horace grinned. "Yeah."

Bruden noticed the bowl of shiny fruit on the dining room table. "That stuff real?" said Bruden.

"The fruit?" Horace laughed. "You want fruit, you eat what's on the kitchen table. *That's* real."

After a few seconds, Horace yawned and lay back on the couch. "Don't be upset if I doze off. Middle of the day—unless I keep moving—"

"I know the feeling."

Horace talked a bit more. Woozie's brother drew the picture above the couch, he said. Woozie had to stop at the store on the way home. Bruden mumbled as Horace commented. If he shifted, he could catch his own putrid odor, released from some enclosed part of his body, the sourness of his own folds and openings.

Then Horace's eyes began to slip back into his head mid-sentence or his eyelids fluttered like they were fragile and light. Before long he was out, the couch sunken under his heavy body, his head on a pillow, his stocking feet on the upholstered arm, his mouth open.

Bruden left the newspaper on the chair. On the rug, his footsteps were as soundless as Ian John's. The banana on the dining-room table was wax, sure enough. In the kitchen, sunny with the afternoon light, he peeled one of the bananas from the basket there. It took him three bites, three bites that didn't satisfy his belly. He dropped the peel in the kitchen sink, still wet from Horace's scrubbing. He could feel the heat from the stove's oven. A calendar on the refrigerator had days marked, notes entered. *Band practice. Young Men. Camp.* Sure enough, Woozie would be an organized sort.

On top of the refrigerator was a quart-sized Mason jar more than half full of coins. A good supply of loonies along with quarters and dimes and pennies. The label on the jar read *Sidney's mission.* Would Sidney miss a couple of loonies? Bruden's long fingers caught one and then another. He replaced the jar and stared at the two coins in his hand. These were what Horace might have given him on the street. He looked at the oven where the potatoes were baking and at the banana peel in the sink. Then with a shrug, he dropped the coins back into the jar.

The carpeted stairs creaked a couple of times, but Horace was dead to the universe.

What furniture Wolfgang had in his house was scarred by Wolfgang's cigarettes. A table was wobbly from a fight Wolfgang had gotten into with two kids who'd broken into the house. That was one night before Ian John came and when Bruden was gone. Wolfgang's house had an empty feel.

Because it had so much furniture, Horace's house felt crowded. Photographs hung on one side of the upstairs hallway. Family photos. A nearly empty bookcase took up the other wall. The few books—*Man's Search for Happiness, The Miracle of Forgiveness,* and others with titles like them—didn't slow Bruden. Hardly any books did.

Behind one open doorway was Horace and Woozie's bedroom, a large room almost filled by Horace and Woozie's four-poster bed. It had a white spread over it and colored pillows piled against the headboard. The open drapes were white, and the walls had blue-and-green-striped wallpaper. Bruden knew he'd never have seen that, not this bedroom in his head—not the plush throw rugs, not the floor-to-ceiling mirrors on the closet doors. Hardly room in it to stroll.

He glanced in two more rooms. One on which the curtains were pulled was filled with boxes, extra chairs. In the other, a girl's room, not lived in either, the bed was piled with clothes, with what looked like sleeping bags and tent poles.

Then, he came to Sid's room at the end of the hall. Could have seen this one without a blink—if he'd tried. A pair of jeans and a couple of shirts tossed on a straight-back chair. A pair of rumpled jockey briefs on the floor with some athletic socks. Woozie must have made the bed. A wall closet along with a wardrobe. When he opened the wall closet, he saw a pile of junk—a discarded radio, tennis racket, baseball glove, CDs, some rolled-up posters, boxes of school paraphernalia.

Sid's clothes hung in the wardrobe. The kind you didn't notice because so many of the kids you saw wore them—baggy pants, baggy shirts, scuffy running shoes. You'd notice Bruden's clothes because they were unwashed and worn. You'd notice the clothes other people wore because they were sometimes fresh and expensive getups. But you wouldn't notice Sid's clothes any more that you would notice Horace's. Maybe you wouldn't notice Sid himself.

On Sid's desk was a Bible. Not only that—an open Bible. Born again? And another one, except it was a Book of Mormon—also opened.

On his walls, Sid had posters. No rock musicians like Bruden would have seen if he'd formed anything in his head, but animals—a purple hippopotamus, some penguins, a wise-looking elephant—saying things you were supposed to laugh at. Maybe Sid was a boy who needed a laugh. Maybe he was a boy who laughed too much.

Bruden took up the discarded jeans from the chair. At first, they felt as though they might have something in the pockets, but a search with his thin fingers found him nothing.

"Who are you? What are you doing here?"

Bruden didn't drop the jeans. He had no intention of showing surprise. "You're Sid." A big boy, taller than his father, in a loose T-shirt halfway to his knees. Still, baggy as the shirt was, Sid looked strong, lithe, quick. Bruden couldn't remember whether he'd seen an athletic trophy or not. Sid had some of his father's features, broad-planed cheekbones, brown eyes you'd call on another occasion earnest, maybe well-meaning. But now startled and angry.

Be glad I'm not Ian John, he could have said. With Ian John's strong hands and knife-clean looks. Be glad it's only this wobbly bundle of bones and sinew called Bruden.

"Did my father bring you here?"

"Your father's napping."

Sid snatched his jeans. "He brought you, didn't he? Get out of here."

"Your father's invited me to supper."

"Not in my room he didn't."

Passing Sid with his grim jaw—*No, I'm not Ian John*—Bruden stopped at a couple of the photos in the hallway. Horace and Sid with—Bruden assumed—Woozie and the two sisters. He peered closely at Woozie in shorts, squinting against the sun. The Grand Canyon. The Mormon temple in Salt Lake. Disneyland.

"Get going," said Sid. "Don't stare."

"Family holidays?"

"You don't need to know about me. It's private."

"What's private?"

"Our lives. Us."

Unhurried, Sid's breath heavy behind him, though he remained at the top of the stairs, Bruden entered the living room. Horace had scarcely twitched, hands folded on his belly. After he sat in the matching chair, when he saw that Sid had moved into the kitchen, Bruden let his head rest on the back of the chair.

He must have dozed off because next thing he heard voices in the kitchen—voices and Horace's snoring. Woozie must be home. "I got salmon to poach," he heard, though Bruden knew salmon was not the subject of the conversation. The two—Woozie and Sid—spoke softly. But not so he wouldn't hear. More like they didn't want to wake Horace. Sid didn't care what buddy-Bruden heard.

"But our lives are private, Mom. We're not on TV."

"I can't change your father," she said. Her voice was clean in tone, her speech unhurried, each syllable making its way at its own pace. Her voice was as strongly inflected as Sid's with pitch and emphasis wide and varied.

"He doesn't have to keep bringing these guys home."

"It's just the last couple of months. Wait, and before you know it it'll be something else. Your father's got good intents. He believes in charity, not a handout."

"So the guy spends the money Dad might have given him," Sid said, "on beer—"

"That's what bothers your father."

"So the bum buys liquor."

"It's the principle, dear. If the man is starving—"

"The guy isn't starving."

Bruden smiled slightly.

"And he smells," said Sid. "They all do."

"Not the old fellow last week."

"Oh, Mom—"

"Just think 'free spirit.' "

She must have kissed the boy on the cheek. He heard a kitchen chair move.

"I'm still waiting for you to clean your bedroom," said Woozie.

"I feel like I should fumigate it now."

"You want to set the table? Forks on the left."

About time. Bruden had been hungry when he settled in Horace's Buick, when he ate the banana, when he searched Sid's jeans. Now, his belly had started its hubbub.

He ate half the salmon, and he could have eaten a second baked potato. "A little man like that," he could hear Woozie tell a neighbor later. "All that sour cream." Tomatoes and lettuce from the garden, tumbled in a salad, went down like nothing. Fresh from his nap, Horace put it away, too. "Must have dozed," he said, as though nobody had noticed.

Bruden didn't flinch at Sid's scowl. The more he ignored it, the deeper it went. But that was Sid's business.

Sid sat across the dining-room table from Bruden, Horace across from Woozie. Bruden would never have formed Woozie in his head. Woozie had a round face, healthy smooth skin, and dark eyes with a crackle to them, and a smile bright as a puppet's. She was as tall as Horace and as heavy, though not so heavy from the waist up. She was heavy in the hips, wide in her denim skirt, her legs wide around.

She liked her free-spirited husband, Bruden could tell, tolerating his open ways with dinner plans. She didn't pull a face at the way Bruden smelled when she shook his hand, giving his fingers a good squeeze.

"I'm Woozie. And I guess you've met Sid."

"Yeah, we've met," said Sid.

Bruden wasn't a talker, so he nodded. He knew that his wasn't an eye for seeing virtues in others. By habit, he'd shape the bad. But it was hard to see right away much bad in Woozie. Not like Sid. Seeing Sid reminded him that he sent out a stink, that his clothes hadn't been changed since . . . the last time. He saw Sids of some sort every day of his life. "We're private," Sid had said. "Our lives are private."

Woozie gave him store-bought ice cream for dessert. Sid said he didn't want any.

"You sure? It's chocolate ripple, one of your favorites."

"I don't want any."

When Woozie put a bowl in front of Bruden, Sid said, "May I be excused? I want to check my bedroom again."

"Maybe pick it up a bit, too," called Woozie as he stomped up the stairs. "Seems like I barely look back and there he is two years old and spoiled by his sisters. Ten and twelve they were then."

"I never look back," said Bruden. "No future in it."

Horace laughed. "No future in it. That's pretty good."

Bruden started to say he hadn't tried to be funny. You didn't get ahead by looking back. Pure and simple.

Woozie told Horace he'd have to remember the line next time he gave a talk at church. Horace had a fine sense of humor, she said, and was always keen for a good clean joke.

After Bruden finished his ice cream, Horace said, "Whenever you're ready. I'll drive you back downtown—or wherever you want to go. But take your time."

"Downtown will be fine."

Woozie stood at the door as he and Horace put on their shoes.

"Thanks for supper," he said. "And—" he tacked on as an after-thought, wishing Sid were there to hear—"for letting me into your privacy."

Wolfgang was sitting on the love seat, watching a TV newscast about a break-in the night before, someone hospitalized, but he followed Bruden into his room with its unmade mattress on the floor.

He listened with wide, unblinking eyes. "You mean he just invited you home for supper—this guy you never seen?"

Bruden patted his belly, putting it on for Wolfgang, who was missing half of what should be in his head. "Just like a five-star restaurant." He fished the coins he'd collected earlier that day from his pocket and placed them in a bowl on a chair by his pillow. He'd hide them later. His own private doings.

The walls and floor were bare in Wolfgang's house. If only Wolfgang could get it into his head about taxes. Too heavy for his feet with three toes missing from a thirty-below night outdoors, the little man would only squint and laugh, showing which teeth were gone.

"You had salmon," he said, "and baked potato and sour cream. And what else?"

"Make that half of the salmon all to myself."

"Like you said."

"Half a salmon?" Ian John was suddenly in the room from out of doors. He was that way, appearing with a phrase, slipping forward without a creak. He sank to the floor next to Wolfgang, crossing his

long legs like Wolfgang. If you knew Ian John and his ways, knew the
real Ian John, you'd think he'd crawled out of a dirty river somewhere.
But just looking at him, not knowing him, the young man with the basketball player's build could have been using a private swimming pool.

Ian John smiled as Bruden repeated his story. Bruden had no fear
of Ian John. What he didn't like were Ian John's smooth face and his
groomed blond hair that one of his girlfriends trimmed for him. A
face that looked open and honest, and eyes—hazel, green-tinted—
that would convince an unwitting listener the words coming from his
mouth were God's truth. You can trust me, buddy.

Ian John whistled. "No lie. And his wife is named Woozie? What
kind of house they have?"

Bruden described the house.

"Where is it, man?"

Bruden held back a second, looking into the deeply colored eyes.
Then he shrugged. "Man, I don't remember. I get lost in them residential areas. One street's like another."

"You're bullshitting me. Where's he live?"

"Why you want to know?"

Ian John chuckled. "Don't make me say it."

"I don't want you to say it. I get lost in those residential areas.
That's all."

Ian John glanced at Wolfgang, who was understanding—maybe
understanding—with an open mouth. Ian John took Bruden's arm.
"Come with me," he said. Bruden stumbled after him into the living
room. Ian John turned on a floor lamp and sat on the love seat, his legs
extended before him, crossed at the ankles. He gestured Bruden to sit
beside him. "Now, let's have it again. You forget. You get lost."

"That's right."

"Then where'd you meet him? This Horace? Tell me about it."

In the darkness last night, Bruden hadn't been able to see how
new, how well cared for, the love seat was. He ran his fingers across the
smooth, patterned surface, violet and dark green, the shapes that lay
between him and Ian John.

Another shrug. "You know where. Here and there."

"Here-and-there where, man? Or is that your private affair?"

Bruden traced a flower. He remembered the way Woozie had

squeezed his fingers, the way Horace's tie twisted as he dozed. He could have drawn a map to their place. But then the picture came strong inside his head: Ian John on the stairs. Not here in this house, Wolfgang's house, but in the hallway outside Horace and Woozie's bedroom. Inside the bedroom, one head to a pillow. One chummy body to each side of the bed, amiable and true. The red numbers on the bedside clock at 2:45 A.M.

"What's the matter, partner?" said Ian John. "You forget that, too?"

"I guess that's it," Bruden said. Horace and Woozie slept soundly, full of rest. Unlike Sid. Ian John might understand Sid. But Horace and Woozie—Bruden could see the rise and fall of their breathing, steady and calm. "I don't remember. Like I forget that, too."

VOLUPTUOUS

Helen Walker Jones

RIGHT NOW, THE VARSITY BULLDOGS are single-file along the thirty yard line of Bulldog Stadium, doing jumping jacks—scissor-flashes of white Spandex against chalk lines on scruffy brown grass. I'm sitting in fifth-period physics, staring out the window, getting a load of Max Whitmer in those stretchy, almost-see-through, girdle-type pants they wear to dress rehearsals, or whatever you call their last warm-ups before the game.

Max and I have been on a total of three actual dates (wrestling match, Bruce Willis combat movie, and—my choice—a snappy FreezePops concert at Snowbird), plus a study session in my bedroom while Mom and her boyfriend bickered in the kitchen. The ticket stubs from our dates are tucked in a diamond pattern around the frame on my bathroom mirror, so I can think of Max while flossing and applying lash-lengthening Kitten Flips mascara. Max and I have kissed only once, and it was last night.

At this exact moment, I'm scribbling some last-minute homework—a one-hundred-word parody of *Crime and Punishment*. My mom keeps telling me, "Valedictorians are not slackers. They don't spend hours contemplating their navels." Mom's hippie-era vocabulary can be sort of amusing—a throwback to the days of ragged bell-bottom pants with a palm tree embroidered on the butt, and a T-shirt blaring *Potential Mothers All-Girl Rock Band* for which she honestly played keyboards.

The clock is ticking on my Dostoyevsky parody, so I keep scribbling, with the paper tucked inside my textbook, writing with a crooked wrist while pretending to listen in rapt fascination to Quackers as he extols the virtues of the Einstein-Minkowski theories of astrophysics. He wrote his master's thesis on Albert and Hermann (he seems to be on a first-name basis with the two of them). Most of the faculty pull double duty—like Quackers, who teaches both physics and English lit. His real name is Mr. Delgado, but he got his duck moniker from walking with his toes turned out.

On loose-leaf paper I conclude my parody:

> *Olga Marmelubsky sat on her bed in the village of Shostakovich, distraught, thinking of the shabbily dressed young man who had torn her heart to shreds. Olga berated herself because she still voluptuously dreamed of marrying him.*
>
> *"Dimitri is like a piece of iron," she whimpered, "and he has broken me like a pebble."*
>
> *Poor Olga asked her reflection in the mirror, "If a dog dies in Moscow but there is no vodka, can there be a funeral held?"*

Maybe Quackers will smile somewhat wryly at our own private joke about the word *voluptuous*—a Dostoyevsky favorite. To me, it meant only one thing: boob job. So I quizzed Quackers, who told me *voluptuous* meant "desiring sensual pleasure." That fits me to a tee.

True confession: Max is the first boy who ever kissed me. Nobody knows this except Ashley Tyler, my best bud. Ashley pledged to be my social coach this year. She clues me in when I'm acting too nutso, in her words. Her number-one piece of advice was, "You scare boys away when you start talking about Lucia di Lammermoor and Albert Einstein. Stick to kung-fu movies and whoever's going to the Super Bowl, and you can't go wrong." Since Ash's advice directly led to Max Whitmer asking me out, I'll be eternally in her debt. The average girl in this high school can walk into a drugstore and ask for cherry-flavored condoms without batting an eyelash. And then there's me—the seventeen-year-old virgin-lipped social retard until Ashley Tyler was kind enough to intervene.

Other than kissing, only one thing renders me physically and emotionally limp: Puccini arias. When Quackers made us read "Euclid Alone Has Looked on Beauty Bare" I told him, "I'm not exactly turned on by angles and hypotenuses, but if you could substitute Puccini for Euclid—*that* I could envision." The class laughed, but I was completely serious. I have this CD of a hunky tenor named José Cura. At night, I replay "Nessun Dorma" dozens of times in a row, imagining myself in a dark opera house with José singing to me, alone, in Italian: "I shall win, I shall win, I shall win!" I suppose that's the macho guy's version of "I Am a Strong and Mighty Woman," my mom's favorite mantra for when she's upset. Unfortunately, the album notes gush about José's beautiful wife and three children, so it's not likely he'll be pursuing me any time soon.

Quackers startles me by asking me to expound on Minkowski's space-time triangle. I stare at his nice brown eyes, his biceps under his pale blue Oxford-cloth shirt, and the thick waves of his almost-blue-black hair in light reflected from the window. I know I'm his all-time favorite student. I actually *read* every single word of *Crime and Punishment*, while everybody else just did Spark Notes. I watched a nine-hour BBC video of it, too. Plus, in all modesty, I admit I inherited a pretty decent brain from my parents, the Plum Alley Queen and the Prince of Garbaga.

Lots of girls in school think Quackers is hot. Do I view him as an object of desire? No way. I don't want him living the rest of his life incarcerated. Besides, he'd have to move on first, you know? Get a Ph.D., instead of teaching in this dungeon for the rest of his natural life.

Despite the fact that my sweetie, Max Whitmer, is basically a wholesome guy who's planning a Mormon mission after high school, Mom thinks of him as a bad boy because (a) she caught him smoking a Tiparillo outside Smith's Food King (before he repented), and (b) he won a contest for good-looking jocks. The prize? A cameo in a cable TV show. Max earned a hefty check, portraying a litter-bearer for a 320-pound Arab sultan. Onscreen, both the sultan and Max (in his loincloth) got devoured by a white tiger. Okay, it happened behind some palm fronds, but you saw blood spurting. Those little incidents colored Mom's thinking about Max Whitmer, totally.

Mom has this new boyfriend—Julius—a dermatologist. "Call me Dr. J," he says, like he's one of the greatest basketball players in history. Mom is smitten with him, even though his nose hairs are his most prominent feature. I nearly barfed when Mom plucked them for him one night while he sat at our kitchen table! I refused to eat there until Mom decontaminated the placemats with liquid bleach.

Julius is Jewish, whereas *I* must stick like glue to Mormon boys, even though (before my first date with Max) Nathan Steinmetz came to my cross-country meet twice, walked me home both times, massaged a charley horse out of my calf, has the cutest chin dimple in school, and can do a right-on impersonation of the vice principal. It's not fair. I still have plans to hang with Nathan after Max goes to preach the gospel. Nathan's dad is, I think, the assistant rabbi at the Congregation Kol Ami. I went to a party at their club once, with my buddy Sarah Light, who's Jewish even if her name doesn't sound like it. Nathan introduced me to his dad, who had a bushy brown beard and an outfit sort of like a Mormon missionary—dark suit, skinny black tie, and white shirt—at a pool party, no less. He told everybody—even teenagers—"Call me Abe."

I don't get why my mom is so hung up on my dating "within the faith," since *she* goes to church only on Christmas, Easter, or if Grandma is in town. People assume we're Catholic—with a name like "Delaney"—but we're not. My ancestors joined the Mormon church in Antrim (up by Belfast) more than a hundred and fifty years ago, and during the potato famine they emigrated to Utah. The Delaneys and their nine kids walked from the Mississippi River to the Salt Lake Valley, dragging their only possessions in a wooden handcart. Mom says that's where I got my bullheadedness, from that side of the family.

All my mother's friends are non-church-attenders and divorced, just like she is. They go out man-hunting on Saturday nights at the Plum Alley, which features a cheesy disco ball, plus drug-addled guitarists, tone-deaf vocalists, and bare-chested drummers. Mom and her cradle-robbing pals ask thirty-year-olds to dance, while wearing stockings with seams that look like miniscule eels crawling along their calves and up under their skimpy miniskirts. Definitely kinky, and verging on perverted.

This apparel is fine and dandy for my mom, but if I try borrowing it, look out! Same goes for her bathing suit—that strapless number with the peekaboo sides. Hot pink with black piping. Trés low cut, as she says, although Mom doesn't have a clue about French R's, and pronounces the word as if she meant a salmon-colored slab of plastic on which you carry your sloppy joes in the high school cafeteria. That swimsuit is off limits to somebody like me who actually has the size-four body to wear it, with no post-childbirth abdominal pooches, saggy boobs, or cottage-cheese thighs. Last April Mom made me purchase a creepy two-piece suit with "boy shorts" instead of a bikini bottom and a top that shows about as much flesh as a nun's habit.

Mom, at fifty-two, is still very sexy looking. She slaves at underwater aerobics, keeps the plastic surgeons in business getting the fat sucked out of her saddle-bag thighs, and continually wears diamonds and pearls to put highlights back in her face. No lie, she pretends that her thirty-fifth birthday was a *recent* event.

Dr. J is always trying to push some new zit lotion on me, insinuating that I need it, which I don't. I have actually been told that my skin reminds certain people of porcelain, even if those people are all named Ethel, Myrna, Velma, and Fanny (my grandma and her pals). So I told him, "Keep your meddling latex gloves off my face." Mom told me to be quiet. If Julius hadn't been there, it would have been "Shut up," but she's ultra-conscious of her image where dating is involved.

My mom may be worried about lights in her complexion, but my buddies and I freak over too-tight thong underpants, kissing with cracked lips or Dijon mustard breath, and having your neck turn blotchy-red when the health teacher gives a frank demonstration of condom usage, employing a zucchini as a model. I've suffered through it twice now, and both times it verged on porno.

Mom's friends all have French-sounding names with three syllables: Evelyn, Sylvia, Jacqueline, Marilyn. It was their mothers' revolt against their own stodgy Ethel, Velma, Fanny, et cetera. Somehow, my name—Grace—sounds more like a ninety-year-old knitter than a kid who'll turn eighteen in a few months. Bad: It's a Biblical name, like "Charity," "Jezebel," and "Delilah." Good: It's short and easy to pronounce—perfect for a marquee, according to my vocal coach, Madame Beatrice Arbizu. She's positive I'll be headlining at the Met before I hit twenty-five. According to her, I have an extensive vocal range, a fine coloratura quality, and expressive hands—whatever that's got to do with it.

Mom keeps Julius around for breakfast after plucking his protruding nose hairs, but she's frantic, worrying that Max and I are misbehaving. I don't know why. My personal chastity standards are posted on my bedroom wall: *No Sex Before Marriage*. There are lots of us teenage virgins around, but nobody knows it since we don't appear on Jerry Springer and Maury Povich. People tell me it's corny to want to be a virgin when I get married, but I don't want anything to compare to, in that department. I never want to lie in my husband's arms, becoming worked up during extensive and expert foreplay, and think to myself, "Wow, my old high school boyfriend was a much better lover than you!" I never want to be fifty-two years old, divorced, and bopping at the disco with my pathetic, face-lifted girlfriends.

I'm juggling my own romantic conflicts, my dream of being an opera singer some day, Mom's frequent love connections, plus my own fiercely competitive desire to be valedictorian of my graduating class, which requires constant effort so that Samantha Freakin' Lewis doesn't exceed my GPA. So far I've had only one A-minus and Samantha's had three, so I'm retaining a bit of a cushion. Nathan Steinmetz is out of the running, after getting mono last March and missing six whole weeks, including midterms.

Somebody yanks on my hair and when I turn around, it's my bud, Ashley Tyler, who discreetly slips a wadded-up note into my palm. "Read this and freak," she whispers. "I found it on the floor by you-know-who's locker." I can't believe people are still communicating in quaint handwritten notes. Ninety-nine percent of the kids I know contact each other by text messaging, including me and Max Whit-mer.

Ash is staring at her shoes as though a tarantula had just landed on the toe. Holding the tightly folded paper, I can almost feel the heat of Max's hands on it. I picture his fingerprints—little whorls verifying that he's touched it.

Last night, when Max came to my house to work on trig, he looked scrumptious as a Ken doll in his low-rider jeans with just a hint of boxer waistband peeking out. Dr. Julius was sitting at the table with his hands folded on a placemat, looking serene and hairy. I rolled my eyes in the direction of my bedroom, as a hint for Max, but he stayed put. I was rather worried about any cosmetic undertakings my mother might be contemplating on Julius's behalf.

"Please," I said under my breath to my mom, "if you're gonna pluck him, do it in the privacy of your own bedroom."

Let me preface this by saying that I absolutely never use profanity. Madame Arbizu insists that I use vocabulary befitting a professional singer, and I make an all-out effort to do so. But Mom misinterpreted what I said. "Young lady," she hollered, "you know I don't allow language like that! Just whom do you think you're talking to?"

"Excellent grammar," Max Whitmer said approvingly, bobbing his head and thumping his textbook with three fingers so it sounded like a galloping horse.

"You have no sense of irony whatsoever," I told him disgustedly.

To his credit, Julius told Mom, "I think you heard wrong, Cynthia."

But Mom was off on a rampage. "If you want to have friends over, you can at least address me with a little respect, Miss Grace Mariah Delaney!"

"You want respect, Cynthia?" Julius said. "Then for heaven's sake, put on an apron and pick up a broom." He laughed at his own cleverness.

"What on earth are you talking about?" Mom demanded, not getting the joke.

Now it was Max's turn to roll his eyes and nod in the direction of the hallway, but before the two of us could escape, Dr. J said, "Tell me, Mr. Whitmer, when you hear the word *mother*, do you think of a woman in slinky black leather and chunky gold jewelry, or do you picture a gingham housedress and a cross-stitched apron?"

I was sure Max had never heard of gingham or cross-stitching, but he tried hard to accommodate Dr. J by saying, "Well, my mother is a very modern and beautiful woman, too, sir, so I'm not really equipped to answer in the way you apparently want me to."

Dr. J was stunned by this. He'd been hoping for a terse "Yup."

Mom said to Julius, "Are you implying that I need to look like a drudge so my daughter will do what she's told?"

"My mother looked like that," Julius said, "and I'll bet yours did, too."

"Why are you dragging *our* mothers into this?" Mom snorted and stared at the ceiling. Her eyes welled up with tears, and she did that little cheek squinch she does to keep them from rolling down. I was sure she was chanting *I am a strong and mighty woman* like she tells me to do whenever I feel like crying.

Max was sighing and leaning into the door frame with both arms elevated, his textbook balanced on his head in the cutest, most alarming way. "Shut up, you two!" I hissed, horrified at what Max must be thinking of me and my home life. I whirled around and ran down the hall to my bedroom to grab my trig text, so we could study in the family room. But when I picked it up and turned around, Max was sitting on my Italian silk bedspread that Julius brought back from a dermatologists' convention in Milan.

"Oh," I said, surprised. "I've never had a boy in my bedroom before." Then I hit my forehead, knowing what Ashley would say about this enormous social faux pas.

Max and I tried to concentrate on studying. Really we did. But Dr. J and my mom were freaking out in the kitchen, like a chapter out of my parents' marriage. Sadly, the reason my parents finally got divorced was because Mom found out about Dad's senseless affair with a toothpaste model. (Mom and I nicknamed her "Bucky Beaver," and Mom really laughed when I asked, "Do you suppose she's toothsome? Or just toothy?") Dad was Bucky's lawyer in a messy divorce. But before that, Mom and Dad had nightly arguments about the thermostat setting and the Visa bill and whose turn it was to empty the "garbaga," which is what my dad still calls it—like it's a delicacy on an Italian menu or something.

And now Julius was flipping Mom's switches just as surely. Finally, as Mom was screaming, "Just get out of here and take your stupid Efudex cream," Max got up from my desk and walked over to the bed, where I was sitting with the advanced trig text open on my lap, put his hands in my super-gelled hair, and kissed me right on the lips. His blond, wispy moustache hairs tickled, and I could see a faint trace of that black stuff he smudges under his eyes during football practice to reduce glare. I didn't close my eyes for a second, because every close-up detail about him was just too wonderful.

Julius was hollering, "Be that way, then, but don't think I'll come crawling back here, Cyn. Women your age are swarming all over me, and I can take my pick."

My lips were tingling, and my palms wouldn't rise up off my silk comforter even though my brain was giving them the command. I was staring into Max's dazzling slate-colored eyes, and the thought occurred to me that in thirty years he would have nose hairs, too, and maybe even tufts growing out of his ears.

My mom burst into my bedroom and said, "Exactly what is going on here, Grace? You know the rules of this house. No boys allowed in your bedroom unchaperoned, ever!"

"I'll see you, babe," Max told me in a soft voice. "Tomorrow after the game. Meet me in the south end zone." I nodded but didn't make a move to see him out. He brushed past my irate mother and out the back door. Through my bedroom's bay window, I watched him trot jauntily down the back steps. The engine of his rusted Nissan roared in the driveway, then pebbles flew up against the bricks on the garage. My mom was still glaring at me, breathing hard and toying with the fake fingernail on her pinky.

But that was last night. Right now, Quackers is discoursing on Hermann Minkowski (pronounced "Hair-mawn," so it sounds like he's Jamaican). The football players have trotted into the locker room for their pregame pep talk, and everybody in class is nodding off. If I make the slightest crackle while opening the note, Quackers will confiscate it.

Finally, it's open on my desk, its edges ragged, the punched holes at the left torn clean through, as if the writer couldn't wait a moment longer. The writing is not Max's. It's loopy, slanted, and the capital I's are exclamation marks, with perky round dots under them.

It says:

Max, PLEEZE don't say ! think your a dum jock. Your real smart besides being athaletic too. YOU OWE ME GUM from 2 weeks ago. If you think !'m one of the cutest blonds in school, well your a stud yourslef! I love your jockeyness. Write me again. And make a interseption for me today. I'll be watchin.

Love, Deb
P.S. HANGMAN.

I can't think for a minute or breathe, either. How could Max prefer this semiliterate dodo to me? The note proves that he has personally commented on her physical attributes, borrowed gum from her, and shares a secret password with her (*hangman*, whatever that stands for—probably a blatant reference to a certain person's male anatomy). Worse yet, my best friend Ashley knew all of this before *I* did! And what is the point of taking trig and physics and music theory, if the stupid girls get the cute guys?

The inside of my lip is bleeding where I accidentally bit it while reading that rancid letter. I never wanted to be a serial dater like Mom. I dreamed of Max and me in a little condo, while I was going for my Ph.D. in vocal performance and he was coaching the Junior Bulldogs to victory after victory. I even thought of giving up Juilliard for him.

I don't know how to do Mom's cheek squinch, so I'm squeezing my eyelids together, desperately trying to concentrate on anything but the agony of being duped and dumped and having tears streak my cheeks. I want to be invisible. I wish Quackers would look right through me, that the bell would ring and I could escape to the end stall of the girls' bathroom. If Quackers asks me to discuss some aspect of quantum mechanics, my melodramatic sobbing will be heard as far away as the locker room. It's true what all those songs tell you: Love hurts. I can't bear to think about Max Whitmer and the malodorous epistle from his secret squeeze. I can't even bring myself to chant Mom's mantra.

I make casual swipes at my cheeks to clear the tears, take deep breaths, and try to think of (a) maintaining my front-runner status for valedictorian, and (b) cultivating my coloratura soprano voice, diction, and knowledge of foreign languages for my future career. It doesn't help. How was I to know that innocuous, big-shouldered, loincloth-wearing Max Whitmer would smash my heart to a pulp? I wish he really *had* been eaten by the Sultan's tiger.

I'm so heartbroken I can't even think about my Dostoyevsky parody, but if I don't turn it in, there goes my G.P.A. Regardless of my psychic pain, I smell Samantha Lewis's juicy-fruit breath, about to overtake me in the valedictorian race, so I'll hand in the assignment. By tomorrow, everyone in school will know about Max Whitmer, the Master of Rejection, and his involvement with that Jezebel.

I'm not lucky in love. Am I predestined to be an unmarried career woman who uses man after man, then tosses them aside like so many empty Pepsi cans and struts away on her stilettos? Fat chance. I'm too much like my mother. I'll be sobbing nightly in my own kitchen, enduring all the crap—the manhunts, the makeovers, the bikini waxes—always seeking my true love, either in a pair of white Spandex football pants or Rodolfo's clingy breeches and calf-hugging tights as he sings to me in *La Bohème* about my cold little hand. I'd be willing to wager my first year's paycheck that Little Miss Anonymous Deb—the girl who thinks enough of herself to use exclamation points as personal pronouns—shall never darken the stage of the Metropolitan Opera House and sing at the top of her voice while pretending to be dying of tuberculosis. But I will. Just you wait.

I'm wondering if Max dated me just so he could crib my trig notes. No way am I gonna meet him after the football game. I refuse to stick with somebody who could fall for the cutesy-poo crap in that note. Maybe in seven or eight years, when Barbara Walters asks me, in my tastefully appointed living room, to recall my first true love, I'll think of Max Whitmer and let one single tear roll down my cheek as the cameraman zooms in for a close-up.

Ashley hands me a follow-up note saying, *Who gives a care about old Max Whitmer, anyways?* She looks at me sideways with that good-hearted Brave Little Toaster grin of hers. Ash is such a loyal pal.

Yeah, I respond in writing, *Given that he's cute, smart, buff, and Mormon—exactly what ! want. Why should ! care about somebody whose little slut writes mash notes to him behind my back? When !'m as famous as Joan Sutherland and Hermann Minkowski, you can bet !'ll have my pick of any guy ! want.* I hope Ashley realizes I'm mocking Max's new girlfriend by using exclamation points. And I sincerely hope she didn't see me wipe my cheeks after I read the putrid, stinking note.

Confessing my heartbreak to Madame Arbizu will be wrenching, but she told me once that I would never be a fully mature singer until I had experienced life to the fullest. So I guess having a broken heart will improve my chances at the Metropolitan regionals next year and in the Juilliard auditions.

I suppose Max—like my dad—was corrupted by a conniving woman. Max was okay with my chastity rules, but his new gal-pal must be hot to trot, pressing her chest against him in the hall, playing tongue tag when they kiss, and wearing stuck-in-the-crack thong underwear—all those verboten things I'd never dream of doing.

I know absolutely that when I get home tonight, Mom will be there with Dr. J, grooming him like a cat. All will be forgiven. Mom and Julius will be crazy-in-love again. He'll be my new prospective stepdad. Maybe there'll be some new clothes in it for me—and I don't mean a spider-weave top and too-groovy bell-bottoms. The outfit I have in mind is more of a ball gown with a beautifully draped white silk bodice and a stiff black taffeta skirt with a cummerbund sash. Madame Arbizu would applaud, just looking at me in that getup. And I'm pretty sure any adjudicator would be able to tell, just by watching the way my chest heaves under that white silk during the crescendos, that I have suffered through and overcome heartbreak of the most devastating kind.

So now I'm shuffling my papers, lining up the textbooks in my backpack, and getting ready for the bell to ring. My fingers are trembling. I take a deep breath to expand my diaphragm, smile despite my sadness, then continue chanting "I am a strong and mighty woman." By the time I've repeated it ten times, I, Grace Mariah Delaney, will pretty much have the rest of my life mapped out, starting with my plan to miss the entire Bulldog football game in order to consult Quackers on the further intricacies of Minkowski's space-time triangle. And later—right before I ask for the new silk-and-taffeta dress—I'll discuss with my mom the deep, cosmic, human need for love, affection, and (as much as possible) the absence of pain.

When everybody has cleared the room, I dial my mom on my cell phone and when she answers, I say, "Mom? Can you come and pick me up? I can't face the car pool tonight." I feel about five years old, relying on my mommy to soothe my emotional trauma.

I toss my Dostoyevsky parody onto Quackers's desk even though he's nowhere around. So long, Olga.

Quackers bumps into me as he bounds through the door of the classroom and knocks my backpack off of my shoulder. "Sorry," he says. "Is there something you need, Grace?"

"Nothing," I say.

I'm already across the hall, twirling the tumblers on my combination lock, when I hear him call from the door of his classroom, "Have you been crying?"

I shake my head and try to laugh in cascades like I do in my "Chiri-

chiri-bin" song. "I'm fine, Mr. Delgado. I just want you to know that
I'm really starting to grasp Minkowski and Einstein."

"You're a true scholar, Grace," he beams. Then he switches off the
fluorescent lights in the classroom, locks his door, and strolls away,
whistling.

I wonder if Max Whitmer will show up at my doorstep after the
ballgame, begging me to listen to his insincere, pathetic apologies and
explanations. Should I tear his heart to shreds and break him like a
twig? Oh, sure. Like I have that kind of power. Eventually I might have
a successful career in opera, but I'll probably never play the lead—
always the handmaiden or the girl-in-pageboy-clothing or the best
friend. Still, I'd be living in New York, making wads of money, hearing
applause every night.

As Mom pulls up at the curb outside the east entrance, I wave excitedly until I suddenly remember that people could be watching. Then
I walk slowly down the stairs, heft my backpack onto the floor behind
the passenger's seat, and say, leaning through the window, "Can we go
get ice cream? Please?"

"Sure, hon," she says, patting the leather seat beside her. "Hop in.
I have great news!" She wiggles the fingers of her left hand and flashes
a huge diamond ring shaped like a teardrop.

"When?" I say.

"Next month. I'm just ecstatic. You can be my maid of honor. Do
you think a nice yellow suit would be appropriate? With a white orchid
corsage?"

"And then we'll move into Julius's house?"

"Of course."

"I do not want to live at the Pimple Palace," I announce. "A house
built from the proceeds of dermatology. That's disgusting. What are
you going to do—braid his nose hairs for the wedding?"

My mom doesn't answer but simply pulls into traffic. At the red
light a moment later, I notice she's doing her cheek squinch, and there's
a puddle of tears at the outer corner of her eye. I've made her cry! I'm
such a jerk sometimes.

"Mom," I say, "I'm sorry I was so mean. You've been through
your share of heartbreak without me adding to it. Until today, I never
realized how it must have felt—being dumped by a man who slept in

your bed for fifteen years straight and cried as he cuddled your new-born baby girl in his arms."

"I'm never going back to your father," she says quietly, sniffing. "Even though he's begged twice." There's a meaningful pause, during which she taps her foot nervously on the gas pedal, causing us to lurch just a bit. "So, do I have your blessing about Julius, then?"

"Sure," I say, trying to sound agreeable. "Julius is an okay guy. And no pimple jokes while he's around—I promise."

Mom checks her mascara in the rearview mirror. "We're gonna be okay, sweetie," she says. "We're gonna be just fine. We're strong and mighty women."

"Oh, yeah," I say. "Birds gotta swim, and fish gotta fly."

"I don't get that, Grace," she says defensively. "I don't know what you're talking about, as usual."

"You know!" I protest. " 'Can't Help Lovin' Dat Man O' Mine.' I sang it last year on the All-State Talent Revue. I won fifty bucks and a certificate to all-you-can-eat shrimp at Sizzler, remember?"

"So basically you're saying I'm a dishrag who lets a man walk all over me?"

"You said it, not me."

My mom would never take my advice, even though I know her marriage to Julius is doomed from the start. Dad's three-month, live-in mistake with Bucky Beaver ended in a whiz-bang midnight fracas—probably because he finally asked her to take out the garbaga. And both my parents have spent the past year out there in the dating scene, relentlessly searching for what they already had in our comfy three-bedroom house. If their luck in the romance department is genetically transmitted, I'm doomed.

How could I ever explain to my handsome, intelligent, lonely parents, or to Max, or to Quackers, that we voluptuous types have to coax ourselves to be choosers in the realm of sensual pleasure, rather than beggars? Otherwise, love can ruin everything. And, more often than not, it does. Just ask me. I am a self-professed strong and mighty woman of the world.

Mom doesn't want my opinion. She keeps on driving, straight ahead into the darkening October evening, oblivious to the roar of the crowd in Bulldog Stadium as we pass by the south end zone, the setting sun striking the huge rock on her finger, spinning prisms over the steering wheel, the dashboard, the backs of my expressive hands.

MEASURES OF MUSIC

Bruce Jorgensen

IT CAME THEN THAT SARA DREAMED of the flood. It had been the news for weeks, cities and towns all along the Front sandbagging streets sidewalks driveways window wells, a landslide that dammed a river and spread a lake over a town. She had gone to sleep several nights thinking of those houses under water, full of water. But the cul de sac was well above the nearest flood zone: nothing to fear.

She woke shaking, to Ryan sitting up peering at her, his eyes dark hollows in the dark, saying "What is it?" and that she was kicking and making odd little yips in her throat, like a pup.

Out of breath, off balance—"Did I?"—she still shook. "It was the water," she told him, water coming at the house in a stream as from a hose to push through the wall.

He put his arm around her, joked, mock-analyzed, comforted till she leaned against his neck.

But still hearing the water thunder coming fainter, far yet steady, no flashback, "Wait," she said, she was hearing it. "Listen."

After a stillness he explained it was the catch basin, it was coming in there, they were controlling the outflow, part of it going down past the temple into storm drains on Ninth East. "Nothing to worry about," he murmured and hugged her, "lie down, sleep," and lay back and pulled her. She yielded her head to the hollow of his shoulder.

She didn't sleep a long time wondering if he did, hearing the flood louder than breath or heart, her mind breached by the dream, a ram of water breaching a wall. This was Sunday morning.

• • •

After church, after dinner, the table cleared and kids dispersed, she asked Ryan to come with her. He was at the piano laboring out a bass part: "And the glory, the glory of the Lord shall be re-veal-ed," finishing the phrase before answering that he still had to pack, and she ought to practice, too, get her cello out. "Fastest packer around, fastest out of town," she chided him, and urged "Come on."

"Where?" he asked.

"Anywhere," she said. "Up to the catch basin."

"Ah—" and wagging a finger he analyzed her ulterior motive, her dreamwork.

"I want," she told him, "your company."

They rode near as they could and left the bikes chained to a street sign to climb the weedy truck-rutted lot sloping to the basin, the high bank with stones half-unearthed by rain. People were there, some walking up, others down, others standing or walking along the bare crest of the dam. She couldn't see what they looked at but the dam only, the wide notch of the spillway with its gray square-scored concrete face, above that the canyon mouth and the rough escarpment, and then lint-colored sky.

She'd worn sandals, so Ryan had to take her wrist and pull to help her up the steep bank. They stood on the dam. She wasn't impressed as she'd thought to be: the water still six or eight feet below the spillway, four or five below the grated mouth of a big corrugated pipe standing up several yards out. Just a glorified chuckhole, she told him. He pointed. "Over there."

She looked then heard as she should have been hearing all along the noise that tracked her dream. Several thousand gallons a minute, he was saying, and they were letting it out as fast as they dared but it was gaining, had been twelve feet down yesterday.

Across the wide basin like a big gravel pit she saw a deep-cut gully, a wash bending out of sight into the canyon, and coming through it a brown torrent tumbling on itself flinging barrelsful into the air high as the banks with that noise windlike rattling and rocklike. She was safe she knew, she could see it tamed when it spread into the basin, the water at her feet lying still as sleep. But everything could move. She watched the stream incessant and ferocious.

Ryan was talking again, as if to a freshman science class, of how this was made thousands of years ago, all the area below a fan delta, rocks and silt carried out of the canyon. "Alluvial," he said. He turned his head toward her. "Our house is built on the same kind of stuff. The old lake terraces."

Bonneville. But she watched the stream. She saw it toss small boulders into the air, heard it mumble. She thought of the empty houses under Thistle Lake and the stripped rooms with water gliding through windows and doors, secret along halls, up stairwells on obscure errands; thought of the ancient lake filling the whole valley, centuries gone before anyone settled on its deep benches. The voice of water and silt and stones fluttering on her skin, strumming her tendons, jarring the beat of her blood.

Ryan packed after the kids were in bed, and Sara more anxious than angry did not pick her usual farewell fight with him but sat on the waterbed in her nightgown cross-legged with covers to her waist and watched him meticulously lay into his carry-on bag his necessities— three changes of garments, three pair of dark socks, two extra shirts, an extra pair of cords, his shaving kit, his tank top, shorts, and running shoes, his leather-bound scriptures. His thin briefcase had been packed since Friday with the paper he would present, copies of the papers he would respond to and his notes on them, the text for his one spring term class, a folder of problems he'd grade on the plane and return when he got back Thursday. He was trying to fit half a dozen books into the bag—physics, novels, biography, she wasn't sure what; reading was his main extravagance, or a vice so regular as to seem governed by natural law. He liked, he said, to have choices. Amused she watched his oblivious mummery. The books weren't all going to fit.

"Amazing," she said.

"Intellectuals travel light."

"Not light enough," she said, and bet he wouldn't open half.

"The point is I could," he said, and set three thinner books aside then took out the thickest to put the thin ones back in, then zipped the bag.

"Tell the kids good-bye?" she asked.

"Oh no—I'm sorry." His usual.

They might not notice, she told him. "It was a couple days last summer before anybody said where's Dad."

"The incredible disposable man," he said.

When he set the bag onto the floor by the bed she felt the absence of the weight keener than the thought of his going while she would be sleeping.

"Not yet," she said. "Astrophysical clown. Come here." She rocked a wave toward him.

He looked up and signed a T: timeout to brush his teeth and gargle?

"Penalty," she warned.

He stepped into the unlit bathroom.

When she heard him tap his rinsed toothbrush against the sink she switched off the headboard lamp.

"Hey," he said. "What?"

"Touch system," she said. "Find me."

Later they sat up to watch random lightning shift along the horizon south to north to west to northwest with low almost continuous thunder.

It was like that, he told her, where she touched him: "Little flashes out at the edges and then closer."

"Will it hit here?" she asked. She laid the backs of her fingers against the slope of his side.

"Probably," he said. "It will be a while."

It was with them a long time, the erratic flaring and the thunder never surely assignable to any one flash. It drew close enough to light the yard, the walls of the room, yet never all the way to them, moving always in stealth and sudden leaps on the clouded rim of the valley.

Later still before Sara slept she was thinking how each trip now left her more alone, more at risk of losing him to hazards of machinery or flesh or feeling. When she did sleep, she had been looking at the still sporadically lit parallelogram of sky out the north window thinking how rain would mist in through the screens and mix its cool after-lightning breath with the tang of dusty wire. Tonight they had slid the windows wide the first time this season.

When Ryan got up in the morning to meet the shuttle, he kissed her awake long enough to hear him say "Good-bye, Stormgirl. Kiss the kids for me."

But she overslept, and barely seeing them bathed and dressed and combed and breakfasted and launched toward school she forgot.

And she felt listless half the morning, left dishes on the table, didn't run, could not think where or what to begin. She took her cello out of the back of the closet and unlocked it from its case, then leaned it against the piano and laid the bow along the keyboard. It was time to start spring cleaning in earnest. But it was the late wet weather, winter dragging on in cold heavy rains, prolonging the confinement she had yearned for in the fall but now felt oppressed by.

She missed Ryan. Absurd since if he were home he would be at work, and she should be used to his conference trips. But his absence this morning was the palpable vacancy of the house and she drifted in it till she caught herself staring at the family-room window seeing only glass.

She started cleaning then and didn't stop till near noon, when she walked out of the house and down to the end of the cul de sac for the mail. The day was clear and the air warming.

Mrs. Francis leaning at the mailboxes greeted her with the fine day, and Sara asked how she was getting around.

"This—thing!" She lifted her walker and shook it. "You get old you get spare parts."

Sara opened her mailbox.

Where had her husband gone so early, Mrs. Francis was asking, and Sara said to New York to give a paper: "Something to do with event horizons."

"Beyond me."

"Sometimes he says it's a little beyond him." Sara shuffled her envelopes: bills and coupons.

Not a thing for her, Mrs. Francis said, but she expected a letter from her daughter any day. Sara hoped it would come, she said, and said she needed to get back to cleaning. Mrs. Francis set her walker a step in the direction of her house. "You have a good time now."

Passing the Morisons' on her way back, Sara saw across the low board fence Darrell Morison hunched in the garden setting out tomato plants. Off this term, as she was, he stayed home while Jan his wife ran endless statistical correlations toward her thesis. Sara admired them both, and recited the phrases Darrell once had told her from his specialty, Boethius: *Naturae rationalis individua substantia*, the philosopher's definition of a person that seemed to omit something; and then as consolation, Darrell had said, for what that might lack, *Interminabilis vitae tota simul perfecta possessio*, eternity as the mind of God knows it, a perfect possession altogether of endless life. Boethius also, he told her, had said temporality imitated eternity by binding itself to the fleeting moment, which bore a faint semblance of timelessness.

She couldn't decide whether that was profound or sad. Back in the house, in the kitchen, she made an omelet. Ryan would sauté alfalfa sprouts and mushroom slices in bacon fat, toss in avocado when the eggs were half done, sprinkle on lemon pepper and grated cheese, make it all up as he went along. Like the quantum universe, he would say; might be one way, might be another, you play it by ear, you look and see. He had invented this while he was gone last summer, sleeping in an attic and getting his own meals in the kitchen of a house belonging to some church members in Ithaca while he worked on radiotelescope data. Sara had tried but could not make it quite right, and not today either. The one thing Ryan could cook, and did.

She sat at the breakfast bar chewing rubbery eggs and remembering awful summer. She had burned the bottom out of a cold-pack canner, burned up a stovetop unit, and the hood on the Rabbit had flipped up while she was doing forty-five on the Parkway and the insurance would not pay because she admitted she had checked the oil that morning and that made it probable she had been negligent. Put that in your endless life. She had written Ryan long letters with all the grim details and told him *If you were my boyfriend I'd drop you like that.* But she got used to his being gone—it was simpler. *It's quieter here,* she wrote him, *more orderly with you gone. Not that we don't miss you.* She had almost dreaded the disruption of routine when he came back, the weight of another personality in the fine-strung web of amenity she had woven with Shannon and Alicia and Brendan. She had even come to like sleeping alone, the restful depths.

Last night, this morning, when they made love she had felt him go out of himself or farther in, seen his face blind and abstract over her, felt herself lift delicate and seeking, felt and heard each breath hum in her throat. They had turned and turned, the bed, the room, she wanted never to stop, she had no words, they poured force and grace back and forth, emptying and filling, wider and wider. In live remembrance warm light sang from her shoulders to her belly.

You married a man, lived with him eighteen years and made children with him, made the love you could, which was harder, and it became daily bread and clear cold water too plain to notice though it fed your life. Then something like this, some good time out of nowhere and lighting the whole sky one moment and gone to memory the next morning so you feared to cherish or wish it to come again. Put that in your endless life. Sara felt like a glass bowl brimful and floating roses, she stood and felt blown apart like a dandelion.

She went back to cleaning. Mid-afternoon, not long before the girls and Brendan would be coming from school, she went to her cello again. For years since graduate school she had played only occasionally and had not played now since last Easter in a string quartet to accompany the ward choir singing Fauré's *Requiem*. Ryan had sung bass in that. Now they had begun learning the first part of *Messiah* for Christmas.

The instrument still gleamed dustless inside its case. She sat on the piano bench, wiped the strings and tuned them, tightened the bow and snapped off a few loose hairs, stroked rosin on it, positioned the cello in the grip of her knees, arched her fingers over the neck and set the bow to the C string.

The first note struck her like a shockwave and sounded her and she stopped. Not knowing if it was joy or desolation she wept.

That night she turned the thermostat down to fifty-five and again left the bedroom windows open. A few days there might be, maybe a couple of weeks, the interval between furnace and air conditioner, when the house could be open, airing.

She had told the girls and Brendan they could watch television if they kept the sound low and left no unnecessary lights on and went to bed immediately after and did not spill popcorn, and they had promised. She was so tired she likely would not wake at two or three and track down their glaring bulbs. She hugged them and asked them to remember Dad in their prayers and went up to brush her teeth and undress.

She knelt for her own prayers and began with habitual words, thanks for what she had, petitions for health, safety, guidance, peace. And broke off unable to think what to say. It was all true and insufficient. Everything, she thought, everything I have, everything. And: I want, I want, I want I don't know what. She was a long time not saying or thinking anything, and was not to remember getting into bed or waiting for sleep, but the dream.

Of a room high-ceilinged with a tall transomed door and walls bare as an abandoned schoolroom, in which she sat in a wide too-soft bed hugging a heavy quilted comforter around her knees, wearing a sheer nightgown, deep burgundy. In the room in profile to her a man stood, suitably tall and dark-haired but slightly stoop-shouldered, wearing a brocaded robe, dark velvet lapels. "Alluvial," someone's voice said. His long fingers let drop a glass and it broke, and he bent to begin picking up the pieces.

How like Ryan, she thought: stopping to pick up, clean up. And she woke then still thinking how he kept everything neat but the desk in his study, which was irredeemably messy; how when the kids were younger and even more disorderly he histrionically cursed them as junior anarchists and minions of entropy.

He had wakened her this morning and called her Stormgirl, sappy as something inside a card, a pop song title. But she took it as a name, herself newly named.

And slept again. And again in the morning when the kids had left for school and she had cleaned the kitchen, made the bed and vacuumed the bedroom and upstairs hall and stairs, she didn't run, and wondered where to begin. She bathed in the tub rather than showering, but without lingering, and put on snug jeans and a cotton shirt cool and almost weightless.

She walked in the still rooms and heard herself humming the phrase Ryan had picked out on the piano: the glory, the glory of the Lord.

She stopped to curl her fingers to the neck of the cello and lift the bow thinking of runs, arpeggios, double stops, measures of music, but she did not play.

Out the family-room window she could see into Morisons' yard, the bared broken earth of the garden, the tomato plants standing upright, their leaves lifted. Light warmed the ground and the day. Sashes on this side of the house had been raised. The air was moving and she thought of it moving through and between the houses finding its own ways.

In her study and sewing room she went to the window and slid the sashes from both ends toward the center. The curtains stood inward with the air.

She turned to her desk where the month's accumulating bills waited to be opened and totaled and paid as far as the money would go. She should begin. She stood with the fingertips of both hands touching the cool polished wood. She felt the air move and looked toward the window. The curtain bellied into the room, its corner stroked her forearm.

She stood watching the slow wave of gauze.

THE WALKER

Matthew James Babcock

YOU COULD SAY THAT MY LIFE AND the Walker's life—well, it's all been a question of firsts. And to be honest, I thought for a long time it was always going to be that way.

Until now.

See, ever since I bumped into the Walker—well, found out who he was (we've never really been introduced, although I feel like I know him better than myself, my daughter, and even my wife, Sage)—he's been around. Around at all my firsts. First love, first driver's license, first hot dog with my dad in Candlestick Park on vacation. The usual momentous occasions in your life that go down in your memory as firsts.

First biopsy.

It's like he's been around forever. Until now.

Which is why I'm worried. I haven't seen him in a while. I look out the window at the glazed December streets, and he's not there. I drive through town—down past the flashing blue and pink neon arrow on top of the Westwood Cinema, Mickelsen's Hardware, the John Deere lot, the courthouse—and I don't see him. I guess it's because now I'm actually looking for him, you know? It's like now that I'm looking for the guy instead of trying to avoid him, he's not there. I miss him, actually. I miss seeing his red and black mackinaw, his grizzled sunken face—kind of grandfatherly. Even though I've always known he's a nut. Seriously, absolutely whacked out of his skull. It's still been comforting, though—creepy and comforting—to see him whenever I've experienced some first in my life.

And I haven't had a first in a while—excluding my wife's recent trip to the doctor's office. So I can't figure out why he's gone, why he hasn't come shuffling around our place in his dirty gray irrigation boots, his orange hunter's hat with the earflaps pulled down, his breath blowing out plumes of evening mist, like some dark night train, endless, timeless. Seriously, the guy's a legend in my book. Just as powerful, just as memorable. A full-blown mythic legend.

Only I haven't seen him for a while.

And that's a first.

I can't stop looking for him. Three or four times a day I part the Venetian blinds in our living room and look out at the hardened December streets, hoping to see his face in the wreaths of Christmas lights, hoping to see him hanging outside the Clean Spot Laundromat next door, cupping a cigarette in his hands, looking off into the frozen dawn for some lightning-colored shard of truth, some answer to it all, like he was always able to give me from a distance. A close distance—always.

"Who are you looking for?" Sage asks me, whenever she catches me staring out the window.

"Nobody," I say, turning and smiling at her.

But he wasn't nobody—still isn't. He's the Walker, and he hasn't walked my way for a while now, now that I'm looking for him, which is a first. And I hope it's not the last.

So what do you do? What do you do when it's a Saturday morning, early, and it's almost Christmas, and a legend has died in your life—well, is on the verge of dying—and you and your wife are waiting for the results of her biopsy to come back from the lab at the hospital in Pocatello? What do you do? I mean, in a way, this is a first. A big first. What do you do when the doctor said the earliest you could find out the results would be Monday or Tuesday? Tuesday at the latest, he said. And so you sit, staring out the window, talking to each other but knowing that it's almost Christmas, which a long time ago was another first, a first for everybody involved—a worldwide first. And all you can think about is, *Hey, this could be it. This could be the last time we're going to look at each other, the last time we're going to say things like, "Dear" or "I love you" or "What are you looking for out the window—I'm right here."*

What do you do when your wife could be on the verge of dying, and all you can think about is some crazy guy you saw walking around and around in circles in the North Park, back when you were just a fourteen-year-old kid taking a driver's education course?

Maybe it's because whenever you run bang up against something that's going to stop time for you, you cling to everything you've ever felt to be timeless, like you're clinging to some kind of talisman that will stay the elements, stop time, ward off evil.

Like the Walker always seemed to do.

So what do you do?

I'll tell you what you do. You get up in the early predawn hours of December, you throw on whatever you find in one of your late grandfather's old war trunks—boots, hat, coat—and you take a walk down to the nearest park and sort it out.

You do what I do.

First driver's education course—September 23, 1984. 11:45 A.M. Jerome, Idaho. My hometown. That's where I first met him: the Walker. I was taking my first driver's ed classes, and we were driving around the old North Park, which was right across from Main Street, facing Towle's Motel and the old, gray stone church—Lutheran, I think, or Presbyterian— where I attended kindergarten when I was six years old. We—me and my friends, Samantha Barnes, Greg Ainsworth, and Brett Thueson— were driving this white Dodge around the North Park, trying to get Joe Mattie, our driver's education teacher-cum-football-coach, to pass us so we could get our licenses. Joe Mattie was a Boston transplant. Don't ask me how he got out to our side of the world, but he did.

See, I'd never met any driver's ed teachers from Boston, anyone from Boston, for that matter. So that was kind of a first for me, too. Actually, I think you'd've been hard pressed to find anyone in my town who even knew where Boston was. Back in the early seventies—or so the story went—Mattie had redshirted at Idaho State in Pocatello as a middle linebacker and shattered the record for tackles in a single season, a record that still stood at the time of my first driver's education course and maybe even stands today. So we were all in this white Dodge, trying to get our licenses, and Joe Mattie made me pull up around the North Park, around past Towle's Motel and my old kinder-garten church.

"Let's see ya parallel pahking," he said. "Right heah, right heah."

"Right here?" I asked.

"Yeah, right heah. Parallel pahk. This is good."

So, I parked. He pulled out his clipboard, jotted some notes.

"You should always check ya mirrah," he said, looking at me, tapping the rearview mirror with his coach's forefinger.

"My mirror?" I asked, looking at Samantha, Greg, and Brett in the backseat.

"Yeah," he said. "Always check ya mirrah. All right, let's go. Remembuh S.M.O.G."

"Signal, mirror, over the shoulder, go," we chanted in chorus.

"Ah," he smiled widely, looking around at us. "Youse guys are learning. That's good, that's good."

Then he saw something.

"Hold it," he said. "See that?" He pointed at something in the North Park.

Greg, Samantha, and Brett craned their necks to see.

"Where?" I asked.

"The Walker," he said, pointing to an empty space between some pine trees and oil-drum garbage cans whose dented lids were chained on.

Only he said it like this: "Wahkuh."

"The Walker's been there," Joe Mattie said.

For a while, we sat there staring at something he saw but we didn't, staring and not saying anything until he finally told me to signal, check my mirror, check over my shoulder, and go back to the high school parking lot.

On the way back, we listened to his story. I drove, and Samantha Barnes checked how many times I checked my rearview mirror.

"The Walker," Joe Mattie said. "He just walks. Around and around. I saw him once when I was a kid growing up in Boston. It was down in this park near my house, the house I grew up in—Schmidt Park, I think it was called—I can't remembuh now. Anyway, it was where they had all the swings and World War II tanks and stuff, you know? Yeah, he was down there, even way back then. He wore the same thing—this orange hunter's hat with earflaps, and this red and black mackinaw, like a lumberjack's jacket. Jeans, I think, old jeans. And he wore irrigation boots, this kind of gray, muddy-colored rubbuh. And he'd walk. All night. Around and around. Eventually, he wore an oval into the grass, and the pahk commission, the local city council, made him stop doing it because they said he was wrecking their grass, see. But that's it. He'd walk around and around, wearing a brown oval, like a race track, into the grass. First and last time I saw him, though. First and last. Until now."

Then we were back out at the high school, perfectly parallel parked.

"All right," Joe Mattie said. "Next time, we'll do highway driving. Take you out past Cindy's Restaurant on I–84 and let you merge."

"Woo," Brett Thueson said. "Can't wait to merge."

And I didn't want to let it show on my face because, well, I was in the company of my friends, people who had an opinion of me. But I had seen what Joe Mattie had seen: an oval worn into the park grass by the tan cinderblock restrooms and oil-drum garbage cans, about fifty feet long, encompassing two pine trees, like a scaled-down high school track circling a football field.

So I didn't say anything.

Which was a first.

But I went down that night. That night, I pried my bedroom window open—I was dressed in jeans, white high-tops, a black hooded sweatshirt, my parents' Kodak Instamatic in the front pocket. I crawled out into the window well. It was a September night, breezy and just warm enough. The stars were out, and I could hear the crickets serenading me with a thrill all the way down in the North Park and beyond. I quietly slid the window shut behind me and scrambled out of the window well.

It was about midnight. But I was wide awake. There was this—I don't know, *energy*—humming in my body, like I was about to do something I'd never do again. But that's the power of firsts. There's these things we do only once, things we *really* do only once, if we're honest with ourselves—marriage, love, the birth of a child, scoring a touchdown against the South Fremont Cougars in sudden death, having biopsies, waiting at home for biopsy results from the hospital in Pocatello—these are the things that we'll never do again in the same way, never again at the same level of wonder, awe, or terror.

That's their power. They have the force, instantly, to change us forever. And that's a long time. Really: forever. Most of the time, we spend our forevers looking back at what we wish we could do again for the first time: first once again, we want to kiss someone beautiful who loved us, outside the high school Valentine formal on February 14, 1986; first once again, we want to take the ball on a sixty strong draw and bulldoze through the defense and break out into the open for a tie-breaking touchdown and clutch a come-from-behind victory at homecoming; first once again, we want to be married, fall in love, start a career, have a child. We want to relish the firsts over and over again, to savor them like luscious white fruit, which is of course impossible.

So we take early morning walks in the winter of adulthood to simulate these firsts in our minds. We sneak out our windows at night, hoping to take a picture of this first, hoping even to secure it, to preserve it—to steal it—so we can keep it forever. But eventually, we find out what I found out that night, which is what I'm still finding out: first is also last. First will always be last. Like with kisses, loves, biopsies, and waiting for lab results to come back from Pocatello by Monday, or at least Tuesday. That's what Sage's doctor said.

We find out this.

Firsts last forever.

That night, I jogged down Avenue C, turned right at Garfield, passed the old silver water tower that loomed like a mute sky rocket in the wide-open September midnight, and headed down Avenue B to the North Park. My weighted breath clung to my lungs, vapory and sweaty. It was a football player's breath, the breath of a young kid trying to hang onto his firsts forever, trying to keep a catalog of first events, ones he never wanted to let die, ever. I jogged past Lonnie Ambrose's house, past Pat Towle's.

Then I saw him.

It was just like Joe Mattie's account of his Schmidt Park, but it was my North Park.

He wore an orange hunter's hat with the earflaps down, and he wore gray muddy-colored irrigation boots with yellow-and-red bands around the tops. Jeans, lumberjack's mackinaw. With a kind of staggering but steadfast purpose, he was walking around and around, treading an oval track into the grass, as if each step would right all the awkward angles in the universe.

I wondered: How long had he been there? How long would he stay? How could he wear a track into the grass overnight? But had it been only overnight? Who was he?

I raised my Kodak Instamatic, aimed it.

But the lens was fogged, so I swiped it clean with a loose T-shirt tail. When I looked up and aimed it again, he was gone. Then he was standing beside me, holding my parents' camera, lowering it, shaking his head no.

"Why?" I asked, pulling the camera away.

"Nobody takes a picture of me," he said.

I couldn't see his eyes, but I could smell his breath. It didn't smell bad exactly, just redolent with time, fragrant with age, like cedar and fresh moss. I could smell things I'd never smelled before in someone's breath. I could smell it all: movie popcorn, a canyon wind, the breath of every December and June that had been and would ever be, peppermint, the smell of a newly cut football field, the breath of children and the breath of marriage vows, and the wind that breathed life into Adam. It was like Eden. But it was the North Park. And there was no Eve.

His voice was young. I mean, by the looks of him, the Walker had to be about seventy, maybe even a hundred. He wore his orange hunter's hat pulled down, so I couldn't see his eyes, but I knew they were under there—checking me out, admonishing me, lecturing me for trying to take a picture of a living legend, for trying to preserve the unpreservable. He shook his head no again.

Calmly, he took back my Kodak Instamatic. It vanished in his fluttering hands. I blinked. Then he said something, rubbing the gray stubble on his hollow cheeks. Well, he started to say something, but then he stopped. I could tell he was trying to make it right, trying to make whatever he was going to say the most momentous occasion of my life. He rubbed his chin, looked off toward the weedy west fringe of the North Park. A police car rushed by, cutting the night in half. Above us, the opal streetlights fizzed and hummed, mobbed by white moths. Turning back to me, he shifted his weight from foot to foot. Unnerved, I examined his old hunter's hat, the mackinaw, the mud-colored boots.

What a weirdo, I thought. *Weird-oh.*

Then I realized why he'd been waiting.

"Not a weirdo," he said. "Just somebody trying to keep it alive."

"Keep what alive?" I said, laughing.

I mean, hey, I was fourteen. I had no respect for eternal, meaning-ful things.

"What alive?" I prodded. "What's 'it'? There's no 'it.' You're a guy in rubber boots who walks around when he should be sleeping. You know, you're probably freaking out a lot of people in this town. What are you talking about—'Keep it alive'? What's that kinda crap?"

He made a gruff sound in the cellar of his throat, as if clearing my impertinence from the concrete floor of the cosmos.

"Just remember," he said, tightening his hat down with both hands. "You heard it from me first."

Then the Walker walked away.

And I went home and never told my parents about how I lost their camera.

First kiss—Jennifer MacKenzie. February 14, 1986. Jerome, Idaho. 548 East 16th Street. Sometime around midnight. Jennifer and I were standing outside her mom's house. We'd been standing outside for about an hour. Seriously, an hour. What had we been talking about? Who even knows, man! I can't even recall, now as I sit here—trying to think about how the lab technicians in Pocatello are undoing the little vials that contain four small samples of tissue from Sage's left breast—I can't recall what, if anything, happened in that hour. But she was beautiful, Jennifer. Beautiful, as Sage is to me now. And as Sage was last night and every night and as she will be every day and night to come. Which is kind of a first, isn't it? Another first, right here, right now (where *is* he, then?).

I mean, how can I in the same flurry of memory see my first kiss and my first and last love both as paragons of beauty, as standards of the same paradoxical thing? Is it possible? Can old codgers in hunter's hats, mackinaws, and irrigation boots really turn your parents' Kodak Instamatic to immaterial vapor? Who knows? All I'm telling you is what happened to me. All this stuff, for the first time in my life. That's all.

So, yeah, it went this way: Jennifer MacKenzie and I are standing under this sheet-metal carport, just outside her mom's house. Her mom, who's single herself, is blasting some Stevie Ray Vaughan— "Darkness, Darkness"—or something like that. I've got this blue ball of electric energy, a valentine dynamo, churning pink and red and yellow and white, down inside my stomach and chest, and Jennifer MacKenzie, all dressed up in her pinkish white satin Valentine formal, is smiling her beautiful smile, smiling with her beautiful teeth. I've already spent an hour talking with her under her mom's carport, but it's time to go, and she's smiling and laughing and thinking I'm funny (I *am* funny, of course, really funny for the first time in my life). She guides my hands to the slender satin dream of her waist and pulls me to her—well, I pull, too. Our hips are close, our stomachs are close, and she's absolutely the sweetest, starriest human I've ever been close to. And her lips. Man, her lips. I can feel her lips on my lips, her teeth close to my teeth. She says this one thing, "Mmm." Like she just tasted something warm and delicious, like a sweet roll slathered in icing, warm out of the oven. Just like that. Not sexy. Not lustful, really, either. Just "Mmm." And let me tell you, that's something I'll never be able to bring back, nor should I really, I guess, except here.

But the stars were out, and we were leaning back against her mom's house over there on the north side of town, out north of Gayle Forsythe Park, past the new baseball field complex, the pitching cages, the high school, and out beyond that was nothing but potato and sugarbeet fields and doddering Holsteins and the absolute edge of the universe where God first put his pencil to his clipboard and made a few notes that set the whole thing in motion, perhaps even putting down a few things that had to do with me and Jennifer MacKenzie, perhaps saying nothing more than "Mmm," perhaps with the pencil tip in his mouth, thoughtful, perhaps writing down *Positive* or *Negative* when he came to the part about a lab test in a hospital in Pocatello. *Breast tissue*, his notes probably recorded. Date: December 12, 1998.

But that "Mmm"—that's all it took. Stevie Ray Vaughan was blaring "Darkness, Darkness" inside Jennifer MacKenzie's house, the stars were out, my body was absolutely jumping with love and energy, and I could feel the beginnings of a universe in the lack of space between our bodies, between Jennifer's soft Valentine's Day formal and my rented crème tux. It was all there—the beginnings, the holding, the "Mmm." Then there was a little wet click, a release, and our lips were plucked apart; she was looking at me, smiling, laughing, wetting her lips with her tongue, and loving me—yeah, really loving me—just for that moment out on her mom's carport under the broken light fixture and the swirling mayflies. And I was loving her.

Then it was her mom.

"Jenn," her mom called, Stevie Ray wailing in the background. "It's time to tell your friend to go home."

"Friend?" I asked. "Am I your friend?"

"Well," Jennifer said, rolling her eyes to the stars. "It's my mom, you know."

"Yeah," I said. "I'll see you at school."

"Okay," she said. "Bye."

"Bye."

Then the screen door opened, and Stevie Ray took her—her beautiful satin glide and flow, her perfume, her lips, her "Mmm." Then I was behind the wheel of my parents' Volkswagen Rabbit convertible, still feeling Jennifer MacKenzie's lips on mine, still feeling her waist, her firm wired-in stomach, her hands pulling my hands, her tapping heart drawing my body and soul up to somewhere way above the potato fields and carports and moms and stereos. I put the Rabbit in reverse, pulled out of her driveway.

That's when I saw him—the Walker.

I'd remembered to check my mirror.

In the night, in my rearview mirror, he stood behind me, wearing the usual: hat, mackinaw, boots. There was a flash: no camera. But he held his hands up, fired off a burst of white light between his fingers and walked off.

Next day at school, Jennifer told me that instead of me she liked Jeff Poole, who drove a red '67 Mustang and wasn't afraid to smoke pot.

Mmm.

Years later, in a college apartment, Sage would blow Jennifer MacKenzie's first kiss out of this known universe and keep it going on, spaceship-style, forever. And I'd go walking out all night afterwards, absolutely sleepless, looking for some drifter in an orange hat, mackinaw, and boots.

First funeral with military honors—Gavin A. Dupree, physics professor and retired colonel. My grandfather. October 15, 1998. Rexburg, Idaho. I remember that I stood in the reception line near the casket down at Flamm Funeral Home. The whole family was there— parents, uncles, aunts, cousins. And our cute red-headed daughter, Shanda Dee, in a white lace pinafore and carmine bow, bouncing in Sage's arms. Sage was wearing a black satin dress and a pearl (fake— gift from me) necklace. About halfway through the reception, an old guy no one knew shuffled through the line. He shook hands with my entire family, smiled. He wore new jeans, had his hair slicked back with Grecian Formula. He'd shaved, but it looked like he hadn't shaved in a while—there were a few bloody nicks in the pliable flesh of his neck and cheeks. He shook hands with me, stopped and looked in my eyes, squinted and cocked his head back as if sizing up a new recruit.

"Knew your grandfather," he said, popping a blue breath mint in his mouth. "Always wanted to get back down and see him. But I guess it's too late. Had some things of his, things I always meant to give back."

"Mmm," I said, casting sidelong glances at my parents, my Aunt Janet and Uncle Terry. "Like, what things?"

"A trunk," he said. "War things."

Then he turned thoughtful, wet-eyed. I realized he was still shaking my hand, a methodical up-and-down hydraulic motion, like our handshake was the thing pumping the tears out of his eyes.

"We were in the 3rd Infantry together," he said. "At the reduction of the Colmar Pocket. January 19, 1945. First time an infantry division was ever given the Presidential Citation. First and last, thank God. Used to go out fishing with him, too. Hunting once in a while. Chopping wood. He loved to get out. Used to see him walking down at Davis Park at all hours. We'd go together sometimes, too. Loved to get his exercise, eh? He was a good man. You'll take the trunk, won't you?"

"Sure," I said, releasing his hand.

"Good," he said, pointing over to where the old war trunk rested on the blue foyer carpet. Next to the trunk stood a pair of irrigation boots, under the hanging coats and umbrellas. "Right over there."

At the funeral's end, he was the only one lingering around, so we coaxed him into taking a picture of the whole family.

"Sure," he said, grinning. "Anything for the family of my old war buddy. Squeeze in, now."

And I wasn't sure if the flash came from the camera or his smile.

Weeks later, Sage and I were sitting on our living-room couch, playing with Shanda and flipping through some photographs of the funeral.

"Hey," Sage said, stopping at one. "Look at this."

"What?" I asked.

"This," she said, pointing at a picture—it was a group shot. The whole fam damly.

"It's the family," I said. "So what?"

"Who's that guy?" she said, pointing to an old man in the back row. He had slicked-back hair, a mile-wide grin, hollow cheeks.

"One of my grandpa's war buddies," I said. "Gave me the trunk."

"What's he doing in the picture?" Sage asked, wide-eyed.

"Came to the funeral," I said, shrugging and looking at her. "Remember? He was one of the last guys there. One of the first guys— first and last."

"Yeah," Sage said, pointing again at the picture. "But what's he doing *in* the picture? He took the picture. What's he doing *in* it?"

First home run—July 23, 1981. Jerome Recreation District Baseball Field. Off Main Street, north of Shaefer's Dry Cleaners and the Northside Tavern. First and last home run, really. Chris DeLucia was pitching for the Gano-Dehlin Huskies, and I was batting for the Volco Blockbusters, coached by Kurt Burton's dad, Ted, and Jeff VanDerBruyn's dad, Lyle. Anyway, it was a full count, and—no, the bases weren't loaded—but I was up to bat, and Chris DeLucia, that hothead, was pitching. The Huskies were up by one, and I remember that Mike Welch was dancing out on second base, not sure if he wanted to try and steal, not sure if he wanted to try and let me hit him in. My coaches, Lyle and Ted, were signaling for Welch to steal third and home, probably because I wasn't a very strong batter. So, anyway, I was digging down in the batter's box there on the Little League field, where all the games used to be played before they built the fields at Gayle Forsythe Park only a quarter-mile from Jennifer MacKenzie's mom's carport of love.

So, I was digging in, looking just as flashy in my gold-and-green uniform as Chris DeLucia in his royal-blue Huskies uniform. He was in eighth grade. So was Mike Welch. I was in seventh. And it was pretty simple. He rifled a fast ball, and I swung. I felt a solid crack. This feeling of connectedness that bloomed in the shaft of the bat shot up my arms and chest and carried the ball and me out over the A&W section of the pea-green home-run fence.

And that was it.

"Great job, son," my dad said, clapping my back.

"Way to go!" Ted Burton shouted, high-fiving me.

"Nice!" Lyle VanDerBruyn barked.

"Woo hoo!" Mike Welch said, slapping my hands in the dugout. "That's a first!"

Then we rode down to the A&W for free victory root beers in Lyle VanDerBruyn's white Econoline van. It was the van we all secretly coveted—red pinstripes, fur-lined seats, tinted bubble windows, mini-fridge, with a poker table and cup holders inside, sleeper cabin on top, shiny chrome ladder and covered spare tire bolted on the back doors. On the way, all the windows got rolled down, and as we cut through the town's main intersection and only stoplight, we chanted, "We're number one! We're number one!"

Afterward, however, I rode my bike back down to the Little League field, past the Northside Tavern, and out into the overgrown grass behind the home-run fence, looking for the ball. The field was deserted. I leaned my ten-speed up against the fence's faded ads: Woods Café, A&W, Jerome Floral. I walked back and forth. I knelt in the heavy windblown grass. But I couldn't find it.

"Hey, kid," he yelled.

I turned.

It was summer, so he had his mackinaw slung over his shoulder, his hat crammed in his back pocket. His jeans were tucked into his boots. Of course, back then, I had no idea who he was. His hair was light brown, receding, like a wisp of hay across his sweaty forehead.

His face was sunken, like a desert floor. Thin, tan—a skeleton with skin. A skiff of silvery stubble glazed his jaw, like snow on summer grass. He squinted, tossed me a baseball.

Then he held up an invisible camera.

"Click, click," he said, smiling.

"Thanks," I said, glancing at him only for a moment.

Then I turned and ran for my bike, hoping it would be the last time I'd ever see him.

And since we're on baseball . . .

First pro game with my dad—June 12, 1983. 4:35 P.M. Candlestick Park: Oakland A's versus San Francisco Giants. On vacation with my parents. I don't know why my dad and I went to the game. See, I was born in San Francisco while my dad was going to medical school. So I think it was something we felt we had to do for some reason, some kind of father-and-son ritual that everybody has to do at least once. Another first and last. We sat in the sun all day, watched a pretty bad game, ate hot dogs, and then we rode the city bus back to our room at the Best Western, and my dad told me about all the hard times my mom and he had endured when they were first starting out: the bills, the low pay, the lack of furniture, the little crackerbox apartment up in San Francisco's Mission District.

On the way back to our motel, we laughed nervously at a roister-ous gang of drunk guys who sat in the front of the bus. The group was laughing loudly—they were schnockered is what they were—preaching, chucking a baseball back and forth, clapping, laughing so hard they choked. Eventually, the ruckus got so bad the driver told them to cut it out or get off the bus. That quieted them down.

Then, a thin guy in a stupid-looking orange hat got up, cleared his throat, reached his hand out to all the tired, dirty people on the bus, and said, "I hope everyone on this bus—is blessed."

My dad looked at me. The bus went silent. Immediately, the drunk crew collapsed into heaps of spasmodic, choking laughter, grinning, rolling around, punching each other. The guy with the orange hat seemed to be the ringleader.

"Yes! Yes!" they shouted. "Amen, brother! Almighty!"

At the next stop, the driver booted them off. As the bus pulled

away, I watched as the guy in the orange hunter's hat talked to his
buddies, who were heavier than the first guy: two of them African-
American, one Caucasian. His two African-American friends sported
navy-blue coveralls, and the other man—a short, red-haired guy—
wore a T-shirt and jeans. I watched out the dirty back window as the
guy in the orange hunter's hat pulled a lumberjack's mackinaw out of a
blue Adidas duffel bag. Then, a pair of irrigation boots. They laughed
and laughed, falling over each other, leaning on each other's shoulders,
slugging each other in the gut.

"Weirdo," my dad said. "Some people just don't know when to
give it a rest."

"Yeah," I said, rolling my eyes, pretending to agree. "I know."

I remember feeling like I'd seen the guy in the orange hunter's hat
before. But I didn't really think about it until a few weeks before this
Christmas when I sat in the living room of my own house, looking out
the window for somebody I knew but had never been introduced to,
thinking this: biopsy, Pocatello, Monday, or maybe Tuesday.

First airplane ride alone—March 12, 1987. TWA flight number 1109.
I was an American exchange student going to stay in Germany. New
York City to Frankfurt. The plane was a DC-10, and about halfway
into our ascent, a guy in the seat behind me tapped me on the shoulder
and handed me a magazine. It was a copy of *Photography.*

"Want this?" he asked. "I'm not going to use it."

I didn't see him, but I could smell his breath.

I was too drowsy to realize what was going on, and so I mumbled,
"Sure," and took the magazine. Then I fell asleep. Somewhere over the
Atlantic, I woke up and started leafing through the magazine. The cabin was filled with the steady nighttime rush and hum of a long flight. I
looked out at the wing, over the streamlined blue clouds sheathing the
planet. I could see lights like shattered fragments of December tinsel
in the distance—below, above. I thumbed through the magazine in
my lap, not really paying attention. Then, in an ad for Kodak, I saw a
picture of a boy and girl, dressed in formal dance attire, kissing under
a sheet-metal carport's broken porch light. I recognized the faces, the
time. The ad said: *All this can be yours forever!*

Startled, I flipped the magazine closed and unbuckled my seatbelt.

Kneeling in my seat, I looked back over, trying to see who'd given it to me. In the seats behind sat three women, all sleeping.

"Excuse me?" a stewardess asked, stepping closer. "Is anything wrong? Can I help you?"

I shook my head.

"No, thanks," I sighed. "Just tired."

"Well, try and get some sleep. It's a long flight."

First airplane ride with Sage—November 30, 1993. Logan, Utah, to Rochester, New York. We were going to see her parents. In Salt Lake, we switched from our tiny prop plane to a Boeing 737. Seated in aisle fourteen, Sage and I held hands. We'd just been married, you know? So, just after takeoff, a familiar-looking woman in a blue-and-gold stewardess's outfit came down the aisle.

"Can I get you two anything?" she asked. "Pillow? Blanket?"

"No, thanks," Sage said. "We're all set."

"No, thanks," I said, recognizing the eyes, reading the gold, winged name badge pinned to her navy-blue uniform lapel. "No, thanks, Jennifer." Then I smiled and nodded to Sage. "We've got everything we need."

In Rochester, home of Kodak, I stayed up all night, watching Sage sleep soundly in our motel bed at the Braidwood Inn. The sheets were navy blue and royal blue, with some green-and-gold swirls woven in, too. I stood near the coffee table, the complimentary notepad and pen in my hands, trying to describe exactly what was going on outside our room. *There he is,* I wrote. *He's out there right now.*

My thoughts, in blue ink, rambled across the pad's cream-colored surface. *He's walking, not anywhere. Around and around and around. She can sleep, but I can't. He's just walking around. He's wearing the same thing: this hat, orange with earflaps, like he's some deer hunter or something. He's got irrigation boots on—this flat, stale gray, muddy color, and the tops are red and yellow. Where's he going to be irrigating, I'd like to know? He's got this mackinaw on, too, like some lumberjack.* Then, in mid-thought, I put the paper and pen down. I walked to the window, parted the dusty brown curtains.

Below our window, he stood in the parking lot between a green Ford pickup and a black Mercedes. He was waving to me—to us.

Then he started walking again, wearing a path into the grass beyond the parking lot.

In the morning, he was gone.

"What were you doing up all night?" Sage asked me, emerging from the shower in a towel. "Couldn't sleep?"

"Nothing," I said. "I don't know—"

"What's wrong?" she asked, coming nearer, letting her towel fall.

"Nothing," I said.

"Nothing?" she asked, pulling me to her. "I know what nothing is, and this isn't nothing."

"It's just that this is a first," I said. "You know what I mean?"

Her eyes searched mine. Strangely, they were the eyes of someone who'd never been kissed.

"A first," I continued. "We'll never pass this way again type of thing? It's epic. I don't know. I just couldn't sleep."

"You're a weirdo. You know that?" she said, looking up at me.

"Yeah," I said, pulling her to me, holding on. "Mmm."

And since the subject is firsts . . .

First of all firsts—November 23, 1993. 10:00 A.M. Logan, Utah. We'd just gotten out of our car, and the guests and family were all somewhere else, probably still down gabbing at the Bluebird Cafe. We were walking up the steps of our new apartment—it was a dive, really. Some guy who worked for Century 21 had bought it—nothing but a big shack—and had slapped a fancy name on it: VanDyke House. Problem was, it was nothing but a fire trap: bad wiring, one door, and only two windows. But it was $275 a month, with utilities, and so we'd taken it. So, we got out of the car and walked toward the steps, and I was feeling like I'd done this before somewhere, only there was this feeling that this was a moment I'd experience only once. But somehow I felt like I'd get to experience it over and over again, like I'd be able to have this first again sometime down the road when all the towns and cities and baseball fields and airports collapsed and burned and flared into a tiny blurred point of light in God's great ever-developing photograph: I'd get to have this again. This first would be my last and last me forever.

We walked, smiling, up the steps one by one, not saying anything, Sage in her white satiny wedding dress, me in my tux. At the door this time, however, there was no music, no Stevie Ray Vaughan. Certainly there was no darkness, darkness. There was only this light that would last forever, pouring through the little screen window (there were bugs, dust—hey, it was $275 a month). This time, I was able to go inside. I didn't have to stay outside the home because it was my home, our home. And Sage smiled, laughing up at me with her eyes.

Outside, Logan showcased a mundane November day. Thanksgiving was on the way. Curved puffs of snow capped the tall, mangled arborvitae outside. I heard some kids call, "Hey, wait up!" I heard cars drive by, the humming of an endless engine in me. Then, the streets were empty. Inside, Sage and I were dressed, but then, little by little, we weren't. She was leading me, and then I was leading her, and there was this lightness, lightness, walking around and around our cheap $275-a-month apartment, inside and out. In the bedroom, I remembered to check my mirror. I saw the curve of my own body in the mirror, the curve of hers, like I'd never seen before, like the edge of the world, curving away and toward us, all of it an evolving photograph that someday would include lab results coming back from a hospital in Pocatello on Monday, Tuesday at the latest. Ours, first. Lasting forever.

That afternoon, when I woke up, I looked outside in the parking lot behind VanDyke House. The snow was melting off the glittering blacktop. I didn't see him.

A trio of auburn sparrows chirped on a cold, black telephone wire outside. Droplets of sparkling, sun-filled water dripped from the wire, near the birds' feet.

"Biopsy!" they chirped.

That day, we took a walk down Logan's Center Street, past the huge nineteenth-century houses, the Needham Mansion. We ate chicken noodle soup and club sandwiches at the Blue Goose Restaurant. We bought each other chocolates and gifts at Coppin's Hallmark. We walked to Merlin Olsen Park, down by the river, and we walked around and around, holding hands, creating the universe with our words.

"Look!" Sage said, pointing to a worn path in the park's north corner. "Somebody's walked around there, around those trees."

"Yeah," I said, looking at the brown oval in the grass. "Weird."

• • •

First child—December 22, 1997. 2:11 P.M. Baby girl. Redhead. Name: Shanda Dee. Johnson City, New York. Helped into our car that day by a security guard in mud-gray boots, grizzled beard. Friendly but restless, in a hurry himself. Took a photograph of us at Sage's request.

First thought—December 12, 1998. No.
Last thought—December 12, 1998. Yes, positive.
First thought again—December 12, 1998. The results will take forever. A few weeks until Christmas. Maybe I'll take a walk. Just down to the park so I can sort things out.

So what do you do?
    You do what I do.
    I grab the first thing I can find to wear—I don't really see what it is that I put on, just some old stuff from one of my grandfather's war trunks—a hat, a coat, boots. Like a man with purpose, I stride into the December chill. Outside, it can't be more than two or three degrees above zero. It's early, gray. Saturday morning. No one is out. No cars on the street. Sage is sleeping; little Shanda Dee is sleeping, too. The roads all up and down 100 West—perhaps throughout the whole town—are encased in dull gray ice. At the end of our driveway, head down, bundled up, I take a right. At the corner stop sign, I hang a left, walking down past NAPA Auto Parts, Papa Kelsey's, and Timeless Photography Studio.
    I don't know what else to do, so I walk. I walk past the business district, trying not to slip on the ice, trying to keep up a pace, trying to keep warm, trying not to think things like: biopsy. Things like: lab results. Or things like: maybe. I walk, trying not to think things like: Pocatello, Tuesday. I walk on legs of stiff ice past a row of old houses behind the rec center. Here, the street rises into an incline, and I have to lean into the hill, like a draft horse trying not to skid backward. I glance up, and a razor wind whips down the street, blowing through the threads of my pitiful excuse for a coat. I think: *It's so dark. I'm freezing! Maybe I shouldn't have come*, I tell myself. *Maybe.*
    At the professional plaza and the doctors' offices, I take a left, walking briskly through the parking lot, passing a few empty cars. Once out of the parking lot, I turn right, heading up Main Street. Heading

where? To the park. Smith Park, the one at the end of Main Street, by the hospital. Tuesday, I think, walking. Or maybe Monday. I am thinking and walking but trying not to think, just walking and remembering how to parallel park, how to make sure to check over my shoulder, give a signal, and then go. I check over my shoulder, lope across the street, hands jammed in pockets like a drifter. *That's the procedure*, I rehearse to myself. *It has to be in that order*, I think, walking.

At Smith Park, I cut through the middle of the snow, passing between the tennis courts and the fenced-in 1901 Best Brand steam tractor, the jungle gyms and swings. I walk, thinking: *biopsy*. It's a tumor, they said. About the size of a quarter. But to me, it sounds like a baseball-sized lump in Sage's left breast, and I want to rear back and take a Hank Aaron crack at it, sending it out over the A&W sign and beyond, out of the known universe.

I walk, thinking, not knowing where I'm walking, head down, my face freezing into a mask gritting its teeth. Tuesday, I think. Or maybe Monday. Would it be Wednesday, though? Could it actually take that long? I cram my hands deeper into the scratchy pockets of the musty coat I'm wearing. My chilled knuckles ring like they've been rapped by baseball bats. My bitten ears sting. The park is empty, blanketed with perfect snow. All around, I see nothing but black December sky, the dimmed houses, and their shoveled walks. I feel hypnotized and dazed by the way it all swerves around my head in an endless loophole of stars and questions, around and around. Houses, sky, December, biopsy—one revolving and forever-developing picture. Soon, however, I sense that the sky is softening, warming, lightening. But it isn't my thoughts. It's true.

I stop walking.

I look around, down at my feet.

I find that I'm standing on what looks like an oval track in the snow, standing where some heavy-footed, downtrodden person has walked around and around in restless agitation. The walking has worn a path into the snow, down to the frozen grass.

Then I see the sky has turned the rosy, frozen blue of a December morning. I hear giddy laughter to my right, and I see two kids, a boy and a girl in winter clothing. They are holding a brand-new sled and a camera. They are looking at me.

A flash—they take my picture.

"Hey!" I shout, running after them. "What are you doing?"

"Get out of here!" the boy yells to the girl, grabbing her red sweater and pulling her by the arm. Like startled deer, they bound toward a nearby house. As I run, I sense that they were making fun of me, and so I hustle after them across the snow of Smith Park, lifting my knees high like a linebacker hoofing it through the tire drill.

Before they can escape into the house—a small, pale brick house with a clean-shoveled walk—I catch them both by the shoulder and spin them around. Brother and sister, I think to myself, vetting them up and down. But when I look closer, I see that they are teenagers: boyfriend and girlfriend. In love, too. I can smell the love. Like the first light and wind reflected off the first December snow. Immediately, I realize the camera and the sled they carry are newly opened gifts to each other.

"Thought you were Santa Claus, mister," the girl says, smiling. "Haven't we seen you before?"

"I live around here," I answer, circling a finger in the air. "Down past Main."

"Thought you were Saint Nick, dude," the boy laughs. "Well, gotta go."

"What were you doing out there?" the girl asks, hanging on her boyfriend's arm. "My mom almost called the cops on Thursday."

"Yeah," the boy says. "My dad is a cop. I almost called *him.*"

"Walking," I say. "I got a lot on my mind."

"Walking!" the boy bursts out. "Just!"

"A lot!" the girl laughs. "We almost called the cops!"

I look at them. They are looking at something, looking at me. They see something I don't.

Then I look at their house. My reflection, in the big living room window—a distant close-up. I check my mirror, check it again. I see myself in the house's mirrored front window, a club-carrying prehistoric fire starter preserved in ice. I see the clothes I'm wearing: some bum's crazy getup. It looks like I haven't shaved for days. I look fifty. My right hand flies to my face, and the teenage lovebirds twitter and chuckle again as I probe the stubble on my sunken cheeks. I watch as the reflection in the window mirror adjusts the orange hunter's hat; screws it down more tightly on his head with both hands; fixes the earflaps; buttons up the mackinaw; stamps his cold feet in the mud-colored irrigation boots to get some blood circulating through his tingling toes. The young couple laughs and smiles at me as I stand transfixed by my own image, by my own first impressions of myself.

"Uh, yeah," the boy whispers out of the side of his mouth to his girlfriend, tapping his temple. "This is a first. Let's cruise, huh? Saint Nick's, uh, a little loose upstairs?"

He tugs at his girlfriend's arm. But she holds on for a question.

"Really," she says. "What were you doing? What are you *doing?*"

And even though her boyfriend laughs at me, mocks me right there in my boots, I say it. And it is delicious to me, like something I've never tasted before.

"Mmm," I say. "Just trying to keep it alive, man. Keep it alive."

TRUSTING LILLY

Coke Newell

WHEN I JUMPED THAT WESTBOUND train climbing north out of Fraser, Colorado, I wasn't intending to come back. Not for her. Not for anybody.

The soggy June fields between Tabernash and the pulp mills were literally hopping with deer mice, and I'd had to scrape back and forth across the long grass with the toe of my boot for a full five minutes before I felt safe in throwing my bag out. Sleeping with mice is one thing; lying down and hearing a couple-three go squish is something else entirely.

It was my second trip through that area with the dog, and I mean a canine: cute little Aussie shepherd unit with eyes the color of the Minnesota sky in late November. Good dog, too. Picked her up at a roadside roof north of Torrington, Wyoming, and I mean a roof. Trucker coming west out of Wisconsin said they called them "ramadas," which I always thought was a brand of hotel. That's what I told the trucker, big fat dude that never quit sucking on the stub of a cold cigar. Never lit it, just sucked and sucked, rolling it around. Spit little bits of tobacco toward the dashboard every half-mile or so, I didn't count. Anyway, that's what I said to him, and he replied, yeah, that's probably why the hotel got its name, Spanish word meaning place of rest or something like that.

So anyway, there's just these two corrugated steel roofs on top of big metal Highway Department posts out there on the side of the two-lane highway in Nowheresville, Wyoming, absolute heaven-in-every-direction Nowhere. Kind of country makes a man feel he's the most blessed important creature ever born, yet the country itself probably never knowing you or any other man ever existed, and caring less.

But here's this dog, just sitting there wagging its tail at me for a good quarter-mile as I come hiking up, me let out at a ranch road three miles back, Bronco Buster heading home to the missus after picking up a cow branding something-or-other back in Lusk. I said, bet you couldn't find one of those at the Ace Hardware in St. Paul, and the guy just looks at me like I'm the dumbest man ever walked.

I bet you couldn't.

So I walk up talking soft. Dog never stood up until I was ten feet away; just sat there wagging its tail, probably guarding the spot for its owner's return, the faithful best friend. Only in the two hours I sat there talking to her before the next car came by and on through the next thirty minutes until one actually stopped, coupla cotton-headed giggle giggle cowgirls in Mama's minivan, and gave us a ride, no owner ever came.

So I called her Princess, and she came with me.

It was that summer I first slept in the wildflower fields south of Fraser. By then I had both Princesses, the one who loved me forever after I gave her a can of Alpo Choice Cuts in the parking lot of a Safeway in Cheyenne and only left me 'cause she got taken, and the other who touched my soul, melted right into my heart and swore she'd never leave me and then did just that not four months later when I told her I wanted to go south and see the Cedar Waxwings come through Madera Canyon migrating south, and she said she wanted to go home to see Jesus.

Well, I'd never been on a road to heaven anyway, and that just served to piss me off at first. I mean, she'd never brought it up before, and I wondered what kind of game she was playing. Which particular comment, voiced, didn't help. We stood there on an aspen-gilded hillside northeast of Santa Fe while Princess One chased spruce squirrels and chipmunks and Princess Two—her name was Lilly Anne Matriche—buried her face in her beautiful knees and cried. Said she'd broken her parents' hearts, freaked out her little brothers and sisters, maybe even put herself at serious risk of life and limb. Possibly even pregnant, although we'd done what we could to avoid that.

We had talked about everything important on earth—meat-eating and war and Iraqi oil and the total boneheadedness of public school and DARE and the merits of relocating to Canada or Australia, either one—but she never told me the God thing. Which is the one thing I did not want to talk about. That and her leaving me.

See, me and the dog had been heading southbound out of Durango on the road that eventually crosses the big rez, and here's this girl selling apricots.

I said, just to talk, "Where's the fruit from?" And she said, oh, I picked it here and around. I'm thinking, yeah, right, no apricots for a hundred miles, clear to Grand Junction at least, and probably not there this early in the year.

But I didn't want to walk on, so I said, "What about the bags?" Perfectly crisp little brown bags, like right out of a grocery store. Hand-lettered sign saying, APRICOTS: DOLLAR A BAG. And she said, straight out, oh, I borrowed these from the City Market. Smiling at me.

God, and I don't mean Jesus, she was beautiful.

I laughed, and she says, "What's your dog's name?"

So I told her that whole story, her practically tearing up at the Ramada Roof in Wyoming thing, a good dog just left out in the middle of nowhere, and I asked her why she was selling apricots. Sitting on a curb two hundred feet from the City Market didn't bug me at all; I'm an entrepreneur of sorts. I just wanted to know: Why apricots? And to talk a little longer. I'd been on the road longer than I cared to think, since life went to hell back home, and I just wanted to talk.

The dog had cuddled right up to her, so close and so quickly I was wondering if maybe the girl was the one who left her in Wyoming in the first place. For about five seconds. But she said, real circumspectly, "I'm trying to get to Portland."

Alone. Out of money.

Well, long story short, which is kind of how ours turned out, I asked her if that was home and she said no way, it's where a girlfriend's family had moved that winter, the place she was going to find refuge. I said, from what, thinking somebody hurt this girl I'll bust their head, but she just told me her family was nuts; I think her words were "religious kooks."

It took a few days to build up some trust. It really freaked me out that she was traveling all alone looking like she did, and only eighteen years old. So I told her so, the realities of crossing the country, and she said no crap, tell me about it. Reluctant to cuss and kind of drawing back into herself. All the way from Baton Rouge in four days, guys offering all varieties of help.

Well, I sat down on the other side of the dog and just looked off to the south.

She said, "What about you?"

And I looked back at her, right into her almond-brown eyes, and said, "I'm going to Portland." Which she didn't believe at all.

But I did. Something in the air there, and it wasn't, I swear, just me wanting to get into her sleeping bag. I had only four years on this girl, but I'd been mostly on the road for seven, and by God or Buddha or whoever cared I was really tired of being alone. Not a single friggin' direction in the world and sick of it. So I committed right there. I said, I mean it, I won't be able to live with myself knowing I left you all alone. A traveling partner to Portland, a few pesos for the journey, and I'll keep my hands to myself.

She looked at me a while, then at the dog, then said okay.

I said back, I'll prove it: we'll camp right here above Durango for a few days, let me make a few bucks doing day labor, sleep in our own tents. And she said, looking right into me: I trust you.

Test me, okay, but *trust* me I thought was a little premature.

"Let me prove it," I said.

And she said, "I trust the dog, and she obviously loves you."

So that's what we did. We stayed right there in the piñon woods above town, she in her bedroll, me in mine. I got a gig unloading freight at the Wal-Mart, me and a bunch of Navajos up from the rez. Way they do it in Durango: cash-daily migrant workers everywhere but the law offices, I suppose, and probably a few there.

Day two I was actually afraid Lilly Anne wouldn't be there when I got back at night, and I told her as much. She said, how 'bout I come down and hang out around Wal-Mart all day so you can keep an eye on me? And I said, I'd like that, but please leave the merchandise on the shelves 'cause a shoplifting rap will wrap our trip up quick. I said "our." And then added: And I'd just have to hang around waiting for you till they let you out.

She kissed me quick on the cheek and said, "You're sweet, Nick, see you tonight."

And she did.

Eighty-seven dollars in our pockets, we made Colorado's North Park on day seven and made out for the first time right there in the Mouse Meadow, Princess One rolling (alone) in the cool afternoon grass thirty feet away.

We never did get to Portland. I convinced Lilly Anne to at least send her folks a postcard from Steamboat Springs, saying, man, if I had parents I'd let them know, girl, they gotta be going nuts. To which she agreed: *Mom and Dad, I'm okay, I'm safe, and almost to Portland. A friend is helping me out, bye.*

We got as far as Craig on U.S. 40, then headed south and west to Grand Junction, where we pitched our tents (gear in hers, bodies in mine) in a farmer's field and picked bing cherries for almost three weeks, then summer apples.

Plenty of food and nearly four-hundred dollars between us, one day we bought a big truck-tire inner tube at a Sinclair station and floated seven hours down the Colorado River, the dog right on Lilly's or my lap most of the way, then all of us climbing out somewhere east of Moab. We followed a slot canyon back into the cool north bank of a low mesa and set up housekeeping. Princesses One and Two both thought this was the finest spot on earth, and I told them both it was. We'd bathe in the river, day-trip into Moab once a week for vittles, hike and read and just lie around, the dog coming to believe she actually owned the place. Until August, when even the slot canyon was hitting eighty degrees before ten A.M. and all three of us were needing some high-country cool.

It was at a country market in Gunnison that some guy buying fishing tackle mentioned the Sangre de Cristos. He and the clerk, talking big fish and deep water. Lilly Anne walked right up to him and said, "What are the Sangre de Cristos?" Saying it real foreign-like, which I suppose it is.

And the guy just stared at her and said, "Mountains, range over east of here."

Lilly Anne said, "How far?"

And the guy looked up to see me coming closer with the dog—they don't even care in Gunnison—and says, "I suppose that depends on where you want to go. 'Bout sixty miles to Poncha Springs, up over Monarch Pass, then south into the San Luis Valley," which he pronounced "Looey." "You can head up into the Crestones from there, not a lot of roads, or clear down to Taos and Santa Fe. All the same range."

We got as far as Red River, New Mexico, before Lilly Anne went to Jesus pieces on me.

She called her folks from a pay phone in front of the Red River Laundromat while I watched a doe mule deer and three identical fawns still in spot cross the highway, just amble right across, four of the fifty-eight residents of that heartbreaking little town.

I shuffled on over near the phone booth, and I could hear her dad crying, actually pleading with her to please just catch a bus or find the nearest airport, they'd pay for the ride and meet her anywhere she wanted. Lilly crying back, then sobbing to her mother, I'm sorry, I'm sorry.

So we sat at a broken-down picnic table near the river and just kind of stared for nearly two hours. She let me hold her hand—in fact she held real tight, but that's as far as it was going. She told me about the call, and we talked about her home and family for quite a while, her Mormon family, always so damn happy and solid and sweet she had decided it just couldn't be real, it couldn't be everything. So she decided to shatter every dream they'd ever had for her and hit the road like a gypsy, hit that daisy-train highway all the way to the West Coast.

But now she was really wanting to go home. Something broken back in Baton Rouge.

Finally I said, baby girl, I love you, what did I do? And she said, it wasn't you, it was these mountains.

I said, "These mountains make you want to go back to Louisiana?"

And she said, "No, what they mean—Sangre de Cristo." And just stared at me like I should know something.

I actually raised my left hand and shrugged, my right hand so tight around hers my own knuckles hurt. I did not want to lose this girl, but there was a ticket in her pocket. Just one. And she still looked at me. I know now what she was doing, probably wondering if I was worthy of her confession. Or if she was.

She said: the Blood of Christ.

I almost said bullshit, but she really meant it; it was coming out all over her face. So I just said, Lilly-girl, tell me about it. But she just shook her head and looked down, so I had no idea what was going on in there.

And then the bus came and my princess kissed me real long, hugged the dog, then climbed on that big bus and went away.

I spent that fall picking fruit in Grand Junction, living in a tent out under the Book Cliffs. Then I got an actual job stacking caramel corn and Twinkies at the Wal-Mart and rented a little trailer home on Grand Avenue near the river for the winter. Me and Princess headed down toward Moab a couple of times just to sit on the lip of the bluff and look off across the canyon, my eyes seeing nothing beyond what was in my head. For weeks the dog was as morose as I was.

Come April we cashed the last paycheck, closed the door and headed back to the Sangre de Cristos just so I could sit at that picnic table in Red River and try to relive, relieve, do anything of the sort. Nothing worked.

She had written her address on a ripped chunk of a cereal box top and stuffed it in my pack, but I never wrote her until right there in Red River nearly seven months later, which was stupid because no way could she write me back. But it was sincere, oh god, it was everything left in my heart:

My dearest Lilly Anne,

I am sorry I have not written before. Now that you are back home, perhaps you no longer care to hear from me, and I suppose I will come to understand if that is the case. But Lilly-girl, I love you. My whole soul hurts daily, hourly, minute by minute as I remember what you are, what we had, and where we wanted to go.

We did love, didn't we.

I hope to write again (and send an address).

In complete love and loneliness,
Nicholas Who Loved You

Me and Princess Number One, who I'd taken to thinking of as Princess Number Two, headed back to the north, taking the long route through Winter Park and Fraser just because I had to do the full circle. And that's where one more ending turned into a beginning, although of what I'm still not entirely sure.

We were walking a back road south of the wood-pulp mill, having spent a cool night full of crickets and scritch-scratch in the Meadow of a Million Mice just north of town. I had just decided that night, and especially that morning when the sun came up over the mountains, that it was time to move on, move ahead, to get back to *Still Life with Nobody* and to nothing, especially not the heartache. Me and the dog. So anxious was I to get gone that we jumped an empty boxcar at the pulp mill on a Union Pacific heading all the way to Portland.

I was hanging back in the shadows until we got out of town, trying to keep Princess right there with me, but at the sound of some kids playing across the field she headed right out into the full sunlit doorway and stood there, wagging her tail. And one of them shot her, right through the brisket. I can't say that they were aiming for her, they may have just been peppering the sides of the boxcars as they went by, the weekly ritual, but she sat down, and then fell to her side and lay there bleeding. I saw her fall about the same time I saw the kid yelling to his buddy and pointing from the far side of the meadow, the Mice Meadow, and I knew something was wrong.

I just sat there and held my dog over my legs as she whimpered and wagged her tail until it stopped. And then I just sat there.

When the train finally stopped in Ogden, Utah, I carried my princess to a shady spot on the Weber River and laid her down as deep as I could in some rocky soil under a cottonwood. At some point I realized I was digging in Mormon soil, planting a piece of my heart. I didn't know much else, but by then I'd had some time to look at life with a long lens, and so I sniffed the wind, threw a few pebbles in the creek, and headed back to the rail yard as lonely as I've ever been.

So now I'm somewhere in the middle of Nebraska, the rails roughly paralleling the North Platte. I'll ride to Omaha, then find my way down to Baton Rouge with only one thought on my mind: Lilly Anne knew nothing more about me than the fact that a dog found me worth trusting. I can't offer her any less about the things I don't, at this point, know for sure.

Zoo Sounds

Margaret Blair Young

A VAGRANT IS PREACHING NEAR THE seals, in front of the pool fence. "The world looks on your outward appearance," he says. "God considers your heart." A toddler in overalls peeks between the vagrant's legs to see the seals. His mother says, "Sir, you're blocking the view."

The vagrant looks at her till she jerks her eyes away. He opens his arms. "Ma'am," he says, "may I witness to you?"

The woman strides away with her son.

But Martha stays. Martha listens. She is behind a bushy pine and doesn't think he can see her. He speaks into the air. "Then there was that fool, built his house on sand. You know that one, don't you?" Suddenly, he is looking straight at her.

She doesn't answer, but she doesn't move either. The man looks so much like Dallen, though his jeans are two sizes too big, his beard a dirty red tuft, his hair a mass of frizz, backlit by the sun and glinting like a rusty halo. Dallen is not that unkempt.

She had seen Dallen the day before. He had sobbed and called her Mommy. "This place—you can't imagine what goes on. Please, Mommy—I've changed! Get me out!"

She promised to do all she could, and told her husband when he opened the door that evening, "We've got to find him a good lawyer, Ross. We have got to do that."

Ross was returning from a bishop's court, which she knew he wouldn't discuss with her.

"Ross?"

He gave her a quick look and a smile that tried to be more than it was. Brushing past her, he said, "Could we chat about this over dinner, please? I've been fasting, and I'm famished." Ross had opted out of Dallen's pain, drugged himself with some spiritual endorphin the way Dallen drugged himself with opiates. He was spending his compassion on someone else's son, hearing someone else's son's confessions, then reading him scriptures on mercy.

Ross moved towards the fridge. He spread mayo on his bread as she spoke to him: "It's obvious to me that that agent—" (she thought an unspeakable word) "—he entrapped Dallen. Baited him." Another unspeakable idled between her mind and her mouth. "He threatened him—threatened his life—if he didn't make the deal."

"Answer me this." Ross arranged his cheese and spoke quietly, his back to her. "Did Dallen buy the pot? Yes. Did he lead the agent to the crack? Yes. Why should we hire a lawyer? To pirouette around his guilt? Why?"

"Because," she said, eyes burning, "he's my son!"

He slid his eyes sidewise to give her a wilting glance.

"Our son," she corrected thinly.

"You'd hire a lawyer for Adam and Eve."

"If they were mine," she answered. "And if it would help!"

He bit into his sandwich and faced her. "I've seen the way God works, Marti. Tonight, I've seen it."

"I'm sure you have."

"There have to be consequences. The wages of sin is death, and the wages of dealing is jail. This may be the greatest lesson he'll ever learn. It may be the only way he comes back. By eating pig slop for awhile."

She tried to nod, but couldn't. "They baited him!" she repeated. "That asshole baited him!"

Ross stopped with the sandwich just before his open mouth. "What did you say?"

She ran, grabbing her purse and slamming the door behind her, muttering down the walk, "Asshole is what I said." Her shoes clacked on the cement. "And shouldn't you close that sermon in the name of Jesus Christ amen, Bishop? Yes, I said asshole."

Though the bad words were usually in her mind, they rarely got out. From the first time Dallen had dumped Cheerios on the kitchen floor, or smeared her lipstick over the bathroom mirror, or pulled his sister's hair, bad words had oozed like thick poison into the vocabulary of her heart. Once, when Dallen emptied the syrup bottle into the bathtub, she had said in her mind, *God damn you.*

The vagrant moves on. Feeders arrive with fish for the seals. Families are filling up the bleachers; there will be a show as the seals earn their keep and let the humans bait them.

Martha watches an androgynous teenager dangle a foot-long herring. A seal leaps for it, and two other seals clap the deck and bark. A middle-aged father wipes the smudge of pink ice cream on his baby's cheek. A mother says to her boy, "Did you see that one jump? This is better than Chuck E. Cheese any day!" The boy rolls his eyes and whispers, "Right."

Martha goes to the aviary, which used to be Dallen's favorite hangout. One Saturday, when he was thinking himself an artist, he had spent four hours there, sketching toucans. And when he showed her his work, Martha dismissed it with "Nice," and reminded him what chores were waiting.

Dallen said then, "I used to have this nightmare. You're chasing me with a vacuum cleaner, and you chase me off a cliff. No kidding."

She found the toucans in the trash the next morning.

This is one of the many incidents she punishes herself with as the toucans cock their heads, measuring her.

The aviary is domed, mostly glass, with netting to contain the birds but give them that illusion of freedom. Inside it's hot, muggy, an imitation of the tropics. A film of sweat starts on her brow, and she supposes the last traces of her makeup will be compelled into wet beads. She remembers Dallen's toucans in detail, and decides they were remarkable, full of life and color and imagination. She will say that to him. She will urge him to be an artist. She repeats it in her mind, *Talent like that—you really should pursue*—as a voice behind her calls, "Sister Hines!"

She turns. It's Stephanie Smith, from the ward. Martha wonders if Stephanie is the first scout of the posse Ross has sent after her. Her watch says 5:25. She has been gone for twenty-two hours. And it's September eighth. Her wedding anniversary.

She says, "Oh." And, "How are you, Stephanie?"

"Don't you love this place?"

Stephanie's father is Ross's first counselor in the bishopric. And a lawyer. Stephanie is Dallen's age and on the chubby side of pretty. Dallen and Steph even went on a date, before everything.

Martha says, "Yes, I love this place," willing her lips to curve into something like a smile. "Is your whole family here?" She sees the vagrant next to the trash can, and he sees her.

"No, just Glo and me," says Stephanie. "Glo has this thing for snakes. I'll take birds any day."

Martha repeats "birds" and eases her eyes from the vagrant.

"So is your whole family here, Sister Hines?"

She thinks, *I have no whole family*, and says, "No."

"Don't you love the parakeets?"

Martha looks at two blue parakeets perched on a banana tree. She says, "Was it your brother's parakeet our cat killed?"

"What?"

"Or maybe it was Joey Faltron's. Dallen was supposed to look after it while the Faltrons were on vacation. Yes, it was theirs. And he left the cage open, and our cat got it. Blue parakeet, like those. Do you remember our cat Linny?"

"You had a cat?"

"I came into Dallen's room, and Linny had her teeth around the little blue head." A green parakeet cackle-chirps, purrs, whistles as it pecks at a seed cone. Martha watches. "You don't think of your pet being a killer. It takes you completely by surprise. You look at it, and you can't—you just can't believe it. And then you remember it really is a cat, even though you're always feeding it from the table. You never saw the signs. It kills birds." Martha manages her bishop's wife's smile like a change of subject, and sits on the stone wall. She has not slept since the night before last, and she has not eaten since she left home, though her stomach is resisting food. Stephanie is nibbling a huge sugar cookie with pink frosting.

"I've never liked cats," says Stephanie. "Maybe that's why."

Martha returns to the parakeet and the seed cone. "I gave Linny away. I took her to the Humane Society, and I don't know what happened after I left. I did that right after I rescued the parakeet. But I didn't rescue the parakeet, did I. It was dead. If I had gotten there five minutes earlier . . ."

"Yeah." She takes another bite.

"If I had seen the signs."

"I had a dachshund got hit by a car." Stephanie shrugs. "Anyway, I love the parakeets."

"I love the finches," says Martha, and she looks at her watch again. Then her eyes drift to the vagrant. "Oh my," she says, "I've got to get home." She stands and backs away. "Good to see you, Stephanie." She executes another bishop's wife's smile.

But she doesn't go home. She goes outside the aviary, notes that the sun is setting, then makes her way to the monkeys. She watches them swing from plastic trees. She notices their poor little outgrown bottoms, red and sore and unnatural. Monkeys always get that way in captivity, she has heard. A marmoset makes kissy lips, swings itself across the fake tree, and laughs mutely. She remembers when Dallen fell from the backyard birch and broke his arm, and she said, "This didn't have to happen, you know. Carelessness, that's all it is."

She left her cell phone at home, so she goes to the outdoor phone booth and looks up *Attorneys* in the yellow pages. Thousands of attorneys. She doesn't dial. She thinks of what she could sell to pay a lawyer. The car is in Ross's name. She could pawn her wedding rings, and then buy them back doing phone soliciting or housecleaning. Or maybe Stephanie's father would take the case for free—if she could get him to understand how things had happened, how the asshole had baited her son. She imagines herself pleading with Brother Smith, but she can hear his answer: "There must be consequences, Marti." In Ross's voice, in Ross's suit, eating a cheese sandwich. It's her guilt he's talking about. She is the one who kept a perfect house but murdered the parakeet. The one who said *God damn you* over spilled syrup. The one who chased her boy off a cliff with a vacuum. God is seeing past outward appearance to her riddled heart, and the monkeys are hooting like hysterical angels. Spider monkeys on a steel jungle gym.

"Anyone who thinks they're descended from one of those needs a good chat with Jesus." The vagrant's voice. "You think that's your great-great-grandpa there?" he says.

"No." She doesn't look at him. "That one's female."

He snorts a laugh. Dallen's laugh was always softer.

"Male and female created He them. But not in His image, not those monkeys. You and me, however, we're in God's image. But you know that. Don't you."

"Sure."

"Ma'am?"

She does not want to face him, but she has no choice. Her body jerks as she turns.

"I saw you by the seals," he says. "I thought maybe you were why God said come here today." He scratches his beard and grins. His teeth are remarkably white and straight, the teeth of an orthodontist's first-born. "Are you?"

"No," she says. "That wouldn't be me."

"Maybe you just don't know it."

She tries to make her voice even and generous. It comes out mean. "Am I supposed to give you my purse?"

"Well, that's not usually how it works, but I guess if God tells your heart—"

She lets herself see how skinny he is. "Do you have a place to stay?" she asks.

"Oh, sure."

"You're homeless, aren't you."

"Me?" When he smiles, his cheeks shine. Though his clothes and beard are filthy, his face is immaculate, eyes azure and lively. The sun, halfway sunk, is so bright behind his head that she has to shield her eyes.

"Where did you stay last night?" She's using the tone that could include phrases like *This didn't have to happen, you know* and *I'm just disappointed in you, that's all.*

His eyes meet hers, and she looks down, away from the light. "Where'd you stay, ma'am?"

She returns her gaze to the monkeys. The vagrant whispers, "God loves you."

"Oh," she half-laughs, "is that right? Is that what He said?"

"And His arms are around you. Even now."

She narrows her eyes and faces him. "Tell him to go away."

He shakes his head slowly. "That isn't what you want."

"Isn't it?"

He says something. He's speaking so quietly she has to strain to hear.
"What?" she says.

"What do you want?" he repeats.

A family—husband, wife, son in a stroller—pass them. The baby's
white hair curls at his neck. Softly, so only the vagrant can hear, Martha
says, "Why did you leave home?"

He folds his arms.

"Did God say for you to leave?"

He shifts his weight and uses a more public voice. "Hadn't found
God yet."

"Did you have a fight with your mother?"

He smiles big again, and Martha smiles too, as much as she can.

"Just one of those things," he says.

"The two are not related," she whispers, glancing away.

"What?"

"Do you have a name?"

"Do you care?"

"Sure I do."

"Jacob."

"Ah. From the Old Testament."

"That's it. Angel wrestler." He thrusts his hands into his pockets.
"And if God tells me to change my name, I will."

"I have no doubt." She can see her image in the glass which
separates her from the indoor monkeys. She looks hideous, thin and
straggly and gray. She is not usually this ugly or this old. "So," she
says, combing her hair with her fingers, "did your mother chase you
off with a vacuum?"

She can see his face in the glass, too. His eyes close as he says,
"No."

It's two minutes to six now. A generic voice announces that the
zoo will close in thirty minutes, and thanks for coming.

So Martha and Jacob leave the zoo. They're a long way from the
birds, but Martha can still hear them squawking and flapping against
the confines of their illusion. She can hear the long, lonely wails of the
seals in the distance. She's sure she can hear them. These are the sounds
she spent the night with. She turns to Jacob and says, "I don't have a
car with me, and I live seven miles away."

When he grins, his whole face shines. "You're inviting me home, aren't you."

"And maybe for a burger before? You look wan."

"Thank you."

"I didn't mean—"

"For the invitation."

"I thought you might be famished."

"You nailed it." He bounces with his steps, leads with his hips.

"Have you been fasting?"

He laughs gently. "Not on purpose."

Across the road is the "This Is the Place" monument. She explains when they arrive, "That's not how it happened, you know. That statue, with Brigham Young standing all sure of himself? It's a lie. He was sick as a dog. Rocky Mountain spotted fever. From a tick, from this little tiny bug. Took all his strength to just sit up in the wagon and say anything."

Jacob puts his hands on his hips, like he's set to strut. "Then why did they have the statue like that then?"

"Oh, to make him infallible. So we wouldn't think we were his illusion. So we wouldn't doubt things. Mind if we sit?" She does not sit; she collapses. Prostrate, eyes closed, she says, "The statue should be like this," and holds her hand up. " 'This is the place, move on.' " She opens one eye. "I hope you're not dangerous, Jacob."

"Me?"

"Because I think if I don't rest, I'll keel over and expire."

"No, no, this is not the place to keel over and expire, ma'am."

"Martha." She opens the other eye.

"Martha," he nods. "Careful and troubled about many things."

"Oh, stop. No more scriptures. You're showing off. You're baiting me."

He considers this, his head cocked like the toucans'. A breeze moves through the grass, parts his coarse hair, and he looks skyward.

To Martha, the sky seems to be receding, the blue getting deeper and darker. "Jacob," she sighs, "I haven't slept in a while. Normally I think scriptures are peachy. But at the moment, they exhaust me. Were you always like this?" Her words slur; her head throbs.

Jacob breathes in deeply and says, "Nah, I've mostly been a lost cause. Left home and went hitchhiking. And somewhere near Boze-man, Montana—ever been there?"

She shakes her head and closes her eyes.

"Well, here I am, hiking, and there's this guy, this stark-naked guy standing on the road. No fooling. He's holding a sign that says REPENT IN THE RAW. Cars are honking him down, and he's just standing there blowing in the wind. So I'm thinking, well, should I duck down some-where? Or just run past him? And the next thing I know, he's right next to me, saying he's been waiting and that God told him I'd be along any minute."

"So you stripped on the spot, right? Went streaking down I-15 together?" Though she doesn't open her eyes, she can tell he's smiling. He doesn't speak until she looks up. Then she sees him. He's on his knees.

"Oh no, you're not praying, are you?" she says, half sitting.

"Nah."

"Because you know what that feels like? Like mockery, is what that feels like." She waits, then murmurs again, "The two are not related."

"The two what?"

Suddenly alert, she says, "Nothing. I'm sorry for interrupting. You met this nudist on the highway and so you—go on, take it from there."

He shrugs. "So I listened. That's all."

"And you had an epiphany? A conversion?" There's a cluster of sego lilies near the road. Martha watches them flutter. The fading light is turning them dingy.

"God said to me, through the stars, and through the trees and in the wind, God said, 'I love you, and if you give me your heart, things will be okay.' "

The sego lilies dance. She can imagine them swaying to Jacob's script. "Well, I'm glad for you," she says, and gets up on all fours. "I think that's real nice." A waxing moon (she remembers the phrase *gib-bous moon* from a report she helped Dallen with a decade ago) is just above the mountains. She feels she could howl at it. She says, "I'm almost ready. We can start."

When he offers his hand, she accepts. He doesn't let go once she has her footing. He is holding her hand like he loves her, and she doesn't mind. They start down Wakara Way, then down Sunnyside. They walk past shops and restaurants, past the old houses, down Thirteenth East. At Westminster College, she tells him about the windows—the old ones the college just gave away to anyone with a truck, because they were remodeling. That was when Dallen came up with his Eagle Scout project. He would build a greenhouse with those windows and grow tomatoes for the poor. She exhales a deep, weary breath and whispers, "The two are not related."

"You said it again."

"What?"

"You said 'the two are not related.' "

"It's a phrase stuck in my head. Sorry."

"The two what?"

Martha glances at their joined hands. As cars approach, she can see herself and Jacob lit up by headlights, can even see her wedding diamonds sparkle briefly, though it's dark enough now that she can't see who's in the cars, can only imagine which drivers are asking, "Isn't that the bishop's wife? Who's that with her?" When she frees her hand, he squeezes, then lets it go.

"Liberty Park is down that street." She points. "There's an aviary there. Bigger than the zoo's. A few years back, someone went in and murdered all the most valuable birds—all the ones whose species were dying out. This person—this terrible person—he executed them." She sniffs. "Like some—some god of chaos."

Jacob clucks his tongue.

"They never found out who it was."

"Well, he knows."

"One of the birds was an eagle. Bald eagle."

"Now that's a shame."

"And it was the day after Dallen gave up on his—though the two are not related." She draws a deep breath and sighs it out. Then the words pour. Her voice is higher than usual, and strained: "But I had told him he owed it to me to be neater and more diligent, and I didn't know he had started the bad things, nobody told me, I didn't see the signs, and I said I was so tired of picking up after him, and that damn greenhouse was dismantling the whole backyard, all my work and my garden, and the damn greenhouse would never be done and he was bringing chaos to my home—but I didn't say damn—and I hated the way things were, that God-damned Eagle project, but I didn't say God-damned."

She takes a quaking breath, and her eyes fill. "It was like his face clicked off. And then the next day—the next day—at the aviary—but the two are not—"

"Martha—"

"The two are not related." She is shivering.

"God," says Jacob. "God, you're in such pain," and he brings her head to his chest and cradles it. When she gives in to crying, he holds her tightly and lets her.

It is fully night when she eases herself from his arms, apologizing, and they begin their walk again. She tells him about the undercover agent who baited Dallen. She tells him she wants a lawyer. She tells him she thinks she's the one who should go to jail. "It's the mothers," she says, "who train the children. When a child fails, it's the mother's fault. I heard someone say that once. In those words."

"They were lying," says Jacob.

"My husband said it," she answers. "My husband, my bishop, my judge." She looks away. "He didn't mean me. Not necessarily. It was years ago. In a talk. When a child fails, it's the—"

"He's wrong," Jacob says gently. "Martha, he's wrong." Even in the moonlight, she can see the copper glint in his hair.

"You left because of your mother," she accuses softly. "Didn't you."

"I left to find good things. That's all."

"She drove you away." She does not want to cry again, though her voice shakes.

"No," he says, but his tone does not persuade her.

"What would you say to her? If she were here, what would you say?"

For a long time, he does not speak. Then he puts his hands on her shoulders. "This," he says. "I'm sorry. I miss you. And you did the best you could."

"Stop it." She grabs his wrists, flings his hands off her shoulders. "Don't do that. You think that's what I want to hear, but it's not true. You want to tell her she's a bitch and a hypocrite. You want to feed her to the lions. She should have her throat slit. Her clothes should get strewn over the park like dead eagle feathers. She—"

"No!" He matches her volume, then smiles generously, even chuckles. "Hold on a minute. That's not how he feels. That's not what he thinks. Honest to God!"

Her elbows are V'ed, fingers taut before her, like she could claw out his heart. With a sigh, she lets them relax, and massages her temples. "I need a lawyer," she says. "Bad." She finds a piece of straw in her hair, evidence of last night, when she sat a few yards from the camel's fence and listened to the caged animals sleep or howl or hoot until dawn. Zoo sounds. The straw has been in her hair all day, she realizes, so even Stephanie Smith must have noticed. "I really need a lawyer."

"Well, there's always Jesus. Head advocate. Public defender," he says. "Come on, let me witness to you."

"Please don't," she says. "You promised."

"Martha."

"Please?"

They walk. The air is sweet with old roses and marigolds. The streetlamps are glowing now, gnats dancing around their yellow lights like pollen.

She remembers, when they pass Kentucky Fried Chicken, that she promised him a meal, so they go inside and she buys him dinner. Her stomach is too nervous for food, though she sips his water. She asks, "Is there straw in my hair?" and he pulls two more bits from her bangs.

"Damn," she says, and abruptly, "Actually, I don't swear. I'm really a very nice person. Well no, that's not quite true." She considers her words. "I seem to be a very nice person. Put it this way: I make a good show of it. And I don't swear but in my heart."

"You are a very nice person," he says to her eyes. His mouth hardly moves, but she hears these words clearly.

She likes that he eats with dignity. He cuts up his chicken and pauses between bites to pay attention to her. He offers her the tomato from his salad, which she declines.

"So," he says after a swallow, "did your son ever grow those tomatoes in the greenhouse?"

"Oh, the greenhouse isn't half-finished. Although I did put our tomato plants there last autumn—you know, to see if the season would stretch under glass. But there's no roof on it. It's just one big hole in our backyard with four glass walls. Uneven ones."

"Still, that must have been a lot of work." He dabs at his beard with his napkin. Someone, she thinks, has taught him manners.

"It'll never be finished," she says. "That's the way Dallen's always been. He dreams big, but he can't finish. He gets it from me and Ross—my husband."

"You're dreamers, are you?"

"Well, we want to be gods, you know. We want to have family reunions where we make galaxies for our wholesome recreational activity."

He laughs and nods. "Yes, I've heard about the Mormons."

"And right now, our son—"

He reaches across the table, squeezes her hand to stop her. "You can handle some mashed potatoes, can't you?" He holds a spoonful near her mouth.

Shrugging, she opens. It's delicious, warm and peppery. Her mouth and stomach moisten to accept, and when he offers her the rest, she takes it. His eyes are much brighter than Dallen's.

"How far to your house?" he says as they leave.

She points to the hill, tells him it's another half-mile. When a police car passes them, lights flashing, she wonders out loud if Ross has the cops after her, and if they should find her now, would they arrest Jacob for kidnapping? Shoot first and ask questions later?

She stumbles on a rock and skins her knee just after the hill. It hurts to walk, she comments, but only a little. And suddenly Jacob is lifting her, carrying her in his arms like she used to carry Dallen to bed. "Point the way," he says. She gives the address, then lets her head lie against his chest. She feels herself bounce with his jogger's steps, and then she seems to be floating, drifting into a dream. A bald eagle has her in its talons, but she has no fear of being dropped. The eagle loves her.

When Jacob sets her down, she realizes she has been asleep, and that they're in front of her house. She calls softly, "Ross?" She does not have her keys, and the houselights are off, though she sees the garden lights in the backyard. She is woozy as she walks there.

"So what shall we do if he's out back?" she says to Jacob behind her. "Should I put a bow around your neck and say happy anniversary?"

Ross is there, in the unfinished greenhouse. He's standing inside the glass, a jar of putty in his hands. The kerosene lantern is on the dirt floor and lights his face from below. His face looks very intent, and old, and lost. He's wearing the same white shirt he had on when she left him, though it's streaked with mud and putty now. The silver hairs shine in his brows and on his head, and she loves him achingly. She remembers the warm stream of his tears oozing between her breasts after Dallen's third arrest, when she said, "If God's giving us this trial, He must know we can handle it," and Ross broke down, groaning, "But I can't! I can't! Not this close!"

She says to Jacob, "That's my husband," and moves toward the greenhouse. "Ross," she calls. "Ross?"

When he sees her, his mouth drops slowly to a grimace of pain and relief. He stands still as she approaches, and they gaze at each other with the glass between. Neither speaks. She can see herself as a ghostly reflection, with Ross—more solid and more unsure—just behind her, their two forms half-merged. Her reflection and his body face her. Both have lifted a hand slightly, either as a half-wave or an instinctive move to touch.

She mouths "I'm sorry," and he closes his eyes like the words hurt him, then climbs up the ladder and leaps from the glass to the earth beside her.

"How could you do that to me?" he whispers.

"I did come back," she says, and lets her other hand rise in uncertain invitation. Ross moans and throws his arms around her, his embrace so hard it hurts her ribs. "How could you kill me like that?" he breathes into her hair. "Do you know what I've gone through? Do you—"

"Ross," she says, and moves her arms around his familiar waist. "We'll talk. We'll talk."

Jacob is watching. His face seems somehow lit from inside, his clothes less ragged than they had been. He makes a simple, graceful gesture with his arms, upward and out.

WHO BROUGHT FORTH
THIS CHRISTMAS DEMON

Larry Menlove

TIM'S WIFE LEFT HIM WITH THREE DOZEN blue spruce still trussed up on the truck and better than fifty juniper, Scotch, red cedar, and Douglas on the lot. She left him when he was finishing up a sale with a stunning customer. He remembered this—and he had a photo of her foot on his phone to remind him. The thing was, this gorgeous woman, with flaxen-honey hair, green eyes, perfect cheeks, and a white-teeth smile that singed the needles of the junipers next to her, smelled like unholy hell: some foreign and eccentric perfume. She was no doubt a beautiful woman, but she smelled like a fancy toilet-bowl tablet. His eyes were watering and he was about to sneeze as the lady handed over a crisp fifty for the nine-foot Scotch that she said would fit nicely in the home's great room.

That's when his cell phone rang. It was Karri. His wife.

And Tim had asked Karri to hold on just a minute. And then he had asked this perfect, yet fetid, customer if she wouldn't mind holding the phone. Just hold it for the moment it would take him to hoist the perfect tree into the immaculate bed of her big Dodge truck. And after he'd done that, the smelly goddess had handed the phone (along with the freshly snapped photo of her foot) back to him with a smile because he had given her a deal on the tree—not that she needed a deal. And off she went to the doubtless warmth and love of her home, her husband, two blessedly ideal daughters, and the spayed purebred chocolate Labrador. And then Karri from down deep inside the electronics and mystery of the little phone pressed against his ear said she didn't love him anymore. Told him she was tired of his silly business ventures and waiting to have his children. She was leaving. Today. She had the cat and all she needed. And that was that. And there he was, dead phone, alone, and the chemical stench of that beautiful woman lingering in the still air of winter.

It wasn't until early May that the city letters regarding the trees started to get ugly. Tim had an acquaintance—poker buddy—on the Payson city council who had pulled strings with ordinances and covered up nonactions for as long as he could. But when it came right down to it, it was bare-naked obvious: Right there in the middle of town there were Christmas trees for sale—in May.

Tim had leased the old parking lot at the defunct Safeway from a businessman in Provo. The man was out of reach due to an extended vacation in Guatemala, and the city had no recourse but to go after the lessee. And in fairness, the city had taken its time about it. It had been a wet winter and spring, and all the merchandise in its fading cheer had weathered it fairly well up until the end of April, when someone had reported a rat scurrying in and around the tired trees. And please, in such close proximity to the public library and the Flying Wheel pizzeria across the street. There was no other course of action. The trees had to be removed.

It was a Thursday. Tim got out of bed and poured himself a crystal tumbler of bourbon and water. It was bottom-shelf bourbon and it was early, nearly noon. He could do nothing about the hour; it was what it was. And the economical bourbon? Well, it was alcohol. His once-comfortable savings were nearing closure, and of necessity he had to make concessions somewhere.

Tim ventured out to the mailbox in his "T" monogrammed robe, gathered his mail, and retreated back to the house. He read the final letter from the city, used the envelope as a coaster. The Payson city fathers had given him until the day after tomorrow to remove all the merchandise from the lot, or they would do it and it wouldn't come cheap.

In truth, the trees were not a priority for Tim. There was the high-def TV. There was his belly, becoming quite illustrious and swollen. And there were his cigars.

By the end of February he had burned through all the lovingly preserved premium hand-mades in his humidor—even the box of Cubans he'd smuggled up from Cancun. And as much as it had torn at his hubris lining, he had walked right into the nearest convenience store and bought up twelve packages of the biggest Swisher Sweets cigars they carried. At home in the den he dumped them into the cedar-lined humidor Karri had given him two Valentine's Days ago. He had checked the humidity, added some distilled water to the water pillow, and, praying for a Havana miracle, had closed the lid.

And so Tim lit one now, right there in the kitchen. Like he had lit up one of the Cubans on a Saturday last summer after lunch. Karri had taken the broom up at him then and swept him out onto the deck into the sunlight. It was funny. Then.

He took a long draw on the miserable cigar there at the table and flicked open his cell phone and scrolled to the photo of the woman's foot. It was clad in a black Mary Jane shoe of sorts with a tiny buckle over the top. The parking-lot pavement was slushy-gray, and the buckle shone like a diamond. Tim looked at the photo of the woman's foot ten, twenty times a day. He knew this snapshot captured the very minute everything fell apart for him. It was the proverbial foot putdown.

Tim licked all along the sweetened cheap cigar until the sugar was gone. And then he dunked the head into his bourbon and sucked on that. He smelled bad. His eyes hurt. His private areas were dank and musty from overuse and under-cleansing. He finished his cigar and took a shower.

He got out of the steaming water and quaffed back his tumbler of bourbon. Then he shaved. When he was done he looked in the mirror and saw a stranger. He saw a man from six months before. A man who risked stability in pursuit of riches in ways he thought were calculated. He saw a man who did not realize then what that risk truly was.

He lifted his eyebrow to the clean visitor in the mirror, gave him a very inquisitive observation. This was not the person he'd come to know and scorn over the course of the last four months. This person might just pick up the phone and call his wife. He might take that risk. Tim was curious to know what the old stranger in the mirror would accomplish on this day.

What he accomplished was measured out in exactly 4,707 calories, 2.2 hours of web surfing, twelve flat hours of television, and three hours of staring at the walls waiting for fate to smolder, lick the edges of his being, and combust.

Tim had last heard from Karri on March seventh. She'd called him from her mother's in St. George.

"What ya doin'?" she'd asked him then, like the past three months of estrangement hadn't even been a week, a day.

Tim took a deep breath on his end of the connection. He had read somewhere on the Internet about confrontation and getting what you want. He had read all of Karri's Oprah magazines that kept coming with their Dr. Phil advice. Tim had even renewed Karri's subscription. He thought he was an expert on recognizing relationship foibles and summits and overcoming. He was prepared for this. Knew what he was going to say to convince Karri to come home, to work out this misunderstanding and make her know that he was a good man, a solid, faithful, loving man.

"Bitch," is what he said.

And so that conversation hadn't gone as well as Tim had planned.

After Karri had yelled and screamed and cried and finally, in a tired and quiet voice, let the word *divorce* creep out into their world, Tim hung up the phone, scratched his belly, and went into the pantry. He foraged the potato chips, the oatmeal bars, the gorp, and a marshmallow brownie mix he was certain that Karri had bought well back before Halloween. And Tim ate. He crunched and smacked his way through mountains of oily processed-wheat flour, peanuts, and whey. He had eaten steadily until the word she'd unleashed that day was choked beneath piles of protein, carbohydrate, and both saturated and unsaturated fats.

It was Friday. Tim rolled out of bed and had his bourbon and cigar for breakfast. He looked at the lady's foot on the phone. Donned his robe. The divorce papers were waiting for him in the mailbox.

Irreconcilable differences.

He didn't know what that meant.

Tim sat at the kitchen table and read through the decree trying to find an explanation. Finally, at the end of the document, he spilled bourbon on the line he was supposed to sign. He held a pen over the puckered smudge, thought he should let the paper dry before flourishing his *Tim Oberman* in the ostentatious hand he used, and got sidetracked by the city letter discarded there beside the divorce decree. Two different sheets of paper: one threatening action for not removing nuisance merchandise; one clearly stating the terms of removal from the union of holy matrimony.

So here it was, he thought. What better time to begin scratching his way out of the passive, suicidal spin he was in? His blood seemed to be pumping a little quicker. The day was brighter. And the ground, bedrock.

Tim went into the den and scrounged through his deep and sometimes dubious business drawer and found the number of the sixteen-year-old kid who had helped him on the Christmas-tree lot all those months ago. The kid had helped unload the trees, set them on their stands, sell them with a smile, and tie them up on car roofs. He was a good solid worker. A first-rate employee until Tim hung out the handwritten CLOSED UNTIL FURTHER NOTICE sign. He remembered the boy was handsome in a Nordic way, all the long hair and the cleft in his downy chin. Tim remembered the hangdog look in the boy's eyes when he told him to go home that day Karri dropped the bomb, told him he didn't need him anymore, told him pissin' merry Christmas to you and yours.

Tim felt bad about that last and was going to apologize for it first thing, but the boy wasn't home. He was at school, where he belonged. The boy's mother had suggested Tim call a fellow by the name of Brick.

"Brick?" he'd asked.

"Yes. Brick," the handsome Nordic's mother had said, and gave Tim his phone number.

So Tim called Brick.

Brick answered with a slow, humble, old-Mormon-prophet drawl, "Hello."

"Hi, Brick? This is Tim Oberman. You were referenced to me as someone who might be looking for a little day work. Is that so?"

A pause, and then the sluggish, retiring enunciation. "Well, yes. I am a body looking for work, yes."

"I've got something for you, if you'd like."

Another pause. "What did you say your name was?"

"My name's Tim Oberman. I got some old, ah, trees to clear out."

"Oberman. Can't say as I recognize the family," said Brick. "You live in the ward?"

Tim adjusted the phone in his ear, took a swallow of bourbon. It stuck, and he choked it down, coughed. "I can tell you're of a good Mormon family. I can hear it in your voice."

"Yes," answered Brick, "I am."

"Me, uh, that is, my family fell away from the church some years ago, might be why you don't recognize us. I'm across town anyway. Wouldn't be in your ward, but I've got these trees."

"Trees?"

"Yes. Had myself an investment enterprise last winter. Christmas trees. Fell on hard times."

"Hard times," said Brick. "I understand, yes."

"Are you available today? Need to get these trees moved ASAP."

"You that one down on the highway by the old Safeway?"

Tim finished the finger of bourbon left in his tumbler, glanced around for the bottle. "Yes. That's me."

For the first time in months, Tim felt like a man. A man with underlings, and he pulled his BMW 3 Series into the hired man's driveway. Tim leapt from the car and walked across the dull grass and vivid dandelions to the front door. The house was submissive, submissive and meek like all the other homes in this rundown district on the west side of Payson. He opened the screen door, which fell loose from the clasp and rattled with no spring or closer. Tim knocked on the weathered front door. He pivoted there on the little porch and looked down the weary street. It was a neighborhood where mere continuation seemed to be the greatest pleasure of life. Tim realized he must have booze on his breath and slipped a mint in his mouth.

He heard a rustling behind the door. He turned to face a much-younger man than he'd imagined standing there in a pair of moss-green slacks and a begrimed short-sleeved button-down shirt that was open at the collar. He appeared close to Tim's own age, possibly even younger. Handsome under it all.

"Brick?"

A long pause. Tim was about to say he was sorry, he had the wrong house.

"Yes." Drawn out, a whole sentence in a word.

"Oh, good, good. I'm Tim Oberman. Nice to meet you." He extended his hand, grateful to be making a business deal—modest as this one was.

Brick lay his moist hand into Tim's.

"Are you ready to move some trees?"

A pause, a moment of slow movement, backing up. "Yes. Let me get my gloves."

In the car, Brick insisted on a short prayer before traveling. He bowed his head, and Tim could hear mumbling and an exhaled amen.

"Thank you," Brick said as he looked up and smiled at Tim.

"Sure thing. We all have our ways."

Brick buckled himself into the black leather seat. "Say, this is a nice car."

"Thank you. I like it."

While Tim drove out of the old neighborhood, Brick dug at his left ear with the tip of his finger. He twisted his hand with quick jerking motions as though he were revving a motorcycle throttle. Then he started in on the right ear. His mouth opened as he did, and Tim saw he was missing a canine. The man had watery eyes.

"You lived here long?" asked Tim.

Brick worked his ear and then examined his finger. Gave it a good look. "Oh, not in this ward, but I've lived here in town most of my life, yes."

"Are you married?"

Brick's head twisted and he looked at Tim full on. Tim glanced over. The look on Brick's face was one of fear and incredulity, a mite lost. Brick turned back to face the windshield.

Tim backtracked, "I mean, ah, if that's too personal a question, I apologize." He faked a cough.

Brick said, "You haven't heard?"

"What's that?"

After a sigh, "It's all over town. The bishop . . . son-of-a—" Brick lifted his hands from his lap in fists, held them there in suspension over his crotch. He lowered them against his legs.

"I haven't heard anything," said Tim. "You having some trouble?"

"Well, yes," said Brick, "but I'm not at ease talking to anyone other than my bishop about my worries. I thank you for your concern, though."

Five minutes later they arrived at the Christmas tree lot. Brick lowered his chin and mumbled some more and unbuckled his safety belt.

The air in the lot was warm and dehydrated. A faint odor of musty pine permeated everything like dried-over forest sweat. Several trees lay on their sides, and there were old newspapers and grocery sacks wrapped around the trunks and tangled in the branches. The trees still held some green in their needles. But it was deceptive. The green was brittle, like old trout bone or diseased and desiccated heart sinew.

Tim and Brick stood beside the BMW and looked over the sad mess of it all. A long piece of red ribbon, burned almost white from sunshine and weather, fluttered in the top of a Douglas fir, one of the tall ones, a ten-footer. It was as though they were returning to some forgotten place, an abandoned carnival or festival. A May Day celebration gone wrong. The big GMC was there at the back of the lot next to the old Safeway. The truck's side-paneled bed was filled with trees heaped up on themselves lying on their sides. Shadows hid, buried inside the branches, deep down in, ghosts of Christmas never was.

The two of them stood there and stared at the lot.

Tim said, "Well, I guess the first order is to see if that truck'll start."

He had brought the key from home, though he'd had to search for it. Finally he'd found it in a half-empty can of peanuts next to the bed. Tim put the key in the door lock of the truck. It wasn't even locked. He opened the door, slid up into the cab behind the wheel, and turned the key. The battery was dead.

"I was afraid of that," Tim said. "How about you move these few trees over so I can get the car in there to jump it?"

Brick took his finger out of his ear and leapt to it. Needles showered off the trees, leaving crunchy paths from where the trees had stood for five months to where Brick was putting them now, bunching them together like condemned refugees, each on its own X pedestal. Tim eased the car up next to the big truck.

While he was hooking up the jumper cables, he asked Brick about his name.

"Is it short for Brickowski or something like that?"

"No," answered Brick.

"No?"

"It's just my name. Last name's Smith."

"Brick Smith. Hmm, that's unusual."

"Just my worldly name. Will have it only as long as I am tried here on this earth."

Tim hooked up the cables and let the Beemer's engine idle a while. He said, "I guess you're wondering why the trees have sat here."

"Couldn't sell them?"

Tim sucked at his teeth, craved the Swisher Sweet in the baggie tucked in the Beemer's glove box. He wished he had brought some bourbon. "I gave it up," he said. "My wife, ah, she and I, ah, we had a separation during the holidays."

Tim hadn't spoken openly with anyone since Karri had left. He had suffered the division from his wife in isolation. His parents and siblings were not very close. A few kind words of encouragement were all he got from them. It was just as well for Tim. He preferred enduring the drinking and awful smells emanating up from his body in a self-imposed seclusion. A few friends dropped by the first month, brought him Christmas gifts, tried to match Tim's drinking while they were there, ultimately giving up or passing out on the couch. They cooed, told him it was going to be all right; Karri would come back. If she didn't, there were a million other superior women out there who would jump at the chance. After all, he was youngish, established, respected, still had his hair and physique. Well-intentioned flattery, but his body was shot through and his hair was a mess. He was forty-two and the city was breathing down his neck to clear out his Christmas trees, of all things, in May. Respected? That description was in some serious peril.

Brick was quiet, his finger poised a foot from his ear. He gazed at Tim. The car idled there beside them.

Finally Brick said, "I am sorry to hear that, Brother Oberman, I truly am."

Tim was getting used to Brick's slow Mormon cadence. He found it soothing in an odd way. It was as if Brick's slow deliberate words held more mass, more value.

"Are you divorced then?" asked Brick.

Tim dropped his chin. He drew his hand over his disheveled hair. He looked up at the truck. He scratched his day's growth of beard, listened to the idle of his car, blinked his eyes. "Got the papers this morning."

"That is a tribulation. I am sorry."

The car idled.

"I guess I could rev it."

Tim got in behind the wheel and pressed the accelerator. The engine whooshed like a vortex, sucking in the air around it and pushing it through its works, converting stillness into energy. Brick slipped into the passenger seat beside Tim.

He said, "I am your kindred in troubles, Tim."

Tim was the one to show incredulity now. "Your wife leave you?"

"I have had my trials."

"Your trials?"

The pause.

"Brother Oberman, may I speak to you in openness?"

And then Brick told Tim a story. A story that astonished him. A story of unequaled perversion, the likes of which Tim had heard only rumor of, full of all the bits and pieces of every dirty joke and every deep buried thought of man. A story of love, hate, brawling, balling, propagation, alcohol and drugs, ruination, and above all, abomination. And at the end of his story Brick gazed over at Tim and said, "That's why I pray now."

"Yes," said Tim.

"Yes," said Brick.

"All this, ah, happened?"

"Yes."

"To you?"

"I am in the process of forgiveness or of damnation," said Brick. "I often wonder which path I am on."

The car idled with the jumper cables snaking from under the hood to the truck's battery in an umbilical connection. Tim and Brick looked out the windshield at the black hood.

"I suppose we should try to get our work done," Brick said. He smiled, and Tim looked over at him. He could see some gleam in Brick's eye, a mote lifting.

The truck started with a backfire and a tremble that shook the trees in the bed as blue smoke rose up from under the truck. Tim moved the car and they got in the truck and drove west to the landfill. Pine needles rattled and blew out in the slipstream.

"Where are your kids?" asked Tim.

Brick fidgeted with his ear. "They are with their grandmother in Salt Lake City."

"Do you ever see them?"

"I haven't much, no." Brick leaned up from the vinyl seat, making it squeak, and pulled his wallet from his hip pocket. He leafed through the scant billfold and pulled out a few photos that were cupped in the shape of the wallet. Brick fanned them out and looked them over. He smiled. "Here they are." He stretched over the long bench seat and held up the photos for Tim to see.

There was a boy, about seven with white hair and crossed eyes; a girl a couple of years younger, missing a tooth like her dad; and an infant that looked to Tim like the very embodiment of peace. The baby was in a woman's arms. The photo showed the woman's lap, an elbow, part of her nose and chin, and a spill of chestnut hair over her shoulder.

"That's my wife holding Chelsie. They're all a little older now."

Tim thought about showing him the lady's foot stored in his phone photo archive.

"Must be hard," said Tim. "Is your wife still around?"

Brick settled back in his seat, put the photos in his wallet, and put the wallet back in his hip pocket. He sighed. "I don't know where she is. Bringing pleasure or pain—or both—somewhere, I am sure." He revved his ear with his finger.

The truck engine droned on. Pine needles glittered into the warm afternoon and settled onto the road.

"Ah," Tim started after a long silence, "how do you, I mean, how does that happen? You know, I mean, I feel like I know what is going on around here. I mean, I'm not a prude or anything. I've been around. I just never knew all that kind of stuff was going on. I mean, this *is* Utah."

Brick watched the fences line out along the field road they were traveling down. He dropped his face and then looked up. "I don't know. It's what's behind doors." He lifted his hands over his thighs. "It's fun, you know. I had a blast. I . . ." He sat there with his mouth open. Words stuck. Then, resigned: "How does anyone know when Satan is at work on them?"

Dust billowed up around the cab as Tim stopped the truck at the land-fill gate next to a tiny shack. A lean man who looked like he was un-dergoing chemotherapy slipped out of the shack and stood with his legs apart and arms crossed and looked in at Tim. Tim rolled down the window and offered the man his driver license.

"Got a permit?"

"I'm a resident." Tim pushed his license toward the man again.

"Don't matter."

"What do you mean?"

"Won't take that much yard waste without a permit." The man turned and went back into the shack and sat on a tall stool. He flipped open a dusty, ruffled *Playboy* magazine.

Tim shouted, "Where do I get a permit?"

"City."

"Hmm," Brick murmured. "Unhelpful little jerk there."

At the city offices Tim got the runaround. No one seemed to have heard of the need for a yard-waste permit. It was a mystery. Finally, he told the snooty man with greasy hair at the front desk to go kiss the mayor. And then Brick added, "And the governor, too."

"I'm sorry. I don't understand why the man at the dump told you

you needed a permit." The man's shrill voice raised to reach their backs as Tim and Brick wandered down the hall and out the door and down the steps into the fine afternoon.

"I need a drink," said Tim.

Brick chuckled, "I don't blame you."

"Well, tell you what," said Tim, "These trees be damned. I'm going home for a nice tall cold Manhattan. You want to join me?" Then he looked at Brick. "I don't mean to tempt you. Your struggles and all."

"Well. I'm coming with you, sure. As for the drink, I prefer straight Scotch."

Tim looked at Brick. Brick was walking to the truck with his head up. He appeared to be grinning, and his shoulders held a degree of straightness—even his green slacks had a jump in them that wasn't there before.

"I've got Scotch," said Tim.

"Single malt?"

"Blended. Cheap."

They got in the cab and slammed the doors. Brick bowed his head and prayed.

"Praise our Heavenly Father, I'm ready for a drink," Brick shouted after his amen, sounding more like a jubilant Baptist than an old Quorum-of-the-Twelve Mormon.

"You sure?"

"I feel the Spirit in this, Brother Oberman."

They drank through the afternoon at Tim's house on the back patio under the deck umbrella. The truck sat out front in the driveway full of Christmas trees. Brick told more stories of sin and debauchery, his suffering for redemption and the need of forgiveness from his children. Tim opened up about his wife and their problems in the marriage. Brick gave advice and clucked his tongue and prayed and quoted scripture and prophets. They drank bourbon and Scotch and beer and smoked Swisher Sweets. They argued the finer points of the Word of Wisdom. They relieved themselves in the hollyhocks lining the patio in full view of Tim's neighbors. Brick bore his testimony. Tim promised to go to church with Brick on Sunday. They got to know each other, agreed and disagreed, made pacts, and before long the sun found its way down in the west and the air gathered cold. They sat in the gloam and felt each other's presence like a warm vapor circulating on currents of barely whispered breath. From out of this slow calm broth they determined what was to be done with the trees, talked it through, saw the plan, the first plan. They waited. At midnight they got to it, shook themselves, rising from the patio like stone men resurrected.

It was two A.M. when they finished. The quarter-waxing moon was long gone down in the west sky. Tim and Brick had piled all the trees in the center of the lot. Their arms were scratched and marked from branches and needles. They were tired, the adrenaline and Christmas songs exhausted from their systems.

"Our finest gifts we bring, pah rum puh pum pum," Brick trailed off and was quiet. They sat in the back of the empty truck. "Shoot, I miss those kids," he said under his breath.

Tim looked at the dark mass of trees in front of them. He pulled out the divorce papers he had stuffed in his pocket.

"You gonna do it?" asked Brick. The last of the Swishers dangled from his lip. The cigar was burning hot and dry; the red spot of coal seemed to breathe a few inches from his face.

Tim slipped off the truck. He walked up to the edge of the tree pile. He was sober. He lifted his torch cigar lighter and flicked it. Butane mingled with the pine scent. Tim held the hissing flame near the divorce decree, read Karri's name typed clearly there on the front page. Plaintiff. His name below.

He had no defense. But he could try.

He let the lighter go out, and he folded the decree and put it back in his pocket as he walked to the truck.

"Plan B, then?"

Tim sat down next to Brick. "Yeah," he said, "I suppose." He took out his cell phone and opened it to the lady's foot. Looked at it and sighed, then: "u-u-A-A-Ah!" He lurched up and threw the phone into the pile of trees. The light from the phone was swallowed up by the branches and needles. "I'll get a new one tomorrow." Tim breathed out and settled back down into the bed of the truck. "I'll call her. And the city, too."

Brick took the cigar from his mouth and studied the hot tip of it. "Not gonna miss these," he said. He leaned up and threw the cigar at the trees. It turned over and over in the air and disappeared in an explosion of sparks as it struck a Douglas mid-trunk.

"You feel like praying?" Brick asked. He stuck his finger in his ear, held it there frozen for just a moment, and then took it out.

"I guess it wouldn't hurt," said Tim.

For a while there was nothing, just the cold silent air of a May night, both men reciting quiet appeals to their respective higher powers. Then the glow started from deep in the pile. And the crackling grew, some pagan deity coming to life. And the men who brought forth this Christmas demon fought the urge to run, to hide, and they leaned back on their elbows, humble and amazed under the tongue of fire that roared all their collective love and hate and fear in a strange and beautiful voice at the darkness above.

OUT OF THE WOODS

Karen Rosenbaum

HERE THEY GO, CARMA WITHOUT HER cane—she'll hang onto Dan if her legs give way—through the glass doors into the maze of parents and teenagers and little brothers and sisters, milling, waving, shrieking, whimpering.

"I can't find the camera," screeches a frantic woman up to her elbows in a canvas bag. Stepping serenely around the woman, Carma and Dan raise eyebrows at one another and attach themselves to the end of the line that snakes through the lobby to the locked high school auditorium. *Their* camera is around Dan's neck. From Carma's canvas bag erupts an enormous bouquet of yellow roses.

"Oooh, roses," a voice behind them squeals. "Who're they for?"

Carma turns and smiles. "Our daughter."

A girl in tight levis and a sequined halter smiles back. "What's her name? What's she playing?" A rhinestone, or maybe another sequin, pierces her tongue. She is tugging on the belt loop of a torpid boy with chartreuse hair.

"Sophie Cusins," Carma says. "She plays the witch."

"Sophie!" The boy stirs and becomes alert. "Sophie's in honors English. She's way cool."

"And the witch!" the girl adds.

"She's been rehearsing for it all her life," says Dan.

"Says her father." Carma wrinkles her nose at him. The girl lets escape a thin, sequin-y laugh.

The doors are pushed open, late, as always, and the throng streams in, the teenagers coalescing in bunches and yelling at each other. Carma and Dan take their usual places, on the aisle, right side, third row, where

Dan's fullback frame won't block too many views. From here, he can bound down to the front at the end of each act, kneel, and snap away.

Carma settles into the rickety folding seat. Even though she left work early and tried to nap this afternoon, her joints throb. She takes a breath and composes her face carefully. "Look at the bright side," those insipid self-help manuals say. The bright side of rheumatoid arthritis is that Sophie has never had to deal with a zealous stage mother like Alicia Sanchez, standing over there in the middle section, flailing her lumpy arms around. Her daughter Maddy looks a lot like her— meaty, freckled. Maddy usually gets those character parts. She's Jack's mother in this production. She wanted to be the witch. But in *this* version of the fairy tales, Sondheim's, the witch turns into a gorgeous vamp, and Sophie has all the equipment to be a gorgeous vamp. She sings better than Maddy, too. Carma doesn't understand why that is. Sophie doesn't seem to work very hard at it. When Grace was in these musicals, she was always crouched over the piano, practicing her part, and her part was never a big part. But Sophie—every evening she sits at that same piano bench, sings her songs through once, then curls up on her bed with her phone.

"Hello Dan, Carma." It's Natalie Green, motioning toward the seats to her right. "Those taken? May we sit there?"

Dan stands and Carma swivels her legs to the side, wincing at the pain in her hip. Natalie and her husband—Ted? Tom?—shake Dan's hand, try to suck in their bodies, and squeeze by. Natalie plops down next to Carma so the husband has to press past everyone to get to the seat next to the wall.

"We almost didn't make it." Natalie fans herself with her program. "We had to arrange for the Sorensons to pick Billy up from soccer, and the babysitter wasn't ready when Tim went to get her, and then Peggy had a tantrum. Oh, you brought Sophie flowers!" Carma's bag is wedged under the seat in front, the flowers spilling out, one crushed by Natalie and Tim-Tom-Ted. "We should have brought Craig something. What do you bring boys?"

Carma tries to remember what part Craig plays. One of the princes certainly; he's such a pretty boy, Sophie has told them with a dismissive lilt in her voice. "Balloons maybe," Carma says, "but I don't know where you'd keep them during the show."

"Oh, balloons." Natalie makes a face. "I didn't think of balloons. Craig says Sophie is just marvelous. She's so talented. You know there's a great group of kids at church now, just like when Grace was in high school. Sophie would really fit in."

Sophie would not fit in, Carma thinks, but she says mildly, "Sophie's free to go to church if she wants to. Any church."

Natalie pretends not to hear the addition. "Craig could give her a ride. We let him take a car. He's so responsible."

"She can always get a ride with Dan." Carma peers through her glasses at her program and checks Sophie's name. For a change, it's spelled correctly.

"We'd love it if you came too," Natalie says hopefully. "If you feel well enough. And you know we make tapes for people who can't come to meetings."

Carma forces a smile. "Dan relays the most interesting bits." She feels Dan's light touch on her shoulder. Knowing how heavy his arm can be, he rests it mostly on the back of her chair. She turns away from Natalie, and the auditorium is suddenly black except for the music light on the piano.

The music teacher drops her hands onto the keyboard and starts to play. When the curtains are drawn, Cinderella and Jack and the Baker are all lamenting their losses. The music is shrill yet sweet, thinks Carma, like sweet and sour. She's been listening to Sophie's songs for weeks. They all sound alike.

The preliminaries over, Red Riding Hood has skipped off into the woods, and Sophie steps forward to witchily harass the Baker with the salient points of his family history and the reason it is to end with him: she caught his father "rooting through my rutabagas." "Don't ever never ever mess around with my greens," she spits out, and the audience snickers and guffaws.

She's always been good at working the audience. Now she is offering to reverse the curse—for a price. She controls this scene, Sophie does. Ah, but Carma knows that before the act is over, the witch will be only a beautiful woman stripped of her magical powers, at which point she'll turn her full attention to the creaky seats and work her *theatrical* sorcery on those in them.

Carma never worries about Sophie forgetting her lines or even losing her composure if she misses a note. When you belt them out, what's a wrong note here and there? This isn't opera. She and Dan just lean back and enjoy the show, wincing only at the other kids' performances. When Natalie's son squeaks out his adoration of Rapunzel, Natalie and Tim exchange little moans and shuffle their feet.

That's how it was with Grace. "You know," Dan said once, "it was more of an achievement for Grace to sing in an octet than for Sophie to be the star."

Carma understands Grace's inclination to gravitate to the back of the stage; she understands Grace's penchant to please. But she can't understand how Grace could put college on hold to marry someone as sweetly bland as Ryan. And a baby now before she is twenty-one. The baby, though—Carma smiles to think about Bradley, fat-cheeked and sunny; she calls him Buddha-ley—the baby is spectacular.

"How is Grace?" Natalie asks after the act-one curtain drops and the whistles and foot stomping die down. Carma does happen to have two shiny snapshots of Grace and the baby lying on the red and blue sailboat quilt that Carma and Sophie, mostly Sophie, had put together and tied.

"He's gorgeous." Natalie stands and shows the pictures to Tim.

"He is, isn't he?" Carma pushes herself to her feet.

"They're still in Utah?"

Carma nods.

"When does her husband graduate?"

"He's got two more years." Alicia Sanchez is pushing her way toward them. Dan has stepped across the aisle and is shaking someone's hand.

"Sophie's great," Alicia gushes. "She's got the part down pat. Bernadette Peters couldn't do it better."

"Maddy's doing well too," Carma says. "They're all doing well." She stands back so Natalie isn't excluded.

"And Craig. Craig's doing just fine," Alicia says, without conviction. "Oh, there!" She points at someone and swooshes up the aisle.

Natalie hands the photos back to Carma. "They're very different, your daughters."

"Yes."

"Is Sophie," she hesitates, "more like you?"

Carma laughs. "I don't think either one is very much like me."

"Sophie has your lovely thick hair."

"With pink streaks instead of gray."

"Kids shout with their hair now, neon colors, everything." Natalie sighs. "I don't know how I'd raise mine without the church." For a minute, Carma realizes, Natalie has forgotten her. Then she remembers and laughs nervously. "Their world is so different from the world I grew up in."

Carma lowers herself into her seat. "Where did you grow up?"

"Idaho. Rexburg." Glancing at the children rushing back to front-row center, Natalie sits down. "You know, my kids aren't like me either. To get up on a stage in front of the whole school and sing with nothing but a piano behind you—I would have died first. I was never any good at anything that people might watch. Sports. One summer I played tennis every morning, and by the end of August I was still missing half the balls and hitting the other half past the baseline."

Carma has to nod. "Sounds like me. I tried volleyball once. And badminton." She laughs. "I was always a klutz. And that was even before the arthritis."

Natalie lowers her voice. "How long have you had it?"

"Twenty years." Carma looks at her hands, covers one with the other. "I was diagnosed right after I had Grace. I couldn't get out of bed."

"Is it—inherited?"

Carma shrugs. "It seems to run in families. The girls *probably* won't get it, but you never know." She pauses. "I'll never forgive myself if they get it."

Natalie looks alarmed. "There's nothing you could do."

"I could have *not* had them."

"No," Natalie says. "You had to have them. We can't any of us know what will happen to our kids. We just pray for the best." Her voice goes up as if this is a question.

Carma answers it with a sigh.

"Is it—do you hurt all the time?"

"No." Carma stops herself from making an accordion fan out of her program. She wants to make copies for the grandparents. "Sometimes it's in remission. I felt great when I was pregnant with Sophie. But afterward it was a lot worse."

Natalie touches her very lightly on the arm. "I didn't know it was so bad. Do you hurt right now?"

Carma doesn't want to itemize, quantify her pain. Suddenly she doesn't want to talk at all. "You get used to it."

Dan creaks in the seat beside her. The theater darkens. Behind them, she can hear two boys talking. "I know Sophie," one says. "Oh, yeah? What do you know?" asks the other. Carma holds her breath. "She's all right." Carma lets her breath out as the piano starts the monotonous jingle that begins act two.

Sophie as Witch is mother-by-bribery, and she is quite a convincing mother, especially after the Giantess squashes her Rapunzel. Carma's glasses steam up as Sophie sings out, "Children don't listen." She is surprised at her tears and can see that Dan's cheeks are wet too.

Their daughters have listened, but it was hard to know what they heard. She and Dan didn't shout. Dan, in fact, always sounded calm, whereas she always sounded, at least to her own ears, whiny. Dan didn't pretend to have answers for all her questions. He honestly didn't have questions himself. "I don't know about religion, organized or disorganized," she wept after he baptized Sophie. "I just don't believe it anymore. I've tried to believe it. I'm not saying it's not true. It's true for you. I even want it to be true for you. You should do what you have to do. And I should do what I have to do. I have to stop pretending it works for me."

Eight years ago now. That whole year the arthritis flared and nothing helped and nobody slept well. Grace was sad. Carma's mother was sad. Dan's parents, visiting from Seattle, were sad. But Dan was shocked when Carma asked if he wanted to divorce her and find someone who could believe as he believed, who could join him in that hierarchical hereafter. And she was grateful that he protected her, as he must have done, from visits by those who wanted to persuade her that she was ruining her family's chances for salvation. "Take the girls to church," she had said. But given the choice, Sophie usually opted to "stay home with Mom."

In Carma's childhood home, it was her father who didn't go to church. The common pattern—believing, determined women; rebellious, indifferent men. But at least she had some kind of precedent.

Carma did what her father had done—if Grace were giving a talk or getting an award or singing in a group, then Carma would go.

But she couldn't go everywhere Grace went. When Grace got that scholarship, the one she gave up after a single year, and set off for Provo, Carma surmised, correctly, that her daughter would eventually be married in a ceremony she could not witness. Twenty-three years after she and Dan had driven quietly to Arizona to get married so that no one would feel left out, Grace and Ryan had driven quietly to Utah to marry so that Carma wouldn't feel left out. "You go," she had insisted to Dan, and he went. A week later, at the reception in Carma and Dan's garden, Grace, in the simple white dress she and Sophie had sewn together, greeted guests with a tranquility that astonished her mother, that separated them in a way the sadness couldn't. Ryan's true-believing family treated—still treat—Carma with profuse, bewildering courtesy.

The light is focused on Sophie, singing, "It doesn't matter now, it's the last midnight." She is singing as if it matters very much. "I'm not good, I'm not nice, I'm just right, I'm the witch," she croons. "I'm what no one believes."

Sophie is not sexually active, Carma is almost sure, not yet. She hasn't had Grace's reasons for chastity, but she has held onto it, up to now. How will she feel when Sophie lets it go? Dan will be devastated. Dan is good. Grace is good. Sophie is good. And she, even *she* is good. Probably. Where do our ideas of goodness come from, Carma wonders. Can anyone get there all on her own, no current church or past church, no great mentors or influential parents, no Dostoevskys or Kierkegaards? Can she get there? And where, oh where, is there?

Dan takes her hand and holds it, touches lightly the fused joint in her ring finger. The finger is swollen so that if she did want to take off her wedding band, someone would have to cut the gold.

"Careful the things you say," Sophie is singing with the Baker. "Children will listen." The rest of the cast is singing now, children themselves, children playing children and children playing adults. Natalie and Tim's prince son Craig swells up his chest and looks, indeed, very handsome. Sophie and Cinderella and the Baker are in the center, and their eyes are shiny and their voices sweet and strong. The piano is barely audible as they all sing, then shout, "Happily ever after!"

No one believes it, of course, the happily-ever-after, but the audience has been transported out of the woods. They stand and shriek and clap and stomp and whistle. Dan is on his knees at the front of the aisle, with four or five other parents, snapping pictures, offering homage. The curtain closes, then opens again, and the whistles and applause resume.

Natalie sits back down beside Carma. "You must be proud."

Carma nods and smiles. "You too."

"Yes."

"Go on ahead. We wait till the aisles are clear." The cast will be in the lobby, surrounded by ecstatic friends. Natalie and Tim edge by her. Up front, Dan is staggering under a bear hug from the Baker's mother, a willowy woman, pretty, young enough to have given birth to the Baker when she was fourteen. A hug like that would break Carma in two. *I don't have to worry about Dan*, Carma thinks. Why is it she doesn't worry? Is it because of the church that separates them? Is it the code that one is responsible for a partner, no matter how she changes? Neither of them had envisioned that she would be unable to pick up either baby, that at times she would be fat-faced and dopey from the drugs, that she would be taken apart by surgeons, that some days she would stare out the window at the laurel hedge and disappear into it for hours. And neither of them had envisioned her arthritic soul.

Natalie returns and crouches beside Carma's seat. "I was just thinking—I guess you've had blessings," she hesitates, "to ease the pain?"

"A lot of blessings," says Carma. She pats Natalie's hand. "And maybe they helped."

As Natalie stands, she brushes Carma's cheek with her lips. "I'll be praying for you," she says, and, eyes lowered, she runs back to the lobby.

Carma says suddenly, silently, to Natalie, to Dan, to God, if there is a God, even to herself, "Yes. Pray for me." Then she smiles at Dan, now disentangled from the Baker's mother. She hands him the bag of yellow roses and pushes up out of her chair. "Shall we make merry?"

"Let's," he says and offers her his arm, and they set out, stumbling just a little, up the empty aisle.

BLOOD WORK

Darrell Spencer

THE MORMON LADY NEXT DOOR TELLS J. J. Cribb she put his hamstring in their temple. It's a curious way to express what she sees as the voucher of her goodwill, but he understands what she means. J. J.'s not been in Salt Lake City for more than two days in the last five years, did grow up here, though, and his mother was Mormon from the word go, an affiliation she often and happily announced. For the last twenty-three years she was alive, she drove herself to the temple twice a week and did temple work. One of her duties was to pray for the sick of every stripe, the halt and lame of mind, body, or spirit. J. J.'s hamstring *is* sore, could, in certain ways, be thought of as sick.

The Mormon temple is a scale model of the universe, boxed to the compass, its cornerstones laid clockwise in the ground. It stands as a point of order in the face of chaos. Only the most worthy Mormons get in, and there they perform sacred ordinances. Their church leaders ask that you and the local newspapers call members Latter-day Saints, not Mormons.

J. J.'s dad, Samuel Cribb Jr., tells J. J. you don't talk to the neighbor lady unless you've got a lawyer by your side. Hire one, if you have to. She and her family—her husband, three teenage girls, and a boy— moved in soon after J. J., his first divorce one day under his belt, moved to Henderson, Nevada. Samuel Cribb's not addressed a civil word to any of the family, and he has no plans to. "Not even after the last dog's been hung," he says.

The neighbor lady's name's Flora. Husband's Leonard, a CPA who keeps accounts for the Mormons and restores vintage convertibles. Flora's russet hair falls like an A-frame from the top of her head, and

she has those reptilian eyes. She wears no makeup. J. J. guesses she's
sixty, but she could be fifty. There's a measure of dread like a night
lamp in her face. Claim around the neighborhood is she's no fun, is
full of mood.

Yesterday, she introduced herself to J. J. just as he finished his
morning run. He'd turned the corner two blocks up from his dad's
place and felt that hamstring nip and tweak he knew too well, that
mid-stride out-of-the-blue kick to the backside of the thigh, not the
rip that knocks you to your knees, but the lodging of a complaint. He
down-geared into a trot-and-shuffle, the on-land equivalent of a dog
paddle. The street below dropped away steep enough to knock you
cartwheeling if you misstepped. A running buddy has told J. J. he is
too tightly wound, has recommended yoga, but only *after* a run, has
argued for nightclub dancing and yelling in the shower. Has suggested
screaming at traffic from overpasses.

J. J. didn't see Flora. He slowed from his trot-and-shuffle to a half-
assed poke-along and then walked from the corner to the fence that
separated his father's yard from hers, and she stepped from the shadows between the two houses. By then, he had hoisted his foot up so his
heel rested on the low cinder-block fence that ran from her backyard
to the sidewalk, and J. J. was flexing his leg. Ivy covered most of the
fence. She said, "My guess is it's your hamstring."

"I'm afraid so," J. J. said. He leaned toward his foot and felt the
hamstring protest.

"Probably the downhills we've got here," Flora said.

J. J. flexed his leg, swung it into place so he was standing on both
feet, and said, "Probably. It's happened before." He told her he'd never
run hills well, up or down, but especially not down, couldn't let go
no matter how eloquently he sweet-talked his brain into relaxing. J. J.
brakes and fights against loosening and lengthening his stride, runs instead like he's jammed cue balls into his arches. He pictures in his head
as incentive and hero that Keep on Truckin' guy, but doing so does no
good. A downhill comes, and he sort of checks up, like a ratchet. He
knows better. He's read the articles. He's lost months of running to his
bad hamstring.

Flora was cutting to stalks the daylilies and rudbeckia that border her yard, readying them for winter. She set her scissors on the

cinder-block wall and said, "Worse thing you can do is to run hills too slow rather than too fast." She tugged off her cotton gloves and placed them next to the scissors. "My boy," she said, "runs cross-country for West High. *Sports* magazine ranked the team number one in the country." She used her hands to show J. J. the hills and gullies, the uncivilized trails, the swoop and drop, swag and pitch that come with running through fields. She said, "You watch the joggers who go by here, and they fight the downhill like they're in danger of it rising up and smacking them. Especially the men, for some reason. They jab at the road. On their face is that look you see on people who are putting a big toe in the swimming pool to see if they really want to go for a dip. You'd think the men are afraid they're going to fly off the planet. The women, for the most part, they glide past our place."

J. J. told her he'd been running at sea level. "Up here," he said, "I'm not sure I'm getting oxygen to my muscles like I should."

J. J. explained that he was Samuel's son, was Samuel Cribb, Junior Junior. The family, to keep phone calls and messages straight, first called him Cribb, then Junior Junior, which was of course quickly turned into J. J. Sometimes, for a joke, his dad was simply J.

Flora said she'd never actually talked to J. J.'s father, which at the time surprised J. J. because, although there was no logic to forge any kind of connection or friendship, the house Flora lived in had been Lester Hirsch's, J. J.'s father's lifelong friend and smoking buddy, two, as they described themselves, reprobate run-to-seed Mormons, born to the faith and a lifetime of agile sidestepping it. Jack Mormons, that's what the Latter-day Saints once called such members. Now they'd be referred to politely as inactives, except Hirsch died.

J. J. himself had walked away from it all when he was seventeen. He'd gotten up in the middle of a Mormon sacrament meeting, excused himself as he picked his way toward an aisle, and left through the front door. The speaker, a church leader in the area, was talking about Satan, saying, especially for the ears, hearts, and minds of the young people, that Satan talks softly. Try this small wrong, Satan whispers. Smoke this cigarette, Satan says. Then he's got you by the throat. Let's steal something, he says. Let's buy porn. Let's shoot up. Small wrongs lead to greater wrongs. J. J. studied the man, his gray suit and tie, his white shirt, his salt-and-pepper haircut and arrested, insignia hair, hair

like a flagship, and recognized that if there was a Satan he was looking at the man, that if there was a Satan he was listening to his soft
tongue. Satan would be the picture of civility. He'd dress and talk *bona
fides*, whole truths and nothing but the truths. Butter wouldn't melt in
his mouth.

Ruby, J. J.'s mother, took his walking away hard. Back then, for
days, weeks, and finally years, sorrow pumped the blood that fed her
heart. She wore anguish as censorious as a shawl. She'd most likely
have put his name in the Mormon temple, though she would not have
told J. J. if she had. The Latter-day Saints must have prayed for his
return to the church.

Flora shook J. J.'s hand when he said he had to get going. Then she
said, "Wait a minute," and disappeared into her backyard. She returned
with an armful of rudbeckia she'd cut and handed him the flowers,
saying, "No need to let those go to waste."

He thanked her.

"Boil the stems in water," she said. "They'll last a good week, maybe two, and won't collapse."

J. J. said, "In a pan?"

She nodded, said, "In a deep one," then pointed at his leg and said,
"I'd ice that now, as much of the thigh as you can, just five minutes."
She pulled on her gloves, adding, "Then moist heat before you run
tomorrow, and ice again afterwards." She showed him a stretch to do
to warm up and cool down, crossed her right foot over her left foot
and tilted herself toward the fence as gracefully as one of her daylilies.
Her hair fell across her face. "Before and after, and gentle, and not
very far," she said. "Hold it right on the edge of hurting for a count
of twenty-five—one Mississippi, two Mississippi—and do both sides."
She adjusted her footing, left foot over right, and swayed the other way,
saying, "Don't neglect the good side just because it isn't hurting right
at the minute. Everything is balance. Nothing over much, you know.
That's Shakespeare."

J. J. tried the stretch, found he had to steady himself using the
fence.

Flora said, "My son sells wrap-around thermo heating pads if you
might be interested."

"I'll see how it goes," J. J. said.

She said, "You need moist heat. Dry won't do you any good at all."

It was when J. J. got back inside that his father told him the neighborhood advice about Flora and having a third party with you, preferably an attorney. It was then he told J. J. he hadn't said anything to any of Flora's family since they moved in. J. J. told him she'd been nice enough, and his father said, "Real bad trouble always is on the surface." Seems she'd even sued Hirsch's family over the house. Samuel buried the rudbeckia in a trash can out back.

Two days later, J. J. just starting a run, was when Flora told him she'd put his hamstring in the temple.

In 1847 Orson Pratt and Henry G. Sherwood, working from a point surveyors established as the Great Salt Lake Base and Meridian, beginning at the southwest corner of what would eventually be Temple Square, laid out Salt Lake City's grid of streets. Brigham Young struck the ground with his cane, marking where the Saints would build a temple to their God, and Wilford Woodruff drove a stake into the spot.

J. J.'s father's house is east of Temple Square up in the Avenues on M Street. Father Junior is a retired surgeon whose latest blood work confirms he's having heart problems. His HDL is low. An early electrocardiogram picked up signs of arrhythmia and most likely heartwall thickening. The hospital wants to do a cardiac catheterization, but Samuel knows too well all the risks. He'd had bouts of angina and is wearing a nitroglycerin patch. He's on oxygen a lot of the time. His saturation level has dropped as low as eighty-four.

J. J., at the end of his first week here, having heated his hamstring and wrapped his thigh in an Ace bandage, having done Flora's stretch, jogs south down M Street. He runs in the road. The sidewalk squares are uprooted and neglected. They look jerry-built and seem confused about their basic function. His route zigzags him about one mile and a half toward the center of the city, first south down one of the short alphabet streets and then west across one of the Avenues, so it's one block breakneck incline, say down M, then across a block, say Fourth Avenue, which is only somewhat downhill. Then south again down headlong L Street, J. J. knowing better but holding his stride in check, restrained and reined in, jabbing, as Flora said, at the pavement, and then he can relax and breeze across Third Avenue, followed next by the tight-assed downhill of K, then easy sailing along Second Avenue.

The houses throughout the neighborhoods are catch-as-catch-can. You name a type of architecture and you'll see it. They're jigsawed together, maybe five feet apart from garage to the neighbor's kitchen window. Eventually, J. J. comes out on South Temple where the Governor's Mansion sits under repair. A Christmas-light fire gutted it two years ago. From here the city flattens gradually, and J. J. runs west toward downtown. Now he sticks to the sidewalks. They're still uneven and crazy with edges, but safer than the traffic, which is four-laned and hotheaded.

Today, a red light catches J. J. next to the Hotel Utah, and he jogs in place. He's kitty-corner to the Mormon temple. J. J. imagines his hamstring in there, women like his mother, like Ruby, ministering to it. Thick women whose carriage is both humble and proud. These are the meek who shall inherit the earth. They are sober and grim. Dignified. Serene. Even their hair is solid as a rock. Their eyes radiate love. Pure light encircles them. No one talks. They rub balm in. Ointments. Aloe. A woman with a nurse's touch applies a poultice. All of it—it's soothing. The toxins flee. The women who look like Ruby kneel and pray. Unction, Piety, Grace, Hope, these are their names.

Against the traffic, antsy, J. J. skips, sidesteps, quibbles his way across Main Street and runs hard along the wide sidewalk that borders Temple Square. You could drag-race at least two cars on it. Temple Square covers a two-acre block. People who come to Salt Lake praise the city's lack of trash and wonder if Mormons are citizens of the United States. It's a fair question, if you think about it. The granite wall around their temple must be twenty feet high. Inside there is the temple itself, and there is the tabernacle, where the Mormon Tabernacle Choir sings. There is a visitors' center where you can ask your questions. Guides will give you pamphlets and Books of Mormon. You can see films about the church. If you leave your name, they'll send missionaries to teach you the gospel. Or you can refer them to friends. Russian? Dutch? Navajo? No problem. They've got people who speak the language.

Every day, J. J. circles Temple Square and heads back up to his father's. This way he puts in four tough miles, up and down hills. J. J.

did his homework when he was a kid, figured, in a teenager's way, that if you were going to build a life on religious belief you ought to know its history. No riding on anyone's coattails for J. J. He took his Mormonism seriously until the day he, as Ruby put it, bowed out. So he read and studied. He knows, for one thing, the *New York Times* once described the temple as frowning. The *Times* said it was barbaric in its refusal to conform to any known school of architecture. It looks Gothic, but isn't. Three towers stand at both the east and the west entrances, each central tower higher than the other two. The temple's built of granite quarried from Little Cottonwood Canyon. The angel Moroni, gold-leafed and fourteen feet high, stands on its capstone blowing his trumpet to announce that God's word has been restored to the earth. One story goes that when the angel was lowered into place on top of the 210-foot central tower on the east side, the church's president, Wilford Woodruff, turned to the man who'd sculpted the statue and said, "Now, Mr. Dallin, do you believe in angels?" Cyrus Dallin replied, "Yes, my mother is an angel."

The temple's façade is covered with icons. There are sunstones and moonstones. There are fifty earth stones that show the seven-days-of-the-week rotation of the earth. Fifty moonstones work out the cycle of the lunar month. There are star stones and Saturn stones, and there is the all-seeing eye of God. There is God's declaration I AM ALPHA AND OMEGA, and a dedicatory inscription begins HOLINESS TO THE LORD.

J. J. heads toward the state capitol building when he gets back to State Street. It's a gut-check climb. His knees hurt. He weaves through traffic, crosses to the sidewalk on the other side of the street. Behind him, somewhere on a spire of the temple, is Ursa Major, the Big Dipper, carved into the granite. According to Truman Angell, the temple's architect, it has a moral, which is that the lost may find themselves by the priesthood of God. J. J. knows we stand before the temple the way we stand before the heavens. We get our bearings from it. His running in the shadow of the temple is a test of his stride, foot strike, and knee bend, the set of his elbow and the rocking-chair swing of his arm. Ruby used to tell him everything on earth is a matter of comportment. She believed in decorum, in good manners, in posture. How you sit in a chair is how you'd sit in the throne of God were you given the chance. How you eat is how you would eat in the presence of Deity. How you shovel. How you sweep. How you walk. Etiquette was more than a word.

Head down, J. J. chugs up North State. It's a clean-air day. He phoned to make sure. His lungs are safe. This trash-free city is under threat to lose federal funding if it doesn't clean up its pollution. Near the top, J. J. feels his hamstring knot itself, and he stops to stretch, one foot up on the curb, one foot in the gutter. He does both legs. He takes the easy downhill to his left, then turns north again past the Pioneer Memorial Museum. The state capitol building's on his right. The climb is extreme, and he can't do anything but lean forward and focus on the road. His chest, it seems, is almost touching the pavement. He turns east and is walking by the time he rests at the top of 500 North.

Across Capitol Boulevard is the entrance to City Creek Canyon. Signs say Do Not Enter, Wrong Way. They're for cars, and the way they're posted they seem angry. Everyone runs here, in both directions. Used to be this was called Gravity Hill, was a place Samuel introduced J. J. to. This is where dads brought their kids to wow them. Couples stopped here to grab at each other. It was open to traffic both ways back then. You'd park at the entrance at what looks like it's the top, and your dad'd point out how steep it seemed to be, how it appeared like you were headed directly downhill. "Take a look," your dad would say, and the kids'd peer out the windshield or hang from a side window. Dad puts the car in neutral, says, "Keep your eyes peeled and a free hand on your heart," and gloats when his big Oldsmobile starts to roll the wrong way, when it starts to roll backward in the direction of what must be uphill. The dad says, "That's one for the books." He says, "That's something to write home about."

J. J. cruises through the canyon. Here and there, at bends in the road, he can see downtown. Salt Lake's building itself a skyline. At the bottom, where the skinny road horseshoes over City Creek and a concrete dam so that now you're climbing Lake Bonneville Boulevard back up into the Avenues, J. J. hesitates, thinking that somewhere along here is a road that follows the river, that winds through Memory Grove, thinking if he can locate it he'll take it through the park so, looping back, he comes out near North State and the temple, adding a mile to his run. He's not paying attention when a car flies around the corner

and skids toward him. He hops off the asphalt, turns his ankle, and is
flung down the grade fifteen, twenty feet on his butt. Kids in the car
yell, but J. J. hears only what sounds like a shot goose. He's almost in
the creek. He rolls so he can sit, and his ankle throbs. He picks gravel
from his hand. He takes off his shoe, scoots down the bank, and eases
the injured ankle into the cold water. He slips his hand into the river.
The water's numbing. Five minutes, then he takes off his T-shirt and
dries the foot, pulls sock and shoe on, and tightens the lace so it will
slow the circulation. He gets into his T-shirt. It's pleasantly damp. J. J.
limps to the road, then walks slowly up Bonneville, tries trotting—it's
okay—so he begins to run. The ankle's fine, but his hand burns, like
he's broken a blood vessel.

Rather than a hunt-and-peck jog down the alphabet streets and
across the Avenues so that he works his way like a crossword puzzle
from C Street to M Street, from Eleventh Avenue to Sixth Avenue,
J. J. stays with Eleventh until he comes to M, then he lopes down it.
He waves at a bearded guy on his porch, expects—why, he doesn't
know—to get the finger in return, but the guy just stares. There's ice
and indifference here, but also an intelligence that could pocket you
and the nine ball in an unheard of combination. The man's beard is
the color of bitter-sweet chocolate. His eyes measure you for a coffin.
He'd eat your young for breakfast. He is smoking a cigar, and there is a
35-mm camera on the porch railing. He's a man who, seated front row
center or behind a pillar in the balcony, could upset the Peking Acro-
bats and their tower of chairs. This man knows how far we as a people
are truly open to deceit and illusion.

J. J. slows between Third Avenue and Fourth Avenue and is walking by the time he reaches the corner. Flora, planting bulbs in her front
yard, sits back and says, "Your knee?"

J. J. glances down. His knee's been bleeding. The blood is dark,
looks like a failed S. He says, "I fell."

"That will happen," she says.

The *Tribune*'s lying at the bottom of his dad's porch steps. J. J. snags
the newspaper and wonders if Flora will put his knee in the temple.

J. J.'s hand is swollen but no longer hurts. Looks as if he's shoved a
walnut under the skin where his pinkie meets his knuckle. He stands at

the kitchen sink, runs cold water on the swelling, and watches Samuel dig around the base of a maple that's started life too close to the back fence. He's digging with a long-bladed tool, one you'd use for flowers, and is working so slowly he could be forty years at this job. Birds hopscotch on his feeders. They nip into tubes of sunflower seeds. J. J. pours a glass of orange juice and takes it outside. Samuel's portable oxygen tank is lying in the grass at his side, but he's not using it. He's hooked the cannula around his neck so the tubing trails down his back.

J. J. comes up behind his dad and says, "Let me give you a break." Samuel leans on his hands. His face is flushed. He's sweaty.

"One hundred percent pure Florida orange juice," J. J. says and offers his dad the glass.

Samuel takes it.

The roots of the maple run under the fence. Samuel's already dug another hole for replanting it. He and J. J. marked a spot where there were no power or phone lines running overhead and it won't crowd the spruce Samuel planted in the spring.

J. J. says, "Rest a minute," and he reaches for the spade.

Samuel waves him away, saying, "I need to get as much root as possible." He hands J. J. the empty glass and starts chopping at the hole. "See those fingers trailing off under the fence, like thread?" he says. "We need them. We don't want to cut any off."

"Will it live?" J. J. says.

Samuel says, "There's no way I know of to tell." He pulls at the base of the tree. It's loose. J. J. bends over, gets a grip about a third of the way up the young trunk—can, for the first time, feel serious pain in his hand—and pulls while his father chops at the dirt. The roots give, then release.

"Got it," J. J. says.

They replant the tree, Samuel tamping, J. J. shoveling. The hole three-quarters full, Samuel dumps in fertilizer. He fills it with water that quickly seeps in. J. J. spades more dirt into the hole, and Samuel spreads it evenly. No way is the tree going to make it. They might as well be planting a fence post. J. J. and Samuel stand, dust themselves off, and Samuel unfolds a piece of paper he's pulled from his back pocket. He's removed the cannula and set it and his oxygen on the back steps. He begins to read. "Job fourteen," he says. "Verses seven through nine." J. J. looks for cues, wonders if he should bow his head. Samuel reads.

For there is hope of a tree, if it be cut down, that it will sprout again, and that the tender branch thereof will not cease.

Though the root thereof may wax old in the earth, and the stock thereof die in the ground.

Yet through the scent of water it will bud, and bring forth boughs like a plant.

J. J. says, "You've got religion."

"Always had religion," Samuel says. "It just wasn't Ruby's." He goes into the garage, returns carrying the paper and a strip of duct tape. He attaches the scripture to the tree's trunk. He says to J. J., "Besides, that that I just did, that's not religion." He takes J. J.'s arm and they walk toward the house. "You're playing golf," Samuel says, "and you come to a par three with nothing but water between you and the green. It's two hundred and ten yards to the cup, which is hidden behind a trap, and you're going to have to nail the biggest two iron you've ever hit or use a three wood, a club you might as well burn for all the use you give it. You take a ball out of your bag—not a cut-up one, and it doesn't have to be brand-new—and you toss it in the water, far out as you can. It's a gift, a tithe. Now, your two iron will carry the water, no problem. You've acknowledged your debt to the gods." J. J. holds the screen door for his dad, and Samuel says, "That's not religion either."

Late evening, and Samuel and J. J. sit on the front porch of Samuel's house. It's wide enough kids could play kid-sized hockey or soccer inside its short retaining walls. The house's brick is plum-colored. Samuel swings on a glider, and J. J. sits on the top step. He's had his hand x-rayed, and it was negative for a break. The walnut-sized swelling is gone, but the red bruise has spread like floodwaters up three of his fingers and across the back of his hand. He pokes and tightens the skin, and his first knuckle hurts.

J. J. says to his dad, "What about the discoloration—does that mean anything?" He holds his hand so Samuel can see it.

Samuel glances over his reading glasses. His oxygen sits like a lap-dog next to him. "You hurt your hand," he says. He stops the glider and says, "For a few days, just enjoy the various colors."

J. J. says, "It looks like blood under the skin."

They can see Flora in her yard. She's either planting for spring or cutting back for winter. Samuel says, "A couple of weeks ago I went down and test-drove a Ford Ranger. Made me feel like a tall person." He indicates how he was sitting above the traffic around him.

"I can see that," J. J. says.

His father, who's about five-six, has put on weight, seems stumpier than J. J.'s ever seen him. Has a belly like the business end of a plunger.

Samuel says, "Question," like he's raised his hand.

"Shoot," J. J. says.

"Junior Junior, what are you doing here?"

"I came to see you."

"Why?"

"I wondered if I could help, if there was anything I could do."

"Like what?"

"Build you something." J. J.'s worked construction since he was sixteen. He rubs his sore hand. He squeezes it into a fist, and the pinkie hurts. He says, "Do you want me to go?"

Samuel's gliding slowly again. "You can stay till doomsday if you want. I never said you weren't good company." He lights a cigarette. His Camels and a Bic have been sitting on the arm of the glider. He blows smoke, says, "Is your divorce official?"

"It is," J. J. says.

"Sorry to hear that," Samuel says. He taps ash onto the porch. "I thought she was a good one."

"She was a good one."

"Better than that first lady."

"She was."

"Funny," Samuel says. "Ha ha funny, I mean."

J. J. says, "She was funny, and she had a great big heart." He cups his hands to show how big Lisa's heart is. "She'd do anything for anyone."

"Amen to that."

J. J. turns to look at his father, says, "Amen to that?"

"You see your kids often?" Samuel says.

J. J. says, "I'm a million-dollar dad."

"Be a five-million-dollar dad," Samuel says.

J. J. nods. If only he could stamp out what his heart feels, its bedrock hurt, its beefs and grievances.

Samuel says, "You don't really want to talk about it, do you?"

"I guess I don't," J. J. says. He does, but won't, not with Samuel, not with anyone. He'd only be vague and tell the lies we all tell, the face-savers. He'd only end up crying in his beer, talking about his loser status in this wide world.

When he turns around, Flora is crossing the lawn, carrying a box the size and shape of a Monopoly game. She's wearing jeans whose white stitching loops over itself like the pull string on a sack of feed.

Samuel stubs out his cigarette, gathers together his cigs, lighter, and oxygen, gets up, says, "She doesn't get in the house," and goes inside.

J. J. meets Flora at the bottom of the steps. "I had my boy order this for you," she says, and she's got the box open. Inside is a nylon wrap you can fill with hot or cold water. Flora shows him how. There's a rubber stopper that seals tight, but it has to be fitted exactly or it won't screw in and you'll get a drip. You feed straps through plastic, then it's Velcro to Velcro. Flora pulls the wrap around her thigh, stands back, and says, "It holds about two quarts, warm water. Just use the tap."

"So this is for the hamstring?" J. J. says.

She nods and undoes the wrap. J. J. holds the box for her, and she notices his hand. "What happened?" she says.

"From when I fell."

She lays the wrap on the lawn and takes his hand, says, "That's blood, for sure. There's no question about it."

He says, "I thought so."

"What'd your father say?"

"He said I should enjoy the colors."

"Did you get an x-ray?"

"I did. Nothing's broken."

Flora picks up the wrap and finishes reboxing it. She presents it to J. J., saying, "Like I said, I had my boy order this for you. It's $37.88. That's with Utah state tax."

J. J. doesn't want it.

Flora says, "I think I told you my boy sells athletic supplies. It's how the track team earns money." She hands him a small packet. "I'll throw in some Breathe Rights." She touches her nose, runs a finger up and over the bridge. "You've seen them on football players. They're for your nose, for breathing." She sniffs hard. "Breathing and performance go hand in hand," she says.

J. J. tells her, "Just a minute," and goes inside. Samuel's not around. Out the kitchen window, J. J. sees him in the backyard. He's filling bird feeders. It's not cold, but Samuel's in a light cotton jacket and he's walking like a comic playing the old man, is carrying his oxygen under one arm. What J. J.'s learned about Flora's boy is that he's a runaway. He's been gone for over a year. The kid had problems, had been huffing gasoline, had slept and eaten in his closet for two months, had been hauled off in handcuffs. Sometimes, when he thought he was God, he got loud. He'd stand in the street and yell commandments. He'd be hospitalized, then come home and walk the streets lethargic as hell. First sign of new trouble was he'd start wearing weird pants, pantaloons, knickers, chaps. The kid had no sense of humor. Finally he was court-ordered onto meds, and he took off.

J. J. writes out a check for fifty dollars. When he gives it to Flora, telling her to fill in her son's name, letting her know the extra is a donation to the track team, saying, "It's a piddling amount," she says, "No, no. We can't do that."

"You can't do what?"

"It has to be the exact amount."

J. J. starts to fill out another check, has written the date and signed it, when she says, "Don't you have cash?" He looks at her. She says, "I have change."

"I don't," J. J. says.

She says, "Okay. This will do," and reaches for the check. He hurriedly writes in the amount. "My boy," Flora says, and she's handing over the wrap in its box, "banged his toe, broke it, and couldn't run for a month."

J. J. checks his hand and says, "That sounds bad." He says, "That'd be a problem."

"Something went wrong during that month," Flora says. They're walking across Samuel's lawn toward her place, and she's waving the check like she's fanning herself. "My boy, when he's running he's fine. Our family is working like a charm then. When my boy is running, life is a rose garden." She stops where the two yards meet. "But during that month the adversary crept into my boy's body, took him over, his soul, his mind, his thinking."

She rolls the check into a tube.

"Not that I'm trying to excuse my boy. The adversary cannot make us commit sin," she says. "Satan can only tempt us. We make the choice. The choices are all ours." She stops rolling the check. "Me," she says, "I choose to rejoice."

"That sounds good."

"It's healthy."

J. J. nods.

"My boy let Satan enter his physical body."

J. J. wants this to end, but doesn't know how to do that. He can't just walk away. His father would say, "Enough," and he'd raise his hands like he was about to push you off a cliff.

"My feeling is," Flora says, "that Satan can possess your body but not your soul. You give away your soul when you don't fight back, when you abdicate the throne God has given you. Your body, I mean, it is the temple of your spirit. It's in the scriptures." She folds the check into her pants pocket. "Satan tempted my boy with alcohol," she says. "He whispered in his ear, because my boy couldn't run, because my boy could barely walk as a result of what he'd done to his foot. Satan whispered in his ear, 'Just try this one time. It'll be fun. You'll feel good.'"

J. J. says, "I'm sorry about your son."

Flora only stares at him. Then she says, "My boy did automatic writing. He'd sit at his desk, and the spirit would move his hand. He wrote down things that had to do with relatives he couldn't have met. They were dead. We'd never told him anything about these people, but he had the facts, facts he couldn't have known."

"I've got to go," J. J. says. He touches his chest, says, "My father's heart, you know. I worry about him."

Flora takes hold of J. J.'s wrist and says, "Let me just tell you this. Just one more thing." She slips her hand into J. J.'s good hand. "The Bible tells us Satan is the prince of the air. There is no place on earth for Satan to land, to set his foot unless we invite him." She lets go of J. J.

"I really am sorry," he says.

She says, "When my boy is running, everything is fine."

J. J. holds up the box and says, "Thank your son for this."

Flora follows him a couple of steps up the lawn, saying, "I go to the temple every day I can for my boy. When I'm not there, prayers are said for him for me."

J. J. wants to keep walking, but he doesn't. He can't even keep his back to her. He says, "My mother believed in the temple. It gave her great comfort."

Flora says, "Around here they say your mother was a wonderful person."

"She was," J. J. says.

"I know that my savior has forgiven me," Flora says. "I choose to rejoice. Every day you have to sit down with your grief. You spend time with it. You invite it into your home the way you would a guest. You talk to your grief."

J. J. turns to go in.

Flora is close. She touches his arm, says, "I know I'm keeping you, but just one more thing." She steps in even closer. "You know how little children go to people who smile. If you wear a frown, they won't come to you. My daughter noticed that. She's an artist. She also noticed that you never see a picture of Jesus smiling, so she painted one. She painted a portrait of a smiling Jesus for the children."

J. J. doesn't know what to say.

"You'll have to come over and see it," Flora says. "The original is in our foyer. We had some prints made, and we sell them."

"Maybe sometime," J. J. says.

"They're prints," she says. "Not expensive. We want everyone to be able to afford one."

J. J. shrugs his no.

"Your father," Flora says, "he won't talk to me."

J. J. says, "He's that way," and now he can leave. He moves up the lawn, then climbs the steps and goes inside without looking back.

At three A.M., J. J. wakes. Something is wrong. This isn't Blondie-and-Dagwood-heard-a-noise-downstairs trouble. This isn't snore and grunt and out of bed to pee. This is someone with a bone to pick, and he's gotten in your head. This is knock-down-drag-out at the center of life.

J. J. finds his father in his bedroom slumped in a chair. He's been waking at night, short of breath, but this is something else. Four pillows, one on top of the other, are pushed up against the headboard. Samuel has pulled on pants, but not zipped them, and he's set out his shoes. They're slip-ons, tasseled, and the same color as the brick of the house. No shirt, no socks yet. "An ambulance is on the way," he says to J. J. "I want to be dressed." He gestures toward the closet.

J. J. selects a shirt, navy blue. Samuel gets into it, and J. J. buttons the shirt for his dad, even the collar. Samuel zips up his pants. "A cardigan," he says, and he points at his dresser. "White," he says. J. J. helps him into it. "Socks," Samuel says. J. J. hands him a pair, and Samuel turns them over in his hand, then flips them aside. His feet are swollen and cyanide blue. "No socks," he says. Samuel struggles to fit his feet into his shoes. He leans on J. J. to stand.

"Jacket?" J. J. says.

They agree on a sport coat.

Samuel's sitting on a padded bench in the foyer when the paramedics arrive. He's hugging his oxygen, has a nitroglycerin pill under his tongue. He wants to walk out, maybe sit in the front seat, but the paramedics put him on a stretcher.

At the hospital, J. J. can't sit still but doesn't want to wander far from the room where they've put his father. Samuel wasn't taken to emergency but to a way station off cardiology, a critical care step-down unit. The door's shut, and the doctor is talking to Samuel. J. J. stepped outside on his own. There's a computer in a recessed window next to the room. FOR STAFF USE ONLY. Taped to the door frame is a hand-lettered sign. It says, FALL RISK, PLEASE BE QUIET. THANK YA! J. J. wonders if that's his father and decides it must be left over. He keeps clenching, then opening his injured hand. The colors are kaleidoscopic. Ray Moss is Samuel's doctor, a cardiologist twenty years younger than his father but Samuel's poker buddy, a reckless five-card-stud man. He carries himself like a soap opera doctor and talks like everything's an alibi.

Moss waves J. J. in, says in passing, "He may have had a stroke. We'll know pretty soon." J. J. is surprised at how good his father looks.

A nurse is checking his lungs, moving her stethoscope like she's hunting water with a stick. He's got oxygen up his nose and is hardwired to a heart monitor, color-coded patches attached to his chest and inside his arms, but he's wearing a shit-eating grin and raising a hand to the room, saying something J. J. doesn't catch. Samuel's speech is slurred.

"What?" J. J. says.

"Rales," Samuel says. He gathers a hunk of his own hair between his thumb and middle finger, rubs the hairs together, and says, "Sounds like that."

The nurse rubs her hair together and says, "Perfect. That's right."

J. J. hears the rales, the sound of hair rubbed between fingers, a crackling. He helps the nurse remove the pillows from the bed, and she punches a remote so Samuel is laid out flat. She zero-balances the bed. It's also a scale. Samuel weighs one seventy. She elevates his head, and the nurse and J. J. get the pillows back under him. She speaks loudly to Samuel, says, "I'm going to run an I.V. push, Lasix." She turns his arm, examining the veins, says, "Nice big veins."

Samuel says, "That's the nicest thing I've heard in years."

She tightens a tourniquet around his upper arm and says, "I always get people on the first stick." She concentrates, aims, says, 'The vein says we're in." She tapes the needle in place, starts the I.V., and says, "You've kept my record intact." She makes notes and then leaves, and J. J.'s father takes his hand and says, "At least it ain't ICU." His grip is weak. He asks J. J. to find him a Coke.

"Is Coke okay?" J. J. says. "I mean, can you have Coke?"

"There'll be a machine," Samuel says. "Or ask a nurse." His ears are pink and backlit by lights on the headboard.

At the nurses' station J. J. asks if his father can have a Coke. He's told it's no problem. He finds a machine down the hall and gets a can for himself and Samuel. He buys a *Time* magazine. Samuel's asleep when he gets back. J. J. can't read, can't really think. He sits by his father and sips his Coke. At one point a guy about twenty comes in and attaches a clip to Samuel's finger. A cord runs from the clip to another monitor.

"What's that?" J. J. says.

"Oxygen saturation." The machine reads ninety-eight. "That's good," the man says, and he's gone.

The word *stroke* scares J. J. It means bedridden, maybe a walker. Means one foot in the grave. Speech therapy. Words will be lost. The past will fade. Memories go. Samuel will forget Ruby's name. Maybe even J. J.'s.

About seven, Samuel opens his eyes and reaches for the Coke.

"I'll get ice," J. J. says.

Samuel nods. Now he's low. He's one indignity from crying.

J. J. pours Samuel's Coke over ice. He unwraps a straw and bends it for Samuel, and his dad sucks in a long drink. He cradles the cup next to his side.

J. J. says, "How do you feel?"

Samuel thinks long and deep on this. Then he says, "Used to be when I slept on my back I woke up with a hard-on."

On his way out of the hospital J. J. holds the door for two Mormon priests. They're sixteen-year-olds who are coming to give the sacrament to Latter-day Saints who've been hospitalized. J. J. knows how this goes. He did it before that day he abandoned the Mormon ship. Later Mormon elders will come and bless the sick. It's Sunday morning. The boys are wearing chinos. One's in cheap dress shoes that look like you'd use motor oil to spiff them up. The other kid's got on city sandals, light-brown socks showing through. His hair is shaved to the skull on the sides. Both of them look smug. Or maybe it's just teenager dull. J. J. can't decide. They're wearing white shirts and the kind of thin knit tie you find in thrift stores.

They'll find a quiet room, and they'll bless the sacrament, the bread and the water. The kid in the cheap shoes will bow his head and say, "O God, the Eternal Father, we ask thee in the name of thy Son, Jesus Christ, to bless and sanctify this bread to the souls of all those who partake of it." J. J. has said those words. He knows the bread is to remind the members of the body of Jesus Christ. They commit to live Christ's commandments and are promised that, if they do, "they may always have his spirit to be with them." This priest will know the prayer by heart. The boy in city sandals will bless the water. It will be given in remembrance of the blood of the Son. He'll read the prayer from a laminated card he carries in his wallet.

• • •

It's still early morning when J. J. parks in front of his dad's house. He's not ready to go in. He can see in his rearview mirror Flora standing on the corner of her lot, on the grass, at the top of the shallow knoll that runs to the sidewalk, and she's got her arms folded across her chest. She's ready for church. Her dress is the color of a peach. It's long, almost touches the grass. Flora's focused on the corner up the hill. Her son's not coming. He isn't going to turn that corner and, running like the wind, shift gears and coast down M Street.

Flora knows her boy knows how to run a downhill. It's second nature to him.

The photographer, he's on his porch, cigar lit, ready to take a picture, tripod, boxy camera, one of those capes hanging off the whole setup, like Brady shooting Civil War soldiers. But he isn't going to get a picture of Flora's son, if that's what he's here for, no shot of the boy's perfect stride, the foot plant exactly where it should be under knee and hip, the elbows set the way they should be set for the slant of M Street.

J. J. sits in his car.

He'll get a start on a ramp today. Stroke inevitably follows stroke— no? He'll build the ramp so it doubles back on itself and has a wide easy turn. The porch is high. He may have to widen doors inside the house. Some he'll take from their hinges. The hallway'll be a squeeze for a wheelchair. He's got to think about his dad's need for privacy. The man always shuts and locks the bathroom door. He keeps doors closed. Everything's dead-bolted. Maybe there's some kind of automatic setup J. J. can install, like they use in office buildings.

The photographer might as well put his camera away. He might as well swallow his cigar.

Flora keeps looking. Her grief is by her side.

The Egyptians built temples. They called the temple the House of Life. Their temple ordered their world. They taught us we can keep chaos at bay if we'll just keep thinking. Chaos is the result of the end of thinking. It was in the temple where the Egyptians thought, where they weighed and measured the enigmas.

There are so many ways to think. A world of possibilities. There's talk itself. Loquaciousness. There's reason. Logic. Math. Dance, that's a way of thinking. There's music. And photography. Photography's got its rhetoric, its choreography.

If we'll just put our mind to it, they say.

Thinking, King's X, time out, a way of saying smoke 'em if you got 'em.

In the temple the Egyptians sang the creation song with the morning stars.

Flora, J. J., and the photographer, they could sing. They could hold hands and make a circle. Or alone. You can dance in a circle all by yourself. Workout videos, when they tell you to circle, they say, "If you don't have room, just circle in place." J. J., he could do that. Or Flora. Or the photographer.

But not today. Not this Sunday morning.

Flora, she can waltz, two-step, even fox-trot with her grief, but in the end she's going to have to eat it.

Think what we want, we all are.

CLOTHING ESTHER

Lisa Torcasso Downing

MARY HAD STOOD BEFORE HER mother-in-law countless times before this. Stood before her more than beside her, the way Esther had always wanted her. *Help me with this roast, Mary; Come sing while I play; Read to me awhile, won't you, dear?* Most women who are bound together by their love for a man who is, to one, the protected and the beloved, and to the other, the protector and the lover, get their heads and hearts all snarled together so that neither reason nor tender feeling can be loosed to a useful satisfaction.

Sometimes, though, life waters people instead of drying them out. Sometimes standing before someone becomes less a stance of submission and more a pose, a position that is neither weak nor strong, but one which simply allows the other to look upon the one. Curiosity, envy, affection all kneaded together like dough, rising quietly in a warm spot on the kitchen counter.

Mary, you have to knead the dough with your knuckles.

Devotion: Mary and her husband Lance had taken in Esther and her husband, George, two weeks before George was diagnosed with stomach cancer, twelve weeks before he died, leaving ten weeks for Mary to learn to pose before Esther, ten weeks to establish the new habit of standing before her.

Rounding down, the years between the death of Lance's father and the death of his mother were sixteen. Mary had plodded along them like a tired horse on a familiar trail, passing detours and distractions with little more than a tail flick, pausing only to provide suck or to again foal. Mary had not been unhappy, and neither had Esther, who enjoyed the pleasure of sleeping a wall away from her eldest son.

And of course, there were the grandchildren.

But the nights often bore down hard on Mary. Her secret fear was that the darkness—that bit which tore into her senses like soil—was attached not to the spinning universe but to her own spiraling mind. Over the years, Mary had shared many things with Esther—a bathroom scale, sometimes a hairbrush, and, of course, the children. Yet, she never shared (wouldn't want to bother her with) every little worry or wonder in her brain, whether it popped in only every now and again or whether it had taken up permanent residence. Simple things had vanished, and though Mary swept under the table for them and hoped bleach would reveal them, she just couldn't put her finger on the simple things Esther always told the children we were on this planet to enjoy.

Certainly the path Mary trod is common, full of head colds, Scout meetings, and parent-teacher conferences, but with Esther always before her to cluck and nod and encourage, Mary moved along with a sense of purpose. She was building a family, a thing she did not at all know how to do, while Lance, especially in more recent years, was off building communication systems in Thailand or Sri Lanka, an important service in anyone's book. The difficult nights were Mary's alone nights, and during them, she lay awake and still, staring up into the darkness and listening beyond the sheet rock for some symptom, any sign, of Esther's life—a cough, a moan, a snore, even the hummed notes of a pioneer hymn; something to assure her that all was well. Any sound that seeped through the wall or under the door into the crevices of her mind came as a sound from heaven, testifying that this path was the chosen one, and Esther, her unlikely companion.

Of course, roads end—sometimes abruptly—and Esther's road was like this. An unexpected and wholly massive stroke put a quick halt to Esther's plans for Sunday dinner. Tonight Lance would've been on a jetliner to corporate in Chicago, but instead he is at home, watching the kids watch him and not knowing at all what to do when Colleen spits at him, then locks herself in the bathroom. And Mary, who should've been at home helping Colleen with her fours times table and Marcus with his solar system report and refereeing her three teenage sons as they fight over the computer, instead finds herself standing before Esther. Finds herself staring down at Esther, staring down at her mother-in-law as she lies upon her back, is laid on a stainless-steel table in a stark back room of the Village Gate Funeral Home.

Mary clutches the overnight bag, examines the green hospital gown in which Esther is clothed. She wills herself not to glance again at Esther's face, not to see what she noticed immediately: that this face she loves—with its small hump on the bridge of the nose and that old-age wattle beneath the chin, with its thin lips and elongated cheeks—has been made unfamiliar through the subterfuge of a mortician's make-up sponge.

Beside Mary stands a woman, and this woman has a voice, soft, smooth. Her touch lands on Mary's elbow, then comes a tug against the suitcase. Mary resists. That which she has carefully packed inside this bag is sacred to her and to Esther: the white gown, the ceremonial vestments worn in the Mormon temple, and the holy garment. The voice again, tender, and Mary comprehends, gives in, releases the case, which the woman places atop the counter behind them.

"I'll show the others in as soon as they arrive." Another touch, this time on her shoulder, then footsteps across tile, the pull of the door and its attending, vacuum-like sensation as the woman withdraws, and then the hush.

There is a moment in every life when we learn, we see, we slam head-on into the comprehension that what we always knew is no longer real, that experience is unduly egocentric, that color is subjective, and that silence cannot be where breathing is found. We have, all of us, we have said, *Sit still, Hold still, Simmer down, Be still.* Even God Himself has commanded it. And yet, when we face the face of death, when we see the ones we've seen every day truly stilled and made artificial by life's last word, only then do we begin to sense how hollow our minds are; how empty, how barren of things known. In that moment—that lonely, isolated, imperative moment—the only thought we can form, the only word we can hold on to, is that one simple word; that odd, unanswerable word. *How?* Not "How could this happen?" nor "How will we manage?" Only, "How?"

Right now, Mary stands in this moment; and that simple syllable is gyrating in her mind, gathering nothing, not even a dusting of sense, but spreading itself thinly, evenly, line upon line, an unanesthetic-like numbness between reality and acceptance. Her hands remain at her sides, and yet she desperately reaches for something to hold on to, an edge into which she can sink her teeth, a ledge onto which she can crawl, something with which she can save herself from facing herself, from looking down and seeing the great nothing that becomes us. When a distant door bangs, from Mary there comes no reaction.

Mary had been only sixteen when she married Lance, himself only seventeen. The ceremony occurred in her mother's backyard beneath a rented arch laced with crepe paper and pink silk roses. She married him before a sparse, outdoor congregation of relatives, voyeuristic ward members, and high school baseball players. The bride and groom, respectively a sophomore and a senior, were nothing more than a pair of everyday kids who had become too familiar with one another, a clumsy pair of kids who confused exotic with erotic, and who believed, for a few brief minutes anyway, that passion might transport them away from the mundane. Of the two, she loved the most, loved with a zeal she felt could heal his wounds and make him visible in the same way that heat in the desert makes the air above the road visible, causing it to wave back and forth, all silvery, and be noticed. An illusion, perhaps; but to Mary, at sixteen, illusion and vision were more than bedfellows. They were creators of life.

George had raged at his son and then wept. Esther had closed the bedroom door and stared.

It had been Mary's mother who begrudgingly made these arrangements and Mary's mother who had footed the bill. But it was Mary who paid and Mary who lived with the consequences. It was Mary's ears that rang with her mother's incessant whine: *worthless whore, worthless Mormons. Don't ruin your life. Don't marry him. No one has to know.*

But of course everyone knew. They may not have known Mary's mother cursed when the girl stubbornly asked if she was coming out to the wedding, may not have realized the woman lay drunk on the sofa throughout, but still they knew. They saw. The fact was undeniable. Mary gave herself away.

Lance's father was not an educated man, but he had had sense and enough connections to land himself a career position in the public relations department of the Church during the early 1960's, about the time things were heating up. The pay, of course, was not substantial, especially for a man with six children, but it had been enough to allow him a mortgage on a five-bedroom rambler situated on a couple of acres outside the city limit. When Lance's wedding plans were announced, George cashed out the meager savings he had accumulated for his son's mission and bought him a wedding gift, a twenty-foot tin can with a bed, a kitchen, and an impossibly small bathroom. He parked it behind the house.

His gift to his "new daughter"—he had swallowed when he said it—was a promise, a finger-in-the-chest sort of promise, which he made to her as he looked Lance in the eye and proclaimed: "You're finishing school." Both he and Lance, both Mary and Esther, knew he didn't mean just high school. "You've got a family," her father-in-law said, straightening up while loosening his tie, and Mary's heart beat and beat and beat. "And you're going to live up to it." He handed Lance the key to the trailer, then walked away and around the few Relief Society sisters who remained, kindly picking up fallen napkins and emptying punch bowls into the garden. Mary's eyes followed him, looked beyond him, and saw in the distance, somewhere over the salt flats, tufted white clouds against the hazy sky. The year was 1977.

1977 . . . Hair was still worn long. The bottoms of blue jeans still belled. The blacks would never hold the priesthood. The Berlin Wall was immoveable, and Mary stood before Esther in a long dress of white lace she'd bought at Deseret Industries using her babysitting savings.

Everyone had gone home in a flash, everyone except Lance and his parents. All Mary had left to do was step inside her mother's house, change into her street clothes, and walk into a new life, become a new wife, and soon a mother—a grown-up. Esther offered to help her, but of course Mary said no. Of course she said no. She said no, and her lip quivered.

Esther took her chin and tipped it up, looked into her pale eyes and they locked eyes. But only for a moment, only for the tiniest, briefest of moments before Mary slammed hers shut. Dear God in heaven, how could she look this woman in the eye, knowing Esther knew all that Mary had done, that she had willingly spread her legs to entice her son, that she had robbed him of his status in the Church, had embarrassed his family, hurt them in a way that no temple sealing ceremony a year down the road could completely heal?

It was all her fault. Lance had been good—the first assistant to the bishop—he had been that good. She had never been anything, not even bad, and hardly ever present. In fact, more days than not, Mary bedded down wondering: Had the day really happened? Did she really exist? Or was her life someone else's dream?

So it was odd, the way Mary opened her eyes when Esther said, "Look at me, child," odd the way Mary responded with both arms to Esther's tug on her hand, an invitation into an embrace, and odder still the way Mary's eyes watered and simply couldn't stop. It was 1977. The world stood somewhere between war and peace. And Mary, this little Mary who had never taken up more space than was absolutely necessary, had seen, in that fragile, unexpected moment, the world turn in Esther's eyes.

Footsteps sound along the tiled corridor, the heel-toe click of pumps, one pair. Mary inhales deeply, smells witch hazel. The shoes stop. Another door closes, and Mary exhales, the sound fading.

She turns from Esther to the suitcase on the stainless counter. It sits between a plastic filing box and a fist-sized clock which is plugged into a socket over the backsplash. She hates having become, by default, the presiding matriarch of a family that the winds of responsibility have scattered like sand. She tugs on the zipper and opens the lid. How she does not want to do this.

But when such things are expected, such things are done. She removes two transparent packages, each marked with the rose-colored symbols of Beehive Clothing. It is her duty to clothe Esther—to hide her most intimate self—in the sacred garments, in their silky white camisole and knee-length bottoms, to adorn her in a white gown and in the robes of the Holy Priesthood.

And so last evening, after the children had finally fallen asleep and as Lance wept alone in their bed, Mary had steam-ironed Esther's hand-embroidered apron; she had carefully heat-creased each fold of the robe; she ran the sash along the length of the ironing board and pressed it to a beautiful sheen. To the temple packet, she had added her own never-used knee-high white stockings. Then today, on the way to

Village Gate, she had purchased at a department store a pair of white satin slippers to replace the worn pair Esther had used in the temple each week.

Mary lays one garment package beside the clock, presses the other against her chest. She turns back to her mother-in-law.

Four other women whom Mary trusts to know better than she how to dress the dead are on their way. But it is Esther who needs dressing, Esther who is dead. And so, with only twenty minutes between now and the appointed time of their arrival, it is Mary who steps forward.

Lance should not have asked this of her.

Her eyes traverse Esther, toe to crown. Where is the trembling hand? That forward tilt of her right shoulder?

When his father passed, Lance had chosen not to participate in clothing him in the temple garb. His great regret remains that he cast that one last dignity to strangers. So with the pronouncement of his mother's death still ringing in Mary's ears, Lance had put his foot down. "We owe my mother this dignity." He had repeated himself at the breakfast table. And in the den. And in the car. He had even told the funeral planner, his fingers pressing tightly into Mary's waist, "We owe it to her."

Inside each Mormon temple is a place which is like no other—a quiet, veiled-in space where initiate blessings are granted, woman to woman; a place where two sisters in faith, two strangers, stand before one another, look one another in the eye and touch one soul against the other, fingertip to flesh, and repeat the words of a blessing and an anointing, the undefiled intimacy of which reflects the very depths of God's eternal love for woman, and through her, for all his children. And Mary has been there.

It is not that she is thinking of this place as she stands before Esther this final time, for the years between back then and now have dimmed the flame of this memory. Rather, she is feeling the experience in much the same way an old woman sitting in a breeze beside the last blooms of summer feels her first kiss, feels it neither in her heart nor in her mind, but all along that tendril we call the soul. In truth, Mary is scarcely aware that her left hand is rising or that her fingers are curled like the petal of a tulip. She is barely aware that the garment package has slipped from her hand onto Esther's forearm, or that her hip presses against the stainless-steel table.

When Mary's fingertips alight on Esther's right cheek, she draws back her hand—the absence of warmth, the lack of response—and takes in the whole of Esther's face. Touching again, she pushes against her subtle sag, a stubborn remainder of that grotesque twist which had marred Esther's face while she lay dying in the ICU. The skin feels cool, the cosmetics waxy and moist.

No. With every breaking sinew in Mary's body, she does not want to do this.

Using the nail of her index finger, Mary scratches at the cleft of Esther's chin until the old age spot shows through. Grandma's chocolate drop. The children will expect to see it.

She straightens, thinks, *How?* Meaning, *How can Lance expect this of me?*

The answer comes—though she neither expects it nor feels ready to receive it—as an impression in her mind, more an image than an actual memory, more like the touch of the spirit than a process of the brain; an answer which allows Mary to see as though through a window back to a day when Esther had stood in the front of a chapel wearing a deep coral suit with a daisy pinned to her lapel and had leaned over a coffin to bestow a final kiss. Not on George, for his coffin had been large, black, and stately.

Suddenly, as Mary envisions a long-ago Esther leaning over a small, white casket, the memory of a once-told story flows back, the tale of Lance's youngest sister, of how Lance had left her unattended in the pool at the house of one of his junior varsity teammates, and of how the angel at the top of the family's Christmas tree had come to be named Kristie: the story of how Lance had disappeared inside himself, where Mary had found him.

Suddenly it is clear: Lance expects because Esther did.

Mary dusts the white gray curls from Esther's forehead.

Sadly, what Mary most wants to know is unknowable. What is knowable, she thinks, as her finger gently twists one of Esther's locks, is that she is the "we" and has always been. Lance never knew it: he never really saw.

She places a hand on either side of Esther and gazes at the chocolate drop.

Lance had come to think of Mary as his partner, the same way he considered the two women in his domestic life a team. But Mary understands the truth: Lance may bring home his paycheck, may sometimes even take her to a movie; but the only thing which leaves him feeling truly alive is sharing the blessing of modernization with strangers in foreign places. He knows his mother baked cookies for the kids and read them Beatrix Potter only because Mary told him, but she didn't mention—and he never noticed—that Esther's bedroom door always closed at eight and that the crumbs which were left were Mary's to wipe away.

Bending her elbows, she slowly lowers herself.

Not that Mary minded cleaning up. Hers was a heart grown in the soil of gratitude, in that relief that comes from having been put alone in the dark, in the dirt, and then feeling the rain of heaven fall.

There is water here, tears in Mary's eyes as she hovers over Esther's face, looking down on the features of the woman who had showered love upon her life even though she never deserved it. A tear lands on Esther's cheek. Good-bye is so hard, so Mary waits . . . holds out for the miracle, for that puff of spent air that surely will arise from Esther's mouth. The fallen tear slowly tracks down Esther's cheek, leaving a trail upon her made-up face. Esther deserves a miracle.

But nature, as it most often will, triumphs over miracle, and soon Mary must exhale, must let go, must feel and hear her own breath slowly escaping her lungs, unanswered. As her exhale sweeps across Esther's mouth and nose, Mary tenderly presses her lips against Esther's cold, unresponsive mouth. She pulls back, hovers inches over Esther's face, and her soul gathers up final intimacies like the sun draws moisture over a desert pond. Then she says it, whispers it really, whispers it like a call, implores, says, "Esther?"

And the response, of course the response remains only—the response remains nothing more than the quiet murmur of her own heart, of her own breath, of her own soul.

This—Mary straightens, wiping her eyes—is the woman who taught her how. With one hand, she clutches the steel rim of the table. How to change a diaper. How to bake whole-wheat bread. The other hand comes to rest on the plastic package from Beehive Clothing, which has come to rest in the crook of Esther's elbow. How to survive. She closes her fingers around the garment package, lifts her chin—

how to forgive—and she scans the air over Esther's body. Though she strains to detect even the faintest aura or apparition or manifestation or sign, Mary understands that Esther is not here, that she can no longer exist in this mortal sphere except in Mary's mind, that she has gone home to those who've gone before.

Resigning herself, Mary lifts the package and tears through the plastic. Certainly the robes of the Holy Priesthood are one thing, a public thing in comparison to this. Mary holds the sacred garment against her bodice. This, Mary thinks, smoothing the silky fabric of the pant, is quite another. This will be Mary's gift.

The tread of Esther's foot had experienced the excess of seventy-five years of wear. The calluses, cracked and white, are all still here, on top of the little toe, on the underside of the big one, on the pad at the base of it. Oddly, pink veins, where there should be blue, traverse the summit of Esther's foot. Her toenails are clipped, filed, and painted pale pink. Mary pinches off the memory of Colleen's slumber party, of seven little girls with cotton between their toes and seven little bottles of glitter nail polish lined up atop an unabridged dictionary. Those cotton balls had been Esther's idea. She begins with Esther's right foot. Mary gathers up her courage as she gathers up one leg of the garment bottom, and then loops the fabric over Esther's toes, which point straight up, a position which seems unnatural considering her state of repose. Enough space exists between Esther's feet so that Mary's right hand slips between them nicely.

Next Mary wills the fingers of her left hand to temporarily release the fabric. She then slides the palm of her hand into the narrow space between the steel table and Esther's ankle. She lifts: the tendon gives, startling Mary, who had supposed rigor mortis to be a permanent state for the human dead. But after a closed-eye moment in which she regroups her determination and chastises herself for the uneasiness in her stomach, she continues, lifting the foot with one hand and sliding the garment past the heel with the other. The foot is not light, but the act is easier to perform than she anticipated. She takes heart, then repeats the motion on Esther's left side.

With Esther's feet properly through the legs of the sacred garment, Mary surveys the situation. Esther's legs are shaved and the skin loose, especially about her knees, but Mary realizes that the thighs beneath the hospital gown remain a formidable obstacle. She hooks both thumbs and each finger into the opposite sides of Esther's right garment leg and pulls it to where the calf meets steel. Perhaps this gift Mary is offering is only a weak outward sign of what she feels for Esther—Mary does the same with the left leg—but at least it is discernible.

With her task on the left side likewise completed, Mary hunches down and force-wiggles the garment between Esther's calf and the steel. Clothing Esther would be easier with someone there to lift the leg, but Mary will not have her gift diminished. In this world in which so little can be known, discernible becomes certainty enough. Therefore Mary continues alone, successfully tugging the hem of each garment leg to the appropriate spot three inches over each kneecap.

From here on, Mary's hands move in secret beneath the hospital gown, pulling, tugging, urging this to end. Thread at the seam pops quietly as Mary contends resolutely with Esther's bulk. In this effort to raise honor to Esther's most private and sacred self, Mary is discovering that the weight of death is a much heavier burden than she ever could have known.

The time will collapse before Mary knows it, and the four women whom she invited to assist her in clothing Esther will arrive, respectfully clad, reverently hushed, shown in by the rail-thin woman who had touched Mary's shoulder. These five will find Mary sitting on the cold tile floor, her legs extended, her head propped against one of the steel table legs. Her eyes will be wide, red; her cheeks damp; and her hair out of place. The four women, her friends, will rush to her, cooing words of comfort, words like, "Mary, oh Mary, you know this is too hard," "Mary, you shouldn't have come alone," and "Sweet Mary, how Esther must have loved you."

The mortuary hostess will roll over a chair for Mary, and the sisters from the church will insist she elevate herself and sit. So she will. The reward for her obedience will be the feel of their soft hands on her shoulders and hair. She will nod that she is all right. Of course she is; yes, all is well. The hostess will leave them. All is well.

"We should pray," one of the sisters will suggest, and Mary will watch them bow their heads.

But she will not join them. Instead Mary will sit in the black chair on caster wheels and stare at this closing rendition of Esther, at her legs left splayed and her hair mussed, at the hospital gown smoothed as flat as Mary could manage. The prayer will end swiftly and the women will turn their attention to the overnight bag and to the white gown and the robes of the Holy Priesthood which remain inside it, undisturbed. Mary, who will use her feet to glide the chair out of their way, will make herself look on their faces as they raise the hem of Esther's hospital gown and gasp, as they pull the green, cotton fabric from her shoulder and whisper in worried glances, as they see for themselves how Mary's good intentions measure up against death.

"Oh, Mary," one of them will murmur, "you can't do this alone."

Mary, whose chair will then rest near Esther's feet, will flick her gaze from the face of this known stranger down to Esther's strange face and remember the last time she had sat beside her. An IV had been dripping while monitors recorded what had seemed important. Though the medical staff had worked, though the priesthood had blessed, though Mary and Lance had prayed, Esther's eyes had still rolled heavenward and fixed themselves eternally there. Only then had Lance put his arm around Mary and led her, weeping, from the ICU.

Today Mary will find no comfort except that which comes from wrapping her own arms about herself. She will cringe as her friends jointly push, pull, and shove the woman she loves into positions amenable to dressing a corpse. The ladies will be discreet, of course, will avert their eyes, will not see what only Mary sees, given her vantage point in the chair, when, during that first violent roll, Esther's hospital gown defies decorum in favor of gravity, opening a glimpse of Esther's faded pubic region. Instantly Mary will think of Lance, of where he came from, bloodied and wet; instantly she will feel in her groin the dark shadow, the black press, which marks the descent of a child; and then, almost as though the one hunted the other, an image of the battered Christ standing before those cursed souls who cast lots for his vesture. Each image, each worry, each fear will tear into her as that cruel and familiar bit has, for decades, torn into her confidence; will tear in and grind out the words, *"You can't do this alone,"* will scrape her insides, *"You can't do this alone,"* will remind her, *"You can't do this . . ."*

But sometimes the voice that resounds in the heart is louder than the one that sounds in the mind. Sometimes words are whispered from soul to soul, from sphere to sphere, and can be heard only when we hold still, sit still, keep the wheels beneath us from turning, and listen for what lives beyond the veil. Such whisperings, such transparent and flawless communication, will come to Mary today, will set a diamond wall around the part within her that is brilliant and divine; will be here soon, will promise her, will say, *"My beloved child, there is no other way."*

And suddenly she will have enough of looking. She will not finish watching the women as they amend what she was able to do correctly herself, as they tug the seat of Esther's garment bottom over her nakedness. Nor will she endure witnessing them untangle the stranglehold that the garment camisole has upon Esther's neck. Instead, Mary will close her eyes, seal them against the nightmare before her, preferring to imagine herself many miles away and many years ago, standing in a temple at the base of a mountain, a temple made golden by the lights which shine at night, wearing a slitted gown and feeling the press of fingers at her hip as a blessing and anointing is bestowed. She will return in her mind to the small trailer, to the foldaway bed, and to the memory of that first set of tiny pink fingers kneading her breast while a matching tiny, pink mouth drinks in life. She will look up in both places, in both times, and beside her she will see her husband. Of course she will see Lance. But before him, before her, she will always see Esther.

MIRACLE

Eric Samuelsen

LUCILLE WENTWORTH SAT IN HER RECLINER working on her cross-stitch, watching Judy and Ray hold hands, sitting across from her on the couch. It was late, past one; they'd talked for hours, the conversation flowing around Lucille like the river around rocks that time she'd gone white-water rafting with her nephew Verl and his wife. She was content with it, she thought, it was all right with her. She wasn't going to raise any objections.

"When was that, Mom? Do you remember?"

Judy, trying to involve her in the conversation again; that was the worst part of a third-wheel night like this one, their attempts to be mannerly. It wasn't anything more than manners, she knew. Still, Lucille would be civil too.

"Sometime in July, I expect," she said, trying for a cheerful tone. "Not long after the fourth."

That was her role tonight, and, like as not, forever, to confirm dates and times of day, to stamp approval, to validate. A court recorder still, she thought, as though miracles didn't happen if not verified by the proper authority. The whole thing was really built on miracles, to listen to them.

Miracles, count 'em up—the extra pork chop, Brother Foxworth's lesson, a lawn mower on the fritz, a stick of jerky in a trucker's jacket. Now it was late and they were still at it, listing all the signs and strange wonders in the heavens. Everything that proved it was meant to be. Well, just look at 'em, Judy and Ray on the sofa with the afghan behind him. She wondered if the afghan still stunk, from when Ray had barfed on it. Another secret they'd kept, Lucille and Ray, one more thing Judy didn't know about her intended. Didn't appear to matter; couldn't nothing break that feeling they had—blessed, like God had kissed them both on the forehead.

Lucille didn't trust it. She had more than just suspicions, that was for sure. She was willing enough to go along with it, with their exclamations of unbelief and amazement, but she didn't feel much like it. Miracles come from faith, and Lucille had no faith in this one. But things had happened, and they couldn't be easily explained. Their presence, holding hands (holding hands, holding hands!) was proof of something or other, and whatever it was, it wasn't her job to break the spell. But a real miracle wouldn't be so risky. A real miracle wouldn't feel so wrong.

"When was that, Mom? What was the day?"

She knew right well what the day was they were talking about; she knew it practically to the minute. The first time she ever laid eyes on him was about 1:15 in the afternoon of July eighth—her years as a court stenographer gave her a good head for facts. Seven months ago to the day, a Sunday morning and the hottest day of the year, there he'd been, in the lobby of the Twenty-Eighth Ward chapel. In he walked, his gray hair plastered against his scalp, tattered corduroys held up by clothesline hanging over his shoulders like suspenders, laces in just one of his battered Adidas, a red kerchief around his neck, a backpack dangling off one shoulder, a thin sleeping bag rolled up and slopping out each end of the pack. Short, stoop-shouldered, at least three days worth of stubble, and reeking of cheap beer and pee. He had a piece of cardboard with LOS VEGAS misspelled on it in Magic Marker, and he was holding a trucker's cap in front of him, standing uncertainly by the door. A bum, in fact. Just a bum.

Lucille had been raised to value neatness and hard work and independence, and while she was willing enough to write out a check for ten bucks and give it to the deacons every Fast Sunday, that was about as much charity as she had in her. She might look at this sort of vagabond, and wonder how he had come to such a pass, and shudder at the thought. But there were shelters for such people, she was overtaxed to support those shelters, and a bowl of hot stew and a hard bench to sleep on could be found there. She drove past men like him all the time, standing by the Kmart parking lot or by the interstate on-ramp. She'd toss him the loose change in her purse if she was stopped at a light when she saw him, then wonder if she'd really helped, or if she'd just given him money to buy cheap booze or drugs, make his problems worse.

Thirty-four years since Mick had died, rolling over his pickup try-ing to make it home through a snow storm, and she hadn't noticed the world standing in line to give her a hand up. She hadn't missed a day's work till she retired four years ago, starting with every lousy job available for respectable women, waitress, teacher's aid, filing and typ-ing and flagging cars on construction sites. Nights, she'd gone back to school, and gotten her stenographer's license, and became recorder of the Third Circuit Court, put in her thirty years on the job. And she'd made the mortgage payment on time every month, kept food on the table and clothes on Judy's back and, every now and then, managed a treat—a trip to Baskin-Robbins or a matinee at the movies, when they could find one that wasn't filth through and through. But she knew how thin the ice had been beneath her, how little it would have taken for her to break through and drown. That was her job, to record human misery and foolishness, the consequences of bad choices, and their final legal disposition.

Recesses, she and the bailiffs used to wonder what would become of the defendants afterward, and speculate regarding what chance they might have to turn their lives around. Often enough, they wouldn't even have to speculate—they saw more than their share of repeat of-fenders. She hated scandals on TV—Watergate or Clarence Thomas or Oliver North—not for the reasons Judy hated them, not because they showed the decline of the world into Last Days levels of immorality. No, what she saw were faces of folks about to lose their jobs; what she saw beckoning was homelessness. It was the one thought with the power to keep her awake nights.

It was silly, she knew—the idea of Haldeman or Nixon or Tenet or Kenneth Lay bumming quarters on the street. Judy had laughed at her once when she had expressed such a sentiment. "Clarence Thom-as, homeless," she'd crowed. "He's a big-name attorney. He'll find work if they turn him down." And Lucille had laughed too; it was, after all, silly. But she'd seen enough doctors and lawyers and successful busi-nessmen brought low in her time to know it was possible. Drink or drugs or sex scandal or money problems; any life could be wrecked. You had to be on your guard.

All those years, it had just been the two of them, Lucille and Judy, her daughter just nine when Mick died. After Judy's birth, the five miscarriages, one right after another, had felt like blows, God down on her for something undefined. After the last miscarriage, she'd stopped going to church entirely. And then Mick had rolled the pickup, and suddenly she'd understood God's infinite mercy, why he'd sent her only the one child, all she could have managed to support by herself. And she hadn't missed church a single Sunday since.

And then Judy had turned sixteen, and her late-night job cleaning the fourplex in Orem, sweeping up popcorn and mopping up sticky Coke syrup after the moviegoers left, had eased things considerably. And Judy had graduated, and Lucille had felt guilty about her grades; low B's and high C's, not good enough for most colleges even if they could have afforded a good one; caused, Lucille thought, by too many late nights working and not enough sleep. Judy had gone two years to Snow and gotten her associate's and then come back home and gone to secretarial school. Dropped out after two semesters, and it turned out she was dyslexic, something the high school or Snow could have discovered if anyone there had cared to look for it. And then Judy had dropped by the Albertson's supermarket to pick up eggs and bread, and seen an ad, and applied, and they'd hired her. And after two years as a bagger and one as a checker, she'd taken advantage of an apprenticeship program they were offering and gotten training as a butcher. And she'd been in the meat department ever since.

And that had been their lives, the years turning mother and daughter into friends, a butcher and a court recorder sharing a home, more roommates than blood relations, companions, sharing bills and chores and conversation, their lives centered on church callings and their cats and visiting teaching and rented movies and gardening. They'd settled. Lucille turned seventy, Judy forty-three.

And then, that Sunday, there he'd stood, in their chapel. A bum, in their nice chapel. All Lucille's fears (not so irrational: butchers did get fired, pension funds got embezzled, homes were foreclosed) made flesh, her deepest anxieties shuffling uneasily in the foyer. Mostly, Lucille hoped someone would have the guts to make him leave. Not easy to do, but that's why men had the priesthood.

In time, probably someone would have; the Twenty-Eighth Ward, in those days before Brandon Fisher became bishop, was not a ward noted for its friendliness. Any other Sunday of the year, Ray would have been—very nicely—sent on his way. Maybe given a ride to the shelter in the back of Mark Hughes's pickup. Or maybe just given directions there.

Except that that particular Sunday, Cyril Foxworth had taught the lesson in Sunday school, on loving your neighbors and Christian charity. And as always when Brother Foxworth talked, Lucille sat on the front row with all the other widows, paying rapturous attention.

So that was the first miracle, that Brother Foxworth taught that week when he wasn't the regular teacher, that the commonplaces and clichés of the lesson were transmitted not through the medium of Brother Kerr's wearisome intellectualizing but through Brother Foxworth's courtly charisma. He was actually a poor teacher, some said—couldn't stick to the subject, much given to long rambling stories, spent three weeks covering five verses. None of that mattered, not to Lucille, nor, she suspected, to Clarice Bowman or Verna Lundquist or any of her other friends in Relief Society. His prophetic white shock of hair, his dancing blue eyes under imposing eyebrows, his impish wit, and above all, his richly modulated baritone invested his every word with authority and charm. "Charity never faileth," he'd intoned, savoring every word, "charity suffereth long," and he'd looked soulfully over them all, walking slowly across the classroom making eye contact right down the front row. And so, an hour later, Lucille Wentworth actually found herself thinking about walking up to the bum in the lobby and inviting him to join them, her and Judy, for dinner.

Thinking about it only, of course. Except, as she stood there thinking, Judy came up to her, a little late as usual; her Primary class always went over. And without Lucille saying a word about anything, Judy had, right out of the blue, asked, "Is there someone we could invite for dinner, do you think?"

Turned out Judy had thawed three pork chops by mistake that morning, and had been sitting all through church wondering what to do about it. Judy knew well enough that pork doesn't keep long, and they weren't the kind to let it go to waste, a good pork loin cut. Be best if they shared it with someone, she said. One extra pork chop, then, that was what had prompted her, that and Brother Foxworth's lingering spell. But still, she could hardly believe she had done it, afterward.

"Be honored if you'd share supper with us," she'd said to the bum in the foyer. His clothes were cleaner than she expected; she remembered that detail.

He'd looked startled by her abruptness.

" 'Preciate it. I really do."

"All right, then," she'd said, and pointed out their blue Impala. Driving home, she saw the curtain flicker over to Springfells' that said Ada had noticed and would be passing the word.

A bum, for dinner, just like that. And that was the second miracle, the extra pork chop, something out of character for them both, Lucille inviting and Judy careless with meat.

Miracle number three, Lucille learned of in the car on the way home. The bum sat self-consciously in the back, the window rolled down despite the heat (he knew he stank, Lucille thought, impressed that he would think to spare them). He asked where he was, what town; he really didn't know. He was actually heading to Las Vegas, he said, when the trucker who'd picked him up suddenly pulled over and kicked him out of the cab. "No idea why," he said, "but I'm much obliged. Just pure chance I ended up here, in this town, but I thank the Lord for it."

Lucille figured he was lying and it turned out later he was. He told 'em about a week later. He hadn't eaten in two days, and as he sat in the truck, dizzy he was so starved, he'd looked over and seen a stick of beef jerky sticking out of the trucker's denim jacket. He'd sat for thirty miles thinking about it, wondering how he could get his hands on it and get the package open without the trucker noticing. He never stole, never, he told them (which Lucille figured for another lie), but this morning he was getting desperate. And you never knew, did you, what the Lord led you to do, the way temptations could be blessings. He'd finally waited until the trucker was occupied signaling to pass and filched the jerky quick as you please. And the trucker had seen it out of the corner of his eye and had gotten furious, which Ray told them he didn't blame him for. And kicked him out then and there. Just pulled over and let him out, right off the 800 North exit, not three blocks from the Twenty-Eighth Ward chapel.

It had taken three miracles just to get him in the door. It took a fourth to keep him there past dinner. Lucille had no intention of it, none whatever. She was pretty mad at herself just feeding him—a first for her and a bad precedent, she figured. But he washed up before eating and did a thorough job of it; that made an impression. And he stood humbly until asked to sit, and sat politely until asked to say grace, and prayed willingly enough, though to Jesus, like a Protestant. It was at dinner that they learned his name and heard the first of his life history.

Ray Ames was his name, from Biloxi, Mississippi. His father, a journeyman welder; his mother, active Pentecostal. Graduated from high school in 1964, and had been lucky enough with his grades to join the Air Force right immediately, avoiding the draft and the jungles of Vietnam. Instead, had spent the war refueling B-52s from a base in South Korea. Got out of the service with training in aircraft maintenance and a Korean bride, and settled down in Atlanta, airport services.

It had worked out well for him, he said, for nearly ten years. He'd told them about his marriage, his life as a respectable citizen. He and Soon Yi hadn't spoken much, but that had been all right; she'd been a good wife, kept the home neat as a pin and spoke when spoken to. Only his mother couldn't stand her and that had led to some tensions, he'd said. He and Soon Yi had had two children, a boy and a girl—they'd be in their late twenties, he said, but he hadn't heard from them in ages. They were back in Korea with their mother, he'd said. The marriage had broken up on account of his drinking, about the time he'd lost his job. He'd liked to bend an elbow with the boys, back in the service, he said, and got into the habit of hitting a bar on his way home from work. And when he did get home, the lack of conversation liked to drive him crazy. So he'd turn on the TV and pop open a beer, and that became his life. Then they'd gotten a federal contract at the airport, and he'd failed a urine test and gotten fired. And it was about then that Soon Yi had left him.

He'd worked a bunch of jobs, he said, enough to keep the house and send a monthly check to Korea. Asked what kind of work he'd done, Ray said landscaping, and some construction, oil changes at a Jiffy Lube, some six years at Sears, doing maintenance—sewing machines and lawn mowers and such. (Lawn-mower repair, he'd said, without any particular emphasis, but that had led to the fourth miracle, the fourth major coincidence and the one that had led to Lucille offering Ray a night's lodging in the spare room in the back.) And then he'd fallen one month behind on the mortgage, and gone on a bender and fallen a second month behind, and from then on things just went downhill for him.

He'd moved in with his sister in Knoxville, he said, when he'd finally lost the house. Lived there for three years, until her husband came into his room one night and told him he'd best be moving on. He didn't blame him neither, Ray told 'em, what with four kids in a three-bedroom and a freeloading brother-in-law to boot. Then Ray had started his wanderin', he said. Just hitchin' one coast to the other.

Lucille had seen his kind in her years in the system, and could fill in the court record herself. Arrests for vagrancy and public intoxication, petty theft and shoplifting; probably a sheet full of misdemeanors. She wasn't too far wrong, it turned out later, though that first night he said he'd quit drinking and had never been arrested in his life. But from the way he said it, he clearly didn't expect to be believed, and as he finished his supper he'd said, with a hang-dog expression, that he thanked them kindly for the meal, but he'd best be moving on.

And Lucille would have let him, except for that lawn-mower business. It nagged her all through supper, from the time he first mentioned it. The coincidence of it all. Again. Because, it just happened that week that Lucille's lawn mower—a Sears and Roebuck, sure enough—was on the fritz. Judy'd had to pull the starting cord harder and harder to start it for months, and finally it had given out altogether. And as Ray Ames finished his supper and his life story, mopped up the last of the mushroom gravy with his bread and polished off his lemonade, Lucille had looked him over more carefully, considering it. He was clean now, and looked peaceable enough. She'd seen no signs of temper or fury from him, and not much spirit either. Just a quiet little man, hair a little thinning, hands a little shaky and he couldn't meet your eye, but more beaten-looking than dangerous. If he could fix the lawn mower, she thought, she'd offer him a night's lodging.

They put him up in the back bedroom, Judy staring wonderingly at her mother as she got the clean sheets from the closet. Lucille couldn't quite believe it either. Making the bed, she kept seeing the newspaper headlines—"Mother-Daughter Murdered by Vagrant." Kicking herself for being so trusting of a total stranger. And no sooner had she finished with the guest room, but she'd talked herself out of it, and she went into the living room to tell Ray she'd changed her mind, and he'd have to be going. Figuring she'd soften the blow with a twenty.

But then she saw him there, sitting on the sofa so peaceable, sitting right next to Judy. And Lucille took a good hard look at the both of them, at him sittin' there by her daughter. Her first thought was that she and Judy probably weren't in much physical danger; Judy was half a head taller than Ray and had broader shoulders. But that really wasn't why Lucille changed her mind again, not why she couldn't bring herself to get rid of him. There he was, a man, sitting on the sofa with Judy. Judy, with her thick ankles and thinning hair, Judy with that moustache that electrolysis just had not done much to get rid of, Judy with the constant skin problems they just hadn't been able to afford a dermatologist for, made worse now from working around meat fat all day. Judy, who'd had maybe one date her whole entire life. The stack of Harlequins under her bed that she didn't think Lucille knew about. The single-adult dances she'd gone to with Velma Paine, up until Velma met Hank Sauer, and then Judy had quit completely. There Judy was, sitting, comfortably chatting, with a man, on the sofa, in her living room. Lucille had thought at that moment that maybe, just maybe, there were such things as miracles, the way she felt at that moment, watching her daughter on the sofa with a man. Or at least she was willing, at that moment, to trust enough to take a chance on getting raped and murdered.

Not that Lucille didn't lock her bedroom door pretty carefully that night, and insist that Judy do the same. Or wake up with a start at every little noise in the house. She had a fitful night of it, knowing he was just down the hall, a complete stranger and a bum to boot. She'd given in to impulse one time too many, she told herself. It ends today. She'd tell him after lunch; get him to fix the lawn mower in the morning, and overpay him for the job. And then, finally, send him on his way.

She could have sworn she hadn't slept all night, but then was startled awake by the sound of water running. Her first thought was panicky—he was in her shower!—but then she realized it was Judy, and that too was surprising. Working with meat, Judy usually showered after work. Lucille got up to see about breakfast—oatmeal or cream of wheat, she figured. But Judy had gotten sausage out to thaw the night before, and had set a package of Pillsbury biscuits on the counter. She couldn't have made it plainer, what she wanted to eat, and so Lucille went along, made the good sausage gravy and a pitcher of orange juice and added a fresh grapefruit each. And watched carefully as Ray and Judy ate together in companionable silence. Judy looked good, for her, clean and fresh—she'd even gone to some trouble over her makeup, usually something she didn't bother with most days. And Ray had spruced himself up a bit, had shaved, and brushed his teeth, and washed his face, and slicked back his hair.

If anything, Lucille probably scrutinized him too closely. He caught her looking at him, and stared down at his food, embarrassed. "I'd-a showered," he said. "Should-a. Prolly a bit on the ripe side, I know. Smelled the sausage cooking, and couldn't help wantin' to eat first."

"It's okay," said Judy. "You don't smell bad."

"I prolly do," said Ray. "Been awhile for me."

"You can shower after you fix the lawn mower," said Lucille. "Be all sweaty anyhow."

"That's right," said Ray. "It can wait." He looked over at the biscuit pan. "Do you mind if I . . ."

"Help yourself," said Lucille.

Ray took another biscuit, added a ladleful of gravy. "I can't tell you how good this tastes."

After breakfast, he helped clear the table, and he loaded his own dishes into the dishwasher. Judy left for work, and Lucille, against her better judgment, found herself making small talk with the man while she washed the skillet—chitchat about the weather and what sorts of flowers should go in the planter on the front porch. Wondering all the while if she was out of her mind, measuring how quick she could get to the meat cleaver on the counter, if it came to that. And just when the conversation ran out of steam, Ray stood up and came over to the kitchen window.

"Let's take a look at that lawn mower," he said. "It's in that shed, out back?"

While he worked on the mower, Lucille found herself at odds and ends. There was always housework to be done, of course, but she'd done the major housecleaning on Saturday, a habit from her working years, and now just had a bit of vacuuming, was all. She knew the neighborhood gossips would be clacking over him; she was half-tempted to dial Ada Springfell's number, just to hear the busy signal. She wanted to keep an eye on him herself, and kept busy looking for chores in the kitchen. But she also didn't want to spy (or be seen spying, which was much the same thing) and so spent her time flitting back and forth between the kitchen and the living room, unable to settle on any project. It was positively a relief when he came to the door, wiping his hands on his slacks.

"Looks like you've got a bad spark-plug wire," he said. "I've cleaned her good, and lubed her, and sharpened the blade, but she still won't start without the part. If you got a Sears in town, I could get her running good."

"Just let me get my purse," said Lucille, and hurried into her room to change.

Driving into town, she found herself again looking at him, at lights and intersections. He sat quietly, hands folded in his lap, looking out the window at the town. It was the closest look she'd gotten at him yet, the sun as bright as it was in the car, and him sitting so near. She could see a jagged scar on the side of his neck, a couple of inches long, she figured. His arm was covered with bug bites, and the pinky finger on his left hand looked broken. He was so quiet, just sitting there, and she didn't want to intrude. But it seemed unnatural not to talk, somehow, unneighborly and borderline rude.

"What's it like?" she asked finally.

He looked quickly at her, a bit twitchy still, a kind of nervous politeness. "How do you mean?"

"Your life, I mean. On the streets and all. Movin' around. What's it like?"

"It's not very comfortable," he replied, "not for someone my age." He shifted in his seat—she could see his hands were still a bit trembly. "Feel like I've been stiff and sore my whole life long."

She left it at that. She knew what he meant; she was seventy-one, and even a good night in her own bed left her back stiff half the time. He was younger, by some twenty years, but she could see the same stiffness, the careful way he got out of the car, the slow, ambling walk, just a touch of a limp. They went into the store together; he found the part quickly, and waited politely for her to make the purchase. And even had the courtesy to hold the door for her back at the car.

Still, she was planning to send him away after lunch; she'd decided, she'd made up her mind. She could feel bad for him, she could see signs of a hard life and feel pity, she could see him with Judy and feel stirrings of hope, she could think that but for the grace of God and so on, but it still didn't matter. He wasn't her problem. She'd put him up for two days, and didn't regret it—bad things could have happened and hadn't and for that she was grateful. But she could still see him on his way. And she would. After lunch.

But then, the whole afternoon, after he got the mower running again, he didn't come back in. First he mowed the lawn, and did a good thorough job of it, raked up the mulch and bagged it. He edged by the driveway and trimmed by the fence. He found a couple of dry patches and watered them carefully. Spent a good hour in the shed before putting away the mower, cleaning and organizing, and when he came back in, it was to ask her what to do with some of the junk he'd found out there. And then, an hour later, when he came back in again, it was to ask if she had a hedge trimmer. She couldn't hardly send him away while he was working. It could even be, she thought, that he knew that and knew, or sensed maybe, that it was best to keep occupied, but it also didn't matter. She didn't have it in her to send him on while he was working on her lawn. Her resolve remained unchanged, of course—anyway, she'd tell him before supper. Or at least afterward. Or, so he wouldn't have to travel at night, the next morning. But then he was gone. She was not backing down, no matter what. He was leaving, that was certain.

He came back in around four. His shirt had come unbuttoned, and his undershirt was sticking to him from sweat, she noticed. She noticed again the air of skittish politeness, the difficulty he had looking at her, as he asked if she would mind it if he took that shower now. She showed him where they kept the towels, assured him they wouldn't mind if he used the shampoo. Then, acting on impulse yet again—she seemed almost governed by impulse these days; it just wasn't like her—she said abruptly, "Why don't you leave your clothes out in the hall. I'll put in a load."

"I've got a change in my backpack."

"I'll give them a wash too, while I'm at it," Lucille said.

"It ain't necessary," he said. "I just got to the laundry a week ago, place outside Laramie."

"It's no trouble," said Lucille. "I'd just as soon run a full load. Never know when you'll next be at a laundromat with spare change."

"It's an unpleasant job," he said, "washing a man's dirty underwear."

"I don't mind it," replied Lucille, wondering just how bad it could be. "Meanwhile, Judy's got these overalls she uses for painting should fit you. I'll toss 'em in."

"I'm grateful," he said, and went into the spare room, came out with an armful of laundry from his backpack. A minute later, he handed more laundry out the bathroom door.

As she washed it, she couldn't help but check it over. Sure enough, the laundry was filthy, showed all the signs of a man with bowel problems who sometimes lacked the means to wipe properly. Something else, too. Blood mixed with the stool. She soaked it all good with Spray 'n Wash, and once she heard the shower stop, got the load started. He came out of the shower, looking suitably abashed in Judy's overalls, which practically hung off his hips; he looked so thin and worn out, Lucille again took pity.

"Take a rest on the sofa," she said. "You've worked hard all day. Judy'll be home soon, and we'll have supper in an hour or so."

By the time Judy came home, he was curled up on the sofa, snoring softly. Judy came in real quiet and handed Lucille the meat wrapped in white paper she brought home every night from work.

"T-bones," she said. "Figured we could get some potatoes baking, maybe barbecue."

"I'll get going on the potatoes," said Lucille, astonished. Judy didn't bring home steak more'n four times a year.

"And I got French-fried onions," said Judy. "Thought we could do that green-bean casserole you like."

Lucille looked at her daughter's impassive face. There was something going on, it was getting obvious, and she figured it could only be the one thing. It worried her, made her wish she'd sent Ray packing right after lunch. There was no place for Ray in their lives, she thought.

She was not about to make a home for him. And yet the house was as much Judy's as hers.

"He's a bum," she said quietly. "A bum off the streets, who we took pity on. We know nothing about him beyond that."

"I know that," said Judy. "I know what he is."

That was better. That was more like it. Lucille hadn't known quite what answer to expect—that's how thrown off she was by all this. The T-bones for supper, Judy in makeup that morning at the breakfast table—it was all out of character. But now, Judy's reasonableness was reassuring—she still had her feet on the ground.

"So you won't mind," said Lucille, "when I send him on his way in the morning?"

Judy looked at her sharply. "Why?" she asked.

"Why?" The question seemed preposterous. "On account of we have to. He can't stay here."

"Why not?" asked Judy again. "How come we can't just leave things the way they are? Him in the spare room and all."

It was literally a new thought to Lucille Wentworth that late afternoon, staggering, new. There were things you didn't do, that was all, park in handicapped or use expired coupons to shop with or wear patterned tops with plaid slacks or not keep your lawn mowed or turn away costumed kids at Halloween. Automatic things you did or didn't do, that the Ada Springfells of the world kept track of and required an accounting for if you were neglectful, not that Lucille minded much what that crabby old gossip thought. Two single women of a certain age didn't invite a bum to live with them. It just didn't happen.

And yet, as they talked about it in whispers out there in the kitchen, Judy's point of view came to seem almost reasonable. It wasn't costing them much to keep Ray there. They could hardly call him dangerous, a skinny old fellow like him. They had the spare room handy for him, and he'd shown, for at least one day, willingness to help out around the house. They could help a fellow down on his luck, help him get back on his feet, and without much fuss for them. There was no particular reason to send him away, and lots of good that could come from keeping him. Explained that way, it began to seem almost Christian, almost like a right kind of thing, however much wrongness it felt all wrapped up with.

"Plus," said Lucille, not wanting to be pushy but thinking it ought to get brought up, "he's a fellow. A man."

"That's so," said Judy impassively. "It likely doesn't mean a lot. Right now, it means nothing at all." And then she looked her mother straight in the face, and Lucille would never forget that look, a look on her daughter's face she'd never seen before, loneliness and pride, shyness and fierceness combined. "But I like him. He seems nice. I don't want him called a bum anymore."

"Well, homeless, anyway," said Lucille; her own stubbornness wouldn't allow her to back down completely.

"Not any longer," said Judy, and it was settled.

They explained it to Ray that night at the supper table. They told him they wanted to have a talk, and Lucille noted his reaction, like all the perps she'd seen in court about to have judgment passed, a *nothing good could come of this* look, grayness and sweaty resignation. But he did perk right up when the news turned out good.

"Well," he said, pleased as punch, to look at him. "Well. I'll try to make myself useful."

"You'll want to be looking for work," Lucille said, it coming out sharper than she'd intended. "We won't charge you rent for that back room there right off. When you've got a job, we'll talk terms."

"That's fair," said Ray solemnly. "That's only right."

"Meanwhile, you're welcome," said Judy, reproachfully friendly. "Let's not spoil things right off, talking money when we've just made friends." And with that it was decided.

They settled into a routine right off, like he'd been living there for years. Every morning, they'd share breakfast, and then Judy would head off to work. Ray would do some fix-it chores in the morning, then Lucille drove him to the employment office. He figured out the bus system pretty quick, and was able to make it to job interviews, grab himself some lunch with the five Judy gave him before she left. Lucille would stay home, catch up on housework and the ongoing cases on Court TV—she couldn't abide soaps or game shows, though she did have a lingering weakness for Sally Jessy Raphael. Evenings, they'd sit in the living room and chat, maybe watch some TV or rent a movie or pass the time playing Scrabble or Yahtzee.

The rest of the week passed like that. Sunday, Ray put on the suit

Judy'd found for him at D.I. and sat solemnly with them through the whole block of meetings, all three hours. In Sunday school, when Brother Kerr asked newcomers to stand up and introduce themselves, Lucille kept it simple: "This is our friend, Ray Ames, who's staying with us for the time being." That was all that needed saying, she figured, and when Clarice Bowman and Verna Lundquist came up to her after Relief Society full of questions, she put 'em off, saying, "Ray's an old friend. We're just helping him through a rough patch." Ada Springfell, she avoided altogether.

By Wednesday of the next week, Ray had a job. LaRue's, a new place in town that sold reconditioned vacuum cleaners and sewing machines and blenders, needed part-time help from a repairman, gave Ray a week's trial. Ten to two, five days a week was all, and they didn't pay much above minimum wage, but it was enough, a start, and a job that had the promise of working into full time down the road. Ray insisted that he pay for his keep, and Judy and Lucille, after some negotiating, agreed to charge him fifty bucks a week.

Not all at once, never one whole evening devoted to it, but a story or a detail or an off-hand remark at a time, Ray told them about being homeless, what it was like. Always kept pretty calm, too, no big sobbing scenes like you'd see folks do in movies, weeping on a psychiatrist's couch, but also not quite conversational. There'd be a kind of tension in him; you could see it in his shoulders. Or he'd look at his hands, play with the rubber band from the evening paper. Telling them what his life had been before.

He told them how you could call a pizza place and order a delivery for some address picked at random from the phone book; and often as not, the pizza would end up in their dumpster at the end of the night in pretty good shape, sometimes even still in the box. McDonald's was bad that way; you hardly ever could find a decent meal from their dumpster. He told how to hitch a ride—off-ramps were okay for panhandling, but on-ramps useless for travel or charity. And you were better off thumbing rides from crummy-looking cars or pickups with a single driver, male. Semis wouldn't pull over for you, but you could sometimes get a ride if you approached the driver just right at a truck stop. He talked about the whole alphabet soup of agencies you could get help from, local, state, and federal, and how you could tell just looking at your case worker how much you were likely to get from her, just the way she'd part her hair sometimes, or how she'd wear her glasses.

When they got to know him a little better, the stories became shabbier—truer, Lucille thought, and a good thing, showing he trusted them. He told about how you could get a Coke machine to give you a free pop sometimes, if you kicked it just right, and about how you always wanted to take a shower and get your clothes washed first if you planned to shoplift, otherwise they'd watch you too close. He told about getting busted for vagrancy, and how it wasn't so bad, getting your three squares and a bed with a mattress, and how some places they'd fine you for it, which made all kinds of sense, fining homeless beggars for vagrancy. You never paid the fine, he said, even when the alternative was a road crew. He didn't mind chopping weeds or picking up litter, when at the end of it was a hot meal.

And one evening, they watched a movie set in a prison, one about an innocent banker who escaped out through the sewage system. It was Ray's choice; he must have had a need to talk about things that night, Lucille figured. And afterward in the semi-dark, Ray told them about jail. It was true, he said, how you had to be careful in the lock-up shower. You had to try to stay away from groups of two or three showering together. They'd gang up, one to hold you face down on the shower floor and one to spread your butt cheeks apart and one to take his pleasure. All the while, Ray's voice a soft buzz in the semi-darkness from back in the corner of the couch with the floor lamp turned off. And Lucille remembered the blood she'd seen on his underwear and something else too, how Judy had caught him buying Kotex at the store and thought it was weird, kind of an unbelievably personal sort of thing to give a girl you really hardly knew.

A tough evening for all of them, that night Ray told about the guys in the shower. As far as Judy knew, that was the turning point; it was that evening she kept referring to as the time it all started to happen, when he trusted them enough to tell something so awful. It made sense to her that after that night, he would begin to look around him more, start to really listen to Judy's attempts to explain the church to him and be willing to take the missionary lessons. Begin to look at her differently as well, begin to appreciate her better qualities. After that night Judy noted a kind of courtliness in his behavior, an extra politeness and courtesy, quite the Southern gentleman in fact, though really he was always polite. The evening threesomes became more of a twosome, with Lucille not exactly shut out but definitely moving out toward the conversational outskirts. Ray and Judy took in a movie now and again, and some evenings they'd leave Lucille to her TV and go out for ice cream. And Ray always paid, said Judy, insisted on it, though Judy made eight times the money he took home from LaRue's.

One night, Lucille came home from homemaking—Judy hadn't wanted to go, Lucille noted sourly—and coming up the walk, looking in the window, saw the two of them kissing on the sofa. She stood outside and watched for a moment. There it was, Ray and Judy kissing. Lucille stood there, knowing what was going to happen. It wouldn't be long, she thought. There'd be a proposal from Ray, and a wedding to plan. Forty-three years old, Judy was still just young enough that grandchildren weren't completely impossible.

If I could be sure, Lucille thought, *if I could be sure that this was really what it looked like, what Judy certainly thought it was, I'd be easy in my mind.* She'd deed the house over to them, move out and get a condo, or move in with Verna Lundquist the way Verna'd been hinting at. Lucille and Judy were comfortable together; it would hurt to lose her. Ray and Judy's increasing closeness already hurt, the third-wheel evenings and conversations and games. But she was seventy-one. Judy deserved better than a spinster life alone with her mom. If only Ray was for real, Lucille could take him supplanting her. But Lucille knew things that Judy didn't.

Two days before the breakthrough, two days before he'd told them the shower story, he hadn't gotten up in the morning. He was probably just under the weather, Lucille had told Judy at breakfast. "He had the sniffles last night, you recall." Judy had nodded, accepted it, told her mom to call her if Ray needed her to bring home some Sudafed from work. "He doesn't go to work before ten," Lucille had said. "I'll get him up in time, drive him in if I need to. Let the poor man have his rest."

She'd gone down the hall to his room. She could smell it, acrid sweet—she remembered it so well from the times she'd done night court—coming through the door. Heard some thrashing around, and knew what it was.

She'd opened the door, and there he was, the room a shambles, vomit all over the bed and the floor and in his hair and down his chest. An empty bottle of Absolut vodka on the floor. Ray half off the bed, legs tangled up in the sheets, trying, half-conscious, to get his foot free.

She'd called him in sick at LaRue's; that was the first thing. She'd saved his job for him, wondering all the time if it was worth it. She'd gotten him up, standing, weaving, on his feet, stupid rictus smile on his face, eyes shifting around. She'd gotten him into the shower and turned it on cold, stood by the tub and gave him a shove every time he tried to get out, even knocked him off his feet a couple times, he was so far gone, stripped him naked while he stood there cussing at her, using words she'd figured she'd never hear again when she retired from the court system. She took his clothes, dripping wet but with the worst of the throw-up off, and got the sheets and pillow case and started a load in the washing machine. She made him stand naked in the shower while she took care of the room, came in once and saw he'd barfed in there too, and she'd had to clean that up. She got in the car and drove down to Smith's, avoiding Albertson's where she might run into Judy, wondering if he'd still be there when she got back but figuring he probably wasn't in shape to go anywhere else. She'd bought some instant coffee for the first time in her life, and rented one of their carpet-cleaning machines, and bought some strong Lysol spray and a bottle of Pine-Sol.

When she got home, he was still in the bathroom, wet and naked, shaking and pale, sitting on the edge of the tub. She got him some clean clothes from his room and told him to get dressed, wait for her in the kitchen, got him some coffee. She cleaned up his room best she could, made one pile for the washing machine and another pile to throw out, and ran the carpet cleaner over the carpet. Scrubbed the walls with the Pine-Sol. He'd wet the bed too, and it took her awhile to wrestle the mattress off the bed, scrub the wet spots with the Pine-Sol, prop it up against the wall to dry off. Sprayed the room with Lysol, the bathroom too. Then went out to the kitchen. Ray sat at the table, sick and pale and shaky, couldn't meet her eyes, took him both hands to hold the coffee mug. She sat across the table from him, smacked the vodka bottle on the table between them.

"Ray," she said to him, "we need to have us a talk."

"I know," he said, so low she could hardly hear it. "I know." He couldn't finish, bowed his head, tears dripping down, the very picture of drunken self-pity, and how often had she seen that in her days?

"We don't have time for that," she said impatiently. "I don't want to hear it. I don't feel sorry for you. Why should you get to feel sorry for yourself?"

"You don't know," he said. "You don't know what I've been through."

She shook her head. "I'm not interested in excuses, Ray," she told him. "Don't have time for 'em."

He didn't seem to know what to say. He shook his head, kept making these little sideways glances at the bottle, took another sip of coffee. "I don't know," he said.

She bored in. "I want to know what you're going to do. Head back down the highway? Like you want to?"

"I want to stay here," he said.

"Which do you want more?" she asked, knowing he'd tell her what she wanted to hear, wondering if he even knew.

And so he said all the right things that morning in her kitchen, made all the right promises. They agreed not to tell Judy, keep the whole thing their secret. He made the most solemn oaths that he'd never drink again, not even a beer, not even Nyquil for a cold. He was done with it, he said, totally, completely, once and for all. She picked up the phone and made a couple of phone calls to old friends in the system, found out where AA met and when. Turned out they had an afternoon meeting, and she drove him down to it, picked him up after. Got his room back in shape by the time Judy came home, and listened while Ray told her at dinner all about his nasty cold, but how he felt a lot better now, thanks. And then watched Ray at the bus stop as he went to work the next morning.

And now it had been four months, and now Ray and Judy were engaged, and now they sat in the living room, making plans and recounting miracles, a couple. Ray's baptism was scheduled for a week from then, the wedding the week following. The bishop was thrilled for them and would do the wedding in the chapel and let them have the cultural hall for a reception afterward, and Verna Lundquist was making a wedding dress for Judy and charging her only for the material, and Clarice Bowman said she'd bake and decorate the cake—she'd taken a class. And even Ada Springfell had said she was happy for them, forcing pleasantries through tight lips like it hurt. Judy was even talking about kids—she'd been to the doctor and he'd said it was risky, but she still could, if they hurried. Ray was full time now at LaRue's, and with a nice raise. Lucille sat, and watched them, and did her needlepoint and wondered. Judy knew by now that Ray was an alcoholic—she went with him to AA meetings and had gotten involved in Al-Anon, though his complete sobriety since meeting her was part of their shared story, myth shaping into legend. And, for now at least, the plan was that Lucille would continue to be with them, that they'd remain a threesome in the house. Lucille agreed to give them the master bedroom; she'd take Ray's old room, she said. It was comfortable enough for her.

It had happened twice more, two more falls off the wagon, two more bouts of six-pack flu Judy didn't know about. All the amusing terms for it—getting a buzz on, two sheets to the wind, hair of the dog that bit me—humorous terms for episodes of betrayal and weakness and defeat. And promises, and vows to do better. Promises that were sincere enough at the time he made them, Lucille thought. Basically, Ray was doing okay. Only three times in three months—it was real progress, basically, considering where he'd come from and what he'd been. And Judy still didn't know—there's a real miracle for you, Lucille thought sourly. What Judy figured was that Ray was susceptible to sudden bouts of illness, hardly surprising considering his years on the street, and that a day's rest made him much better. Lucille was not about to tell her different. Though it was gonna be hard to hide when the two of them shared a bedroom.

But he'd quit for good by then; he'd told her so himself. And maybe that was true, too, like all the other miracles. Maybe this is what salvation looked like, small steps forward and back, not a sudden leap to someplace new. Maybe it's like God giving you a jumpstart every now and then, when you need one, knowing your battery's still faulty, but getting you away from there to a place where you can take care of it.

She was willing to believe that anyway, she thought. Willing to help shape the story the way Judy believed it. She could take being supplanted, if what replaced her was real and good. She was content with it, she thought, it was all right with her. Maybe it was possible, maybe Judy's belief in the whole Ray story and the whole Ray miracle would be enough to sustain it. But looking at Judy, her daughter, sitting there with Ray, her fiancé, reminded Lucille once again just how high the stakes were, and just how much she was gambling.

BREAD FOR GUNNAR

Phyllis Barber

NO ONE SEEMED TO KNOW THE MAN, not even me, and I tried. His name was Gunnar Swenson, but that's all most people knew about him. He lived on the corner of our block in a small gabled house with chimneys on both ends. Who knows how long he was there before my husband Heber and I and our four children moved next door?

We'd come back to Salt Lake City, discouraged by the red clay country to the south. We tried to help build the settlement of St. Thomas for Brigham Young and the Lord, but Indians and scorching sun didn't seem to want Mormons in that part of the world. Gunnar didn't seem to want us around, either. Whenever I was out in my yard, he'd never turn his head in my direction.

"Hello," I shouted. I leaned against his fence and shaded my eyes with a neighborly hand. "Hello, there." But he never paid a mind to me. Nor to the carriages and horses passing our houses. He spent his morning hours digging the soil, sifting it from his shovel, picking out every weed. But the strange thing was, after raking the soil finer than powder, he didn't plant a single seedling.

One morning while I rinsed the breakfast dishes, I put my nose flush with the window glass to watch him more particularly. He kept turning the soil over and over again, raking it, refining it, for no apparent reason. He was always preparing, but never growing anything—no flowers to pick or green peas to snap.

This reminded me of St. Thomas, where nothing grew—not our crops, not our sketchy trees, not even our marriage. Heber tried to hide his disappointment, but I think he was annoyed I wasn't the stalwart woman he thought I was in the beginning. "Heber," I pleaded, "I'm choking to death in this place. Take me back to irrigation ditches and some real mountains. I hate the bleached desert and creeks that run dry when the rain stops."

I begged until Heber had no other choice.

"We failed the Lord," he reminded me the day we stuffed every crevice of our already-overloaded wagon. "If I didn't love you the way I do, I'd stay and finish the work."

"I'll make it up to you," I promised him. "I'll do good works for God."

For just one brief moment, in the middle of his trying to understand me, he looked as if he wished he could wash me off his skin. He stared at me, hard and uncompromising. "God would give you strength if you'd let him," he said, and then swept the floor harshly. I suspected it was me he wanted to sweep out of the house. He needed a hardier woman, a partner to strive with him and help him find approval in God's eyes. But why think of that now? Spilt milk.

Pulling away from the window and back to my chores, I used my fingernail to scratch the hardened yolk from the last plate in my dishwater. Then I looked out at Gunnar, the soil falling from his fingers. I leaned close to the glass once again. He was exceptionally tall, stoop-shouldered, massive, and blond. Maybe he'd been a farmer in the old country who lost his property in the big drought and converted to Mormonism to answer for his losses. Maybe he was a descendant of a North Sea Viking with no faith in the land. To see him sift the fine soil through his large fingers reminded me of the fairy-tale giant who held small people in his hands and watched them quiver like leaves. I couldn't stop wondering about Gunnar's hollow husbandry.

On the following Sunday, as the weekly parade of Mormons walked past our house on their way to Sunday school, my family and I joined the procession on the well-trampled path. As we passed Gunnar Swenson's front gate, I said, "Wait a minute, Hebe. I'm going to invite Brother Swenson to go with us."

Heber smiled as I lifted the latch, approving my impulse to tend to lost sheep. But as I pulled the gate open, I saw what moved like a shadow sliding out of view on the west side of the house. Sure it was Gunnar, I dropped my hand and peered into the shadows at the edge of the house that now seemed absolutely still. Even the leaves on the vine had stopped rustling, as if collaborating in Gunnar's invisibility.

"Strange," I said as I turned back to Heber, who was boosting Jonathan, one of our two-year-old twins, on his back for a ride. He took a few galloping steps, sang a child's tune about Banbury Cross, laughed with Jonathan, then waited for me to catch up.

"Bishop Miller's been trying to get him out of that house and yard and back into activity," Heber said. "Nobody's had any luck, but if anybody could do it, you could. You're an angel of a woman. Most of the time, that is." Heber put his arm around my waist and pecked my cheek.

"How long's Brother Swenson been in the valley?" I asked, brushing the unruly hair from Jonathan's eyes.

"Scandinavians been coming here in droves for fifteen years now. The bishop said something about a sweetheart died or maybe left Gunnar for someone else. Doesn't know for sure. Come on, we'll be late."

One August afternoon as I was fixing lunch with newly baked bread and preserved apricots, I watched Gunnar set his shovel, hoe, and rake against his house. After lifting a bucket from his porch and stuffing two paint brushes into his back pocket, he walked along his white picket fence to the corner of the yard. There he squatted on his haunches and began to paint. Painstakingly, he pressed the brush against the wood until it fanned over the broadening face of the picket and spread the most amazing shade of red I've ever seen, a wild sort of parrot red, a splotch of half-formed flying bird trying to rise up out of Gunnar's yard. Picket after picket turned red until both sides of the front fence had no white to show.

Then, even more odd, late that afternoon while I sat on my front porch with the twins and my mending, Gunnar walked out of his house holding a stack of calico strips in his hand. Keeping my face turned to my stitching and the boys, I watched him tie every other picket with a strip of calico, loop the material around the wood, and fasten it in a bow, as if his fence were some kind of valentine. In two days, the entire fence bordering two streets, the alley, and our house was bright red and wrapped in calico.

"Heber," I said at dinner, my peas halfway to my mouth, "have you ever seen such oddness? Calico ribbons on a red fence?"

"I don't know how he stays alive or gets paint and ribbons." Heber dabbed his mouth with his napkin. "I guess the bishop drops a food basket off late at night once a week, and there are those take pity on him in unpublished ways. Speaking of unpublished, I should tell you the stake president wants to talk to me tonight. I'll be gone a while."

"What does he want, Heber?" My attempt at sounding calm failed. Heber's cheeks grew red, like Gunnar's fence. I saw my oldest daughter Elsie look up from her food, her ears alert.

"I'm not sure."

We both knew what might be happening. Lately, the stalwart men in the church were being asked to restore the work of Abraham to build up the kingdom with more wives to father progeny as innumerable as stars, uncountable as sand by the sea. "You know he's been calling more of the brethren to live the Principle," I said under my breath because of my little pitcher with big ears sitting at the table next to me. "Elsie, finish your peas," I said too sharply.

"I don't want another wife in this family," I whispered, trying to keep my sudden anger intact, squeezing Heber's fingers until I could feel my fingernails sink into his flesh. Elsie kept her eyes down, but I knew she heard every word. "Do you hear me?"

Heber shrugged and excused himself from the table. "Only the best men get called for that. No need to worry about me."

I cleared the table, tucked Jonathan and Jethro into bed, read a story to Elsie and Liza, brushed my hair silky, and stretched out on top of the crocheted coverlet, a wedding gift from my mother. Another wife? Oh God, please, don't ask that from me. Things have been hard enough. I tossed from side to side until my hair was tangled again.

I don't know how long it was before Heber tapped my shoulder and said, "Better wake up and get dressed for bed. You're freezing." His face was beaming down on mine as if lit by a piece of the sun. He was a handsome man, my Heber. He had a straight, strong nose, a broad back, a penchant for nobility. "The Principle," he said as I sat up, rubbing my eyes. "We've been chosen, Anna. Brigham Young has given his blessing." Heber was happier than since we'd been called to St. Thomas, glorying to know God still loved him.

"To me," he said as he patted my hip and settled into the mattress, "serving God is more important than my life! We're blessed, Anna. Doubly blessed."

The Principle, I said to myself all night as I tried to find a place in the bed where sleep would bless my churning mind. After a time, the words became a rhythm in my head: *prin-ci-ple, prin-ci-ple*, like the wheels on the train I could hear on clear nights. I finally dropped into a restless sleep where I saw a crowd of women keeping me from Heber. They pushed me away and held his hands in vise grips. *He's ours now*, they said. *He's mine*, I shouted back, *he's mine!* I shouted all night in my dreams.

I washed the breakfast dishes, my dishcloth circling to the same rhythm I'd heard all night. The sound was so loud I couldn't pay attention to my unkempt children—Jethro, whose nose was running, Jonathan, whose face was specked with breakfast food. I wanted to give myself over to God and Brigham Young and Heber, but I couldn't, not in my mind, not with my body. This was my family. Heber was my husband. We didn't need anyone else. Why did we have to do what Abraham did? He lived a long time ago.

I pulled the carrots out of the bin, scraped the skin, then grated them savagely into a bowl. *I won't do it. No one can make me do it.* Then I caught sight of Gunnar with a pile of boards stacked against his house, the hammer in his hand rising and falling onto the head of a nail. He seemed to be building a staircase on the side of his house. But there was no door or landing anywhere in sight. His stairs had no destination. Just before sunset, he stopped abruptly, carried his tools away, and left seven stairs going nowhere. "What a fool," I said to my reflection in the window. "Men are fools!"

During the month of September, Heber decided on the woman he wanted for the second wife that the Lord, through the wisdom of the church officials, commanded him to take. Her name was Naomi; she was eighteen years old and had a tiny waist and the beauty of a woman in bloom. "We've come for your blessing," Heber said softly as the three of us stood together in the parlor.

"You leave me no choice," I said. The girl blushed and moved closer to my husband.

"I've come to love Heber," she said, looking up at him as if he were a lion in full mane. "I know I'll learn to love you, too," she added and blushed again. Right there in my parlor. The three of us.

I tried to remind myself that God works in mysterious ways, but I spent many numb hours at the sink, pulling the parboiled skins from tomatoes and peeling cucumbers. Thank goodness for Gunnar.

As the weather was changing, his projects became even more peculiar. The latest was to shingle one of his chimneys with gold-colored tin. One by one, he tapped nails into each shingle until his whole chimney was covered. Through the steam of my boiling cucumbers, I saw him hoisting a blue Swedish flag on his flagpole. Then he fastened a nose-gay of cut paper flowers: pink, blue, yellow beneath the finial. I almost burned my chin in the rising steam trying to figure what he was up to.

That night, after we lowered the flame on our bedside lamp, I rolled over to face Heber. "Shame, wasting a life like that," I said.

"What life?" Heber said, yawning and folding his reading spectacles on the lamp table.

"Our neighbor's. Have you seen those paper nosegays on his chimney?"

"You are endlessly curious about that man, aren't you? Kiss me good night, my Anna." He kissed my forehead. I kissed the top button of his underwear. Then I rolled on my back and found the best part of my pillow.

"Those flowers are for the woman you told me about, I think. I'd like to be loved like that." All I could hear was Heber's steady, relieved-to-be-close-to-sleep breathing.

"My life is wasted, too. Me being replaced by another woman, especially someone so young and attentive to your every need. She makes me feel like her mother. And you could be her father. That's not right, Heber. The way you look at her. That's the way you used to look at me."

Heber breathed deep from his chest. He was gone, and I was left with the raging feelings that wouldn't give me rest. *I can't do this, God, I can't.* But after I said that so many times, my mind wandered to what Gunnar's sweetheart had been like. Was she a beauty men adored, was she pock-faced or shy, a burgher's or a poor farmer's daughter? What about Gunnar could have captivated her? And if he loved someone once, why wouldn't he notice anyone else, especially me, out in my yard every day? I felt like the invisible cloth of the emperor's new clothes when Gunnar wouldn't look up and acknowledge me standing there, trying to break the silence with a bunch of radishes in hand, pulled just for him.

As soon as Heber would be finished remodeling the small home on Fourth South Street for his second wife-to-be, about late November he judged, the marriage would take place in the new temple. I'd get to stand in one of the marriage rooms where the two of them knelt and gazed at each other over the altar, their longing observable in the space between them. I'd be asked to accept this woman as Heber's wife. And because I honored God's wisdom more than my own, I'd give my husband away to another woman, to God's kingdom here on earth. But why?

This was my family! The cavity of my heart was a leaden bowl as I stood at my kitchen window and watched leaves float to the ground, victims of the frost's bite. And it weighed even more when I tried to keep busy pulling strings from beans, teaching numbers to the twins, and watching what Gunnar did next. This time, he was standing on his front porch with a pair of scissors in his hand, shaping hearts and flying birds out of paper, gluing them to his window pane. I was mesmerized by the care he took with the tiny scissors as he trimmed the rounded arcs. He was like an overgrown child cutting snowflakes at school, so much larger than the task he was performing.

I wanted to go to him, comfort him, pull him away from the wasteland of his futile projects. But Jethro came down with a fever that same day. I watched Gunnar from the bedroom window while I cooled my son's head with a wet washcloth. After dragging a ladder to the side of his house, he went back inside and brought out a large framed picture. He climbed to the roof, hammered a long nail into one of the sheets of tin on the chimney, and hung the picture way up high. I couldn't make out what it was until later that afternoon when I went out for Jethro's tonic. Hung at the top of his chimney was a brown sepia tintype of Gunnar's house. Mounted on both sides of the frame were more nosegays of paper flowers—more pink, blue, lemon yellow petals cut from stiff paper and wired together.

As I turned into my yard, I decided to be bolder with Gunnar. Do unto others, I thought. He must want some company. A friend. Soon, I promised myself.

A more determined autumn moved into the valley that night. The wind picked up after sundown. It blew especially hard after I went to bed, hooting around the corners of the house and keeping me from sleep. I reached over for comfort, but before my hand reached the other side of the bed I remembered Heber was working late at her house-to-be. I listened for the sound of his hammer on the wind. Maybe it would float into the bedroom and haunt me and make me cry again, but instead, I heard singing in between the gusts. Swedish words in a sweet high voice. The sound pierced into my loneliness, and I turned the warming brick with my left foot to find the remaining heat.

Turning on my stomach and folding the pillow over my ear, I could still hear the high, penetrating song filtering through the dark. "Close your window, Gunnar," I said out loud. "I don't want to hear your pining!" The chilly night was inappropriate for love songs. I rolled toward Heber's empty spot and circled my nonexistent husband with one arm. No response. He'd never sung love songs to me—five years in the clay country, four children, two miscarriages, always backbreaking work to do. As I nestled against Heber's pillow held close to my breasts, I envisioned a princess in the dark in a dense forest. She had tree-length hair. She was dressed in white, waiting in a tower for a voice to call her name and nothing but her name. Anna, I heard on the wind. Anna, a part of Gunnar's wistful melody until Heber trudged up the stairs, sat on the bed to unlace his boots, and fell into the mattress and quick sleep.

The snow came that next day.

Through a screen of gentle flakes, I watched Gunnar from my upstairs bathroom window. I brushed my long, dark-brown hair while he pulled a rocking chair from inside his house, sat on his front porch, wrapped himself in a wool shawl, and sanded a piece of wood resembling half a flower vase. His knees covered with a ragged quilt, he sat there the entire day as the snow deepened, smoothing the wood patiently. From various windows of my house, sometimes holding Jethro, whose fever was close to breaking, sometimes standing with a finger across my lips, I watched him rub the surface as if it were a baby's skin.

Finally, as the blurry sun dropped behind the Oquirrh Mountains, he glued the vase to his front door. Then, through the steel-blue light, I saw him stuff a bouquet of paper flowers into the vase, probably pink, blue, and yellow, though the dusk made them colorless.

I knew it was time for me to go to him. I'd rise early the next morning, in enough time to bake bread before the house woke.

After the bread was done, I unlatched his gate carefully and balanced on my toes to keep the new snow out of my shoes. The sidewalk seemed long. Kicking against the porch step to shake the snow from my shoes, I noticed something I couldn't have seen from my window. The outline of a heart and the initials GS and AS were carved into the porch pillar; tiny squares of blue paper had been glued together in the shape of a mosaic bird perched at the top of the heart.

After knocking three times, I called his name. "Brother Swenson, it's your neighbor, Sister Crandall." I knocked again; still no answer. "Please answer, Brother Swenson—it's Anna Crandall. I have bread for you."

I was ready to bend down and leave the bread wrapped in the flour-sack towel, though I hated to leave it out in the cold just fresh from the oven, when I saw a tiny opening in the door, one eye peering out. I swallowed and nodded my head in greeting. "This is for you, Brother Swenson. I thought I should say hello after all this time being your new neighbor."

The door opened wider. Standing a good foot above my head, Gunnar Swenson stared out at me. His pale blue irises looked like star sapphires. His coarse blond hair had stubborn cowlicks sticking out in spikes. I felt my chest constricting.

"Anna?" he asked.

"Yes. Anna Crandall."

"Anna?" His white blonde eyebrows faded into his pale face and all I could see were his eyes, like asterisks. They frightened me.

"I'm Anna Crandall. We moved in last spring. I'm sorry to be so long in saying hello."

"Anna?" he said again. "Why did you leave me? Did you fall off the boat?"

"No," I laughed. "I've never been on a boat. I'm Anna Crandall. Your neighbor." I pointed to my house.

"Anna. Come in." He trembled like a leaf in the wind. Only frail things were supposed to tremble like that.

Before I allowed myself to cross the threshold, I examined the interior, dark and smelling close. His boots sounded hollow-heeled as he crossed the room and fingered paper flowers stuffed into vases of every kind—quart jars, olive jars, ceramic candy dishes. In some places, the wire stems of the paper flowers were stuck into modeling clay to hold them erect.

"Come in."

I held onto the frame of the door for as long as I could before my feet walked into a different world. As I closed the door behind me to keep the cold from Gunnar's already frigid room, I felt an overwhelming iciness.

The ceiling was covered with nosegays of paper flowers, the same pink, blue, and yellow stiff-papered flowers gathered into bouquets on the chimney and the front door. Each nosegay was fastened upside down to the ceiling to form a canopy. Spun spider threads ornamented the blossoms and gave them a silvery, wispy look. A grayed lace curtain divided the living room from his bed. Two windows, a mantel, a miniature chest of drawers, a small cast-iron stove, and one rocking chair, the cane seat of which looked like a bowl for tired bones, settled deep between the frame—all seemed incidental in this sea of flowers.

"I have flowers for you," Gunnar said, his eyes not registering my face but looked past my shoulder into another reality. "I have poems. Sit down, Anna."

He moved the rocking chair to me and reached over to an alabaster knob on a small drawer and slid it squeaking out of its place. He lifted a yellowed piece of paper, folded into a square inch and curled at the corners.

"We've been hoping to see you over at church, Brother Swenson. Everyone wants to get to know you."

"Church?"

"The church, the ward house. You remember."

"Was ten years ago I come from Sweden. Missionaries tell me about Zion, and then I meet you on the boat, Anna. And then you go away."

"Anna Crandall. I'm your neighbor. I just moved here with my husband last spring. Heber and I've been talking how we should get over here and get to know you, but I got caught up with my children, my preserves and garden and settling in. Please forgive me."

All the time I talked, Gunnar was unfolding this tiny square of paper. He used his fingernail to peel each fold from another. Intent on his work, he hadn't heard a word from me. I wanted him to look up so I could say, Hello from your neighbor, and be on my way, but he didn't offer me the chance. He picked at the paper carefully. It looked as if it would split instantly with rough handling, especially at the folds. Gunnar finished the delicate operation and started to read without giving me the opportunity to leave his house.

"Anna, many years I say, Anna, fill my days with your smell. The moon changes while I wait, fullness to slivers. I feel the slivers of you in my heart that won't let you be gone from me. Never will you be without flowers." Gunnar looked up at his ceiling and counted the nosegays hanging there. "Twenty-four, twenty-five," finally "thirty-seven." Then his white-blue eyes turned in my direction, but focused over my shoulder on some place far from this room. Spiked star-eyes filled with visions of flying birds. Gunnar was shaking, this big man who should have been telling everyone what to do. This massive body, which could have its way with people in any dispute, shook as if there were no warm place anywhere.

"Brother Swenson," I said. "Do you see this bread? I baked it for you. I made it with honey."

"I wait for you on the ship. I wait by the rail on the port side. I walk back and forth until Orion goes down to the water. You say you will come and be my bride in Zion. Why you go, Anna? Do you fall in the water? I listen for your voice, 'Gunnar, save me. Gunnar,' but I don't hear you, so maybe you go straight to the bottom."

Maybe I should have eased out the door, but I watched him tremble, like I myself had done at my kitchen window and in my bed at night. "Gunnar," I said firmly, forgetting propriety. "Listen to me."

"Anna, I keep calling. You don't answer."

I bent forward to pull myself out of the chair, to reach out and take his hand. I didn't think about it or I wouldn't have done it, but I stood right up to him and took his hand, as big as a calf's head, into my small ones. "Gunnar." I stood on my tiptoes. "Listen to me."

He turned to pick up a vase full of flowers. "For you, Anna."

"I am not your Anna. I'm your neighbor."

"My Anna." He covered his ears with his forearms, burying his head between his elbows. "No talk."

When his hands fell back to his sides, I held them again and stroked the tissue-paper skin and the blue veins. I held his hand to my cheek and warmed it. "You are so cold, Gunnar. Why don't you light a fire?"

"Now you are here, Anna, I light a fire."

"Why don't you come out to church, Gunnar? There are other women. You have so much love to give."

"We need a fire, Anna, to keep you warm. I keep you warm. You'll be happy here."

Gunnar bent over the hearth to a stack of split logs mummified in spider webs. Cupping his hands into a small bucket, he transferred dry pine needles into a nest between the logs. Then he pulled open another drawer and unraveled stacks of scrap paper, blue, pink, and yellow, placing them carefully over the logs. He fumbled in a small glass for a match and struck it on one of the fireplace bricks. He stood there, holding the match between his fingers, letting the fire burn until it charred his fingertips.

"Gunnar!" I said. "Drop it on the fire." He smiled at me, the kind of smile where one's face belongs to something else. Blue smoke spiraled. He lit another match.

"Do you need help?" I stepped toward him to take the match. He held it up, out of my reach, and smiled that dispossessed smile again. His smiling cancelled my wish to put my hands on his shoulders and make him all right; his smiling made me shrink toward the door. He held the match higher and higher, the flame burning close to his fingers again. "Light the fire, Gunnar. I've got to get back now."

"Days go by, I wait," he sang in English. It was similar to the song I heard him singing the other night. "I wait and I wait, and I rock my arms for my love, for my love." As he lit another match, holding it up and away from me, the flame leapt into the bower of flowers, away from Gunnar's hand. The flame curved into the paper stamens and folded petals and browned them, blackened them, and the entire bower of nosegays came alive for the first time.

"Gunnar," I yelled at him. Gunnar watched the flames leap across his flowers. The heat spread to the lace curtain and browned it to ashes that flaked to the floor and drifted onto his bed, sparking the fibers and the rough floorboards to life as well. "Run, Gunnar!"

And Gunnar lunged forward, suddenly, lunged toward me and grabbed me in his arms. He hugged me until I couldn't expand my ribs to find a breath. "Gunnar!" I tried to scream. And I looked up at him, and his hair was on fire and he seemed an angel of destruction, an angel of the Lord coming to tell the world to obey or be destroyed in the last days.

"I love you, Anna. I prepare for you like the virgins with lamps. You are my love."

I pulled away from him. "We've got to get out of here." But he seemed to have turned to a pillar of stone. His hair was on fire, his feet rooted to the wooden floor. I grabbed the flour-sack towel. The bread tumbled to the floor. *Wrap Gunnar's head. Stifle the flames. Smother them.* But as I reached for Gunnar's head, he put his hands up to keep me away from him.

"Gunnar!" I shouted. "You're burning to death!"

His huge arms were the masters of the room, the masters of me with my flour-sack towel trying to whip the flames from his head. His huge hands, held up as guards, kept me away while the corona of flame burned brightly around his head. The cracks between the floorboards were narrow rivers of flames. The flowers were curling away from their centers, their carefully cut edges crumbling. Anna's bower—bouquets, valentines, bluebirds, poems hidden in drawers, lace hanging to protect the bridal chamber.

"Let me help you," I begged over the crackling of the fire.

He just smiled, oblivious to the fact he was burning alive. And something happened, something so awe-striking I was humbled in that strange house with the paper flowers and folded poems. Gunnar's hair burned like a torch, but the fire didn't touch his face. His face glowed white, and that rocking chair with the sagging seat, it glowed white too, like the great white throne. Gunnar sizzled with whiteness. I could hear that sound and knew I heard the power of God.

"I love you, Gunnar," I said suddenly, surprising myself. I drew close to him and looked into his eyes, filling with the power I sensed in him. "Anna loves you more than anything in the world. I'm here with you." I put my arms around his waist and held him as if he were the only man I ever loved. He bent to kiss me, the crown of flame on his head. And I felt the fire pass through my lips and deep into me until I was his Anna, his long-sought love dressed in white like the princess with tree-length hair.

"Forever," I said, then broke away, out of the house and the flames, back to the safety of my home. I grabbed my twins into my arms and rocked them while the fire devoured the seven stairs, the gables, Gunnar's tin-covered chimney. I watched the front porch cave in as the neighbors made their too-late attempt at a fire brigade. I didn't offer my help. I held my babies tightly until there was nothing left to burn.

Gunnar is with me, nonetheless, as I stand at the kitchen window today, wiping plates dry and looking at the charred ruins of his house. I can see him standing in the fire as if nothing could touch him, smiling with the bliss of a thousand years of peace while the house folded into itself and turned his paper garden to ash.

I can feel him, floating by my side, whispering Anna in my ear. And in this weak moment, on the morning of the day I'm supposed to go to the temple with Heber and Naomi, I'm almost overcome by the enormity of his devotion.

But as I lift the dripping flatware from the dish drainer, I can see Gunnar's face in flames, finally crumbling to the black ash of obsession. My Anna, my Anna—all he can say. All he can think. Even though I know there's no satisfying that kind of longing, I'm still mesmerized by it. I want to believe. I want to hear Anna in my ear, buzzing in my head. I want someone to love me that way. Only me. Anna, Queen of All Women. But even as I pray in my secret heart for such purity, I have questions. Wiping a spoon with my checkered dishtowel and dropping it into the wooden drawer, I wonder.

These dishes aren't mine; the house over my head is a loan; the children are God's. Heber is a gift, not my right. I don't want to burn in the flames of my having to hold everything tightly in my cupped hands, things that don't belong to me or to anyone else, for that matter.

"Not my will, but thine, be done," I say to myself as Heber opens the door for us to walk to Naomi's new house and then to the temple.

I say it again as I watch Heber and Naomi kneel across the altar from each other, fresh devotion on their faces.

I don't cry. I don't recoil. I take Naomi's hand in mine as she stands. The new wife. The new possibility. I close my eyes and take a deep breath, inhaling God's mysteries.

THE CARE OF THE STATE

Brian Evenson

IN LATE AUGUST RUMORS REACHED ME that on the morning of August 23, eleven days after his sixtieth birthday, Brother Prater had put an end to his life. The *Daily Herald* clipping my mother sent me reported that his death had occurred at a short distance from my and his hometown, where the railroad tracks curve through a stand of aspen before passing through fields. Prater apparently stepped out of this stand of aspens, knelt, and placed his head on one of the rails. None of the newspaper accounts I subsequently tracked down indicated whether Prater's head was positioned so as to look toward the oncoming train or away from it. Perhaps this fact could not be determined, though it strikes me as being of the utmost importance.

The obituary which ran in the *Herald* a day later was titled "He is with Christ." Not surprisingly, it contained no mention of the fact that Prater had taken his own life. Instead, the obituary spoke of the dead man's church service, his dedication to and care for the members of his congregation, his love of family, his love of God, his astounding openness and patience. It degenerated into increasingly generic praise, until, almost by way of an aside, the last line of the obituary stated without further explanation that for two years (1986–1988) Prater had been "under the care of the state."

It was this curiously disconnected, unexplained final statement, coupled with the unusual manner of Prater's suicide, which led me to reconsider my sketchy impressions of my former bishop. He had always struck me as stalwart and faithful, stable in every way. When I was a teenager, he had often been held up to me as an example. There had been no indication that he would ever be under *the care of the state*, whatever that phrase meant.

After receiving the *Herald* article and the obituary, I telephoned my mother. She did not know, she said, what "under the care of the state" meant either. She had been as surprised as I was upon first reading the obituary. She could not, though she had considered it at length, remember Prater being absent from the ward for two years for any reason at all. In fact, during the period of absence mentioned in the article, he had been bishop. She remembered having seen him every, or nearly every, Sunday. She remembered having heard, however, that in 1985 or 1986 or 1987 Prater had resigned from his job as an accountant with Wilder, Benson and Moscuvy to go into business for himself. She wasn't sure of the details, didn't know what type of business, but it hadn't lasted more than a year or two, and then he had rejoined his former firm. Perhaps, she suggested, the state had assisted him in some unknown but invaluable fashion during that period.

Two months later, when I found myself still thinking about Prater—his perpetually firm bishop's handshake, his head on the track facing away from or toward the train, both his hands grasping the sides of the pulpit, his ear to the rail listening for the train's approach—I made arrangements to return home for a few days. My mother picked me up at the airport. As we drove the fifty miles home from the airport through a landscape of dead grass and rock and frost, my mother recited the usual litany of news—immediate family, then extended, then friends and ward members—quickly moving from the familiar to people I knew only vaguely or not at all.

"What about Prater?" I asked.

"No news," she said. Then added, "He's still dead, if that's what you're asking."

I suggested that was not what I was asking.

"I see that you're not here to see me at all," she said. "You're here to see Prater."

"You sent me the clipping."

"That has nothing to do with it," she said. We drove a while in silence, climbing up over the icy, gray rim of one valley, falling into the next.

When we finally reached home, I put my suitcase in my childhood room and walked to Prater's house. It was a simple brick affair, identical in all important particulars to the houses around it. Prater's wife seemed not displeased to see me. She remembered my name, asked about my current life, asked about my mother, offered me a glass of water. Her husband's death, she told me, had been a complete surprise. He was doing well. He was successful in business, she wanted me to know, and he had been happy in every way. He had nothing to hide, she claimed. She had every reason to believe, she said not without a trace of hysteria, that he had not committed suicide but had been killed. When I asked her what evidence she had for this, she chose to speak instead of her husband's service to the church, his dedication to and care for members of his congregation, his love for his family.

I asked her if she had written his obituary. She nodded her head. It needed a wife's touch: it had been her duty.

I was puzzled by something in it, I told her, by the last line's mention of "under the care—"

She was shaking her head before I could finish. It had been a mistake, she told me, the one thing she had not in fact written. It had been either inserted by accident, transposed from another obituary, or was some kind of cruel joke, in very poor taste. She had called the paper to complain as soon as it appeared, but it was already too late. I must not believe it, she said. It had nothing to do with her husband.

I apologized, took a sip of water, and we passed on to other topics. She spoke generally, about the ward and the neighborhood, until she seemed calm again, then I asked her what business her husband had been involved in for the few years he had broken with Wilder, Benson and Moscuvy.

She became agitated. She reached out and grabbed my hand. She was sure, she said, that her husband had been killed. He had not committed suicide. In any case, she said, taking my glass and leading me toward the door, I was not to believe anything that they were saying about her husband. He had been as perfect as a man could be, she said. God could testify to that. She had been glad to see me again, she said firmly, but now she had other matters to attend to.

I spent the next few days in the company of my mother. I told her about my visit to Prater's wife, her anxiety. She refused to comment at first. There couldn't be any truth to what she had said, I suggested. Clearly it was a suicide.

"It's her right," said my mother. "She's in mourning."

"There's something she isn't telling."

My mother shrugged, stayed on the couch holding her magazine, looking out the window. Eventually she told me that what I was lacking was empathy. What she lacked was a proper sense of curiosity, I told her, then asked to borrow her car.

I spent the early afternoon in the library, looking at the other obituaries that had appeared alongside Prater's. The phrase *the care of the state* fit no better in any of these obituaries. I searched forward and backward a few days, found no obituaries to which it might possibly appertain.

By late afternoon I had made my way up Second North to the *Herald* office to meet with James Mullen, the editor who oversaw, among other things, the obituary page. I showed him the clipping and asked him if he remembered it.

He took it, peered at it cursorily, handed it back to me.

"No," he said.

I explained to him the problem with the last line, reminded him that Mrs. Prater had called to complain. He looked at it more carefully.

"I remember it now," he said slowly. "Are you with her?"

Mrs. Prater? No, I wasn't with her.

"Who are you with?"

Nobody, I told him. I was a former member of Prater's congregation. I wanted to know why he had killed himself.

"Why do you want to know?"

"I don't know."

He sat playing with his tie, knocking the end of it against his knuckles.

"I didn't look over the obit," he said. "My assistant did. Charles Decker."

"Can I speak to him?"

"He's gone now."

"Gone?"

"Fired. Over that particular obit, matter of fact. He was a decent assistant all told, but had some peculiarities. He wasn't altogether well."

"How did the line slip into the obituary in the first place?"

"He put it there. He wrote it."

"Why?"

"Because he said it was true."

"Was it?"

"Yes," he said. "In fact it was."

"But you fired him anyway?"

He leaned toward me, tapped the obituary. "These things are not about truth," he said. "They're about something else entirely."

The state mental hospital sits in the foothills in what was once the area east of town but which is now part of the town itself. When I had been a boy, it had been isolated. Every year, either in some strange attempt at therapy or out of resignation, they had run a haunted house, allowing certain of the inmates to dress up as monsters. Now it was less conspicuous; there were houses near the grounds, a water park with multiple slides on the hill just above it.

Mullen's directions allowed me to find Decker's particular building without difficulty. I followed the long drive up toward the main structure, a long gray-green building with barred windows, but turned before reaching it, then parked and walked past a chapel to a sturdy cinderblock house near the fence. It seemed an ordinary house, though on closer inspection I could see that the window frames were nailed down. The glass of the windows was not glass at all but two sheets of thick Plexiglas with a wire mesh between, the Plexiglas scratched, burning with sunlight. The door itself was made of metal, painted to suggest a wood-grain pattern. The name BRIGHTON HOUSE was on a greening iron plate above the door frame.

Decker, I discovered, was a warder of sorts for a group of more stable patients living in this halfway house. On their way back to society, the patients lived there, interacting, free to come and go during the day as long as they took their medication on schedule and returned at night. Some of them held jobs and went out regularly. Others could not be convinced to leave their rooms. He had no other home and was obliged to be on the grounds all but six hours of any given twenty-four-hour period. He had no family, no girlfriend.

"They don't keep warders here long," he told me. "Unless they're me." We sat in his bedroom, a small room with a private telephone line and another metal door, this one dented and scratched on the outside.

He had been a warder for twelve straight years before moving to the *Herald*, three times longer than anyone else had lasted. Eventually the job made anyone crazy, he said, and for the last two of those twelve years he had been substantially madder than any of those he supervised, though he claimed he was quite sane now. He had, he said, in the last two years of his previous stint as warder, begun to appropriate the symptoms of other patients, as if mental illness were infectious.

When I asked about my former bishop, he told me Prater had lived in Brighton House from 1986 to 1988, after a severe breakdown (the details of which Decker had never been told) and in the middle of a bout of depression. He had been a bishop at the time and had been counseled by his psychiatrist to give up his church position because of his declining mental health. In the end, he had agreed to give up his calling, take a leave of absence from his job, and go into treatment, his psychiatrist arranging a stay for him at Brighton House.

Except it wasn't that simple, Decker said. Prater's wife didn't want him to resign as bishop, and he himself didn't want to resign either. He needed it, he felt. It ratified his existence. To resign would only throw him deeper into depression, he feared. Yet, if his breakdown and struggle with depression were generally known, he would be forced to resign as bishop. He needed to find a way to receive treatment while at the same time continuing to serve in his church position.

After several months of living in Brighton House, he confided to Decker that he had not resigned as bishop after all. He continued to preside at church on Sundays, telling nobody that he was no longer living at home. He had individual and group sessions at the state hospital during the day, but made sure to show up near his home every day around five carrying a briefcase to maintain the illusion that all was well. He had dinner there and then returned to Brighton House, where he would have dinner as well. He had let nobody know about Brighton House, and continued to act in his role as a bishop as if nothing had happened. Sundays would find him depressed and exhausted, overwhelmed by the weight of his calling, and Monday and Tuesday it was usually all Decker could do to coax him out of bed. He was hardly getting better, perhaps getting worse.

He began to hide in his bedroom during the day, terrified that someone who knew him from church might see him. He would go out only with his face swaddled in scarves, removing the scarves only once safely away from the hospital grounds. He invented a profession for himself—an entrepreneur involved in latex—and eventually began to speak about it, even around Decker, as if it were real. When Decker reminded him that it wasn't real, he would become irate. Once he spent an entire night banging on Decker's door with a stone, yelling that he was going to kill him. Then he retreated for his room, refusing to speak or move for almost three days. Decker could have had him committed to the main facility, but didn't.

"It's like that sometimes," said Decker. "You get used to it." He pulled out one of his dresser drawers and held it out to me. It was full of earplugs of all different sizes, colors, and noise resistances. He extolled the advantages of each. "With this one," he said, touching one, "I couldn't hear him at all." Sometimes he kept them in for days at a time, he said. He would walk around Brighton House or out on his errands and communicate with people just by guessing what they were saying. It usually didn't make any difference, he said: the connection was just as genuine, or just as phony, depending on how you looked at it.

He took the drawer away from me, held it on his lap as he continued to speak. There followed for Prater a range of shifts in behavior, he indicated. One day he would curse God, the next he would spend entirely on his knees, praying. He became obsessed with plants, reading books on the indigenous species of the region. He learned to speak eloquently about how this land had once been desert and wilderness and needed to be returned to desert and wilderness. He came to feel the nonindigenous plants were a kind of insult and set out selectively uprooting them. When the gardener complained, he was asked to stop and did for a time, despite his anxiety. One night when Prater did not come back for his medication, Decker went in search of him and found him on the lawn with a carpet knife, cutting up small hunks of sod and chewing them up. He had to be sedated, and there was talk of moving him to the main facility. Instead, he was prescribed a slightly more potent medication and eventually managed to restrict his destruction of nonnative plants to areas outside of the asylum fence.

As he spoke Decker kept putting in earplugs and taking them out, piling them to one side, on the bedspread. I found this disconcerting. It was about this time, he said, that Prater's obsession with stones began: the theological significance of stones. Jesus was the rock of the church, the Ten Commandments were set in stone, the stone had been rolled away by the angel to release Christ from the tomb. At his worst, Prater couldn't utter a sentence without saying the word *stone* or *rock* or mentioning some particular type of stone; he was always speaking of what was next on the *slate* or taking things for *granite* instead of granted. He began to gather stones, bringing back handfuls and pocketfuls of them at the end of the day, until eventually all his drawers were full of them and there was a layer of stones spread over his floor, the room itself slowly filling. If he, Decker, had not put a stop to it, Prater would have filled the room to the top.

He put in a pair of earplugs and stood and led me to the door. He ushered me out of his room and down the hall. In the common room were four men, all relatively normal in appearance. They stared at me until I had passed by. I went out the front door, Decker behind me.

"You see," he said, stepping onto the grass, speaking slightly louder than he had been. "None of this should be here; it's unnatural. There should be nothing but dirt and scrub and the taller dried grasses. I can understand that. Prater was right. But the stones are a little harder for me to understand. I'm not a religious man."

We began to walk. He had left before Prater had, eventually getting a job at the newspaper. Prater, he heard, had eventually cut off his relationship with Brighton House, pronouncing himself cured, and had gone back to accountancy. Prater wasn't stable, Decker insisted, but he could do a good imitation of stability. Then, almost a year ago, Decker had proofread a notice for the paper saying that Prater had been released from being bishop, someone named Kyle Hodges being called in his place. It won't be long now until he's back in Brighton House, Decker had thought.

By that time we had reached the gate. The sun had begun to set on the other side of the valley, torn in half by the peak beyond the lake, the lake itself inflicted with a blinding sheen of gold. When notice of Prater's suicide arrived, Decker said, he realized that he had been wrong. Then the obituary had come in: no mention of the suicide, no mention of any of Prater's difficulties, just the same old stuff. It was as if, even though dead, Prater was still hiding. "So I decided to out him. But don't think it was for him or for some higher moral purpose. It was for my own good as much as for his."

He shook my hand slowly. "He could have been any of us from around here," he said. "I could have been him. You too, or you wouldn't have gone to all this trouble." He held my hand an uncomfortable moment, then turned to move back toward Brighton House, his shadow cast long over the grounds. He stood in front of Brighton House turning his ring of keys over and over in his hand, the sun glinting off them until it slipped below the mountain, leaving both of us alone in the gathering dark.

LIGHT OF THE NEW DAY

Darin Cozzens

33

THEY WERE KNEELING AT THEIR CHAIRS, on kitchen linoleum worn especially thin in the region of each kneecap. Arranged on the tabletop, eye level between them, were two bowls, two spoons, two glasses, a plate of unbuttered toast and three boiled eggs, a pitcher of milk, jar of jam, and a seldom replenished sugar bowl. In the center of the table, resting on a folded dishtowel, was the steaming pot, whose contents he never let himself know until *after* the prayer.

We bow before thee, Heavenly Father, thankful again for the light of the new day.

In her seventy-three years' worth of new days, certainly as long as he could remember, there had been no variation in the opening line. Even now, in mid-December, a full three hours prematurely, Edrus Penroy praised the sunrise in prayer. Even early in her widowhood, amid all the dark worries about the farm's fate, she had begun her prayer by invoking the light of a new day.

Nor did its staples vary. The first category of things to pray about was food. Whatever was in the pot, oatmeal or wheat mush or rice flavored with cinnamon, augmented by whatever was on the chipped plate, was blessed to nourish and strengthen them. Then, after the transition to the hungry and needy, the staples poured forth: grateful for health and strength, mindful of sins and shortcomings, in need of wisdom and guidance. The list was long. She prayed for the sick and afflicted. She prayed for missionaries and soldiers. She prayed for the leaders of nations. She prayed for a troubled world. Finally, hunched for warmth in her lemon-colored housecoat, she prayed for loved ones—for protection and safety on his two sisters, much older than he and settled in places far distant from the farm, and on their good husbands, and on her eleven grandchildren.

The only variation in her prayers lay in the particulars associated with each staple. And these were dictated by the events of the season—military invasions, depressed crop prices, births, deaths, weddings. Ten years ago, for example, when his father died, she included themselves for a month or two among those who needed comfort in their mourning. And just in the last few weeks, her prayer had asked blessings on the forthcoming spring weddings of three of the younger tier of grandchildren, most recently the one named Myron.

He had heard every syllable a million times. But on this morning in December, just as he was ready to say amen and get to his breakfast, she paused, then uttered syllables new to both of them:

And please bless Hewell . . .

Only twice in his life had the condition of Edrus Penroy's only son prompted more than a brief particular. At age seven, he almost died from fever and croup. Then, at thirteen, forgetting his dad's caution, he climbed off the tractor without stopping the PTO and banged his shin against the baler's spinning driveshaft, would have been pulled in and mangled if the leg of his jeans hadn't shredded in the first fraction of a second and torn away clean from leg and boot both. "Thank heavens for worn-out britches," Edrus Penroy had said.

But on this morning in December, with no sickness or accident in recent memory, she went on at such length, in such a peculiar, pleading tone, as to make him a staple all his own. Please bless Hewell and comfort Hewell and guide Hewell. In what way? To what end? Thanks to a sustained vagueness, calculated or otherwise, he could not know until almost the last sentence: *Inasmuch as Myron has found a helpmeet, in like manner, please remember Hewell.*

Despite the marriages of four or five other grandchildren in the last few years, it was the announcement of Myron's that finally called attention to Hewell's singleness. This was the Myron who left college a month into his first semester to live in the mountains until snowfall, the hunter who ate deer liver raw, the boy who hated suits and ties and crowds and, for those reasons, didn't leave on his mission to Ecuador until he was twenty-five—and then only with considerable coaxing.

And this was the returned missionary who never had spoken ten words to a girl, much less dated one. A good boy, but always a little strange, a source of concern for his parents and grandmother. It was going to take a special young lady, everyone agreed. But, not six months after flying out of a place called Guayaquil, with a firm resolve to follow his mission president's counsel and get on with life, he found her. Sue the rescuer. Sue the beloved. And now look at him—engaged and squared away, studying accounting or business or whatever a forward-looking Mormon boy studies, clerking part time in a department store, serving as scoutmaster in his church ward, eating his meat cooked. Sue the miracle worker. And *where* did he find her? Nowhere farther than a young-adult dance.

Even veiled in prayer, Edrus Penroy's logic was easy to figure: first, if Myron could find a wife, anybody could; and second, if his method worked for one hard case, surely it would work for another.

34

By the light of a new day in late May, Hewell found himself kneeling but, with last night's wallflowering on his mind, only half attentive as she ran through the day's particulars: bombing in some European country, a beef market that had found yet another bottom, a dead aunt on his father's side, the birth of Myron and Sue's first child, one year to the day after their marriage in the Idaho Falls temple.

Inevitably Edrus Penroy approached her new—and, by now, well-honed—staple. But, on this morning, this staple included a new particular, if you could call it that.

And please direct Hewell, please bless his . . . efforts.

They both knew what she meant by the word. As on mornings in his long-ago childhood, Hewell fidgeted—from hunger, from discomfort in his knees, at the memory of a dance he shouldn't have attended in the first place, at her habit of making God the go-between in this conversation.

At the conclusion of the prayer, after some wordless scooting and shifting, the old chrome-legged kitchen chairs supported the one other posture they existed to support, and a quick peek in the steaming pot solved the morning mystery. Wheat mush. He had hoped for rice with cinnamon.

Hewell's mother refastened the safety pin where the lemon house-coat had been missing a top button for the better part of a decade. Without looking at him, she unscrewed the seal-band on the mason jar of chokecherry jam, then laid both band and lid upside down beside the sugar bowl.

"Have some jam, Hewell."

"No thanks."

Edrus Penroy nudged the jar toward him. "There's nothing wrong with this jam," she said. "It'd be good on that toast."

"Yes, ma'am," he said, shelling the first of his allotted two eggs. "But I'll just dip it in my mush."

"You say that every morning."

"Because that's what I *do* every morning."

"Suit yourself."

She took up a spoon, very deliberately lowered it through the jar's mouth, and gave it a slow twist. Yet for all that, the amount of jam she dabbed on her slice of toast wouldn't have covered a soup cracker. Still, the reason the jar had lasted since January went beyond frugality. In her kitchen, whatever quantity of sugar a recipe called for was automatically halved.

"Just remember," she said, with a tinge of ominousness, "I've got two dozen jars of this stuff in the cellar."

Using her spoon as a trowel, his mother began spreading the dab of jam toward the bread's edge. Still without looking at him directly, she spoke of the day's work, of the bean planting and harrowing awaiting him.

"Soon as I get myself dressed," said Edrus Penroy, "I'm going to hoe in the garden till Co-Op opens. And then I'll go get you more seed."

Given the "efforts" she had asked God to bless, there was more on her mind than jam and bean seed. Hewell shelled his second egg, sugared his mush sparingly, and awaited the morning's real question.

"So," she asked finally, obliquely, spreading and spreading until the chokecherry jam was more color than flavor, "how was the dance?"

Neither the shrug nor the labored shoveling in of mush put her off.

"You were back fairly early."

"Eleven o'clock don't feel so early," he said around a mouthful, "when there's thirty acres of beans waiting to be planted the next morning."

"Did you have a good time?"

"A dance is a dance, Mom."

"I bet you didn't even ask anybody," she said. "Knowing you, you probably spent all your time at the food table."

She was right. Twelve summers holding a cup and little paper plate or napkin. Twelve summers' worth of chips and dip, brownies and chocolate chip cookies, barrels of punch. What would she do with broccoli and cauliflower *raw* on a serving platter? Or real cheese and something besides bargain-bin soda crackers? Or root beer floats? Or *buttered* popcorn?

She chewed her toast inscrutably, said, "Did you at least *talk* to anybody?"

"Old Newton never showed up. But I did see Gary and that cousin of his—Lon, I think his name is. They're building guard rail over by Gillette, came clear over the mountain just for a dance." He glanced at his mother, said, "That's desperation for you."

"I meant," she said, "did you talk to anybody in a dress."

"I know what you meant," Hewell said. "And I think you probably know the answer."

Now she looked at him, said, "I might have guessed." She tightened the lid back on the jar of chokecherry jam, would have used a pipe wrench had one been close at hand. "You know, Hewell, the Lord helps those who help themselves."

"The Lord isn't the one you gotta ask to dance, Mom."

Her hands fell away from the jar as if they had been slapped. "Well, what a thing to say."

For several moments, the only sound in the room came from his own eating—the spoon in his bowl and the crunch of toast. Yet by the time he dared to look directly across the table, her face showed more grief than anger.

"I'm sorry, Mom—"

"All I know," she said, her eyes welling with tears, "is that, in this life, you have *got* to keep trying. Sometimes trying is all you *can* do."

While her wheat mush congealed, she studied him morosely. "Do you have any idea," she asked, "how you come to be here?"

He knew the story.

"Even when the doctor said there wasn't a one-in-a-million chance I'd ever conceive again, your daddy and I *refused* to quit. Twenty *years* after we got your sister! Do you know how long twenty years is, wanting something every night and day of it—neither one of us getting any younger? But we weren't just praying. We were doing our part; we were trying."

In their life together, she had, more than once, ventured into such disclosure—describing, for instance, the history behind his father's hernia operation or her own eventual hysterectomy. But on this morning Hewell was not so much discomfited by her words as he was moved. Resting his forearms on the old eating table, he leaned toward her, said, "I *am* trying."

She snorted. "That's what you call staying home from their outings and giving plumb up on Sunday-night firesides? Like a doggone hermit? Looks to me like you're down to dances as your last hope—at your own doing."

"Mom, listen," he said. "Listen to me. Girls young as the ones at these things ain't interested in me."

"Self-pity won't help you none."

"Is it self-pity to tell the truth?"

"You just haven't found the right one."

"Mom, it's ten years of this, and I haven't found *any*body. Not since Gwen."

Abruptly she looked down at her bowl. "I don't really think you had anybody found then," she said.

"Suit yourself, Mom."

"You can't expect it overnight," she declared. "I never have. And you still got plenty of good years to look."

With one last morsel of toast, he wiped his bowl clean. "And where else would you suggest I do all this looking?"

"I didn't say anything about where else," she said. "There's no need for where else—not for a good boy like you, never married, clean in your habits. Not if you'll get off your self-pity and do some asking. There's going to have to be some of that before there'll ever be any courting. That's the way of things, in case you didn't know." She sighed and resolutely patted the tabletop with both hands. Then she scooted her chair back, stood, began stacking their breakfast dishes—all while looking at him with what could only be called pity.

"It's plenty early in the summer," she said, finally turning toward the sink. "There'll be lots more dances."

35

Midmorning of a day in June, after moving irrigation water on the barley and corn, Hewell rode the unpadded dish seat of the old Mc-Cormick, monitoring the cultivator assembly bolted to either side of the tractor's front end, keeping each of six rows of fragile new pintos centered between a pair of close-set sweeps. Get the weeds and not the beans, she would say at the slightest evidence of "cultivator's blight."

Already the day was hot, and riding a creeping tractor was tedious, soporific work—leaning first to one side of the steering wheel, then the other, vigilant for a snagged rock or alfalfa root bulldozing the beans. Just yawning or daydreaming, you could take out ten or twenty yards' worth. *Keep your eyes open, Hewell.* Down the field, then up. Sixty, maybe seventy, rods each way, at a crawl.

It was a long time till noon and the big meal of the day. Boiled potatoes, scrambled eggs, Swiss chard stewed until, on the plate, it was little more than a green puddle with stems. Maybe macaroni plain— she didn't believe in melted cheese—maybe beans or peas, *maybe*, if he was lucky, a pan-fried hamburger patty or a pork chop. No ketchup. No apple sauce. No horseradish. Just the flesh of the good beast, cooked like a slab of leather. And let the rest of the world waste their pennies on pop or lemonade. Tap water was good enough for Edrus Penroy. She had never forgotten being newly married during the early years of the Depression. No matter how many meals she had to build around eggs and boiled edibles from field and garden, she was always vehemently grateful to have *something* on the table. To her, even bitter jam was a blessing.

As was refuge from the elements—beneath a roof in dire need of reshingling. And a bed to sleep in—though how she ever had managed to fit a husband on a mattress barely double-cot wide, and how that mattress had accommodated all that trying, was an abiding mystery to Hewell. And wherewith to clothe herself. Home-sewn pants with elastic waistbands (two pairs of polyester, one of light denim), two Sunday dresses (summer and winter), of course the flannel housecoat faded to a dull lemon color, and essential footwear: a pair of rubber snow packs for barn and field boots, white canvas tennis shoes for everyday comings and goings, and lace-up black oxfords for church, for funerals and weddings.

Coming at last to the drain ditch at the end of the field, Hewell clutched, put the tractor in neutral, and hopped off to stretch, jog in place, revive himself for the long run back upfield. Looking at all the ground covered and all the ground left to him, he felt as if he were looking at his life. Forever one direction, an eternity the other. Too short and too long, too. He burped oatmeal and climbed back into the dished seat.

She prayed for health and was inordinately healthy. Skinny and wind-blown, a little arthritis, but healthy. No bowel malfunction, certainly. At a young-adult fireside a long time ago, Hewell heard a food-storage expert warn that an abrupt shift to whole wheat could actually prove dangerous to someone with an unconditioned digestive system. Compared with themes related to dating and romance and conducting your courtship on a spiritual plane—the usual fare at such gatherings—whole wheat didn't seem like much of a topic for a group of red-blooded singles.

A fireside is a fireside, Mom.
What'd they talk about?
Surviving on cracked wheat.
I could've told you everything you need to know about that.

In cobble, the click and chink of cultivator tools was a welcome sound. It meant the sweeps and shovels, though rattled loose on their standards every once in a while, were finding their way under and between and *through* the rocks. It was the quiet you had to worry about, when the big ones got stuck in the tools and dragged along for the ride.

Go to dances, do your part. That was her answer. Meanwhile, blink or yawn, and another summer was gone. There was no making her understand, this woman who had married four months before her seventeenth birthday and never knew the joy of even one young-adult dance, let alone fifteen years' worth. A tank of gas and a long drive to a church house in Lovell or Greybull or Burlington or even as far away as Worland or Thermopolis—just to stand two or three hours at the periphery of a dimly lighted gymnasium, completely detached from the throb of music, studying the dancing couples as if through the glass of an aquarium. She had no way of appreciating the wariness, the banding together, the wide skirting if he happened to be standing between them and a group of new arrivals, guys fresh home from missions or on summer vacation from BYU. If he happened to be standing along their way to the refreshment table, they took another route, spoke to him only if they mistook him for a chaperone or a janitor waiting to sweep.

At nineteen, he had wanted to go on a mission. He could have had his share of dog and humidity stories. At some Sunday evening fireside he could have been the one reporting on his "experiences," fielding the questions of admiring young ladies. *Were the people receptive? Did they have four seasons, like we have?*

Despite what she said to everybody, despite one of her prayer's particulars in that era, she really didn't want him to go. Just wait, she kept saying, until fall, until after the beans are out. Or until after Christmas, when the cattle come in off the fields. Or until the planting's done. Just wait, Hewell. You're my youngest; it took me too long to get you. You have no idea how hard this is.

So he turned twenty, then twenty-one, and the boys his age started coming home. At twenty-two and twenty-three, he would have been old to begin a mission, but he could have gone. There was still a chance. But then, just about the time he was going to tell her—now or never— his dad collapsed right there in the muck of the milk barn, carrying a bucket of rolled oats, and the whole question was settled forever.

36

As on numberless other rounds up and down the field, the McCormick came finally to the ditch. Hewell clutched, throttled down, then stared at his hands on the steering wheel. That girl last night had stared. He had just thrown his plate and napkin away in the big trash can beside the refreshment table, still had a mouthful when, not skirting or rerouting either, she walked straight toward him. They all looked young, but she was hardly beyond adolescence.

"Are you here for Heather?" she asked in her helpful, all-business, not-so-adolescent voice.

"Who?"

"You're Heather's dad, right?"

Never again. Even if his weathered face and balding head didn't betray him, the hands would. No missionary or college student fresh home had his hands wrapped around the handle of an irrigating shovel four or five hours a day, silt ground into the callus pad on each thumb and forefinger—impossible to scrub out, May through August.

Self-pity won't help you none.

"There's other kinds of missions, Hewell," said Edrus Penroy a week after the funeral. His dad died in late March, just before barley planting, with the spraying and cultivating and irrigating and cutting and baling and harvesting stretching ahead as far as the eye could see. "A mission isn't everything."

And he had listened to her.

"There'll be other girls," his mother had said. "This Gwen is not the only fish in the pond."

In his early twenties, when he should have been on a mission or due home from one, he went out a few times, thanks to the charity of some nice girls. They took pains, however, to let him know that charity was all they felt. But then, at a fireside a couple of summers later, during refreshments and mingling, a girl named Gwen came up to him—and she wasn't looking for anybody's father. After five years in a music room at Nyman R. Spafford Elementary School in Salt Lake City, she had heard, through relatives, of an opening at a school in Ralston, Wyoming. Better pay and a change of scenery. "Does that make sense?" she asked. She was the only girl he had taken out more than one time, the one and only female he had brought to the house.

"A music teacher?" said Edrus Penroy, after waiting up for him that same night.

"What's wrong with that?"

"She's too old for you."

"What's a year or so?"

And too educated. And she's a city girl. And she's hunting marriage.

"You hold *that* against her? Tell me who at those firesides ain't hunting the same thing."

"There'll be other girls."

"Hey, stranger," Gwen said the very last time she called him, "I haven't heard from you for a while."

There would be other girls, his mother said.

And he had listened to her.

39

"Hewell?" she asked, pushing the jar of crabapple jelly toward him. "You do *like* girls, don't you?"

41

Hay dust filled his ears and nostrils; leaves stuck to the sweat of his face and arms. But by four o'clock on an afternoon in mid-August, the knotters had tied a thousand knots—five hundred bales in a row—without a miss. Not bad for the old New Holland, bought the summer before his dad died, used even then.

"Because if you're that . . . *way*, Hewell, it can be cured, you know."

He had said *no thanks*—to the jelly—and she misconstrued. And once persuaded, she was a hard one to disabuse. He had assured her: he liked girls just fine; it was them that didn't seem to like him very much.

"Well, since you stopped going to the dances, I just got to wondering. It's hard to see you so lonely. Sometimes hormones need an injection or something like that."

It was bad enough half the world wondered—nieces and nephews at family get-togethers full of cheerful pity (*How's it going for you, Uncle Hewell?*), all the people at church looking at him, week after week, year after year, wifeless on a back pew, asking themselves what else could possibly keep a red-blooded Mormon man single this long.

Pivoted halfway around in the tractor seat, one leg drawn up, swaying easy to the plunger rhythm of the flywheel, Hewell watched the unbroken flow of the cured windrow—up and off the slightly yellowed stubble and into the burnished steel mouth of the baler. At that point, the process was a racket of teeth and tongs and blades, so that whatever ended up in that mouth was swept without a handhold into the dark gullet of the plunger chamber.

He was halfway down one of the field's last windrows when he spotted the bull snake surfing the windrow. The spectacle always fascinated Hewell. A quick, darting slither left or right would carry him off the windrow, between the tires, and out of danger. But by some instinct beyond understanding, a snake surfing for its life couldn't see escape half a body length away, kept coming back to the windrow's center—exactly the position of greatest risk. As always, at the first flagging of an amazing stamina, one of the baler's pickup teeth caught the tail end and flung the whole body upward; then a boost with another tooth, and inward it went, a writhing loop bounced toward plate steel on which scales would find no purchase, to be swept along with stems and leaves toward plunger knives that could shear a two-by-four without a shudder.

In the summers since his apprenticeship with their first baler, the ancient John Deere that came within a thread of tearing his leg off, Hewell had seen a hundred snakes baled—mostly water snakes and bull snakes, but sometimes rattlers. Sometimes he stopped the baler to go back and see. No matter how carefully he noted the spot, he always had to search four or five bales before he found the loop of scales and skin protruding between compressed leaves of hay—or, on the knife-cut side of the bale, the sheared segments. Often he was lucky to find even a nose or tip of a tail. Once in a while he didn't find anything at all, at least not until January, when the bale, deprived of its twines and broken in a trough, spooked the nearest two or three cows with the scent of something besides cured clover or bromegrass.

Only once in a dozen times did a snake get as far as the pickup teeth and somehow escape. But on this day in August, with Edrus Penroy's hardest question so clear in Hewell's mind, this one did it. After the first flinging contact with the pickup teeth, its tumbling body, like a boomerang of dog chain, found a current of gravity that drew it back down along the cresting windrow. Though the tips of several other teeth made just enough contact to buffet and disorient, every progress was now down and away from the dark chamber. And suddenly, finding the thatch of sun-cured alfalfa once more beneath its scales, the snake angled sharply from the line of the windrow, skimmed off into the stubble, and was gone.

A thousand sound knots in a row, and the knotter picked that moment, the moment of the snake's escape, the same moment a truck turned down their lane, to miss one. In consequence, the next bale issued untied from the machine's plunger chute and ruptured on the ground. And not at the far end of the field, either. Had her window been rolled down, the driver of the Ralston Light and Power truck probably could have heard Hewell's lamentation as he throttled down and climbed off the tractor. And had he looked up a little sooner from his fiddling with the knotter, he would have realized he had an audience, would have realized, *before* she went by, that the audience was not his eighty-one-year-old mother, who had gone to town after more twine and was due back anytime.

His lamentation gave way to something else when, on the return leg of the meter-reading circuit, the Ralston Light and Power truck slowed, then stopped just across the ditch from where he was still clearing clogged twine from the knotter fingers. The driver rolled her window down, smiled, and hollered something friendly.

Hewell tried to nod a nod worthy of so wonderful a greeting.

With the truck already inching forward, she smiled again, and waved, then was gone ahead of a plume of dust dancing merrily through heat waves.

At supper, chewing unbuttered corn on the cob with teeth unexamined by a dentist in the last fifteen years, Edrus Penroy said, "Did Ralston Power check the meter today? They usually come on the fifteenth."

"Yep," Hewell said, forking, at one time, a half-dozen slices of unbuttered, unbreaded, unflavored zucchini, "they sure did."

When the light bill came a week later, Hewell suggested that he pay it in person.

"A stamp's a whole lot cheaper than gas to their office," his mother said. They had prayed—Myron's wife, Sue, was due any day with her fourth baby—and were now eating breakfast. Thanks to fog and a steady rain, the light of the new day was not impressive. She said, "I don't see why you have to go clear to the far side of town just for that."

He reminded her that she often paid in person.

"I don't make a special trip of it."

Since the patter of the first drops shortly after midnight, he had lain awake thinking. But now, of all times, his reasoning couldn't *seem* calculated.

"It's raining, Mom."

"There's plenty to do right here at home," she said. "You can work in the shop."

Yes, he supposed she was right. He would soon need to start cutting beans, might as well mount the knives on the McCormick while he had a chance.

With great maternal satisfaction, she troweled lime jelly on her toast. Hewell worked cautiously at the shell of a boiled egg.

"The knives!" he said suddenly. "I won't do much mounting without them. And they're at the blacksmith's. I took them a week ago, to get them hard-faced."

"Will he have them finished?" asked Edrus Penroy.

Hewell was more than sure he would. He had had all that time. And what better day to take care of such an errand? Then he could stay busy in the shop forever and ever.

He peeled the second egg. And—since Ralston Light and Power was just across the road from the blacksmith's shop . . .

"Now you're talking a little sense," she said. "I may teach you some smarts yet."

At the payment counter of Ralston Light and Power, he asked only whether the change in their meter reader was permanent. But the lady clerk was gabby, and that one question was enough: the new meter reader's name was Benita—Spanish for something like Bernice—just got the job, drove over from Cody every day—that's where she lived—was very religious, didn't party at all—but was the nicest girl, and a *hard* worker—had two or three kids but was divorced from the father—still had his name, Sievers, but hadn't ever remarried. And not because there was a single thing wrong with her.

42

Every month of her first winter as meter reader, on the day her route was to bring her down Road 15A, toward the electric meter of E. Penroy, he found reason to be in the proximity of the field next to the road. Any reason would do. In November, for instance, he carried a hammer and can of staples and walked the fence along the ditch bank—a fence so far gone that the chore was meaningless, like setting out to reshingle a house whose rafters had long since rotted.

"What in the world are you messing with that old fence for?" his mother asked during another supper. "It ought to be torn down."

"You're right," Hewell said, piling his bowl high with stewed cabbage. "I thought I could spruce it up a little, but it's got to go." He assured her he'd get to it in his spare time—which happened to present itself on the same day for each of the next three months. During this same period of his life, he added to his private prayers some particulars of his own: *Please let the Ralston Light and Power truck break down somewhere nearby. Please let one of its tires go flat.*

In March, with every strand of rusted barbed wire rolled up, every stray staple combed from the undergrowth, every rotted post stump dug from winter-hardened sod—the ditch bank as clean as the dawn of creation—he resorted to burning dead grass in the field's drain ditch. The smoke obscured, but did not discourage, the smile and wave.

"What in the world are you burning down there for?"

In April he hunted all afternoon for wild asparagus among the charred stubble. When the Ralston Light and Power truck passed, he wanted to flag it down and give his findings to the driver. But he could not risk his mother's scrutiny. Not yet. Instead, he settled for the wave and the smile, savored them like water in the desert. Instead, when he went in for supper, he emptied the half-full lard bucket on the kitchen counter.

"Nothing better than fresh asparagus," said Edrus Penroy, setting a pot of water to boil.

He wanted to tell the driver of the truck: *You give me hope. I carry your phone number on a card in my wallet. I live thirty days at a time just for your smile and wave.* And he wanted to tell his mother: *I've met someone, and I'm going to try to see her on some sort of courting basis.* Maybe that would convince her—his hormones were A-okay. If only he could explain, make her understand how, one afternoon a month, that ditch bank tilted toward the North Star and became a paradise in waiting.

But he could not afford to spoil this chance.

She's Mexican, Hewell. You don't even know her. How many kids already, and who's their daddy? And I don't suppose she's a Mormon.

So what was left? Waving and waiting? And if so, waiting for *what*?

42 ½

Two more months passed. Another season changed. The electric meter kept turning. And in all that time the Ralston Light and Power truck never broke down and never had a flat.

So first thing in June, when the summer's first crop of hay came off the fields (about a week too early), Hewell made a stack where he had never made a stack before—just beyond their little plot of lawn. It crowded their parking space and looked out of place, but it also blocked any clear view between the house and the big light pole. This was the light pole whose cowled hundred-watt bulb, thirty feet up, provided something to look to on moonless nights. It was also the pole to which the electric meter was bolted.

"But why on earth right *there*?" asked Edrus Penroy after the first run of bales was placed as the stack's foundation. "Sixty years, and we've never put hay there. What were you thinking? I'll have hay dust coming in every time I open a window. And you know it don't take much to give me the cough. One of these days I won't be able to shake it. I'm an old woman, Hewell, but you work and worry me like I was a chore girl." She gave him a hard look. "I swear, I wish you'd said something first."

"Well, do you want me to move it?" he asked, with just the right blend of defensiveness and submission.

"No, I don't want you to move it," she said. "No need to compound the problem by making a wasted effort of it. But you promise me you'll feed this one first between now and next winter."

He promised. A promise that gave him six months at most, six months in which her arthritis and cough and low blood pressure weren't likely to get a lot better—or a lot worse, either.

When the Ralston Light and Power truck rolled into the yard on the fifteenth of June and pulled behind the new haystack, driver side closest to the pole, there was a lard bucket of fresh apricots perched on the meter. Standing behind the shop, between the chicken coop and vacant brooder house, in new pigweed already threading its way through pipe and angle iron and sucker rod on his dad's scabbed-together metal rack, Hewell watched. She noticed the bucket first thing, the fruit heaped above the rim, and looked around several times before reaching for it. Then she sat for a long time—baffled? worried? scared?—looking down at the seat where she had set the bucket. Another long interval passed before she came back up with the clipboard and pen and read the meter, before he saw the amenable smile.

That night, and many nights thereafter, he imagined her hungry, fatherless children eating good food provided at his hand. He lay awake thinking of all the fruit and produce he could give her. And he thought of other things, too—the curve of her neck, the swell of her blouse. No, he didn't need any injections.

In July there was a lard bucket of tomatoes—and more. Atop a pair of hay bales stacked at the base of the light pole were short boards of various thickness, and atop those, a bucket of cucumbers and a full peck of green beans. Using his own truck window as a guide, he had fashioned the pedestal's height exactly. Thus she could reach the bucket and basket without even opening her door. In August— peaches, more tomatoes, new potatoes, and sweet corn. In September, after just one light frost to help the flavor—a big Hubbard squash and a basket of apples with a note tucked among the fruit. She set the basket on the floorboard of the passenger side, and then she was holding the note, written on the only piece of colored paper to be found in Edrus Penroy's house. From his place behind the shop, among angle iron and ripe pigweed, amid the drowsy afternoon cluck of chickens, he went over every syllable in his mind:

I'm not trying to bother you or be weird. I just hope you like fruit and such.

His one regret was the signature: *Yours truly, Hewell Penroy.* It sounded dumb enough even when it wasn't directed at a female. What did it mean, anyway? But then he saw the head tilt and the concentration of writing, saw her reach her own folded slip of paper (from a Ralston Light and Power message pad) through the window and wedge it in the meter housing.

Long after the truck was gone, the boards and hay bales back in their regular places, all discoverable evidence of the moment cleared away, he stood behind the shop reading and rereading her words—*I love fresh fruit and vegetables. Thank you so much*—and the telephone number that, until this moment, had been just a number.

He was going to have to tell his mother. This sneaking was no good, this hoping she wouldn't detect his inattention and distraction, praying she wouldn't come around the haystack one afternoon to find him building his monthly altar of hope. Which made him wonder what he could put on that altar next month. It was fall, the nights were colder, the garden mostly down to dying stalks and vines. A few more squash maybe, and the pumpkins. Maybe a little sack of clean pintos. But that was it.

He was going to have to tell her.

Her name's Benita, Mom. And if you don't like it, that's too bad.

For three weeks he carried in his wallet the folded slip bearing the Ralston Light and Power logo, studied it two or three times daily. Then, against the urgency of the meter reader's next trip down their lane, he awoke one morning resolved to tell her at breakfast, steeled for what he thought was coming.

On that same morning, October twelfth, Edrus Penroy came from the stove hobbling, holding the handle of the steaming mush pot with both hands. For the first time in Hewell's memory she did not kneel to pray. "I'm a little footsore this morning," she said, lowering herself onto a chair, catching her breath at every movement of her lower leg. "I believe the Lord will make allowance." And in her prayer, after giving thanks for the light of the new day, after petitioning the three-thousandth time for Hewell to find happiness, she made a rare reference to a particular of her own physical well-being: *Please bless my big toe, Heavenly Father. It's hurting me some.*

Perhaps out of humility or shame for a debility—or both—she was understating. As a matter of fact, the toe was swollen dark purple and oozing pus, and the bright line of fever already had reached her ankle.

"What's this?" he said.

"Oh, it's nothing," she said. "Have some jam, Hewell."

"Why didn't you say something?"

It was no cough or arthritis or low blood pressure that had bested her, but a toenail gone bad. At the first sign of trouble, she had numbed the whole foot in a bowl of ice cubes, then yanked the nail with a pair of pliers. But despite her experience with homemade operations of this kind, the usual week of salt-water and vinegar soaks hadn't cured anything. "Listen, Mom," he said, expecting a fight, "you'd better let me take you to see a doctor."

But she didn't fight; she only mumbled at the pain as he helped her to her room to dress, and again when he handed her a wet washcloth for her face and hair brush for her head, as if any touch anywhere, even at the opposite end of her body, registered in the inflamed toe. She winced when, lifting her like a child, he slid her onto the truck seat, and all the way to town she was pale, her forehead clammy with perspiration. She wore a tube sock on her sore foot, but no shoe.

"You should have come in a lot sooner," the young doctor said. "Infection like this is bad in anybody, but for a lady your age—"

"My age is none of your business," said Edrus Penroy. "I was curing croup and earache before you or your mom and daddy, either one, were even born. I raised three kids with never a broken bone or an overnight in the hospital. And where was all you doctors' good advice when I was trying to get *him*?" The question, accompanied by her pointing to Hewell, meant little to a thirty-two-year-old doctor who was new in town. "None of it worked anyway," she said. "Hot, cold, special schedules—in the middle of the *day* even—we tried everything. What did the doctors know? Nothing. It was a long prayer and a miracle got him here."

The doctor gave Hewell a look of utter bafflement.

"Ma'am," he said, "I'm just saying you've got a staph in a bad place, and it has a pretty good head start on me." He looked again at Hewell, this time with a grave expression.

"I may be stringy as an old hen, but I'll heal just fine, and I'll do it without a lot of overpriced pills and nonsense." Eyes bright, face flushed, she was babbling now. "Just a shot of penicillin's all I need. And while we're here, is there some kind of shot you can give my boy?"

43

On the fifteenth of October Edrus Penroy was in the hospital with Hewell at her bedside. After the surgery to drain her leg, she seemed addled, afraid, almost panicky.

"Don't go, Hewell," she muttered. "Don't leave me in this place."

To do the milking and feeding at home over the next ten days, he had to sneak away, early morning or after dark, and hurry back before the sleeping pills wore off. He had had no time for squash or pumpkins, hadn't even left a note. But one evening, late in the month, passing the light pole on his way to the milk barn, he found the card and flower—still fresh—and tire tracks that did not belong to the Ralston Light and Power truck.

I heard about your mother, and I want you to know I'm praying for her.

Several more weeks passed. The electric meter kept turning, the haystack between it and the house went down bale by bale, tier by tier, and, despite a second operation, Edrus Penroy did not recover. Hewell's note, tucked in the meter housing on a stormy afternoon in mid-November, was short: *Thank you for the flower and card. I'm sorry I don't have anything for you. And I'm sorry I haven't called. My mother has been real sick.*

Sick as she was, her death, two days after her eighty-third birthday, took the doctor by surprise. He had urged against calling Hewell's sisters home, especially during the Thanksgiving holiday, had argued that their mother might linger for a long time, might even get better. Sitting at her bedside on that last night, Hewell knew differently.

"We got you here by a long prayer and miracle," his mother whispered in one of her last lucid moments. "After all that, I don't want you living out your life like a hermit."

"I won't," he said.

She could not hear him, was not really looking at him. "It's no good being alone in this world," she said, blinking long, then gazing into the dimmed light overhead, then blinking again, "no good at all. But one of us was going to *have* to be—that was the problem. And I didn't know if *I* could bear it." Tears flushed the rheum of age and pain from her eyes, then spilled into the furrows of a face soon to be relieved of all its wear and grief. "I'm so sorry, son," she said. "I am so very sorry."

And Hewell Penroy, single and alone in his middle age, was sorry, too.

In the first few days of December, his sisters arrived, went through their mother's belongings, cleaned the house from top to bottom.

"You really need some new linoleum in this kitchen," the oldest one said. "It's worn through all over the place. And look at that pattern. This is the twentieth century, Hewell."

"I don't see what you two were living on," the other sister said after a trip to the grocery store. "There wasn't one thing in the fridge."

Over the next day or two the old house filled with Edrus Penroy's grandchildren and great-grandchildren, gathered now from places far distant for the funeral of a woman they hardly knew. Hewell gave his bedroom to Myron and Sue and as many of their five children as would fit, and slept on a camp cot in front of the shop's coal stove.

"How goes it, Uncle Hewell?" he was asked at every meeting with a member of the next generation.

By the end of the week it was all over—the viewing, the funeral, the graveside service, the Relief Society lunch at church, the family dinner that night, the distributing of a frugal woman's belongings.

"She'd want you to have this," Hewell said, handing a full case of chokecherry jam to each sister.

"What will you do now?" one of them asked.

What he had always done—eat and sleep and work, one day after the other. That is what he would continue doing, the same schedule he had followed for twenty years, save for one thing. And that one thing wasn't buying the farm, taking care of the legal papers to get it in his name—though, thanks to his sisters' approval, that would happen soon enough. He was thinking of something else.

On December fifteenth, despite his best efforts to sleep late, Hewell was up at five o'clock. First thing, he went to the switch in the utility room and flipped on the yard light—the first light of this new day, albeit artificial. One more feeding and the stack by the light pole would be gone, six months and a week from the day he had placed the first bales, seven years since the last young-adult dance, ten since he had stopped attending firesides, twenty since his final resolve to get on a mission. Would she ever have known how long that was?

From the light switch in the utility room he went the refrigerator in the kitchen and pulled out a carton of eggs, a cake of cheese, a package of link sausage, and a square of butter. From the freezer, orange juice. From the bread box, a full loaf. From the cellar, potatoes. For the next forty minutes he peeled and grated, broke and beat, sliced and cooked. Out of long habit, he started to set the table with two of everything—plates, glasses, utensils—and suddenly caught himself. Yet after a moment's thought, he made no changes. With melted cheese dripping from an omelet, from atop a platter of hash browns, he knelt at his kitchen chair and gave thanks for food and shelter, health and strength, for the life of his mother, a person both flawed and decent—and for electricity.

At last, after a long night of darkness, the December sun cleared the horizon. Dishes washed, chores done, Hewell filled out his morning cleaning up the remnants of the haystack, chopping dead pigweed behind the shop, and burning it in a big pile by the garden. Then, on a whim, he rummaged through the clutter in the brooder house and found a mostly empty bucket of red paint, another of green—frost-ruined and watery, but with pigment enough for his purpose. Over the shop's stove, he softened the bristles of a brush, then painted alternating rings up the light pole as high as he could reach.

At noon he went in the house, ate two pork chops—one with barbecue sauce, the other with horseradish—then set to work on a fudge recipe clipped from a very old magazine and kept (how many decades?) at the bottom of his mother's cedar chest. Somehow his sisters had missed it, tucked away in an envelope with some family photos and a ticket stub from a 1940 Gold and Green Ball.

The first ingredient Hewell pulled from a shelf of the utility room was sugar—a fifty-pound sack of it. He was careful to use the heaviest pan in the house—the mush pot—on the old stove's fickle burner, careful to stir in exactly the amounts the recipe called for, and a little more, careful to stir the hot candy patiently with a wooden spoon. By the time the chopped walnuts sank into the spoon's swirl, the pot's rich odor had filled his nostrils and the house and the whole world.

Later, with the fudge cooling in its pan, he showered, shaved, put on a new shirt and pair of jeans, combed such hair as was left to him, and waited the last hour he would ever wait for this moment. When the Ralston Light and Power truck finally turned down the lane, he put on his good coat, took the plate of fudge wrapped in bright foil, and stepped outside to meet it coming.

WHITE SHELL

Arianne Cope

THERE ARE PIECES OF WHITE SHELL sifted with the sands and soils of Dinetah that confuse newcomers and outsiders. Tourists look at the shells like puzzle pieces, trying to force them into what they know. A gift of the ocean in the depths of a parched desert? "If they looked past themselves, they would realize the place they stand was once covered by a shallow sea," Mary's grandfather said. "And it is they who do not belong."

Even those who do belong on the reservation survive only if they are able to adapt to the desert's hostile personalities that push forward, turn under, circle overhead like vultures. Few things survive the grip of the sacred land. Grandfather is one of them. His skin is soft and warm like worn denim, the same color as the lofty mesas. His limbs are like the branches of lone twisted trees. His gray hair is as soft as owl feathers. His eyes are patient, slow-moving clouds. Like coyote, spiders, yucca, Grandfather lasts. Mary does not.

Like high passing storm clouds, Mary is forced beyond by encroaching winds before her time. She watches the sacred land retreat from view, afraid it will forget her, knowing her footprints on canyon floors and atop mesas have already blown away.

Mary steps gingerly into her new land from a small gray bus with sagging, rusty bumpers. The bus's engine idles impatiently behind Mary, waiting for her to go inside her new home. But Mary only touches her toes to the greenest grass she has ever seen, just off the sidewalk, as if she is testing the temperature of unfamiliar pond water. There are boys with painted faces playing with bows and arrows and slings in the front yard of the new-looking house. It is a long brick house with a low-pitched gable roof. Bigger than the trailer in Snowflake and much bigger than the round hogans Mary is most used to. Up and down the street there are houses of similar shapes but different colors. Mary wonders if there are really people in all of them, living so close together.

"Hey!" one of the boys yells. "She's here!" They all run over to Mary, stop a couple yards away. One light-haired ambassador continues closer. He is wearing smears of red face paint and carrying a plastic tomahawk. "We were just playing cowboys and Lamanites. You wanna join? You'd be the only *real* Lamanite we've ever played with." Mary has no idea what Lamanites are. She studies the freckles on the boy's face and figures he is two or three inches taller than she is and two or three years older.

Just as the boy opens his thick, chapped lips to say something else, the front door of the brick house opens, and a woman comes out the front door wiping her hands on a white-and-green checkered apron. She catches one of her black pumps on the top porch step and nearly falls face first onto the concrete path leading to the street. "Whoa!" she yells in surprise, then turns and keeps walking, muttering death upon her shoes. The woman's grimacing face suddenly lights up with what Mary perceives as put-on pleasantness when she makes eye contact. "How *are* you, sweetie?" she asks when she reaches Mary. The woman's eyes examine Mary from top to bottom. With a wave of her hand she signals for the bus driver to leave. "Thank you for your trouble of dropping her off directly, Brother Bean!" The bus driver nods before putting his engine in gear.

As the bus pulls away from the curb with a grinding sound, the woman stoops down to Mary's eye level. She is wearing lipstick the color of blood, and her light hair is done in shiny waves. After a moment or two Mary has not said anything, and the woman speaks again. "Well, Mary. My name is Diane Jensen, and my husband's name is Walter, although he's not home from work yet. He's no doctor, but what we have is yours. We've been looking forward to this day for the *long*est time! Have you eaten? We've already had our supper, but I saved you some. You like meatloaf?" The woman pauses for moment, awaiting a response from Mary. She continues cheerfully when she does not get one. "Just wait till you meet the girls. You're going to *love* it here. Come in and I'll show you all your new clothes and your room." The woman pauses for a moment. "Well, sweetie. Do you like red? I figured you'd have . . . *dark* hair, you know, so a lot of your jumpers are red. Won't that be nice? And the boys, don't worry about . . ." Words bubble faster and faster out of the woman like the jumping of a jackrabbit oblivious to an approaching truck before . . . crunch!

Silence.

The woman's mouth closes, and her eyes squint a little. Mary sees it on her face. First confusion, waiting for some kind of response—a yes, a hello, a smile even. The woman repeats herself. Then becomes concerned. Finally, she says, "Can you *hear* me, dear?"

The woman whispers about it with her husband that night. Mary hears through the cracked door of her new bedroom. "Nobody said she couldn't talk. Should we call her mother? Maybe she's deaf and nobody notified us."

"Would her being deaf make any difference in us keeping her? What would the Savior do?"

"Well . . . *no*," the woman says after a moment of thought. "It won't make *that* kind of difference." Then she pauses for a moment. "She does respond," she continues slowly, thoughtfully, "in a kind of *way*, with her eyes . . . when you speak to her. What if—"

"Don't worry about it," the man's deep voice jumps in. "She'll come 'round. Don't need to cause her more trauma. She's pretty young. Maybe too young for this kind of thing. Already left her mother and father and home and has to swallow all eleven of us in one shot. It'll just take time for her to . . . adjust, you know, for us to teach her the gospel and good manners. Best if we do it real slow, and . . ."

The man's voice becomes softer now, too soft for Mary to hear. So she climbs into her bed and lies there, staring at the dark ceiling until she hears the radio come on, and the sound of the announcer replaces the woman and her husband's whispering voices.

Mary turns from her side to her back on the fold-out bed, tunes out the radio announcer, and tries to think of something else. The mattress's coils squeak under her weight. She has never slept on a bouncy mattress like this before and feels strange lying up so high. All she had was rolled sheepskins on the floor in hogans with her grandparents or even with Mommy in the trailer. And the bed she used at winter school in Chinle was made of fencing wire that barely bent at all even when Mary jumped on it.

Mary watches arrowheads of light from a passing car's headlights dance across the ceiling. She is alone in the room. "Just for tonight," the woman told her. "To help you ease into things." But Mary suspects it has more to do with her scraggly hair and the way she smells. A doctor at the bus stop in Richfield extracted a handful of lice from Mary's hair and gave her a shot, pronounced her healthy. But even after giving her a bath, Mary's new mother seems hesitant. She touches her only when necessary and at an arm's length the way Mary imagines one would treat soiled, reeking underpants.

Tomorrow the two sets of bunk beds on the other side of Mary will fill with her four new sisters. For now the girls are giggling in sleeping bags on the floor of the next room with the boys. The woman said Mary would have five new sisters and four new brothers. One of the girls is a tiny baby that sleeps in a cradle next to the woman's bed. "I won't trouble you with all of them at once till morning rolls around," the woman told Mary when she tucked her in.

Mary plays with the buttons on her new pajamas—a red-and-white plaid flannel top and matching pants. The buttons feel cool and smooth in her fingers and click-clack when she taps two together. She turns back onto her side. The bed squeaks again. Someone shuts the radio off, and she hears her new parents' voices progressing down the hall to their bedroom. The rhythmic sound of the man's hoarse laugh penetrates the wall near Mary's bed before she hears the creak of a closing door. The man's face is still foreign to Mary. He has brown hair. That is all she knows because she could not bring herself to look at his face when she was introduced.

A moment later the baby cries. It sounds muffled through the walls, like the sound of a distressed kitten. Violet is the tiny girl's name. Mary remembers because it matched the pureed plums smeared across Violet's face and high chair when Mary first saw her.

Mary falls asleep much later after all the noises—the water running in the bathroom, someone coughing, the baby grunting—slowly quiet like a dying fire and she can no longer even strain to hear anyone's breathing. But she jerks awake after barely slipping into the other side of consciousness. Her body is covered with a film of cold sweat, and her legs and arms are twitching. She is unable to relax again and find the secret place of sleep without the sound of Mommy's shallow puffs next to her, leading her there with some sense of safety.

"Mary, I want you to call me Mother as soon as you feel comfortable," the woman says over breakfast the next day. Mary does not like how casually this new mother uses her given name. In Arizona she had been called, simply, *awee*, or baby. Nearly everyone on the reservation went by a nickname to protect the sacredness of their given names. Mary turns her face from her new mother's smile and looks at the large oak table. There is more food spread out than Mary's used to seeing in a month. Things Mommy and she would have been lucky to find while scrounging in the garbage piles of even the richest Arizona white men. There are two cold bottles of milk, a ceramic saucer filled with country gravy, two plates stacked high with cream-colored biscuits, and a bowl of ripe pears and peaches.

Mary's new mother slides a fried egg on Mary's plate and hands her a pear. "Eat." Mary holds the fruit to her nose and pulls the sweet rainwater smell of its thin, yellow skin into her nostrils. She has the urge to slip it into her pocket and grab another in case there is no food later, but she is worried someone will see her and become angry.

"These are all your new brothers and sisters," Mary's new mother says, introducing each of her children quickly. Mary looks around the table at the communal stare of nine pale, freckled faces. "You may call them your brothers and sisters." Mary feels the almost tangible heat of the children's inquisitive expressions burn rings of embarrassment on her cheeks. She has never had a sibling and cannot imagine calling anyone Mother but her own . . . Mommy.

Mary looks down at her fried egg, stares at the asymmetrical shape of the broken yellow yolk until it blurs, but she cannot keep her thoughts from rolling away from her like a dropped ball of yarn. Mary remembers Mommy's warm kiss on her cheek before she had boarded the bus in Arizona. A burst of wind had turned the wet, red lipstick mark instantly cold. "It's a long ride to Utah, *awee*," Mary remembers Mommy saying in Navajo while holding back tears. Then Mommy changed to English, which better masked her emotions. "Be a good girl. They say you'll change buses in Richfield and a nice man will bring you to your new family. You just used the bathroom, right? Don't want you making them make any special stops." Then the bus's folding door closed softly between them and that was all. Mary found a window seat near the front as the bus lurched into gear. She lifted her hand and caged the kiss mark on her cheek as if it were a startled moth. Her other hand reached up and pressed against the window pane as she watched Mommy's body—her arm raised in a motionless gesture of good-bye—shrinking smaller and smaller until it was a dark speck merging with the horizon.

Another child who was going to Utah on the same bus, a boy a couple years older than Mary, ran to the door after his parents slipped from view. He banged his small fists on the door. Rattle. Rattle. Rattle-rattle-rattle. No one responded. His lost, shiny eyes, like a frightened fawn's, seemed to look right through Mary as he found a seat in the back of the bus. Mary shivered as he passed.

Mary and the boy are two of nine children going to Utah for the school year. Mommy had explained it all to Mary a dozen times before she sent her away. "It's the chance to get educated and get ahead. To fit into the modern world outside the reservation." This was after weeks of exasperated attempts to find out why Mary had lapsed into what Mommy called a vocal coma after the return of her daddy from the war.

Mommy left Daddy sleeping on the gold sofa and brought Mary back to the reservation for a few days so that Grandfather—the *Hataa-lii*, or medicine man trained in healing methods passed down over centuries—could perform the hand-trembling chant used to diagnose ailments. Mary kept her eyes closed through the entire ritual. "It is not her head, her fingertips, her limbs, or the tip of her tongue. She is hurt deep in her spirit," Grandfather said when the ceremony was finished. "Beyond even the reach of the Holy People for now."

So when Mommy returned to the trailer house and two overweight, pimple-faced *Gaamalii* missionaries knocked on their door and explained how the Mormons were in the tentative stages of starting a placement program for Navajo children, Mommy immediately volunteered Mary to be shipped north. "I think they want them to be at least eight years old, and, well . . . *bap*tized," the missionary explained, tugging on the knot of his thin red tie. "Honestly, I brought it up only as a way to start talking to you about other things. Have you ever heard about Christ's coming to the Americas? A record left by ancient people witnesses that he is the light and life of the world." The missionary held up a set of scriptures before he continued. "Christ said, *I am the God of the whole earth, and have been slain for the sins of the world.*"

But Mommy said she was not interested in Christ's coming to America or anything else about a religion preached by young white men unless it could give her daughter food and clothes and education and save her from whatever was frightening her to silence. "She'll be seven this year. She's really bright," Mommy said softly, so as not to wake Daddy and risk chasing off the missionaries.

"Well, seven's still not old enough to be *bap*tized," one of the missionaries said, punching his leather scriptures with his right fist to punctuate his pronouncement. "I'm *pretty* sure they're going to require that she has to be eight."

Mommy's eyelids lowered and her chin began to quiver. "Please."

He would see what he could do.

Three weeks later that turned out to be good enough. Mary remembers Mommy using an artificial voice of cheery English from then on. "You know, even Snowflake is named after two *Gaamaliis* with the last names Flake and Snow. And your father's father's sheep still graze on Mormon lands in Aneth. You don't remember when we lived there, do you? Well, you were born on the state line under a half-moon with your head in Arizona and your feet in Utah. That was a way to bring opportunity and peace to your life." Mommy stopped speaking for a moment and smiled sadly. "Then we wrapped your little body in sheepskin and placed you next to the fire under the bright moon with your head facing the flames . . . to warm you." Her voice cracked. She paused again, then quickly shook her head as if the memories filling it were marbles, easily rearranged. "They're going to pay for your food, you know, your clothes, and your school. It'll give me a chance to save some money and get out of . . . and come for you." But the only thing that made the news sting a little less to Mary was the promise of summer visits. And Mary's promise to Mommy was to never forget her own family and *Kiiyaa'áanii*, the towering house clan.

On their way to the bus stop Mommy repeated in Navajo "The House Song of the East." Not in the smooth, seamless chant-singing that grandfather uses; she spoke the Navajo words plain, naked. "Far in the east, far below, there a house was made; delightful house," Mommy said. "God of Dawn, there his house was made; delightful house. The Dawn, there his house was made; delightful house. White corn, there its house was made; delightful house. Water in plenty, surrounding, for it a house was made; delightful house. Corn pollen, for it a house was made; delightful house. The ancients make their presence delightful; delightful house." Then Mommy added something not repeated to her by her elders, her voice breaking and her eyes unblinking and shiny. "My daughter leaves me now for better things, a new home; delightful house." Mommy stopped and looked at Mary, gestured with the raising of her eyebrows for her to join. But Mary remained silent, speaking the words only in her mind. *Before me, may it be delightful. Behind me, may it be delightful. Around me, may it be delightful. Below me, may it be delightful. Above me, may it be delightful. All, may it be delightful.*

But now Mary is here at the Jensens' breakfast table with her new Mormon family, and she does not want to remember Mommy any more. She turns her attention toward anything that can snag her thoughts on the present, like the tight feeling of her scalp from the two braids her new mother has made of her hair, how she is unable to wiggle her toes in her new rigid shoes. She watches Violet drop her bottle off her high chair, then cry for someone to pick it up. "Rat-tle, rat-a, rat-ling," Violet says when her bottle is retrieved, shaking it so hard milk comes spraying out the nipple.

The way Violet says the last word, with a glottal in the middle, is like the Navajo consonant sound meaning grass. This turns Mary's gaze out the window on the other side of the kitchen, through which she can see the small half-acre backyard. It is well into September, but the grass is still green. She thinks she sees a walnut tree in the back corner of the yard. Grandfather planted a walnut tree near his summer hogan as soon as he received word of Mary's birth. It was her tree, inching up over the years with her. Mary looks over the Jensens' back fence at the mountains—*nahasdzáánbikáá' niilyáii.* They are splattered with dull patches of rust and copper. It is still a desert here in Utah like in Arizona—Mary can tell by the sparse vegetation in the foothills— but nothing like the sheer rock on the reservation and the parched land that breathes in puffs of orange dust. Mary thinks of her grandparents who are harvesting corn in Canyon de Chelly, preparing themselves and their small sheep herd for winter. Grandfather's teeth look like the varying shapes and shades of the white and yellow *naadą́ą́* kernels they have finished harvesting. The memory of his partly toothless smile sends an aching pang up Mary's spine. But even if she were on the reservation, she tells herself, she would be leaving Grandfather to go to school during the cold months.

Mary pulls her eyes back to the table and cuts a tiny bite of the white of her egg. She holds the fork awkwardly in her fist, it being her first attempt at eating with utensils. Fry bread served as fork and spoon at home. And suddenly, even with all this food in front of her, a piece of fry bread is all Mary feels like eating.

"You excited for school, kids?" Mary's new father asks. He wipes his mouth on the rolled sleeve of his red flannel shirt.

"Yeah!" some of Mary's new younger brothers and sisters say enthusiastically. The older girls sigh with teenage aversion. "That's my gang," the father says. "Now let's gather in the front room."

The younger children run from the table and through the kitchen's open doorway. Mary's new parents and the older children follow. "Come on in with us, Mary," her new father calls over his shoulder. Mary leaves her nearly untouched breakfast behind and walks cautiously after her new mother into the living room. Everyone is kneeling in a circle and folding their arms across their chests. One of the boys elbows one of the girls, and their father orders him to stop. Then it becomes silent, and Mary's new father smiles at her. "Come. Join us, Mary." Mary kneels where she is, in the doorway. "No. Over here," her new father says, holding back a laugh. He scoots sideways on his knees to make a spot for her. "I'll say the prayer today." At that everyone bows their heads and closes their eyes.

Mary has not heard the word *prayer* before but quickly realizes it is similar to *sodizin* in Navajo. Mary copies their posture but keeps her eyes open. "Our kind and gracious Heavenly Father," her new father says before clearing his throat. Mary does not know whom he is addressing but imagines it is perhaps a grandfather who is deceased. The boy elbows the little sister next to him again. The girl does not yell, but scoots out of firing range. "We kneel before thee today as a family with grateful hearts," the father continues. "We thank thee for this new day and the good meal we've enjoyed together. We thank thee for providing us with a good home in which to live." The mischievous boy has opened his eyes and unfolded his arms and is inching toward his sister again. Because her eyes are now sealed with reverence, she does not see him approaching. "We thank thee for each other and for the opportunity we have to share our blessings with Mary, who has come to us from Arizona." Mary's face becomes hot at the mention of her name. One of the older girls peeks and smiles at her, then quickly, guiltily, closes her eyes. Mary's new father continues, "We thank thee for the gospel and for Jesus Christ and for the atonement." Mary does not know who Jesus Christ is. She has heard the name before and knows it has something to do with Christian churches. Perhaps it is white people's name for First Mother. "We ask thee to send thy spirit to be with us this day." The boy has reached his sister now and yanks her hair. By the time she screams, he has darted back to his place and is closing his eyes tightly. Mary's new father does not open his eyes or stop the prayer as she suspects he should. He just pauses and clears his throat before continuing with louder, slower words. "*Help* us to keep the spirit of con*ten*tion out of our home. The spirit that Lucifer would wish to prevail here. Help us to know thy will, Father. Again we thank thee for all that we have. And we say these things in the name of our Savior and Redeemer, Jesus Christ, amen."

Mary's new brothers complain all the way to school. The two older girls are in junior high, and the other girls are too young for school. So it is just Mary and three boys heading to the local elementary behind Mary's new mother. They are all in a row at first, like a parade of little ducks, the boys walking stiffly in their new clothes as if their legs are encased in denim casts.

"Will you still let us play night games?" the youngest boy asks. Mary's new mother is staring off into the street, her thoughts on something else.

"Fat chance," the oldest boy says. Then he turns his attention to Mary. "So who is your teacher, Mary? Are you going to be in the same class as Tom? He's a first grader too, you know." He points to Tom, the youngest boy, who is behind them untucking his starched collared shirt from his dark jeans. The boy keeps speaking even without an encouraging response. "Do you remember our names yet? I can say them all really fast. Listen." The boy dives into a list of his brothers' and sisters' names, his included, Bobby, in one streak of breath. "SherryEvelynBobbyGregTomLindaJohnNancyViolet." He dramatically gasps for breath when he is finished. Mary nearly smiles, and this seems to satisfy Bobby. For the rest of the walk to school, things are comfortably silent.

Mary's new mother brings her directly to the office at the front of the red brick schoolhouse. A short man in a green suit greets her and says, "I'm Principal Douglas. Welcome to Spanish Fork's Reese Elementary." He takes off his glasses and steps uncomfortably close to Mary, squatting down to her level. "It's a great idea the church is developing. You're definitely the youngest I've heard of, though." He pauses for a minute with a warm, concentrated smile. "Maybe many more students will follow in your footsteps next year, eh?" He stops and rubs his shiny bald scalp as he waits for Mary to nod or shake her head, but she does neither. Mary's new mother smiles nervously. "Well, thanks for bringing her down. I think I can take it from here, Mrs. Jensen."

"Yes. Thank you. Let me know if there are any problems."

Principal Douglas nods, then turns to Mary as if her new mother is already gone. "Let me introduce you to your teacher, Mary. I think you'll really like her."

Mary is in the same class as Tom, Mrs. Minor's. Their little classroom has green tiles for a floor except for one corner where a large red carpet is spread, curled up at the corners. Every student's name is printed on little pieces of blue or pink paper and taped onto the top of their desks. Mary's name, in pink, has a little bluebird drawn on the top of the "a." She likes it very much. All the boys in class are dressed much like Tom in new collared shirts and dark jeans or pleated tan pants. The girls' scabby knees peek out from under dresses or jumpers, and they wear white knee-length or lacy ankle socks.

Mrs. Minor starts out the day with what she calls singing time. "How about reviewing our ABCs?" she asks, then begins singing the letters of the alphabet. Mary has never heard of things called letters. She knows language orally only, English or Navajo. "A, B, C, D . . ." Mrs. Minor begins singing animatedly. Her gray curls bob slightly every time she drops her flaccid right arm on the down beat. ". . . W, X, Y, and Z. Now I know my ABCs . . ." Mrs. Minor stops the song early. "Mary, won't you sing with us?" She gives her an encouraging smile. Mary stands silent, her bladder suddenly throbbing with a desperate need to urinate. "Now let's *all* sing." Mrs. Minor starts another song Mary has never heard. "My Bonny lies over the ocean. My Bonny lies over the sea . . ." When Mary does not join, Mrs. Minor looks at her with raised eyebrows. She stops the singing mid-sentence again, and says, "Mary, when I tell you to *do* something, I expect you to *do* it or there will be consequences." The song starts again, but Mary does not open her mouth. She feels the warmth of her urine slowly spreading down her white tights and into her shiny black Mary Janes. Mrs. Minor does not stop the song again.

For the rest of the day the lower half of Mary's body is engulfed in a hot, itchy sensation as her urine dries. The boy who sits next to her plugs his nose in disgust when the strong odor of old pennies reaches him. Mary holds her legs together as tight as she can to try and keep the smell from spreading further.

"Mary?" Mrs. Minor asks while all the children are picking up their bags and papers at the end of the day. "Do you think you could ask your . . . *parents* to come with you tomorrow morning, a little early. Your mother perhaps?" Mary stares blankly at the wall. Mrs. Minor scratches her wrinkled cheek with one of her painted fingernails. "Or . . . maybe . . ." She sighs. "*I'll* just try to *call*." Mrs. Minor pats her short, stiff curls and pulls her lips into a tight red bud for a moment as if she is considering saying something else. But after a moment she says, "You may go now."

Mary picks up her bag and begins to walk toward the door where Tom is waiting for her, picking his nose ineffectively with his thumb. "Oh, wait!" Mrs. Minor calls as Mary walks out the door. "You forgot your picture, Mary. It's still sitting on your desk. All the other students are taking theirs home." Mary turns and looks at the picture she has drawn with crayons, a black circle swirling like a dust devil around a little bluebird. She turns silently and walks away with Tom as Mrs. Minor waves it after her.

That night the telephone rings after Mary has been put to bed. Mary's new sisters are busy having a pillow fight, and she cannot hear what is said. But Mrs. Minor pretends not to notice when Mary does not verbally participate in class the next day or any day after that.

Mary hears the word *Lamanite* again on Wednesday afternoon in a light brick church several blocks from the Jensens' home. Only this time the word is not used in reference to her directly but as part of the lesson in the Primary class where her new mother has brought her. The elderly woman teaching the class—Sister Paulson, she asks to be called—instructs Mary's new brother Tom to read a verse from a plain black book. Everyone in class has an identical copy.

"And it came to pass that the Lamanites came up on the north of the hill, where a part of the army of Moroni was concealed," Tom reads from the book, slowly and with difficulty. Mary does not follow his words, only gathering that they are explaining some major war. Mary has seen churches before but never been in one. She used to wonder what they were doing inside. Dancing? Singing? Meditating, perhaps? But she never imagined congregations meeting in musty classrooms to learn about wars, the worst thing she can think of, taking away daddies and sending them back angry.

Tom finishes the verse, and the teacher reads a paragraph from her lesson book. No one listens. Two boys are leaning back in their chairs and trying to push one another over. A red-headed girl is prying open the classroom's tiny window. Tom is staring at a large yellow booger clinging to the end of his pointer finger. After a thorough examination he rolls the sticky snot between his thumb and finger until it dries and crumbles onto the carpet. Sister Paulson sets her book down and asks the children a question about what they have been reading. No one even looks at her, much less raises a hand to respond. The large white clock measures the silence. Mary counts one, two . . . forty-six, forty-seven, before Sister Paulson repeats the question.

Mary is ashamed for her peers. On the reservation she was taught that elders are wise, and when they speak, you listen. Sister Paulson stares at the class with baleful blue eyes. No one notices the warning but Mary. Suddenly Sister Paulson raises her voice, angrily. "Class!" Everyone instantly sits straight and looks ahead. "Do you listen to a word I say?"

"Yes, Sister Paulson. We listen," says one of the boys who had been fighting.

"All right, Wally, then what have you learned today?"

"We're supposed to read our scriptures, say our prayers every day, go to church, and act like Jesus."

Sister Paulson scratches her graying hairline and sighs. "And what does Jesus *act* like, Wally? If he were here, would he make noise in my classroom? *Wal*ter?"

"Yes!"

All the other children burst out laughing.

"That's *it*. You can sit in the corner until class is over. The rest of you can open your scriptures and take turns reading the lesson's verses over again." Sister Paulson crosses her legs, sighs, and says under her breath, "You'd think you have no religion at all, let alone the truth."

Mary watches the children open their books and pretend to read for a few moments until they revert to their earlier behavior. She is confused by their conduct and even more by what Sister Paulson is teaching. The word *religion* that Sister Paulson used does not exist in the Navajo language. Grandfather told Mary she was expected to keep her life in harmony with nature, but he didn't use words like *good* and *evil*.

"Why can't you act more like our new student?" Sister Paulson says near the end of class, surprised when her students listen. They all quiet and turn to Mary, whose face grows hot. "It is her first week here, and she has more reverence than all of you." Sister Paulson looks at Mary and smiles with crooked, yellow teeth. Mary folds her arms and looks down with shame, away from the faces of her classmates. Like most Navajos, Mary hates being singled out, especially with praise. At least Sister Paulson did not use her name directly.

While Mary tries her best to seem invisible, Tom leans over and whispers something to Wally. They both giggle.

"What's so funny, Tom?" Sister Paulson asks, adjusting her large brassiere under her blue suit jacket. Tom looks sheepishly at his feet. "What's so *fun*ny, Wally?"

"Tom said Mary doesn't even know how to take baths."

"That's it! Both of you, stand in the corner," Sister Paulson says heatedly, raising her painted eyebrows. "I'm *sorry*, Mary."

And there it is. Her name.

Mary is more troubled by the teacher's direct approbation than Tom's words. After all, it is true. She had never seen a bathtub with running water before this week. Turning on the water that comes out of the silver faucet with such force frightens her.

Just then the bell rings, and Sister Paulson sighs in relief. "No running in the halls!" she calls as the boys dart like desert roadrunners out of the classroom. Mary is the last to leave.

The Jensens are back at the same church on Sunday afternoon for what Mary's new mother calls sacrament meeting. Three older men in suits, white shirts, and ties greet a line of people waiting to enter a large room filled with wooden benches. Mary joins the rest of her new family in line but does not look at the men or shake their hands when she reaches the front. Not just because the men frighten her, but the idea of shaking hands as a greeting is intimidating. People don't shake hands with strangers on the reservation. They only touch palms with good friends. Luckily time is short and the men quickly turn their attention elsewhere.

Mary files into one of the front benches with her new family just as the meeting is about to start. They fill the long bench from end to end. An old woman with puffy white hair at the front of the room plays a large wooden instrument. The way her fingers move reminds Mary of Grandmother's fingers working wool through her loom. The younger children immediately pull out coloring books and little bags of corn flakes to entertain themselves. After a few moments, the three men who stood at the doors greeting the congregation walk up to the front of the room. The congregation's whispering slowly begins to quiet. One of the men, a short bald man in a black suit and blue tie, steps up to the podium and begins speaking. "Welcome, brothers and sisters. We are pleased to see so many here today. We'd also like to welcome any visitors." He looks directly at Mary, making her heart strike against her ribcage like an attacking rattlesnake.

This same man stops Mary in the hall after the meeting. He gives her a copy of the same book Tom read from in class on Wednesday. "It's yours, Mary," he says smiling. "We're glad to have you with us. I'm Bishop Barlow. Let me know if you need anything, anything at all." He juts his hand out and holds it in the air in front of Mary, hoping she will reach out and take it. She does not. Instead she turns the black book over in her hands. On the spine of the book Mary sees words in gold, but she cannot read them. She is uncomfortable and does not like how the man steps up so close to her and speaks so loudly.

After dinner that evening, Mary's new mother reads from the black book. She explains a little about it to Mary in slow, loud words before they begin, as if Mary is hard of hearing. "This is the Book of Mormon. It's an account of the people in ancient America—your people. You'll probably love learning about their history. The book tells us how to live, and it tells about when the resurrected Savior came to visit the Americas after he died in the old world. We've only just started reading it again as a family. We read from as often as we can, like the prophet tells us. It's divided into different books that are an account of different times. We're just now getting into the second book."

Each child takes a turn reading a few verses out of the book except for Mary and the baby, Violet. Even the second-to-youngest girl, Nancy, who cannot be more than two, repeats the text after her father whispers it into her ear. They read about how a group of people lead by a man named Nephi separate themselves from another group of people led by Nephi's wicked brother named Laman.

It seems strange to Mary that this fair-haired, fair-skinned family thinks they know more about her people than she does. She has never heard of the men they are reading about: Nephi, Lehi, Jacob, Laman, Lemuel. They are not Navajo names. There is no mention of First Man or First Woman, the four sacred mountains, or the four worlds.

Mary's new brother Greg reads about what God did to the wicked brother Laman and his followers: "*And he had caused the cursing to come upon them, yea, even a sore cursing, because of their in . . . in . . .*"

"Iniquity," Mary's new father jumps in when Greg cannot decipher the word.

"*Iniquity,*" he continues. "*For behold, they hardened their hearts against him that they became like unto flint; wherefore, as they were white, and exceedingly fair and delightsome, that they might not be enticing unto my people the Lord God did cause a skin of blackness to come upon them.*"

Greg looks up from his scriptures. "That's where your dark skin comes from, Mary."

"Hush," Mary's new mother says, her cheeks pinking with mild embarrassment. She looks into Mary's confused face and explains, "This happened a long time ago. It was because of this people's wickedness. It's nothing *you* did exactly, dear."

Mary does not understand why her new mother is acting uncomfortable for her. Mary's skin color is commonplace on the reservation. Of course there were certain places off the reservation that would not serve Navajos, but that was as much for fear of fleas as skin color. Yes, she has already noticed that her skin is different here and causes the children at her new school to turn and look at her, the adults to whisper. But she has never thought of it as a mark of wickedness like this book says.

That night while Mary brushes her teeth awkwardly, copying the motion of her sisters, she remembers the words *exceedingly fair and delightsome*. She compares her dark skin to the reflection of her new sisters' light skin in the mirror. Mary's top lip is thicker than her bottom. She has no lines on the smooth plane of her face except for a single shallow crease on each eyelid while her sisters have dimpled cheeks, lines under their lower eyelids, and two curves connecting the corners of their mouths to either side of their noses. Mary's nose is longer than theirs, flatter. Her eyebrows are dark, straight lines with only a finger's width between them, while one can hardly tell her new sisters have eyebrows at all. Mary's eyes—like polished obsidian in the bathroom's bright light—are nothing like the transparent blue of her new sisters' eyes. Mary's high cheekbones are lost in the child fat of her face, less pronounced than her new sisters' yet more dominant. She has such a round face. Like Daddy's face, she realizes. An icy feeling pricks the back of her neck and ears. And she feels a little uncomfortable and confused, wondering if these girls' milky skin *is* something that would belong to her if not for her peoples' sins. Why did she not look more like Mommy, at least, if not like these girls?

Mary remembers how Mommy tried to act like white people. The way she used to talk about the customs and culture of her parents as outdated. Her given name was not even Lily, but Girl of Slight Form. Mommy said by the time she was fourteen she was wearing red lipstick and short, fitted dresses instead of long flowing skirts like other Navajo women. Mommy hitchhiked to Phoenix every year or so and came back with bags of stylish shoplifted clothes. She called them Betty clothes. "Don't I look like a real Betty in this?" she would ask Mary when she tried something new on. Mary went to Phoenix with Mommy a couple of times. She helped sneak things out of stores by shoving silk stockings in her underpants, tubes of lipstick in her ratty socks. "Everything in this world belongs to everyone," Mommy explained to Mary. "No one can own anything. Everything should be shared. I help people share their nice things with me. That is the fair way."

It takes Mary a moment on her way to her new bed, but she is still able to recall Mommy's appearance in detail. Her big brown eyes. Skin that glowed with a golden undertone. She curled her hair, kept it shoulder length, unlike the straight, long, windblown locks of other Navajos. Mommy tried to curl Mary's tangled hair once. The black ringlets were straight again within an hour.

Mary runs her tongue over her clean, crooked teeth. Mommy had naturally straight, white teeth—a reservation rarity. "You are the prettiest mother," Mary told her once, reaching out to touch her hair. Mommy pulled her hand away. Then she told Mary the story of Changing Woman, the lost baby who became *Asdzáán*, the spiritual mother of Navajos. "Changing Woman was constantly becoming new," Mommy said. "So I knew if I was really her daughter, I could change into anything I wanted. Even a Betty."

The only thing Mary remembers about Mommy's appearance that is at all unsettling is her eyebrows, plucked away and painted on in little forged arcs that make her look permanently, unnaturally happy. She thinks of Mommy's long neck, tiny nose, and painted lips, then hangs the pretty conjured image on the wall of her mind and falls asleep gazing at it.

Mary awakens just after six, immediately alert. Something seems different. The house is strangely still and bright and cold. Safe. The air smells fresh like cold milk. Mary shivers as she pulls back her covers and swings her thin legs over the bed's edge and feels her dark hairs stand at attention to the cold. She heads to the window to discover three weeks of dry November now suffocated in winter. Behind the parted purple curtains there is half a foot of fresh snow dispersed equally over everything as if it fell as a blanket of bleached wool in one collective thump. Its whiteness is washed silver with the light of a cashew moon. Mary tiptoes out of her bedroom, careful not to wake her sisters. She slips out of her pajamas, leaves them in a heap in the kitchen, and slides out the back door. She staggers down the concrete porch steps while bitter bolts of cold shiver up and down her naked body, then pauses for a moment, smiling, as she looks at the backyard transformed. The sun is just beginning to rise over the peaks of Maple Mountain with a hopeful glow of pink and green, outclassing the moonlight with greater glory.

Mary ventures out into the fenced yard and stops near the walnut tree. She bends over and scoops up a handful of snow and starts rubbing it into the goose bumps on her skin. A ritual snow bath. When Mary was too small to scrub herself, Grandmother used to wash her with snow like this to clean her and bring her blessings from the Holy Ones. Mary could never stop shivering. Even when she was old enough to bathe herself, she still hated the coldness.

But this morning Mary does not fear feeling frigid. After her whole body is rubbed red and dripping, she stands directly under the walnut tree and showers herself with shards of freezing snow by shaking its branches. She spins—arms open—dances under the snowing tree, trying to catch the glinting white flecks on her tongue. Her ear tops, toes, and fingertips burn crimson with cold.

The tree is bigger than Mary's walnut on the reservation. She used to sit under it every morning after completing the age-old childhood custom of running to the sun. The earth seemed alive beneath her, a kind of friend and protector. Mary feels a connection to this tree too, like the branches above are reaching to scoop her up and take her back to the sacred land.

After the tree's arms are emptied of their snow, Mary sprints eastward the way she used to on the reservation, with her open arms greeting the new morning sky and its weakening stars. Her lungs suck in icy air and exhale it warm back to the world. And Mary feels for a moment that she is back in the middle of the endless Dinetah instead of on a half-acre plot of patchy, frozen sod. She runs as fast as she did one year before, at first snow, scissoring through the reservation with tiny legs. The sun rising like a bright stringless balloon in the . . .

Thud!

The Jensens' back fence suddenly damns Mary's flight. She clutch-

es a wet wooden post to keep from falling. But she wants to keep running. Until her heart is beating in her thighs and temples. Until her legs
buckle under her.

"*Mary!*" a voice suddenly screams. Mary's heart jumps, and she
loses her footing. She falls on her bare bottom in the powdery snow
and looks up to see her new mother's figure on the back porch. "What
are you *do*ing? You're totally *naked!*" Mary is frightened by the shocked
stare of her new mother's face as she pulls her pink robe tightly
around her body and marches across the yard in her slippers. "Give
me your hand," she orders when she arrives at the fence. Mary sits
still with her arms wrapped around her body. "*Give* me your *hand!*"
There is a hush just for a moment before Mary sees her new mother's
arm rise high above her head. Then a hot burning smack slams into
Mary's face. Her new mother draws her hand back and rubs it slowly.
Her words come out in a heavy wave, "Mary, I can *only* put up with
certain *things*. But this is just . . . out*land*ish! Don't ever let me find
you sneaking out of this house alone *ever* again. With or with*out* your
clothes on." She takes a deep breath that slows her outburst. "Look.
I'm sorry. I don't know what they do on the . . . just don't do it here.
Here we *never* take our clothes off where other people can see us."
She looks around to see if any neighbors have witnessed the morning's surprises.

Mary's new mother's face is still flushed and frenzied, but she does
not yell it when she says again, "Give me your hand." Instead of waiting for a response, she simply grabs Mary's icy palm and leads her into
the house and down the hall to the bathroom.

Mary is left standing naked next to the toilet while her new mother
disappears for a moment. She returns holding clean white underwear
and an outfit under her arm. Mary's hand is rubbing her sore cheek.
Her new mother sees this, and her eyes soften. "Now, honey," she says
warmly, repentantly. "Just climb in the bath, and you'll feel much better. I'll have a nice hot breakfast for you when you're finished." She
hesitates by the doorway for a moment as if on the border of two
worlds, while her snowy pink slippers leak puddles on the floor. Then
she walks briskly back to Mary, tenderly kisses the top of her head, and
rubs a big circle on her back. It is the first time she has shown Mary
physical affection. But it is the lingering sting on her cheek from the

slap—not the tingle on her scalp from the kiss—that tells Mary this woman really is her mother now.

"How about a haircut?" Mary's new mother asks cheerfully. Mary has just come home from school and knows her hair is tangled from the harsh January wind at recess. "I think all that hair is getting to be too much for you to take care of." Mary has feared this moment for months. She does not want short bobbed locks like her sisters, but dares not protest. Her new mother spreads sheets of newspaper on the kitchen floor and sets a chair on top of them. "Sit here." Then she puts a large bowl on Mary's head and quickly cuts around it with the same black scissors from the kitchen drawer she uses to cut fat off chicken and coupons out of magazines.

Snip. A clump of soft darkness falls and curls on the ground. Snip. Another. Mary's eyes fill with tears. Grandmother never cut her hair shorter than her shoulder blades. She would be furious if she saw the growing pile of hair lying on the linoleum like a faceless dead animal.

The whole thing takes only five minutes. "You're done," Mary's new mother declares, pulling the bowl off her head and dusting a few hair clippings off its rim. Then she looks at Mary. The slits of her new mother's smiling eyes pop open in surprise. "Oh, no."

Mary reaches up to feel the fresh, feathery ends of her hair. She realizes suddenly what went wrong. "The bowl must have tipped or something," Mary's new mother says, pulling each side of Mary's hair to her chin. There's at least three inches' difference in their length. "Well. Let me even it out. This will just take a second, dear."

Mary begins breathing rapidly as the scissors start circling her head again. How much hair is she going to lose? She wonders if she should have run and hid before all this began.

But then it is over. Mary's new mother dusts clippings off the scissors, then her hands. Mary's heart skips. She jumps down on her hands and knees and begins frantically gathering up the cut hair from the newspaper. Her new mother laughs. "Just fold it up like this and toss it in the trash," she says, pulling the newspaper away from Mary. As she lifts it, some of the hairs fall onto the floor. Mary starts picking them up one at a time. "What are you *doing*, Mary? Here. Just use the broom. If you don't get every single one, it's okay."

Has she not heard of the yee naaldlooshii? Mary wonders. Skinwalkers. They look like regular people by day, wear dark cloaks at night while doing their dirty work. Their alliances with evil spirits make them tricky foes. If they find Mary's hair, they will work their evil magic on her. Grandmother always told her, after trimming her hair with a knife, "Just one piece of hair overlooked, carried off with the breeze, can mean your destruction."

Mary watches her mother toss the trimmings in the garbage can. Several hairs fall like shredded feathers. But when her new mother says, "Go play while I get dinner ready. I don't need you crawling around my feet," Mary leaves, filled with trepidation.

She goes straight to the bathroom. Staring back at her in the mirror is a girl with a ridiculous bob just below her ears. The girl in the mirror lifts her hand and brushes her fingers across the blunt strands. Their ends turn out in different directions like spliced wires. The girl's hand drops. Her dark eyes are distant and unreadable. But her heart is humming like a frightened desert swallow.

That night Mary hears a dog bark in the distance and is sure the skinwalkers are coming for her. She pulls her blankets up over her head, but the tiny tent's oxygen supply depletes quickly. Mary tries to breathe deep to make up for it, but her fear has tightened her throat. In. Out. Destruction. Disharmony. In. Out. She listens for a long time for the skinwalkers.

Finally Mary cannot take it anymore and she emerges for fresh air. She opens her eyes and looks around. A little moonlight is filtering in through the curtains. Everything seems still outside. It is quiet except for the breathing sounds coming from her sisters' beds. The water heater rumbles and hisses from down the hall. Mary nestles up against the wall and listens for something else.

Maybe they have not found her hair yet. She still has time.

Mary sneaks out of bed, opening the door slowly so the hinges do not squeak. She tiptoes down the hall and into the kitchen where she gets down on her hands and knees, searching for hairs. Her new mother swept after dinner, but there are still a few trimmings against the wall. Mary opens the pantry door and spends several minutes pulling hairs out of the broom. Then she lifts the lid of the garbage can and peers inside. She sighs, her fear returning. Someone has taken the garbage out. How many hairs could have been scattered on the way to the street? Mary considers venturing outside to search for them, but one look out the back window into the cold darkness is enough.

Back in bed, the gathered trimmings now safely hidden in her pillowcase, Mary wonders why the skinwalkers have not come. The rest of her hair could be blown anywhere by now. Then she remembers her new mother's cool oblivion to Mary's horror after the haircut. *Maybe*, Mary realizes, *maybe skinwalkers do not trouble white people.* The idea is comforting. Perhaps her being in the same home as the Jensens is some kind of protection.

But her mind lurches again. What about when she is wandering alone at recess? Or walking home from school? Will they come for her then? How will she ever be safe?

Mary's question is answered the following week in Sunday school. A girl reads a passage of scripture about the Lamanites. "*And the gospel of Jesus Christ shall be declared among them,*" the girl reads. "*Wherefore, they shall be restored unto the knowledge of Jesus Christ, which was had among their fathers. And then shall they rejoice; and their scales of darkness shall begin to fall from their eyes; and they shall be a white and a delightsome people.*"

The other students seem oblivious to the passage, but Mary feels as if a large weight lifts from her. *They became white.* So maybe if she is good enough, she will turn white. Then the skinwalkers will never again be a worry. And then, maybe, she can grow roots strong enough to keep from being plucked up and transplanted again.

Mary is not sure what the word *delightsome* means but imagines that a delightsome person is someone everyone likes. She would like to be that too. *This is Mary. Isn't she delightsome?* Mary imagines her new mother introducing her to strangers. Then Sister Paulson's voice interrupts her thoughts.

"Why did Heavenly Father take the curse away from these people?"

The girl that read the passage answers without raising her hand. "Because they stopped acting like their moms and dads." Mary turns to her.

"That's right, Cindy," Sister Paulson says. "They let go of all their old evil ways."

• • •

Mary is in the bathroom studying her reflection as she has done every night for months. She pulls back her hair, pinches her cheek, squints her eyes. But even under the bright lights, Mary still looks like the darkest person in Utah. Her forehead wrinkles with confusion.

"Mary!" her new father calls from down the hall. "Are you done in there? I'm taking the other kids to get some milk. You can join us." Mary thinks of the rows of candy at the grocer's and excitedly flips off the bathroom light.

They do not stay long. Mary's new father seems anxious to get back home. When Mary is about to exit the store's double glass doors into the early spring air behind her brothers and sisters, a store clerk follows her and taps her on the shoulder. "I don't believe this belongs to you," the clerk says, pulling a bag of M&Ms out of the pocket of Mary's jacket. Mary's new father turns around and frowns.

"Mary?" her new father asks sternly. "Where did you get this? Did you pay for this?" Mary studies the buckles on her shoes.

The clerk thrusts his hands in the pocket of his apron and says, "I saw her take it off the shelf, but didn't want to say anything until I saw you leave the store."

"I'm *so* embarrassed," Mary's new father says nervously. "I can promise, though, it *won't* happen again. Mary, say you're sorry." He pauses. "*Mary*, say you're *sorry*." The store clerk looks at Mary with lowered eyebrows. Nearby shoppers have stopped pushing their carts now to stare at the confrontation. Everyone, even Mary's youngest brothers and sisters, is quiet, waiting.

Finally Mary's new father apologizes for her. "She really is sorry. She's just scared. She's new here and doesn't even speak to *us*." He pats Mary on the back like a disobedient puppy.

When Mary gets home, her new father orders the other children to bed and asks Mary to come in the kitchen. "Mary. What you did was *wrong*. Taking things without paying for them with money is against our Heavenly Father's teachings. I wish you would have apologized. Why is it you still won't speak? You're safe here." Mary clasps her hands together behind her back and looks down. No. She is not safe here. Not yet. Her new father sighs. "Now I hate to do this. I really do. I don't want to hurt you. But I spank the other children when I really need to teach them a lesson. So this is only fair." He takes Mary by the shoulders and pushes her facedown over a chair, then rolls up the sleeve of his red flannel shirt, and with a swift smacking sound, spanks her bottom with his large hand.

When he raises his arm to strike again, a memory flashes in Mary's mind of her own daddy, two days after he came home from the war. Mommy was gone. Daddy paced in front of the gold sofa with torn cushions. His thin legs hardly looked up to the task of supporting his thick torso, especially when he was drunk and wobbling. Mary watched him closely. He seemed to have the outside world clinging to him like an odor with his new American accent and swear words, the way he moved quickly, jerking, like an irritated soldier instead of a nice Navajo father. Even his name had changed to Harry, a loose-fitting English nickname for his given name, New Heaven. "You have no idea!" he yelled at Mary. "No idea about my work in Saipan. You think anybody else notices? Hell, no!" He swatted the air in front of him. "Those stinking codes. Everything in the whole stinking world is written in stinking code. I don't know why they needed me to make it worse. Are you listening? Are you listening to me!"

Then Daddy raised his hand above Mary, but she did not have the sense to do what she does to her new father now. Mary turns and sinks her teeth into the arm holding her down. She bites deep but does not break her new father's skin. She runs.

"Ahhh!" Mary's new father screams just as she darts out the back door. "Oh, Mary! Oh, gosh." Mary looks back over her shoulder long enough to see the curve of little pink marks she has left on his white forearm.

Mary flies down the steps and across the yard. But before she reaches the back fence, she trips and belly flops on the grass under the walnut tree. She does not cry, but her body is shaking. She remains facedown on the ground, like a human star, as if she is trying to stretch her limbs enough to sense the earth's roundness.

Mary opens her mouth to say something, but then closes her lips. She looks up at the kitchen window and shudders. Even though she is alone outdoors, she does not want to go back inside, skinwalkers or not.

After a few minutes, the rapid beating of Mary's heart on the raw-hide drum of her chest begins to slow. Or is it her heart at all? For a moment, Mary cannot decipher if the beating is coming from her body or the earth upon which she lies prostrate. *Th-thump. Th-thump.* Mary breathes in deeply and fills her lungs with as much air as she can. Holds it. The ground inflates against her body, and the walnut arms overhead bend lovingly toward her. The ground smells like wet newspaper and is cool where it touches Mary's skin. The pointed tips of grass blades tickle her chin and right ear. Mary exhales, and the land heaves in sync as they rotate together a thousand miles an hour toward sunset. Mary closes her eyes and holds on for the ride, her fingertips curling into the soft soil as if gravity has been momentarily suspended.

The night sky slowly unrolls itself protectively over Mary like a thick sheepskin. She does not turn over to see the emerging stars, but their outreach to earth leaves pinpricks of light on her back, like points on a map. Grandfather said the stars were placed on a blanket and flipped into the sky, where they stuck in all the right places—a guide to all the laws one must obey to walk in harmony. Mary wonders if the law of taking things when you have no money is written in the stars, and she failed to read it. How many other laws has she unknowingly broken? The sky must have been rearranged on her trip to Utah, and she will have to relearn it before she can transform like the Lamanites in the Book of Mormon.

Mary's mouth opens again. She moves her lips silently as if priming a pump, then presses out a barely audible prayer. She tries to speak the words like her new family does when they kneel together. "We ask thee . . . we ask to help me be delightsome. And we ask thee to please keep me safe from skinwalkers until I change." The prayer is addressed to no one specifically—God, Jesus, or the Holy People. Mary just releases the words like a kite to get tangled in whatever heaven they reach first.

She imagines what it will be like to get her new white skin. Maybe she will crawl out of her brown covering like a rattlesnake out of its scales, leaving behind a delicate sheath to dry in the sun and crackle under the feet of some later wanderer.

Until her skin does change, Mary decides even her new God will not detect a glint of her old, evil Lamanite ways. She will hide them so deep that if a fragment ever emerges, anyone, even Mary herself, will see it as only a confusing puzzle piece from eons ago, bleached anonymous and sifted in the sands of her mind.

Mary rolls on her back, expecting the confusing canon of the Milky Way to greet her. Instead, shining straight above is the moon like a fragment of white shell in a sea of darkening navy. The same moon she was born under. The same moon she gazed at on the reservation while Grandfather sang. Mary tries to push these thoughts out of her consciousness. It is not hard. Hovering in her mind is her new father's disappointed expression from the market, his pale face eclipsing the past.

Mary reaches toward the heavens with her right hand, wanting to pluck the lunar shard from the sky. Silvery moonlight kisses her outstretched hand. She bends and straightens her fingers several times like the accelerated motion of primrose petals opening and closing to days and nights. From wide to tight. Changing from dark to light. Brown to . . .

White. Mary smiles.

Hymnal

Lee Allred

Swift to its close ebbs out life's little day.

Earth's joys grow dim, its glories pass away.

The prelude had started without him. Sam could hear the music seeping through the church's thick oaken outer doors high up on the second-story landing.

He sighed. He had meant to be on time for the end of the universe. He had arrived before anyone else—his wife Ellie or the sixty-eight others now seated inside—but he couldn't go inside without one last look.

Change and decay in all around I see;

O thou who changest not abide with me.

He climbed up the rain-slicked stairs. Dark-green moss oozed like putty from cracks in the concrete. His rain-soaked dress shoes squelched with each step.

The sky, what there was of it, was the leaden gray of an Oregon November. Rain drizzled from low-hanging sheet clouds, coloring the asphalt streets an inky black. Up the hill was where Sam's house should have stood sixteen trillion years ago.

Only an empty void gaped there now. Sam hadn't the heart to recreate it.

Should they have gathered somewhere else? No, this was the place. Here, here in this rundown, second-hand church of pink-beige stucco, he and Ellie and the others would watch as the universe died.

Eight trillion years after Earth died, eight trillion left before the universe joined that death, came the day of decision. Not many of them were left to make it, only Sam and Ellie and old Charlie.

They found Charlie alone at the Boundary. The line marked the approach of total entropy, the universe's creeping heat-death. The old man squatted there tossing pebbles into it like a little boy skipping stones across a pond.

Sam glanced at Ellie before he spoke. "No one else is coming," he told Charlie.

Charlie grunted. "Given up, have they? All of 'em curled up and died, have they?"

He flung the rest of his handful of pebbles. As each pebble struck, the careening of its atoms rippled energy outwards ever-so-briefly until all heat and motion were leeched out.

He stood and dusted off his hands.

"*Spirit, nearing yon dark portal at the limit of thy human state, fear not.*" He shook his head. "Tennyson," he said, " 'God and the Universe.' Amazing what muck the subconscious will dredge up, given half the chance."

He stared out across the nothingness.

The music transitioned to the opening bars of "For the Beauty of the Earth." Ellie's way, Sam supposed, of reminding him it was time to come inside the chapel.

Sam stood on the landing and looked back that one, final time.

Across Main Street sat the red-brick First Presbyterian Church whose towering grandeur shamed the shabby squatness of his own chapel. The Moose Lodge lay kitty-corner, still badly painted in that dirty lime green that no one, not even the Mooses, liked. The shining chrome of Newberry's back entrance glistened in the rain. Across the Umpqua, towering above the sleeping town, stood Mt. Nebo, its craggy face marred by a painted American flag and the high school senior class's graduation year scrawled underneath. ROSEBURG. 1970. It was all there. Every detail. Just as his memory pictured it.

Of course it was, Sam thought bitterly. He had recreated it himself from that memory, a memory perfected with the aid of the very atoms that had once made up this scene.

He turned toward the door, knowing that as he turned, everything he had just gazed upon would cease to be. Every atom, every wave of light would slow and die, giving up their life to buy Sam and Ellie and the others just a few more moments to find the answer.

Now only the church, a tiny building in a vast dying universe, was still safe, still vital. Only those inside still alive.

No. That wasn't true. Of the seventy beings inside, only Sam and Ellie were still alive.

Eddies of approaching entropy lapped at Charlie's feet. "What about Turley?" Charlie asked without turning around. "Or Sanchez? Or that stringy old biddy Hallister?"

"All of them," Sam said. "Hallister, too."

Nothingness swirled scant valences away from Charlie's feet. He did not step back, but tensed as if he meant to leap forward.

Sam put a hand on Charlie's arm to pull him back. Charlie shrugged it off. "Eda, too," Charlie mouthed. He lifted up a foot to step forward.

"Charlie," Ellie said in her quiet voice. "Please don't."

The old man hung his head.

"*Please.*"

Charlie slowly lowered his foot and stepped back. He put a gnarled hand to Ellie's hair. "*Most blameless is he, centered in the sphere / Of common duties, decent not to fail.*" Tennyson again.

His hand fell to his side. "I can't believe you're the two that are left. The rest of us were tougher, you know. Meaner, smarter, greedier. Hasn't mattered in the end, has it? One by one the rest of us have all given up, while you two still stand there hanging on, as full of hope as that first day. You two had each other, had each other from Before, and that has made all the difference."

"You're still here, Charlie," Ellie said.

The old man almost smiled. "Yes, I'm still here. I must have had something to live for, too, eh?"

The old man held out his palm. Above it appeared a schoolchild's model of a Bohr atom. "I spent my entire life seeking after this," he said. "The cold, rational, obsessive pursuit of knowledge."

The Bohr atom began to change, began to refine itself, layer after layer, to grow more detailed, retracing the history of Man's quest for the knowledge of the universe. Protons and neutrons and neutrinos. Quantum theory with its quarks and charms. Tachyons. Wavicles. The grand miasma of Chaos Theory and the iron-rod unyieldingness of the Order Theories undergirding it.

Faster and faster it flashed, past the last stages of Mankind's understanding before Mankind's death, through the simplicities of the Unified Theory Einstein could only fumble at. Down through each level of existence, past the ken of human understanding until at last it reached the final level, the smallest discrete iota of Being.

There, above his hand, swam the jots and tittles of Existence. Each self-aware, each straining for the call of its own True Name.

Then, of their own volition, the iota forming the model atom shuddered as one and fled Charlie's presence for the safety of Sam and Ellie.

Charlie's open palm clenched into a fist.

"Do you realize how meaningless it makes me feel? To have spent my whole life—even from Before—scrabbling after the secrets of a grudging universe, finally conquering them all—only to have those same secrets come easily to you, seek you out without your even having to look for them?"

The fist curled open and dropped to his side.

"You have everything. And I . . . I have nothing."

The model atom faded away.

More to himself than to the universe, he whispered: *"Let Science prove we are, and then / What matters Science unto Men?"*

Sam slipped quietly into the chapel. The congregation was made up of their seventy—Turley and Sanchez and all the others he and Ellie had pulled back out of the Boundary, iotically reinfusing them for the final moment.

Though outward ills await us here,
The time at longest is not long.

Sam cat-footed up the aisle. Charlie, seated in the back row, turned his head to look at him.

Charlie did so for the same reason he deliberately held up a dog-eared copy of Prather's *Notes to Myself* rather than a hymnal: to prove that he was his own self, not merely the puppet of Sam's reconstruction.

Eda Hallister sat in the pew just behind Ellie. The old woman wore widow weeds. An ugly feathered pillbox hat sat perched on her bunned-up gray hair. A black veil draped down from the front of her hat, too sheer to conceal her tear-stained face.

She did not so much as blink as Sam passed by, but stared straight ahead at the hymn board with its cardboard letters indicating which hymns were to be sung. She held her hymnal with a white-knuckled grip as if as long as the music sounded, the universe could not die.

His purpose has not failed.
His promise is not foiled.
Oh, but it has failed, Sam thought. *Oh, but it has.*

Charlie stared at the Boundary. "It's not a question of whether it can be done. It's doable, all right. Just a question of whether or not it makes any difference."

"You mean you don't know?" Sam asked. "I thought you knew everything there was to know about the universe."

A flicker of the Bohr atom reappeared between them. Not Sam's doing; the iota themselves were mocking the old man.

Charlie batted the atom away. "*This* universe," he said. "What you're proposing is another universe altogether."

"We don't have any other option. Except, that is, of simply giving up. I'm not prepared to do that. Neither is Ellie."

"Well, maybe I am. Maybe I see nothing wrong in just sitting down and knocking back a few cold ones as existence spins itself down."

"Charlie—"

"*We're talking about heat-death of the universe here.* It's not something you can fix. Haven't you learned anything from your little friends?"

Charlie turned his face away. "I've learned every mystery of the universe but one," he said. He fell silent for a few moments, then quoted Tennyson again:

Death closes all, but something near the end,
Some work of noble note, may yet be done,
Not unbecoming men that strove with Gods.

He turned back toward them. "All right, I'll help."

Ellie reached over and patted Sam's hand as he slid in beside her. She pulled his hand toward her and rested it on her leg. Rain from his sleeve wept onto Ellie's dress.

"You're late," she whispered.

Sam made to speak, then found he couldn't. His head jerked in a clumsy nod.

"Don't let it happen again." Her words were meant to be a mock scold, gallows humor, but her joke fell flat even as she uttered it. The organ played all of two notes more before she covered her face in her hands.

There was still a little time before the optimal moment to act.

Charlie spent that time thinking about Before. Sam could see it wash across his face, his eyes. No. He was thinking of Before and After, of that brief interval between the two.

He said to Sam, "You've never asked why I'm always quoting Tennyson."

Sam already knew the reason, but Charlie gave it anyway.

"We could have saved them," Charlie said, "if we'd but known. But no, we were too busy fleeing Earth, too new to our abilities, not yet knowing such as we could not be killed. Not yet knowing such as we could save them all, teach them to become like us."

"Charlie—"

"I heard them call, those poor doomed fools. Those handful of scientists on Pluto Station. Starving, drowning in carbon dioxide and their hopelessness. Watching as the Shoemaker-Levy-type comet struck the Earth. Knowing that the rest of Mankind was dead, that there would be no relief ship, that they were it."

A tear trickled down Charlie's face. The first Sam had ever seen.

"They did not call for help, oh, no. They knew, long before we *knew*, that the universe was empty. No, they turned their huge radio dishes to the stars in the vain attempt to keep Humanity alive long after Mankind had died. No, they broadcasted to the stars, hoping against hope that one day someone would appear to hear. They broadcasted everything in their database. The human genome first, then mathematics, history, literature, the arts—the sum total of human experience.

"And then at the last, with their last breath, the last stuttering of their batteries, they broadcast their final message, their final defiance against death. Tennyson's 'Ulysses':

We are not now that strength which in old days
Moved earth and heavens, that which we are we are—

He wiped at his face and could not finish the rest of the stanza. He did not need to. Sam already knew the words.

Sam pulled a hymnal from the back of the pew in front of him. He ran his fingers across the blue-black vinyl surface. His fingertips skidded across the tiny checkerboard weave, squeaking softly. He breathed deep the damp-caked odor of its ancient paper, its sturdy binding and glues dating from a time when books were meant to last.

Ellie had argued with him at first. Other editions had been issued, relegating the 1950 hymnal to the forgotten dustbins of secondhand stores. The horrid, pretentious green edition with its niggling correlated footnotes and sanitized lyrics. The even more flaccid edition after that.

This was the edition Sam knew best. This was the edition of which Sam knew every page, every song number, every ligature, long after its replacements were relegated, too, to the same dustbins.

Which hymnal edition mattered to Sam with an intensity stronger than he could explain. For him, the songs from this hymnal, the printed words and notes on these pages, held a power far beyond the iota of any printer's ink. These songs were real in a way the ones in the green edition never could be.

When other helpers fail and comfort flee.
Who like thyself, my guide and stay can be?

Sam opened the book and held it up with one hand, his fingers spread across the back, the thumb mashed down against the spine.

He held it gently at first, but with each passing note the grip became no less desperate than Hallister's, his hiding behind the opened hymnal no less helpless than Ellie's hiding behind her cupped hands.

Charlie explained to Sam and Ellie what needed to be done. Charlie could not do it himself; the iota would not do it for him. But they would do it for Sam and Ellie. For Sam and Ellie's sake, one third of them would cast themselves into the Boundary to give up the energy needed to reverse the course of the universe.

Sam and Ellie called forth the True Names of the universe's iota. The universe halted in its mindless expansion, then hesitantly turned back upon itself, drifting back toward the center origin point.

The cyclic theories of the universe—a Big Bang expansion, then a collapse back into a Big Bang—had been discarded long ago, back in Sam's youth.

Now, in desperation, hoping to jump-start a dying universe, the three of them were altering the universe to fit that discarded theory, not knowing whether it would actually work.

They waited.

"Tennyson wrote the one perfect poem of the English language, you know," Charlie said as they waited. "Quite ill, he had nearly died during a boat crossing to the Isle of Wight. Later his nurse scolded him to write some sort of thanksgiving for a miraculous recovery.

"Oh, he wrote a poem, of course, But when he finished he flung the page of scribblings at her, and the nurse fled sobbing out the room. Tennyson had written his own death song. 'Crossing the Bar.' "

Charlie watched the universe collapse. "It's the one perfect poem because its imagery is true for every delusionary pantheon Man has ever invented. Charon, Ra and his boat, Lincoln's dream portents, the Nazerene Pilot asleep in the boat's bottom. *Twilight and evening bell / and after that the dark!*

"Everything dies. Even the universe. Even the God Tennyson so wanted to believe in, killed by science and Darwin. Tennyson's entire corpus was a struggle against that death, against his doubts. His masterpiece 'In Memoriam' is by its very title a surrender to Death. Everything dies. Even us."

He turned to seek some crumb of hope from the newly ordered universe. "No. That isn't true. Beings such as we can't die, can we? We'll simply lie inert, drained by unconquerable entropy, waiting for a new restorative infusion of energy that will never come."

Charlie stopped. He sniffed as if sensing a sea change in the air. Then he knew, they knew, what they had known all along.

"It won't work." Charlie raced through the calculations. "There simply isn't enough oomph to kick over again into another Bang." All they'd changed was the speed of entropy's creep.

Ellie spoke first. "Maybe we could try something else—"

"Something else? Something else!" Charlie turned on her. "There isn't any something else left to try. Or maybe that precious God of yours has finally spoken up?"

"Maybe He has," Sam said softly.

"What then?"

"I don't know. Yet."

Charlie's voice was bitter. "Godhood was once defined as the ability to reverse entropy. He must not exist then.

"That," he said, as he pointed at the Boundary, "cannot be reversed."

He spun on his heel and walked away.

The light streaming through the chapel's stained-glass windows faltered, then stopped. The Boundary had reached the outer wall of the church. The organ notes trembled, hesitated, drowned out by choked-off sobs.

The yellowed glow of the indoor lights, glass globes each suspended by three rusted chains from the cracked and peeling vaulted ceiling, lent a final gloom to the plaintive chords of "There Is a Green Hill Far Away."

Why couldn't it have happened sooner, the event that had changed them all?

With only a little more time they could have deflected the comet as easily as swatting aside a mosquito. Then they could have changed all of Earth's population as they themselves had been changed. With the finest minds from a pool of billions to choose from, some solution surely could have been found.

He and Ellie might know everything about iota and the universe Charlie knew, but Charlie had been smarter Before, and whatever talents one had Before were magnified After. Charlie could use that knowledge far better than Sam or Ellie could. Sam and Ellie and Charlie and the rest had all tried their best to find an answer, but in the end what were the seventy of them? Merely flotsam from a nursing home.

Seventy patients of a government hospital's Alzheimer's ward. Crabbed boomers. Endless strings of broken marriages, divorces, live-ins had left them alone in their final years. Only Sam and Ellie had been different, had had each other. Each an only child, unable to have children, they had wound up as alone in their fidelity as the others had in their fickleness.

Perfect test subjects without any relatives to sue if things went wrong. The drug was supposed to cure their Alzheimer's, to reestablish neural links.

Instead, it *established* new links. And kept establishing them. Hundreds of them. Thousands. Millions. On and on without stop.

Sam and the others had realized their new potential at the same time their frightened creators did. Not yet fully understanding or having mastered their new status, the seventy of them fled. In their panic they had fled not only their captors, but their corporeal existence and Earth itself.

Fear not thou the hidden purpose of that Power which alone is great,
Not the myriad world, His shadow, nor the silent Opener of the Gate.
Terrific, Sam thought. *Now he has me quoting Tennyson.*

At the back of the chapel wisps of entropy seeped through the foyer door.

Charlie couldn't really hide from them. Not when they could name the current resting place of every iota. But he could let them know he wanted to be left alone. Sam and Ellie did so.

But after too long a time had gone by, however, Ellie grew worried. Against Sam's better judgment, they sought Charlie out.

Charlie had expended a huge quantity of energy to push aside the Boundary, to form a bubble of live space next to where Eda Hallister lay inert.

"Just a little sooner," Charlie said, staring at her lifeless form. "Just a little sooner and there could have been more than just a used-up wino and a white-bread couple right out of Ozzie and Harriet fighting against the end of the universe. What is the purpose in that? Where is your precious God now?"

"I don't know," Sam said, "But—"

" 'But He exists,' " Charlie finished for him. "You sound like Job."

Charlie turned. "Job. The trusting fool. There Job was, suffering by God's own hand but insisting on God's goodness, desperately seeking answers. Finally, when God does show up, what does God do but give Job not answers but more questions."

Charlie spread his arms to encompass the universe. "Well, we have all the answers now. And what did we find? Nothing. An empty universe. No life at all beyond Earth. No life on Earth left after that comet. It's all meaningless.

"Sure, we could reconstruct trees and deer and chirpy little songbirds. We could seed an empty universe with life. And what good would that do? They wouldn't be real, just puppets dancing on our strings."

A second tear formed in Charlie's eyes. "I could reinvest Hallister here with life, but would she be real or just a puppet?"

He turned away. "I've no wish to play a Calvinistic God. God's no better than any of us now. He hasn't any more answers than we have."

Sam let out a long, slow breath. "The answers are there. Somewhere."

"And we need you to help us find them," Ellie added.

Charlie softened for just a moment, then snorted. " 'It's not too late to seek a newer world.' Push off!"

"But—"

"Listen. I know you two better than you know yourselves."

He reached out a hand as close to Hallister as he could come. "You'll go on looking for an answer until you run out of time, until the very end. Then, when you realize there isn't an answer, you'll reconstruct something to give you comfort for those final fleeting moments. A church, no doubt. Sit there singing hymns or some such. Probably drag the rest of us in there, too."

Ellie tried to smile. "Only if you want to be there."

The old man snorted. "Oh, sure, sure. No atheists in a foxhole and all that. Just make sure when you pull my strings, don't have any hymns coming out of my mouth. Give me that much dignity at least."

A third tear. "Speaking of gifts. I'm going to give you one last gift now. You'll need all the energy you can get to find those answers. *'Little remains; but every hour is saved / From that eternal silence, something more.' "* He choked on that last word. "More? Another eight trillion years more won't be near enough."

Charlie took a step toward the Boundary. "You know, if there really had been a just God, He would have seen to it I'd have discovered poetry before I discovered hooch. More kick to it."

A last tear. "Funny. They're just words strung together. And yet, there's a power in them that could light up a night sky. Find some way to save the words."

And with that, he stepped into the Boundary next to Hallister, pushing the last of his life energy toward Sam and Ellie where it could yet be used.

Sam realized he was crying.

Not Ellie. Ellie stood there, her ashen face filled not with grief but rage. With a voice that shook the firmament, she cried: "O God, where art thou? Where is the pavilion that covereth thy hiding place?"

"Where?" echoed across the cosmos. "*Where?*"

The echo died.

No answer came.

One by one the people in the back pews moved toward the front to escape, if only for a moment, the creeping Boundary. Charlie moved all the way up to sit next to Eda Hallister. He'd dropped his copy of Prather. Now it was just a pile of dead atoms inside the Boundary. He hesitated, then reached for Hallister's hand. She gave it to him, then pushed up her veil and tried to smile. So much time, so many what-could-have-beens wasted in doubt.

Charlie's smile reminded Sam of Tennyson and of T. S. Eliot's remark on "In Memoriam": "It is not religious because of the quality of its faith, but because of the quality of its doubt." No other poem, another critic had written, had opened so many doors.

But how could doubt, not faith, open doors?

Job had sought answers, but God had not given any. "Gird up thy loins like a man," He had thundered at Job, "for I will demand of thee, and answer thou me."

Job had known the answers all along.

"Where wast thou when I laid the foundations of the earth? Declare if thou hast understanding. Who hath laid the measures thereof, or hath stretched the line upon it? Whereupon are the foundations thereof fastened? Who laid the cornerstone thereof when all the morning stars sang together and all the sons of God shouted for joy?"

How do you reconstruct that cornerstone? How do you reverse entropy?

"Hear, I beseech thee, and I will speak," Job had shouted back to God. Faith *and* doubt.

Job had known all along. *I have heard by the hearing of my ear. Now my eye seeth.* "I will demand of thee and declare thou unto me."

But God never had declared the answers to Job, had he. He didn't need to. Job knew all along the words God left unspoken.

Funny. They're just words strung together. And yet, there's a power in them that could light up a night sky.

The words and notes on these pages held a power far beyond the iota of any printer's ink.

I have heard by the hearing of my ear. Now my eye seeth. Sam, too, had known all along. So had the doomed men and women of Pluto Base.

Poetry is nothing more than mere words strung together. Painting, nothing but blobs of pigment placed just so. Music, only varying pitches and tones sequenced both together and one after another.

The painter doesn't create colors, the writer words, or the musician sonic wavelengths. They take what exists and organize it, but they still create. So, too, did God, who created the world not out of nothing but by organizing it.

But in that organization, in those poet's words, in those composer's notes a power is created from nothing, a power that defies entropy. Tennyson had been dead two hundred and fifty years when Pluto Base sent out their last message. Tennyson had been dead eight trillion years when Charlie had stepped into the Boundary. Yet those words still held a power that will withstand the end of existence.

Sam set down his hymnal. He didn't need it anymore. He took hold of Ellie's hand, then Eda Hallister's and Charlie's through her and on and on until hand in hand they crowded up on the stage around the organ, the last circle of light against the dark.

With a call to the iota, the organ stopped what it was playing. The solemn comfort of "Abide with Me" wasn't needed any more. What was needed now was the fire and the triumph of the Hosanna Shout. The organ began the clarion call of "The Spirit of God Like a Fire Is Burning."

Sam kissed Ellie, and then together in a voice that reshook the firmament they sang:

The visions and blessing of old are returning
And angels are coming to revisit the earth.
We'll sing and we'll shout with the armies of heaven,
Hosanna, hosanna!

And each of them, seventy voices, sang or shouted words to beat back the darkness, whether those words be the Kaddish or the Lotus Pearl or the words from an old discarded hymnal. As they sang, as they shouted, the tendrils of the Boundary turned and fled, Death itself died.

Seventy voices, for Charlie, with Eda's tears fresh on his cheeks, stepped forward, too, with his words of power, the words most precious to him, Tennyson's *Ulysses:*

We are not now that strength which in the old days
Moved earth and heaven, that which we are we are,—
One equal temper of heroic hearts
Made weak by time and fate, but strong in will
To strive, to seek, to find, and not to yield.

QUIETLY

Todd Robert Petersen

JOHN HAD NEVER DEDICATED A GRAVE and did not expect that he would be called to do so this soon after joining with the Mormons. He had not been a member for very long and was still frustrated. The white leaders didn't seem to understand why he would be, with the Spirit and the brethren in Salt Lake as his guideposts. Still, writing down the name of the village on a scrap of paper, he accepted the branch president's charge, fully aware that a white American would be afraid to venture outside the cities, even with the U.N. troops on patrol.

The branch president told John that he would know what to do when he got there. This was unsettling somehow, but as he prepared himself for the journey west of Kigali, he began to feel better. The instructions given in the priesthood manual said to address Heavenly Father, then state that the ordinance would be performed by the authority of the holy priesthood. He was then to dedicate and consecrate the burial plot as the resting place for the deceased and, if desired, pray that the place would be hallowed and protected until the resurrection, asking the Lord to comfort the family. Finally, he was to express thoughts as the Spirit directed, before closing in the name of Jesus Christ. Simple, really. A prayer. That was all there was to it. He thought there might have been more, something not in the book, because white prayers still seemed dead to him. For John, spirit had always flown more freely in the breeze than in a book.

John had been told that Marie Dusabumuremyi's husband, Immanuel, was killed by Hutus, though it hardly mattered now who killed who first; in his country, neighbors killed one another with dull machetes, left each other faceless in the dust. John was not surprised to find that no one spoke of these things in the general conferences. Perhaps the trials of the American pioneers were more important, he wondered.

Marie had found her husband hanging upside down in a tree three days earlier, fastened by his ankles to the limbs with yellow and black electrical wire. She told the branch president that Immanuel had been gone all night, that they were both newly baptized after having met two American missionaries in Pretoria. The branch president told John that the Dusabumuremyis had been saving their money for a journey to the temple in Johannesburg. He also told John that at night, people spoke of hearing gunshots and jeeps tearing around. He spoke as if it were unimaginable to hear those kinds of things.

John was wearing a white shirt and took along his scriptures, the manual, and—not wanting to depend upon the hospitality of others—a half-loaf of bread. When he stepped off the bus that took him to the edge of Kigali, he saw two boys sitting on some crates and tires, sniffing at rags they held under their noses. He thought of telling them to go home, to do something decent for their parents, but he just walked on, wondering if someone was going to find them in the morning curled up into two little cold balls.

After twenty minutes, a truck came by and the driver offered him a ride. He climbed in back, and as they drew farther and farther from Kigali, John began to wonder again why Jesus Christ never came to Africa and why blacks weren't allowed the priesthood for so long and why God had suddenly changed his mind. These kinds of questions, John remembered, turned people against the prophets, so he turned his thoughts toward the missionaries who'd taught John that God was the same yesterday, today, and forever, which didn't really help. *It is strange*, John thought, *that twenty years ago I couldn't have blessed that grave. The American would have had to do it himself.*

Being Zimbabwean made it easier for John to move around, something the branch president took into account, no doubt. The American did not seem to understand that things were different for blacks than they were for the whites in the church. Perhaps he was too young to know. The American apologized for some things in the church and for all the things that seemed to have taken so long. John told him that the times were the times. He said that John was too simple for the world of today. John said that he guessed he was and followed his remark with silence. The branch president seemed vexed by the fact that John was, at the same time, oddly resistant and strangely compliant.

John looked out from the back of the truck upon the sun, which was just starting to burn down into the clouds. What glory was that? A slow death in dust and filth? The day led to slaughter? It seemed wrong to read from the manual when the time came. There were no priesthood holders in that village then, African or otherwise, and John was the closest as far as that branch president knew.

Using what was left of the light, John reread the instructions in the manual, memorized them. There was one man who had lived in the neighboring village, but he had taken his family into Tanzania, working in Dar es Salaam until he had enough money to take them all to Salt Lake City. He wanted his children to grow up in the American Zion. *He should have known that since blacks finally have the priesthood, it needs to stay here in Africa*, John thought. But he knew that he couldn't hold the desire to escape against anyone.

Most of the small shacks in the Dusabumuremyis' village were covered with rusted metal roofs; only a few had windows. Marie's home was nowhere close to where the branch president told John to find it. When he finally did, the widow was not there. A nervous neighbor said that Marie had gone to mourn with Immanuel's family. They told John that if he went up the path, he would find their house near the water pump. It took John only a few minutes to get there. He knocked and called after Marie. An old woman's voice scratched, "Go away."

John said that he had come from Kigali to bless Immanuel Dusabumuremyi's grave. A silence followed, and he glanced around at the sky, which was still darkening. A few clouds to the west flared orange in the low sunlight, and across the way a mother strolled somewhat cautiously toward her house, a child slung across her back. She eyed John. He smiled back at her. She lowered the basket from her head and ducked into her house just as a breeze rustled the leaves of a tree that rose up out of the middle of the village. Some unknown and alien bird called out while a bat swooped down into view, changed direction suddenly, and disappeared back into the abstraction of the trees and rooftops.

John sat down outside the house and asked God what He would have him do, and as he prayed, the sky continued to darken.

After an hour, stars began to shoot across the firmament. After another hour still, a latch rattled and the thin door shuddered open. A leathered face appeared. Her eyes were yellowed at the corners. Her hair was almost completely white, and she was wearing a T-shirt with a sunflower printed in the center, a threadbare cotton skirt, and dirty canvas tennis shoes.

"Go away," she said.

Behind her, someone who could only have been Marie lifted her head. She held a bundle in her lap, and she was looking straight into John's eyes. John grew nervous and scrambled to his feet.

"Go away," the old woman repeated, then she closed the door. A girl walked by with an empty basket against her hip. John grimaced slightly and looked down. In the distance, a flare seared a white line across the night sky, burst brightly, then fell back to earth. As the darkness settled back around, the stars reappeared. The wind changed, and John caught the sickening scent of garbage. He hung his head and asked for God's help, but when he said amen and opened his eyes, the door was still closed.

He knocked again.

Nothing.

A neighbor peeked out of his door and stared at him. It was still impossibly hot, and John wished he had worn a thinner shirt, but it seemed right at the time to dress formally. He looked down at the cuffs, and where the white cotton stopped, John saw only the vague outline of his hands disappearing into the darkness. It occurred to him suddenly and quietly that he should ask the neighbor what he knew. As John approached, the man's wife pulled the man inside and closed the door.

John wanted to turn back and go home, but it would have been at least a three-hour walk to Kigali. *Some sleep before the church meetings tomorrow will erase most of this*, he thought. Looking back into the sky, he threw up his hands, squatted down in the pathway, and waited. No one came out of the house. He opened his bag and took out the bread. As he unwrapped it and lifted it to his mouth, John was stopped. He tilted his eyes upward, then rewrapped the bread and stood.

A slight breeze started up as he crossed back over and knocked on the door again, not thinking it would open. It rattled, and in the skewed, yellow light, the old woman appeared again. John gave her the bread and turned away without catching her eyes. She closed the door, but before John had gone five steps, it opened again.

"Mormon," she said.

He stopped. "My name is John," he said, turning to face her.

"You love God, John?" she asked, tucking the bread under her arm.

He said yes and then scratched the backside of his neck, though it didn't itch.

"You love Jesus?"

He nodded.

"Then why do you say that you will *be* a god one day? Marie says she will be God and have her own planet, and I tell her God is God, who else?"

John shrugged and said that he was not sure. "I just believe it because it is true," he said.

"What did you come for?" she asked, pointing her chin at him.

"I came to bless Immanuel's grave," he said.

"Do you *know* Immanuel?"

He shook his head. "I know *of* him," he said.

"Why, then?" she asked. "Why come to do this?"

He shrugged and said, "An angel will cut off my head if I do not do what I am told." John did not know if this were true, but it seemed like the kind of thing God would tell an angel to do—at least, it seemed like the right thing to say because it seemed as if he had heard it before, once, in a discussion. The old woman opened the door a little wider. Her face was twisted and her breathing heavy.

"It is Immanuel's church, too," John said, and from inside he heard Marie start to speak. The woman quieted her and then dug one knuckle into her ear. She was troubled. The breeze picked up. "We will bury him tomorrow. You will come pray then," she said nervously and somewhat dismissively. "You will pray then."

John told her that he would, and then he waited for something more to be said. Marie rushed up to the door, but the old woman shut it, leaving John to stare at tin corrugations in the darkness.

• • •

In the rubber-black air, he imagined the white of Marie's teeth and eyes and the dark loam of her skin. She was beautiful. He looked around at the quiet village, took off his shirt, walked over to the fence, and draped it over the wire. He lay down in the dirt alongside the house. It was cooler there. With his head resting on his bag, he closed his eyes and wondered when the gunshots would start.

He dreamt that Marie came to him as he was lying on the banks of a river, half in and half out of the water. She rose up out of the current with her arms crossed and her hands covering her breasts— that was all he could remember at first. Dawn came slowly and without color. He stood slowly, trying to work the knots out of his neck and back. It was not yet hot, but it was going to be—worse than yesterday. He brushed the dirt off his chest and shoulders and thighs. He was hungrier than he had ever been before. The whole town, he could see, was set about in slender trees, and at the west end of this path there was a well with a rickety covering of wood and sheet metal.

He walked down shirtless and ran the hand pump until the water flowed out, ducked his head underneath, and drank until his belly hurt. He stopped and gave thanks for the well and for the quiet of the night, then he went back and put on his shirt. It was still clean and white, and he imagined that somehow he wouldn't look like he slept in the dirt. A few women and children went down to the well and filled up old cans and plastic jugs and shuttled them back into their houses. They were all shoeless and cautious as gazelles. They seemed to know right where John was without looking.

"Mormon," he heard someone say from across the road. The neighbor woman from the night before called to him, and he went over. "Take this," she said, and she handed him a small cornmeal cake and then disappeared back inside her shack. John said thank you to the door and started to eat the cake. As he turned around and raised it to his mouth for a second bite, a naked boy, perhaps three years old, looked over at him from the pump. John lowered the cake and motioned for the boy to come over. His sister was busy with the water and did not notice that her brother had wandered.

"We should share it," John said, breaking the cake in two and handing the boy half. He looked over at his sister tenuously and back at John, then took it. "There," he said. "You have some."

John ate his part quickly, watching the boy, who was deliberate with
the food, catching falling bits with his other hand and scooping them
to his mouth. When his sister was done with the water, she looked over
with some alarm and called back the boy. John stood and told him to
go along. She came up and without looking took her brother's hand
and dragged him up the road and around the corner.

John's dream from the night before was beginning to follow him
around. Marie's hair had been coiled up on the top of her head with
small sea shells woven into the braids. Wide gold hoops trembled in
each ear, and her lips were pomegranate red. As she approached, he
rose up to meet her and found that his hands and feet were stuck down
in the mud, which set around them like cement. Struggling against it,
he looked up at her in time to see her navel rise above the water. A
cloud of birds circled behind her head and landed on a shoal in the
center of the river. More birds took the place of those that landed,
and the sky sizzled pink on blue. The wind generated from the bird
wings blew waves of river water onto his chest. As Marie continued to
rise, she dropped her hand from one breast and covered herself below. Strange modesty for a goddess. Some beast roared in the distance
like a hippopotamus, and rifle fire cracked from somewhere across the
river.

At the Dusabumuremyi house, John gathered up his scriptures and sat
down to read from the Book of Helaman, when he noticed that the
neighbors were beginning to gather in the street.

"Mormon," the old woman said, "come with us." A small procession filed out of the house. Marie was veiled and hunched over. John
rose and followed, fumbling with his books. The people proceeded
quietly and ceremoniously out of the village, past a small church with
a small, crooked cross on the roof peak. A cemetery populated with
small headstones and grave markers of carved wood fanned out behind the church, where a single grave had been prepared. It was surrounded by small mounds marking those who were freshly dead.

Immanuel's body was wrapped in a white cloth and bound with
strips of the same material. John could not remember ever seeing such
a burial. The old woman beckoned him, and he came. Bowing his head,
he began the prayer and became lost in it, saying things of which he

had no immediate recollection. He closed in the name of Christ, and when he looked up, he saw that everyone was looking at him. When he said amen, they echoed him, and four men come forward and meticulously lowered the body on thin sisal ropes, which they hauled back out once Immanuel had settled at the bottom.

After the men coiled the ropes and passed them to one man, everyone turned and left, even Marie. No one was crying, not then and not at all during the funeral. In normal funerals, John was used to at least one woman rocking back and forth, keening. But this time he was left standing there, not recognizing the funeral, the ceremony, or anything that had happened. It was altogether unfamiliar.

As John walked out of the village, he stopped at the Dusabumuremyis' house and stared at it. The sun burned above the trees, and he winced at the brightness of it. The moon and the stars were better for him at this point, the coolness of nighttime and the freedom of dreaming. As he walked past the pump, the damp smell of the mud made John recall his dream. He tried to think past it toward what might have come to pass in the dream were it not a dream. It occurred to him that he had sacrificed the love of a woman who shared his faith for peace of mind, and that knowledge made plain the sad truth of his desire. Suddenly, he was spinning in the wide mouth of infinity, stretching his hand forth and pulling it back, ascending and spiraling down like a man quietly but decidedly torn.

THANKSGIVING

Angela Hallstrom

BETH: LISTENING

"TAKE CARE," SAYS MY GRANDMA TESS. She is the first one to leave after Thanksgiving dinner because she can't drive at night. She has two hours' driving to do, north to Uncle Russell's house in Logan. She's worried about me. She wonders how I will bear up. She covers my hands with her own, and her skin is paper dry.

"Things seem hard right now, but you'll see your way through. You're my Beth. You've always been a strong one," she tells me.

I'm lucky to have a grandmother like her. I don't get the feeling she's lying to me. I don't get the feeling she's telling me only what I want to hear.

We stand by the open door, and sunlight streams through her thinning hair.

"I'm hanging in there," I tell her. "Really, I am."

"You can do this," she says. "Yes, yes. You can."

Today, no one has said Kyle's name out loud. During dinner Aunt Christy said, "Do you think he's well enough to be trusted around the baby?" Everybody knew who "he" was. But I didn't look up from my turkey.

Finally my mom said, "Who knows, Christy," in that great tone she gets when the subject's about to be changed.

No one has said his name, but in his absence he seems just as powerfully present as he always has been. Everyone feels it. My sisters keep sliding the conversation around, trying to avoid topics like love and marriage, mental health and single motherhood. My dad keeps coming up behind me and putting his hands on my shoulders. Really, they may as well all just be saying, "Kyle, Kyle, Kyle." A big family chant.

I keep listening for the door. I told him not to come. I said, "Kyle, it's for the best. You know how my mom gets—it's nothing personal, she just wants some peace—but you can spend time with your own mom. You can see Stella tomorrow. You can see me tomorrow. We'll talk then, I promise, we will, but today is not the day. Today is not the day."

He yelled at me. "Heartless," he called me. "Home wrecker."

I said, "Kyle, you are not yourself. Can't you see that you are not yourself?"

KYLE: OUTSIDE

Kyle imagines the family inside the house, laughing, eating, Beth and her sisters teasing each other and telling their inside jokes. His father-in-law, Nathan, in his chair at the head of the table, his mother-in-law, Alicia, sitting just barely on the edge of her seat, tense as a cat, ready to jump up and get somebody butter or salt or more ice. All of them pretending they don't miss him, that he never existed, that they're better off now without him.

He knows the food they've been eating because he's had Thanksgiving at this house practically every year for the last eight years and it's always the same food, yams with the marshmallows on top, homemade stuffing with cranberries and pecans. Kyle always got a drumstick. He got one and Nathan got the other, because they were both dark-meat men. "A real man likes the dark stuff," Nathan would say, and it made Kyle happy, knowing that his wife's father thought of him as a real man. From the moment he first met the Palmers he's been trying hard, doing his best to be the kind of man he should be. He'd be lying if he said all the effort to seem cheerful and focused and strong hadn't worn him down a little, but he'd been willing to do it for her. For them. For all of them, the whole family. And what good has it done him? All they do is listen to Beth and her side of the story, her little tales she tells: Kyle did this, Kyle did that, like she's Little Miss Innocent, like nothing's her fault.

And now she gets to sit there at the table as if she never did anything wrong and he's left alone, parked in his car two blocks from their house, abandoned on Thanksgiving by the family that said he belonged to them, the family that acted so charitable and kind but really they were just waiting for him to slip up. Waiting for a mistake so they could pull out the rug and watch him rattle to the floor and say, See, you never were good enough for us, we never asked for you, we measured you and found you wanting.

Like at Stella's baby blessing last month, his own daughter's baby blessing, he comes and wants to be a part, that's all, but everybody's so hung up about his clothes, how they're not appropriate for church, but what do they expect when his own wife leaves him, abandons him to fend for himself in their little apartment, and he has nothing, no money, no love. Who wouldn't show up in shorts and a T-shirt if not just to make a statement, so they could see what they've reduced him to? And then when he goes up to the podium to speak and keeps talking, pouring out his heart about his sweet little daughter and his wife who has left him, and her family which has betrayed him, the bishop takes him by the elbow in the middle of it all to lead him away from the microphone and he looks down and there's Beth, sobbing, crying, holding his beautiful little daughter wearing her beautiful white blessing dress, and he's thinking, what does she have to cry about? Why is she the one crying when she's kept everything for herself and left her own husband with nothing?

She keeps telling him, "Just get back on your medication and then we'll talk." Get back on your medication and then, maybe, then, someday, then, then, then, but he tells her they're poisoning him with it, he can feel it in his blood, eating at his cells, chewing little holes in his molecules to let the poison inside. Sometimes he thinks she's in on it—Beth, her family, the doctors, all of them, plotting together to poison him with those innocent-looking pills. He's even said to her, "Are you trying to kill me?" That's what he said the night she left him. "Are you trying to kill me?" All she could do was say, "Kyle, please, Kyle, please," the baby carrier hooked over her arm, Stella crying inside—and her father, Nathan, waiting for her in the car on the street so he could carry her away.

But they can't get rid of him as easy as that. He's earned his place.

He has a right. They were there at the temple, they can't have forgotten when he was bound to their daughter—and so, yes, to them, to all of them—eternally. Meaning: Forever. Meaning: Without end. They're hoping he won't show up, of course, hoping he just burns himself out and disappears like a curl of smoke up into the sky. But he is a father, a husband, a member of this family. They cannot cut him off like a dead branch on a tree and leave him out in the street. And he will show them. He will behave. He has ironed his clothes and brought flowers for his mother-in-law and he's planned what he'll say to Beth—"You look beautiful, as always"—and then they will see that they shouldn't be afraid of him.

Beth: Uncoupled

My older sister Marnie and I are putting up Thanksgiving leftovers. We're in our parents' kitchen, and all three of her boys race past us screaming.

"These kids are running circles around me," she says. She's not being metaphorical. Her boys are screaming good-natured screams— screams of joy, you might call them. But still.

I am putting up the pies. I take slices from each leftover pie and squeeze them together into one tin, pumpkin and French silk and lemon meringue side by side.

"They should sell pies this way," I say. "It makes more sense. The variety. People would snap them up."

"Well there you go," Marnie says. "Your million-dollar idea."

"I've been saved!" I say, and she laughs. I haven't told her about my money mess—well, Kyle's money mess, but since he's my husband, it's mine too—but I know that she knows. My mom's a talker and my sisters are worse. Secrets are hard to keep. For example, I know that Marnie's husband Mike makes $94,000 a year in his job as some kind of finance guy for General Mills. When Marnie heard I'd left Kyle, she was nice enough to call me up and ask if I wanted to come stay with her in Minnesota for a while—"Get away from it all," she said—but I told her no. First of all, I'd feel in the way. Second, I don't know if I could stand it, really, living with their cute little family in their brand-new house, watching Mike swinging in the door from work at the end of the day and Marnie kissing him on the cheek. At least that's the way I imagine life goes at Marnie's house, and I don't know how much of it I could take.

Marnie points a spoon at my baby, Stella. "I don't think that child has made a peep in twenty minutes," she says. She pats her pregnant stomach with her free hand and smiles. "I put in an order for one like that this time. Hope God remembers."

Stella sits propped in the crook of the couch, gumming on a board book. She's a good baby, wide-eyed and calm. A lap-sitter, Marnie calls her. She's six months old and has yet to roll over back to front, but they tell me not to worry, so I don't.

"The mysteries of genetics," I say, and Marnie knows what I mean. Take Marnie and Mike—obedient, even-tempered types, both of them—and all three of their boys started screaming as soon as they left the womb and haven't stopped since. And then you have me and Kyle. You'd think we'd be in for it, but we end up with this sweet baby girl, as even-keeled as they come. She's been sleeping through the night since she was four weeks old.

"You deserve your Stella," Marnie says. "She's lucky to have you."

Of course she's not, I want to say. Don't be ridiculous.

"See?" Marnie says, and I look where she's looking, at Stella's round face. "See how she watches you, wherever you go? She can't take her eyes off you."

I know, I know. Children see everything.

"Open your eyes and look at me," he'd say when we fought. He wouldn't let me turn around, walk away, glance at the floor or the sky. The last time we fought, before I left him, he grabbed me by the shoulders, tight. Shook me a little. "Look at me!" And I did: his green eyes lit with fury, his skin tight across his cheeks. Even then, a handsome man.

We are almost finished with the silver. Marnie stands at the sink with her arms in the hot soapy water and I stand beside her, rinsing and drying.

Mike comes up behind Marnie and smoothes his hands over her round belly. "Nap time?" he says into her ear.

Upstairs, their boys are thumping and jumping. I keep listening for howls of pain.

"Ha," Marnie says. "Right."

"I think Grandpa's been looking pretty anxious to go to the park, don't you? Give me five minutes, and we'll have ourselves some quiet."

He leans down, and I hear him as he kisses her on the neck. I pretend to disappear.

I am in a house of couples: halves of wholes, yins and yangs, eternal pairings. Marnie and Mike are here today. Tina and Jimmy. Aunt Christy and Uncle Rob. Everybody's touching each other, even my mom and dad. Alicia and Nathan. I've heard it so many times it's almost one name, Aleeshyanathan, like something you'd call an Indian princess. They seem to be touching a lot lately. I swear they hardly touched at all when I was a kid, or at least I didn't notice it, but now I see them all the time. Like now: his hand resting lightly against her back, her head tilted against his arm.

I'm lucky I have Stella to hold on to. My Aunt Christy keeps telling me, "Why don't you put that child down?" She says I just might spoil her. But I need her weight on my hip, her skin on my skin. She is mine, and I am hers. Her heaviness keeps me pinned to the earth.

A few weeks ago my mom caught me crying in the bathroom. "You'll feel better in time," she told me. "You've made the right decision. A hard one, but the right one. You deserve to live your own life. You and Stella, together—you can make a good life."

I didn't answer her back. I just nodded like I agreed with her, mainly so she wouldn't worry. She thinks I should divorce him. She hasn't said it in so many words, but I can tell that's what she wants me to do. I can't talk about it, myself. Don't even like to think about it.

But I have abandoned him. My husband for eternity, and I've left him to himself. There are times I think I'm a terrible person. My mother tells me, "There's only so much you can do." She says, "You've got to think about your daughter." And I do. Constantly, constantly. I think of Kyle and I think of my daughter and I think of myself. I stay up half the night in my old twin bed at my parents' house listening to Stella breathing and sighing in her crib, and I wonder if I've ever made a good choice in my life.

So this is what I tell myself. Kyle and I—our story—it's like this news report I remember from last winter about a skier who got lost in the mountains. For days, the whole community was looking for him. They had search teams, helicopters, police dogs. But then a big storm came and blanketed any clues they might have found with a fresh layer of snow. The temperature dropped. They held a press conference and said, "We're calling off the search; we'll have to wait for springtime, for the thaw." The lost skier's father stood up in front of the cameras with his eyes full of tears and said, "It's the hardest thing I've ever done, because I know he's buried out there somewhere, but it's much too dangerous for a person to venture out in these conditions."

I think of Kyle, my Kyle, buried deep, surrounded by cold and blinding white. I've been digging and digging. I don't know how long I'm supposed to keep digging until it's okay for me to stop trying to find him.

ALICA: INTUITION

Alicia stands by the front door holding Christy's coat.

"Thank you so much for having us," her sister-in-law says. "The meal was delicious. Everything, perfect."

"Well, I wouldn't say perfect," Alicia says.

"Yes! Perfect!" Christy leans in. "And no surprise guests," she whispers, conspiratorially, in Alicia's ear.

Alicia can't wait for Christy to go home. It's been a peaceful day. Uneventful. Nothing like the baby blessing when Kyle barged in during the sacrament, his hair all disheveled, his eyes wild and frightening. She's sure her extended family has spent many entertaining hours dissecting that whole scene, and she's glad today hasn't provided Christy with any more material.

When Beth moved back home with the baby this summer, Christy had called Alicia, breathless for details. Almost giddy.

"Bipolar?" she asked. "Isn't that the disease you see on television movies where people have all the different personalities?"

Alicia could hardly bear answering; Christy could be so deliberately clueless. "No, Christy," she told her. "It's the disease geniuses sometimes get. Van Gogh. Virginia Woolf. It's a particular struggle for the sensitive and the intelligent."

Today Christy has tried to bring up Kyle and his situation at least half a dozen times. During dessert, she told Alicia she had gone online and looked up lithium, and she said, "It doesn't sound all that bad to me. It's a wonder why he won't stay on it!" Luckily, Beth was out of earshot, upstairs nursing the baby.

Christy's husband, Rob, is outside waiting in the car. Alicia hears him rev the engine.

"You've got a lot on your hands," Christy says. "I don't envy you. A distraught daughter *and* a baby at home! I don't know how you do it."

"We'll be fine, Christy. Don't you concern yourself with us."

Rob honks the horn.

"That's my cue!" Christy says, then reaches over to kiss Alicia on the cheek. She scuttles to the car, carefully balancing her load of Thanksgiving leftovers.

Alicia walks out onto the porch and waves as their Buick rolls around the corner and out of sight. The air is cool against her naked arms. The trees are bare; the ground is brown and dry. November is a terrible month, she thinks.

She wonders if Kyle is hidden somewhere, spying on the house, watching her. She wouldn't be surprised if he were. And it wouldn't frighten her, either. It would mostly make her sad. She wishes she could go back in time eight years to Beth and Kyle's sophomore year in high school, the year they met. Maybe, if she had known what to look for, Alicia could have seen the signs. She could have warned her daughter. Instead of agreeing with Beth, seeing Kyle as interesting and brilliant and emotional, she would have had the good sense to recognize he was more than just a passionate kid. But she was almost as swept up as Beth had been. Here was this boy who came skidding into their lives at full tilt: so smart, so funny, so full of ideas. He'd help Alicia with dinner, doing crazy things like adding Tabasco to the spaghetti sauce and then saying, "Isn't this the best spaghetti you've ever had in your life?" And they'd all agree that yes, yes it was. On Mother's Day he would always send her a card, even before he and Beth married. Sometimes he would write, *Thank you for bringing Beth into this world.* Other times, *You're the mother that I never had.* Although he did have a mother: an unpredictable, difficult woman who'd raised Kyle all alone. That's where she'd told Beth he should go today.

"He has a mother," she said to Beth. "It's not like we're all he has."

"Yes, we are, Mom," Beth had answered. "And you know it."

But Kyle is not the boy she remembers. The tall, handsome, laughing boy who took her child to the prom, who turned nineteen and dressed up so strikingly in his dark-blue suit and served a mission, who came home and said to her and to Nathan, "I would like your daughter's hand." She can't say when the obvious changes started. Six months after Beth married him? A year? The doctors told them diseases like this sometimes come on in early adulthood. There's no way they could have known. But she *should* have known. She feels betrayed—by her own intuition, by God—that she hadn't somehow sensed disaster.

She looks down her normally deserted street and counts the cars lined up along it. Over a dozen are bunched in front of her neighbors' houses. And who are the people that her neighbors have let inside? Grandparents with Alzheimer's, alcoholic uncles, mean-spirited sisters. She knows her neighbors, knows their stories. She knows they have opened their doors on holidays to all sorts of difficult people who come underneath their family umbrellas. But she can't. Not this time. She has kept her door deliberately closed.

The worst part is she doesn't feel guilty for doing it. Because first and foremost, she is a mother. And a mother must protect her child.

BETH: ROMANTIC

From my upstairs bedroom window I can see my mother, coatless, standing on the porch. She keeps looking up and down the street. I can't help thinking that she's watching for him. Waiting. I told her, chances are, no matter what we say, he'll still show up. But I don't think he'll dare if she's standing right there. He's afraid of her. Only her. Even at the height of his mania she can stop him dead in his tracks.

My mom is a beautiful woman. Prettier than me. She's kept her hair long, just past her shoulders, and she colors it to the same deep reddish brown it was when she was my age. I used to feel sorry for her, that she married my dad. Isn't that funny? I thought she sold out. He was a good dad, sure. Steady, dependable. Nice. But he seemed like an awfully average husband. When was the last time he swept her away on a romantic trip? Wrote her a poem? When I married Kyle, I even wondered if she was jealous.

Kyle's latest romantic gesture was to buy us two one-way tickets to Australia. A few weeks after I had Stella, he came bursting in the door.

"It's a place of mystery! Full of excitement! We can live by the ocean. Live off the land!"

That's when I knew he'd gone off his medication again. I didn't even ask him how he'd paid for the tickets or if we could get a refund. I just silently nodded my head and thought, *I don't think I can do this anymore.*

NATHAN: DIRECTION

Nathan wants to get away from the house. It's not that he doesn't love them—his daughters, his sons-in-law, his wife—but by nature he's a solitary man. A lover of quiet. Even now, late in November, he tries to get outside and walk at least once a day. So when Mike asks him if he'll take the grandkids to the park down the block, he's glad for the chance to get some fresh air. He puts the boys in their coats and lets them bolt out the door. He keeps them in sight as they tear down the street, but he doesn't call out to them to slow down or wait or hold hands. He lets them go. He thinks, boys need to run.

It's when he rounds the corner to the park that he sees Kyle in his dusty red Honda, sitting. The engine is turned off and Kyle is staring, immovable, his eyes fixed off in the distance. The boys are at the park now—clambering all over the jungle gym, shrieking on the swings— and even though Kyle is parked just across the street, he gives no in- dication that he sees them or hears them. His profile stays frozen. Nathan feels suddenly nervous and ashamed, as if he has sneaked up on somebody, as if he's in a place he's not supposed to be. He is unsure if he should gather up the boys and head home. Pretend he never saw his son-in-law. But he has seen him. And even though Kyle hasn't so much as tilted his head, Nathan's sure that Kyle has seen him too.

Nathan sits on the cold metal bench near the swing set. Marnie's boys are hollering, "Grandpa! Watch me slide!" and they don't even recognize their Uncle Kyle sitting across the street in his car, listening and not listening. Watching and not watching. The afternoon sun hangs low in the sky, and the wind sends dry leaves skittering across the sidewalk. It's getting chilly. Nathan wonders how long Kyle's been sitting without the car turned on. He wonders if the boy even realizes it's cold.

He's got to go to him. There's no getting around it. No matter what Kyle has done—all the ways he has hurt Beth, all the lies he has told, and his stubborn refusal to stick with the therapy and at least try, at least *seem* to try, to get a hold on this illness that started strangling him so slowly that no one in the family thought to notice until it was out of control—no matter what, Nathan is responsible for this man. He opened his door to Kyle when he was still a kid. Watched as he burrowed himself deep into their family. And Nathan let him do it. Encouraged it, in his own way. And now he is responsible.

He walks toward the car, his eyes on Kyle's unmoving face. He comes up to the window. Taps it. He can see the shine of tears across Kyle's cheeks.

"Kyle," Nathan says.

Kyle closes his eyes. He keeps his chin set firm.

"Can I just talk to you?"

Slowly, Kyle turns his face to Nathan. He opens his eyes. They are tired eyes, bloodshot and sunken. Weary. He doesn't move to roll the window down.

"What do you want to say?" Kyle asks. His voice is quiet, muffled through the glass.

Nathan considers how to answer this question. That he's afraid for Kyle? Afraid *of* him? That, somehow, he wishes Kyle would disappear and wonders how to save him? That he doesn't know what to say?

Behind him, Nathan can hear his grandsons' voices, clear and brittle in the air.

"Grandpa!" they're calling. "Push us!"

"I just want you to know that you're not alone," Nathan says.

Kyle leans his head back and lets out an angry burst of laughter. "Really?" he says. "You think so? Well you could've fooled me."

It isn't until Nathan is almost to the house that he hears the engine rumble. He doesn't know what it means, if Kyle is leaving or coming. And he doesn't know what he wants it to mean.

He has always been a man of direction. A giver of advice. "Here," he likes to say. "Do this, follow these directions, one, two, three." Then, what had been broken could be fixed. What had been complicated could be understood. He remembers when Beth was a child, how easy it had been to rescue her. If she fell off her bike he could scoop her up, dust off her knees, and kiss her head. Tell her, "Keep trying, keep doing your best—in time it will get easier." But not anymore. She is beyond him. Her life, her story, no longer his.

But he prays for her. For Beth and Kyle and little Stella. They are a family. He asks God to be gentle. It's all that he can do.

KYLE: ELECTRIC

He turns on the car and thinks, stay or go, go or stay, claim your life or run away. Always he's thinking like this. In little poems. Little songs. He's been writing a lot of them down in a notebook that he's brought to show Beth, because sometimes she has such a hard time listening to him, really *hearing* him, and he remembers how she used to love his poems, way back when. He would give them to her, and she would cry and say things like "I love you," like "What would I do without you?" It has been months since he has kissed her, months since he has touched a girl, even, any girl, and he thinks his skin might be starting to go electric with unused tactile energy. He's almost afraid to touch her now. Zap! What if he touched her and an electric current shot out from under his skin and got her? Zip zap! Maybe it would make her more afraid, or maybe it would make her remember the powerful kind of love they share, the very real and, yes, shocking kind of love they have between the two of them. He's always said she's scared because their love is too strong and he is too real. That's why she wants him on that medication, because he's just too real without it, but he's tried to explain that it's the real him she fell in love with anyway and there's no way she'll ever love the other him, the sad, slow, fat, dull—the lurching mannequin he is on those pills. She'll leave him anyway if he takes them. He knows it.

So if she would just take a chance, take a dive with him, go for a ride with him, let her hair flow free and wild with him and love him like she used to, like he knows that she still can. He thinks of Nathan, his face in the window, his sad, pale face. He said, "You're not alone." Not. Alone. If anyone could still be in his corner, it would be Nathan, a good man, a man who maybe sees beyond the surface of things. A kind man. The only father Kyle has ever known. After Stella was born he told Nathan, "I want to be a father just like you." But Kyle was on his meds back then, and even though he kept trying to be a real father—a true man, like Nathan—he didn't have the energy, wouldn't have the energy unless he got rid of the pills, and maybe Nathan understands that. So he hopes Nathan answers when he goes to the door, or Beth, but not Mike, that Minnesota son-in-law with his button-down shirts and his big meaty handshakes and his questions—*You got yourself a 401(k)? An IRA? You heard about that IPO?* Last time Mike asked him a question like that, Kyle spelled out his answer, N-O, which he thought was pretty funny, and it flustered that Mike for a minute. If Alicia answers the door, he's brought her the flowers. White roses, her favorite. He doesn't know what he'll say to Alicia—just hand her the flowers and look in her face and hope she recognizes that it's only him, only Kyle, the boy who loves her daughter and loves her family and just wants them to give him a chance.

BETH: IDLING

When my dad came home from the park he told me right away.

"I thought you should know," he said. "He doesn't look well."

I keep thinking, how long? How long has he been around the corner, sitting in his car? All day? Since before the rest of us were even awake? I wouldn't be surprised if he pulled up at four o'clock in the morning. Some nights he sleeps only two, three hours; he gets an idea in his head and he can't stop thinking about it, can't keep himself from jumping out of bed and acting on it. But then, in a way, I knew he was out there too. I could feel him from the minute I woke up.

I step outside our front door. The street is quiet. I hear, very faintly, the rumble of an idling engine. I wait for him.

KYLE: BEAUTIFUL STRANGER

He puts the car in drive, steps on the gas, curves around the corner. Then he sees her standing on the porch, her hands stuffed deep in her pockets, her hair pulled away from her face. She is wearing lipstick, a deep red he has never seen on her before. Her lips are the only color against her pale face. She looks like a woman, like a grown-up. Kyle thinks, *This beautiful stranger—she knew I was coming, she's come out to meet me, she's going to welcome me home.*

THE PALMERS: PATIENCE

Inside, the family has been warned. Nathan told them, "Kyle's outside, and I think I gave him the impression it's okay to come over." Alicia has gone to her room. Marnie and Tina—the sisters—they both agree it's for the best that he come inside. After all, they argue, what are they going to do? Lock their doors on him forever? Stella's his daughter. It's Thanksgiving. He has a right. Christy and Rob and Grandma have all left, so who does Mom think she needs to impress? It's only Kyle. No matter what, he is still Kyle.

The sons-in-law, Mike and Jimmy, decide to watch football. They will smile at him, say hello. Speak if spoken to.

Beth opens the front door and leads Kyle inside. His face is flushed and spotty. In his left hand, he holds a bouquet of white roses. He lifts his right hand and waves.

"The fam!" he says.

Nathan rises from his chair and shakes Kyle's hand. "Good to see you," he says.

"Been a long time," Kyle answers, then laughs once, short and hard.

Marnie says, "Pie! We have pie for you. We have extra. There's plenty."

"Can I take those flowers? Put them in water?" Tina asks.

"Actually, these flowers are for Alicia. And where is my beautiful mother-in-law? The lady of the house. Has she deserted us? Up and flown the coop?"

The sisters look at each other.

"She's resting," Nathan says.

"Or," Kyle says, "is she playing hide-and-seek?"

Outside, the sky is turning dark. Clouds are moving in.

"A storm is coming," Tina says.

"It's a good thing," says Nathan. "We certainly need the moisture."

Everyone nods, earnestly, eagerly. Upstairs, a baby cries.

"There's Stella," Beth says. "I'll go get her."

"No," Kyle says. "No, let me. I mean, can I?"

Beth looks across the room at her father.

"How about you come with me," she says to Kyle. "We can get her together."

They climb the stairs to Beth's old bedroom, Kyle clutching the roses in his left hand. Beth's room is painted butter yellow. It's still decorated like a high school girl's: trophies on the shelves, pictures from school dances. In every photo it's just the two of them, Beth and Kyle. Never anyone else. Different poses and outfits and hairstyles, but always they're the couple with their arms around each other. Heads tilted in close.

Stella's crib has been pushed against the far wall, the only place it will fit. The baby isn't crying loudly. Whimpering, mostly. Patient. Kyle comes to the head of the crib and looks inside. The baby is on her stomach, struggling, pushing up against the mattress with her arms.

"Well look at you," Kyle says.

Stella stops crying at the sound of his voice. Lifts up her head and sees him.

"Look at you so strong," he says to her, his voice gentle, singsong. She breaks into a grin.

"How'd you get there on your tummy?"

Then, from the doorway, Beth. "She's on her stomach?" she asks.

She walks over to Kyle and stands beside him. They peer into the crib together.

"She really is on her tummy," Beth says. "I was starting to worry she'd spend the rest of her life flat on her back. The doctor said not to worry about her rolling. Said it would come in her own time. But I wondered."

"Sometimes you've just got to be patient," Kyle says.

"True," Beth says. "Very true."

Kyle slides his hand, slowly, along the railing of the crib, until his pinkie touches Beth's. She doesn't move her hand. "When you love somebody, I mean," he says. "Especially. Patience."

Downstairs, the family is happy to hear about Stella.

"What a champ!" Nathan says.

"She'll be running you ragged before you know it," Marnie tells her sister.

Tina brings Kyle his pie. "I remembered you like pecan," she says.

Kyle sits at the table. He is the only one eating. Someone has turned off the television, and the family listens as Kyle's fork clinks against his plate.

"I think I see some flurries," Tina says. "Look. Outside. It's about time."

The family looks out the window. Delicate white snowflakes drift by, lonely, so slow a person could count them coming down.

"It seems, in my day, there used to be so much snow. By Thanksgiving time we'd have had a few good storms. But anymore even the weather's unpredictable," Nathan says. "Can't even count on the weather."

Outside, the flakes twirl in the wind. Kyle has stopped eating his pie.

"I'd like to show my daughter the snow," he says.

The family turns and looks at him.

"Does she have a coat? I'd like to put it on her. Take her outside. Show her the snow. The two of us."

The family looks at Beth.

"You want to show her the snow?" she asks.

"I would like to, yes. Very much. I'm her father."

KYLE: SNOWFLAKES

Kyle sits on the swing at the far end of the yard, holding the baby on his lap. He points at the sky. The baby's eyes follow his finger. He pushes the swing with his feet, slowly. It is not too cold, and the breeze is very light. The snowflakes are in no hurry. They spin and tumble and land on the baby's coat. He can't remember ever seeing a snowflake up close, and it looks just as it ought to, symmetrical and complicated and beautiful, the way God likes for things to be. He whispers to the baby, "Look." A snowflake has landed on her sleeve. "Look how pretty." The baby will not look. She keeps her chin tilted up at the sky. The sky is a mystery. And snow. And God. His little daughter understands this. Her tiny hands are getting cold. He covers them with his own. Leans his cheek against her head. Says, "We can keep each other warm."

BETH: WINTER

It is getting dark. I move out to the patio where I can watch them better. Behind me, in the house, I hear my family. I can't pick out what they're saying. I can hear only the tenor of their voices, their laughter and their silences. I bring my legs up and wrap my arms around my knees. Watch my breath turn to white. The swing creaks softly, marking even time.

Between Kyle and me is a path of scattered roses. He didn't drop them all at once. He made himself a trail, like Hansel. He knows I am watching. I can see his silhouette, his dark shadow, rising and falling. His back is to me. He has his arms circled around her.

I listen for Stella's voice. The smallest whisper of sound, the tiniest cry—I will hear it and go to her. The night is that silent. That still.

But then I hear a song, very faint. It's Kyle, and he's singing:

For health and strength and daily food
We praise thy name, O Lord.

A Primary song. A Thanksgiving song. A short one, sung in a round. I remember singing it with my sisters.

He gets to the end of the line and takes a breath. Begins again:

For health and strength and daily food
We praise thy name, O Lord.

I can see his face bent toward the sky. I come up behind him.

"Sing with me," he says. He doesn't look at me. He looks up, and the snowflakes land on his cheeks, his eyelids. "It's such a pretty song. But we have to sing it together."

"Kyle," I say. I reach out for Stella. He keeps swinging.

"For health and strength and daily food," he sings, and waits. This is where I should come in.

"For health and strength and daily food." Again.

I can't sing with him. I listen to the moaning of the swing, the air pushing through the trees.

"Have you ever smelled her hair?" he says. "It smells just like the morning."

He is crying.

"Kyle," I whisper. "Can I have her? Can I have Stella?"

"It's not good to be alone."

"Can I have my baby?"

"I only ask for small things. The song. It doesn't sound right when you sing it alone. It's not complete. It's a very sad song when you sing it all alone."

"She's getting cold."

He stops the swing with his feet. I crouch down beside him, and Stella looks up and smiles. She lifts her arms to me.

"I would give you anything, you know," he says.

"I know," I say, and grasp Stella beneath her arms. Pull her to me.

"We love each other," he says.

He turns to me. His eyes are wide and luminous in the moonlight. His face shines, smooth and white. I reach out and touch his hand. His skin is like ice.

"I've got to get her inside, where it's warm," I say.

"I remember," he says. "You've always been afraid of winter."

"You should come inside too. You're freezing. I can feel it."

He shakes his head. "I don't feel the cold."

"Kyle."

"And the snow is very beautiful."

I leave him out on the swing. I walk with my daughter toward the house, and it's lit up and warm, a deep yellow glow against the night. I hear Kyle's voice rise again in the air, singing, and I hear the creak of the swing and the scuff of his shoes on the hard ground. I don't look back at him. The roses have disappeared in the snow. I tuck my daughter up tight against my chest, open the door, and take her inside.

WOLVES

Douglas Thayer

WHEN HE WAS SEVENTEEN, DAVID Thatcher Williams and his cousin
Cleon, who was also seventeen, hopped a freight in the Provo yards
to start a trip to Washington, D.C., to visit David's Aunt Doris, his
dad's sister. Just before they started back, Cleon was offered a job and
decided to stay (good summer jobs were hard to get in Provo in 1940),
so David came home alone. He knew that if he stayed at night in the
big hobo jungles, he would be safe enough. David's Uncle Charley,
who had hopped freights to Denver, Cheyenne, and Los Angeles the
summer he graduated from Provo High, gave David and Cleon a lot
of good advice.

When David left Washington to return to Provo, his Aunt Doris
gave him three dollars, which he carried in change to pay for his food.
In the jungles the hobos cooked together, and if a hobo wanted a bowl
of stew or soup he had to put something in the pot or chip in a nickel,
a dime, or maybe even a quarter. A dime bought a loaf of bread in
those days.

David lived three blocks up from the railroad yards. Hobos
knocked on his mom's door to ask for food. His mom, Mary, always
fed them; they sometimes did odd jobs for her. When David and his
friends were younger, they rode their bikes down to talk to the hobos
in the jungle at the bottom of Second West and listen to their stories,
and the boys also hopped freights for short rides. Most of the hobos
had families and were looking for work. Some were college graduates
who had good jobs before the Depression. At night, falling asleep
in his darkened room, David listened to the whistles of the passing
trains.

David's dad, Frank Thatcher Williams, ran the laundry at the state mental hospital in Provo, and hobos who had gone insane were brought to the hospital. David's dad sometimes brought patients to the house for holidays or family picnics. Some had to be told to eat or, at Christmas, to open their presents. One patient who had been a hobo sat staring at the front room wall for two hours, his eyes blank. Sometimes he couldn't remember his name. In the hospital medical wards, patients lay in bed for years, fetal and wearing diapers.

The *Herald* occasionally carried a short article about a hobo found dead in a jungle or along the tracks, his body mangled. Some bodies carried no identity papers of any kind, and the sheriff could not always be sure if the death was accidental. The county had to bury these men. In the bigger jungles the hobos organized committees to keep order. Men who preyed on other hobos were called wolves.

At seventeen David was tall and thin with thick curly blond hair just like his dad. David was a hopeful, happy boy and always smiling. He was an Eagle Scout, sang in the high school a capella choir, played basketball and softball, and dated any number of girls. Before David and Cleon left for Washington, David's dad brought their families together to kneel in prayer and ask the Lord to watch over the two boys and bring them home safe.

David's mom was expecting a baby, and David wanted to be back home before it was born. David's mom smiled when he said to be sure and have a boy. He had three sisters and wanted a little brother.

The third day coming back alone from Washington, David was in Nebraska outside of a little town called Gothenburg. It was the last week in August. The corn in the vast dark fields was high. It was late evening, almost dark. David walked the tracks looking for campfires in the wide band of willows bordering cornfields. A hundred yards out, paralleling the tracks, a creek cut through the willows.

Hobos liked creeks so they could get cleaned up, wash their clothes, and have water for cooking. David had been told there was a jungle along the creek. He'd also been told it was a good jungle; people from the small towns sometimes dropped off surplus vegetables from their gardens for the hobos to eat. In some towns the police would threaten the hobos and drive them away if they were found walking the streets or begging for food.

Although above him the night sky was clear, far to the south David saw flashes of lightning and heard distant thunder. Going out to Washington, he and Cleon were caught in storms in Nebraska and Iowa. They'd never seen so much rain before in their lives, the rain coming down in sheets for hours, flooding the land, the thunder terrible and constant, the flashing lightning turning the skies bluish white, the wind lashing the corn and willows.

David saw two fires flickering deep in the willows and trees, which were already black in the fading light. He hesitated; he knew it wasn't the big hobo jungle he was looking for. But he'd been walking for hours. He was tired, dirty, and hungry; he hadn't eaten all day, and he didn't carry any food or cooking utensils with him, just a bowl and a spoon, which every hobo had to have. He didn't want to be caught out in the open if the storm hit.

David decided if the group of hobos was big enough to need two fires, he would be all right. He figured he knew what he was doing; he and Cleon had made it all the way to Washington without any trouble, and he was better than halfway home now.

He dropped down the grade but couldn't find the trail through the high, dense willows. Knowing the general direction to the fires, he pushed through. Finally, ahead of him he saw the fires flickering.

He stood back in the willows and looked into the clearing. He saw three men, one sitting, smoking and reading, the magazine turned to catch the light from the fire nearest a lean-to, one smoking and playing a game of solitaire at a table, and one standing by the cooking fire and eating from a bowl. Under the lean-to, which was covered by canvas, was an old mattress with a blanket spread on it. Three chairs and a table had been made from lumber scraps. Laundry hung from a rope stretched between two small trees. Steam rose from an open pot and a covered coffee pot on a grill over the cooking fires.

David was surprised that four or five men weren't around each fire, yet everything seemed okay. The three men had made an effort to build themselves a home out in the willows, but then David was just a tired, dirty, hungry, green seventeen-year-old kid anyway.

He stepped into the clearing and helloed the fire. A hobo had to get permission before he could walk up to a fire.

All three men stood up. "Come on in! Come on in and welcome!"

The tall man, who had been eating, put the bowl down on the table and waved David in. The two men smoking took the cigarettes out of their mouths. As he got closer, David saw that the three men hadn't shaved for at least a week. Their pants and shirts were shabby with wear. Two of the three looked middle-aged, maybe a little older; the third, the smallest, looked much younger, perhaps not yet twenty. The two older men carried folding sheath knives on their belts.

"Hello, kid. You look all worn out. You alone?" The tall man stepped around the fire.

"Yes, sir. I need a place to camp for the night, if that's okay. I saw your fires. I can go on though."

"You're more than welcome, kid, more than welcome. Not a good idea to camp all alone out here. Take your pack off. Must be heavy."

The three men gathered around him. The tall man asked David his name and where he was from, and David told them. They did not tell him their names; they did not offer to shake hands. Hobos liked to get to know a person before they talked much about themselves.

All three men smiled.

"Yeah, they're real happy to see you," the young man said, "real happy, real happy. Yes sir, real happy. So am I, real, real happy. Yippee."

"Shut up." The tall man turned back to David. "He's a little simple. You look hungry, kid." The tall man turned toward the fire where the pots were steaming. "Why don't you have a bowl of stew and then take a bath in the creek? You look like you could use a bath. There's a nice hole for taking a bath."

"Thanks. I'd like to get cleaned up. I've got a dime to pay for my supper."

"Oh, that's okay, kid. You keep your money. Sit down and eat. Got a bowl and a spoon?"

"Yes, sir. Thank you."

The tall man offered David a cup of coffee, but he said he didn't drink coffee.

The tall man talked to David while he ate. The young man stood next to the table, grinning but silent. After David finished the first bowl, the tall man filled his bowl again.

"There's plenty, kid, there's plenty. Got to keep your strength up."

"You sure do. You sure do. You sure do."

"I told you to shut up."

The camp was deep in the willows; David didn't see any path out. All the big jungles had worn paths through the willows and weeds.

After David finished eating, the tall man walked him back to the creek.

"You got some soap, haven't you, kid."

"Yes, sir."

"Good. Come back to the fire when you're ready."

The tall man came back twice while David was standing in the waist-deep water.

"Just checking, kid. Don't want you to drown. You're taking a long time."

"It's really nice to be clean again."

"Sure it is, kid."

When he finished taking a bath, David put on clean shorts from the clothes in his backpack and stood in knee-deep water next to the creek bank to wash his dirty clothes. He wanted to have clean clothes to put on just before he got home. He didn't want his mom to think he hadn't tried to stay clean. He wondered if the baby had been born yet and if he had a little brother.

"Hey, kid."

David turned to see the two older men standing on the bank. The tall man had cut a willow and was peeling the bark off with a long-bladed folding knife. The other man carried a coil of thin rope. The tall man folded the knife and put it in the black belt sheath.

"Yes, sir?"

"Come on, get out. You take too long. What you washing your clothes for? Get out."

"Better do what he says, better do what he says, better do what he says. Better, better, better."

David turned. The young man was on the other side of the creek.

"Have I done something wrong? I'll just get the rest of my clothes on and go. I don't want to bother you. I'll pay for the bowls of stew."

"Just get out, kid."

When he waded from the creek carrying the shirt he'd just wrung out, the man who stood behind him slipped a noose over his head and snugged it against his neck.

"What are you doing? What—"

"Kid, we don't want you to ask any questions. You just do what you're told, and we'll all have a real good time" The tall man had moved a little off to his side.

"I don't want—"

The slashing blow with the willow across his back was so sudden, so unexpected and savage, that David dropped the washed shirt and almost fell to his knees, his vision blurring to white.

"I told you, I told you, you better do what he says. He's mean. He does things to people."

"Shut up. Now, kid, all you have to do is cooperate so we can all enjoy ourselves."

Understanding finally what they wanted him for, his whole body tightening and shrinking against that knowledge, for he had heard of such things, David said no again.

The second blow across his back was more savage than the first, and then he felt the noose tightening around his neck, lifting him to his toes. The other man had thrown the rope over the limb of a small tree and pulled it tight.

On the second night they started to torture David, and he knew they were going to kill him, had to kill him. They were drunk on three bottles of wine they'd sent the young man to town to buy with David's money. They burned him with their cigarettes and with pieces of fence wire heated in the fire, laughing when he flinched, asking him how it felt. The tall man with the black hair whipped him with the shaved willow and threatened to cut him.

The rope tied to the lean-to frame, the noose still around his galled and bleeding neck, David was weak, in shock, but still conscious, still able to feel the pain when they burned him. But he didn't scream anymore.

David did not fill his mind with hate, plan revenge, righteous murder, but he thought of his mom and dad, his sisters, the new baby, his grandparents, his uncles and aunts and cousins, his neighbors and friends, bringing their faces and their laughter to his mind. He thought of family parties, reunions, picnics, Sunday dinners, and fishing trips with his dad. He thought of Christmas and Thanksgiving and all the good food, and playing basketball for Provo High, and dancing with girls, and receiving his Eagle Scout badge, and going to church. But mostly he thought of his mom and dad hugging and kissing him when he left for Washington and telling him how much they loved him and to come home safe. David prayed, and he kept repeating his name to himself—David Thatcher Williams, David Thatcher Williams, David Thatcher Williams, David Thatcher Williams. . . .

All evening and into the night he'd heard the thunder, the wind picking up, and then the rain came, great sheets of rain pounding the earth, putting out the fires, and then the fierce wind tearing the tarp off the lean-to. Outside the lean-to, drunken, falling down in the darkness, cursing the rain, the wind, each other, the three men searched for the tarp, their cursing rising to meet the pitch of the storm.

The creek rose, the cool water coming up over the old mattress on which David lay in his shorts. Fumbling with the rope, David loosened the noose and pulled it over his head.

David crawled slowly away from the wind-muffled cursing. In great pain, he entered the dark, bending willows, the water from the rising creek a foot deep. The palms of his hands were burned, so he tried to stand, but the soles of his feet were burned too, the cool water not easing his pain. He fell, stood up, fell, crawled, made his hands into fists to crawl, saw himself in the great flashes of lightning. He came to willows edging the flooding creek and crawled into it, the deep, fast water carrying him. David did not think about wanting to die, or needing to.

He crawled out on the far bank. Standing now, walking on the sides of his feet, holding onto the willows, he pulled himself forward. He saw in the flashes of light the dark wall of a cornfield, the tops bending in the wind. He knew the three men would search for him there, spreading out to follow the rows until they found him. They had to find him; they had to kill him. He turned, moved into a wide band of waist-high grass, and crawled into that, let the grass beat down over him, and lay staring up into the darkness.

Fitful, sleeping, perhaps unconscious at times, feverish, the burns becoming sores, some already infected, the pain increasing now, David lay covered with the long grass, waiting until he saw finally the pale morning light coming down to him. The rain had stopped, but the dark clouds hid the sun. David heard yelling, cursing, as the three men searched for him, the voices fading and then coming back on the pulsing wind.

He crawled into a thick patch of willows and lay curled. Listening, he waited, willed himself to wait. Mosquito-bitten except where he was covered with thick mud, the mosquitoes in gray swarms above his head, growing numb to pain, David slipped away into darkness and then came back, slipped away and came back. He heard the rumbling and whistling of nearby trains. He saw his arms, legs, stomach, the burn sores and red insect bites like the marks of a disease, the sores swelling, red and black, some as big as nickels. He prayed he would not die and that somebody would help him.

In the late afternoon, the only sound the gentle wind, no voices, the clouds still hiding the sun, David followed the creek. Crouched, arms held out away from his body, he moved very slowly because of the numbness, kept stumbling. He lay down in the no longer flooded creek, but he dared not touch his body to rub away the dirt. He waded to the other side, where he knew the railroad tracks were, but stayed in the willows.

He found a farm road, walked along the grassy edge, but he was falling down now. The fever, a heat in his face and head, was spreading through his body, bringing back feeling except for his numb feet. Stooped, he saw across a field a small man on a tractor. The man stopped the tractor and stood silhouetted looking at him. The man was short and thin and wore a hat. David stumbled forward. When he fell, he crawled until he could push himself up again.

He saw a man walking down the road toward him. The man stopped and looked, bent forward, came farther. David saw it was a boy, not a man. He wore a yellow straw hat. The boy came closer.

"Gee. Gee whiz. What happened to you? What's your name?"

David looked at the boy.

"Gee. I'll get my mom. She'll help you. She always helps everybody. She'll bring my dad too. He'll come, and my big brother, Will. Wait. Just wait. Don't go anywhere."

The boy turned and ran up the road. He didn't stop to pick up his hat when it fell from his head.

Standing next to a barbed-wire fence, David reached out and gripped the tight top strand with both hands so he would not fall.

It didn't hurt. Flies lit on his lips and under his nose. They lit on the sores. He saw under the mud the red welts on his chest, stomach, and thighs where the tall man had whipped him with shaved willows. David's whole body pulsed with the fever from the growing infections, the beginning delirium masking the pain.

When the boy's mother and father and older brother came, they had to pry David's hands loose from the wire.

"No, no," the woman said, "no, no. Dear God, no."

She was a large woman. She wore a blue apron over her dress. She touched David gently.

They broke a bale of straw in the back of their pickup truck and laid him on that. As the pickup moved slowly up the road, the woman knelt by him smoothing his hair, waving away the flies, and praying for him. He lay on his back. His elbows resting on the straw, he held up his bloody hands, the blood running down his wrists. The woman told him her name was Mrs. Meyers. David closed his eyes and slipped down into the grayness.

When he opened his eyes again, David lay in bed on a rubber sheet. Three women had pans of warm soapy water, and they were washing him and putting salve on his sores.

"What's your name, son? What's your name?"

David reached out to touch the woman in the blue apron. He spoke very slowly. "Mrs. Meyers, Mrs. Meyers."

"No, your name, your name."

David looked up at the woman.

"It's the shock and the fever. It's a wonder he isn't dead. Look at his neck. Who could have done such a thing to a boy?"

"His poor mother."

A woman with a stethoscope around her neck was giving him a shot in the arm with a large hypodermic needle. Slowly the remaining pain ebbed, and he slipped into the morphine darkness. For two weeks, delirious, he moved in and out of the darkness. He heard voices when he came up out of it and sometimes the whistle of a train far off, saw shadows, but felt no pain, his body vague, heavy, swollen, hot, indistinct. He could not speak.

Whenever his eyes opened, the women held his head up off the pillow and made him drink. They spooned broth into his mouth, the warm liquid spilling down his chin and onto his neck and bare chest. He knew that under the sheet he wore a diaper. The women put salve on his infected sores, on his neck, and on the welts from the beatings. Some of the infected sores had to be lanced. His hands were bandaged. Three little boys stood in the doorway. David saw vases of flowers and sunlit windows.

"You must eat, son. You must eat."

"What is your name? Where do you live? Who are your people?"

David did not know the answers to these questions. He remembered the boy coming down the lane toward him.

David stared at the women. He sank back down again into the darkness. If his eyes opened in the night, he saw Mrs. Meyers sitting by his bed in her big chair. Her hand lay on his bare wrist. She would stand up out of her chair to kiss him on the forehead and smooth back his hair. She talked to him. He heard her prayers for him. He did not speak. In the darkness he felt his hands inside the bandages. His eyes closed. He heard the faint, far-off whistling of trains.

One evening he could keep his eyes open. He lay on his back under a sheet. He stared up at the white ceiling. He was very weak. He heard two women talking. One of them was Mrs. Meyers. He turned his head toward the voices. He saw Mrs. Meyers and another woman he'd seen before, but whose name he didn't know. He watched them. He listened. He saw the black scabs on his arms.

"Look, look, he's awake. Martha, look."

"Praise God—at last."

They came to the bed. They talked to David. They sat on either side of the bed. Mrs. Meyers kissed him on the forehead and smoothed his hair. The other woman put her hand on his arm.

"What is your name, son? We need to know your name. Your family will be worried about you. You must tell us your name."

He did not answer Mrs. Meyers. He couldn't speak. He stared at her.

They talked to him, entreated him, begged him, asked repeatedly for his name, his father's name, where he was from, but he did not answer. He stared at them.

The other woman stood up. "He's gone." She crossed her arms over her chest. "He's gone, Martha. Look, you can see it in his eyes. The poor boy. Little wonder, really. Such a nice boy too."

"No," Mrs. Meyers said, "no." She shook her head. Tears slipped down her cheeks. "It's the shock, the fever. We have to be patient."

"It's as plain as the nose on your face, Martha. I've seen it before. My Delbert's got a brother like that named Fred. I've told you about him. Nothing you can do, worse luck. Makes you worry about your own kids. Of course you're not thinking about anything like that when you're getting married. Funny. The families take turns bringing Fred home for Christmas. Just sits there at the table like a stump. You have to cut up his turkey for him; sometimes you have to feed it to him. You're lucky if he don't piss himself. Just like a baby, really. Makes the kids nervous. Of course I don't mind. Used to it, I guess. You can get used to anything. Have to." She looked down at David. "Such beautiful hair for a boy. Too bad that he won't be passing that on. He'll end up in the state hospital in Lincoln or some other place. You've done everything you can to locate his family. Maybe he has no family. A lot of 'em don't."

"No," Mrs. Meyers said, turning to David, putting her hand on his, "no, no, no, no."

"No," David said, whispering the word, closing his eyes against a horror he understood only instinctively. Then louder, "No! No! No!" And then he was shouting, not at the woman, but at the possibility of what she had said. Forcing himself up on his elbows, finding the strength for that, he kept shouting, "No! No! No!" Mrs. Meyers took him in her arms, holding him, David holding onto her, shouting, until the shouting turned to weeping.

In the night when David woke up, Mrs. Meyers sat in her chair, her head resting on the bed, both her hands on his arm. He thought her very beautiful.

David became stronger. He no longer had to wear a diaper but could wear shorts and a T-shirt. Except for the lacerated palms of his hands, all the sores had scabs now. People brought him gifts of candy, flowers, new shoes, pajamas, and clothes.

David's memory came back slowly, first what happened in the hobo jungle, his whole body stiffening against what he remembered. He tried to black it out, refuse to remember, pushing it back down deep. He closed his eyes, turned on the bed to push his face deep into his pillow, brought up his hands to wrap the pillow around his head. Lying awake in the night, staring up at the ceiling, he told Mrs. Meyers what the three men had done to him, his eyes filling with tears as he spoke.

"Oh, dear God," she said, "oh, dear God." She took his hands in hers and kissed them.

The sheriff came to talk to him. The bodies of two boys had been found in the last two years, one in Nebraska and one in Iowa. The boys had been tortured and murdered, their throats cut. There had been a short article about David in the county paper.

A man from the big hobo jungle east of Gothenburg came to the house to talk to David about what had happened. David didn't know even the first names of the three men who had brutalized him; they hadn't used their names. The visitor asked David to describe their clothes, belts and belt buckles, their knives, teeth, hair, rings, scars, the color of their eyes, the sound of their voices, the color of their blankets, asked him the same questions two and three times, took notes. The man wore a felt hat, a brown suit with vest, a white shirt, and a tie—all shabby. The man's name was Walter W. Simms. He said he was a member of a special committee of gentlemen selected to look into the matter.

"Son, at one time I was a police officer in Chicago. We intend to see this matter out. There must be justice in such cases." He wrote down the Meyerses' address.

One afternoon sitting out on the Meyerses' front porch in the sun looking down at his open, healed hands, David knew that his name was David Thatcher Williams and that he lived in Provo, Utah. His whole life came flooding back to him so that he had to close his eyes and hold his head in his hands against the joy of it.

His dad and Cleon came for him. They'd been searching for him for over a month, going from one hobo jungle to another between Provo and Washington, showing David's picture. Cleon had quit his job in Washington to help search for David. The assistant superintendent at the state hospital, a Mr. Startup, had loaned David's dad his new Buick to drive. His friends at the hospital took his shifts in the laundry so that his dad was kept on the payroll while he was gone.

David cried when he saw his dad. David's dad, his eyes brimming with tears, hugged and kissed David. Cleon shook his hand and then put his arms around him and held him. David's little brother had been born a week before his dad and Cleon came to Gothenburg. David talked to his mom on the phone.

When they left Gothenburg, Mrs. Meyers hugged David and kissed him. Mr. Meyers shook their hands. David's dad thanked Mr. and Mrs. Meyers over and over again for their kindness. David's mom phoned and thanked Mrs. Meyers. The Meyers boys all said good-bye and brought David gifts. Mrs. Meyers had fixed them a big lunch basket for the trip. The family waved him out of sight. All along the road, neighbors stood by their gates to wave.

It was early evening of the second day when they drove into Provo and turned up Third West from Highway 89. Neighbors stopped watering their lawns or left their newspapers and knitting on their chairs to walk down from their porches to wave to David. Bishop Matthews, bishop of the Sixth Ward, and his two counselors were at the house. Some neighbors brought gifts of food or bouquets of flowers. His sisters came running out of the house, all four of his grandparents walking behind them. His uncles and aunts drove up in their old cars, his cousins jumping out to run over to him. Everybody hugged and kissed him and told him how wonderful he looked.

David went into the house to his mom, who sat in the rocking chair holding his baby brother. She stood and, moving the baby to one arm, she kissed David on the lips.

"He's beautiful, Mom."

"Yes," she said, reaching up to touch the red, indented scars on David's face, "he is."

David's mom took his hand in hers, turned it to look at the palm, and then pressed it against her cheek. David began to cry. His mom pulled his head down to her shoulder. She whispered to him and stroked his hair. She told him to sit down in the rocking chair, and she put his baby brother in his arms.

Later David's dad called all the family into the house to join in prayer and thank the Lord for David's safe return. That night his dad came into his room and lay beside David until he fell asleep. His dad did that every night for two weeks. If David sat too long, or started to cry, his mom asked him to help her; he took care of his baby brother a lot, changing his diaper, feeding him a bottle, and taking him for rides in the baby buggy.

David didn't want to go to church, but his mom said he was going. The ward members shook his hand, patted him on the shoulder, told him how good he looked, and said how nice it was to have him back home. Every week David went to Dr. Clark's office to talk to him. Dr. Clark was the family doctor. He was past seventy. He'd had a practice in Provo for over forty years, but still made house calls night or day. Bishop Matthews came by the house to sit and talk to David and had him come to his office on Sundays to talk.

David's friends came to get him to play basketball and softball and go to parties. David's mom made him go. But David wouldn't go on dates or go swimming. He started high school, but he had to drop out because he would suddenly start to cry in class.

David's Uncle Harold, who was a plumber, hired David on his crew to dig trenches for water lines and sewers. He pushed David hard; it was all pick-and-shovel work. David liked the hard work. At night he did his high school lessons. His mom helped him.

The other three men on the digging crew all swore, smoked, and drank. They were all older and couldn't get better jobs. They were all divorced. Hank had been divorced four times. They told David funny stories about their own lives and the lives of other men they'd known. They were full of funny stories. David listened to the stories, but he didn't often laugh.

David's dad brought patients home from the state hospital to share Thanksgiving and Christmas with the family.

Two days after Christmas, David received a letter addressed to him at the Meyerses' and then forwarded, the envelope bent and smudged. David had just gotten back from an ice-skating party and was sitting at the kitchen table with his dad when his mom handed him the letter. David put down his glass of milk. His mom had made a fresh batch of oatmeal-raisin cookies.

Inside the envelope was a clipping from an Iowa newspaper reporting that three men had been found hanged from a big dead cottonwood tree near the railroad tracks a mile west of the town of Grinnell. The men carried no identification. Their hands and feet had not been tied. The picture showed the tree with the three ropes hanging down. The nooses had been cut off. There was no note, just the clipping.

David handed the clipping to his dad, who read it.

"God rest their souls," his dad said. "God rest their miserable, damned souls."

"What is it, Frank?"

David's dad handed the clipping to his mom. She read the clipping and put it down on the table.

"What a terrible thing," she said. "What a terrible, terrible thing."

David looked at his mom and dad. He didn't say anything. He took another oatmeal-raisin cookie from the plate, ate it, drank some milk, and took another cookie.

David started back to Provo High in January. He didn't want to go to gym and have to shower, but his dad said he didn't know why not.

BUCKEYE THE ELDER

Brady Udall

THINGS I LEARNED ABOUT BUCKEYE a few minutes before he broke my collarbone: he is twenty-five years old, in love with my older sister, a native of Wisconsin and therefore a Badger. "Not really a Buckeye at all," he explained, sitting in my father's recliner and paging through a book about UFOs and other unsolved mysteries. "But I keep the name for respect of the man who gave it to me, my father and the most loyal alumnus Ohio State ever produced."

Buckeye had stopped by earlier this afternoon to visit my sister, Simone, whom he had been seeing over the past week or so. Though Simone had yammered all about him over the dinner table, it was the first time I'd actually met him. When he arrived, Simone wasn't back from her class at the beauty college and I was the only one in the house. Buckeye came inside for a few minutes and talked to me like I was someone he'd known since childhood. He showed me the old black-and-white photos of his parents, a gold tooth he found on the floor of a bar in Detroit, a ticket stub autographed by Marty Robbins. Among other things, we talked about his passion for rugby, and he invited me out to the front yard for a few lessons on rules and technique. Everything went fine until tackling came up. He positioned himself in front of me and instructed me to try to get around him and he would demonstrate the proper way to wrap up the ball player and drag him down. I did what I was told and ended up with two-hundred-plus pounds' worth of Buckeye driving my shoulder into the hard dirt. We both heard the snap, clear as you please.

"Was that you?" Buckeye said, already picking me up and setting me on my feet. My left shoulder sagged and I couldn't move my arm but there wasn't an alarming amount of pain. Buckeye helped me to the porch and brought out the phone so I could call my mother, who is on her way over right now to pick me up and take me to the hospital.

I'm sitting in one of the porch rocking chairs and Buckeye is standing next to me, nervously shifting his feet. He is the picture of guilt and worry; he puts his face in his hands, paces up and down the steps, comes back over to inspect my shoulder for the dozenth time. There is a considerable lump where the fractured bone is pushing up against the skin.

A grim-faced Buckeye says, "Snapped in two, not a doubt in this world."

He puts his face right into mine as if he's trying to see something behind my eyes. "You aren't in shock are you?" he says. "You don't want an ambulance?"

"I'm okay," I say. Other than being a little light-headed, I feel pretty good. There is something gratifying about having a serious injury and no serious pain to go with it. More than anything, I'm worried about Buckeye, who is acting like he's just committed murder. He's asked me twice now if I wouldn't just let him swing me over his shoulders and run me over to the hospital himself.

"Where is my self-control?" he questions the rain gutter. "Why can't I get a hold of my situations?' He turns to me and says, "There's no excuses, none, but I'm used to tackling guys three times your size, God forgive me. I didn't think you'd go down that easy."

Buckeye has a point. I am almost as tall as he is but am at least sixty pounds lighter. All I really feel right now is embarrassment for going down so easy. I tell him that it was nobody's fault, that my parents are generally reasonable people, and that my sister will probably like him all that much more.

Buckeye doesn't look at all comforted. He keeps up his pacing. He thinks aloud with his chin in his chest, mumbling into the collar of his shirt as if there is someone down there listening. He rubs his head with his big knobby hands and gives himself a good tongue-lashing. There is an ungainly energy to the way he moves. He is thick in some places, thin in others, and has joints like those on a backhoe. He's barrel-chested, has elongated piano player's fingers and is missing a good portion of his left ear, which was ground off by the cleat of a stampeding

Polynesian at the Midwest Rugby Invitationals. I can't explain this, but I'm feeling quite pleased that Buckeye has broken my shoulder.

When my mother pulls up in her new Lincoln, Buckeye picks me up and the chair I'm in. With long, smooth strides he delivers me to the car, all the time saying some sort of prayer, asking the Lord to bless me, heal me, and help me forgive. One of the more important things that Buckeye didn't tell me about himself that first day was that he is a newly baptized Mormon. I've found out this is the only reason my parents ever let him within rock-throwing distance of my sister. As far as my parents are concerned, solid Baptists that they are, either you're with Jesus or you're against him. I guess they figured that Buckeye, as close as he might be to the dividing line, is on the right side.

In the week that has passed since the accident, Buckeye has turned our house into a carnival. The night we came home from the hospital, me straight-backed and awkward in my brace and Buckeye still asking forgiveness every once in a while, we had a celebration—in honor of who or what I still can't be sure. We ordered pizza and my folks, who almost never drink, made banana daiquiris while Simone held hands with Buckeye and sipped ginger ale. Later, my daiquiri-inspired father, once a 163-pound district champion in high school, coaxed Buckeye into a wrestling match in the front room. While my sister squealed and my mother screeched about hospital bills and further injury, Buckeye wore a big easy grin and let my father pin him solidly on our mint-green carpet.

I suppose there were two things going on: we were officially sanctioning Buckeye's relationship with Simone and at the same time commemorating my fractured clavicle, the first manly injury I've ever suffered. Despite and possibly because of the aspirations of my sports-mad father, I am the type of son who gets straight A's and likes to sit in his room and make models of spaceships. My father dreamed I would play for the Celtics one day. Right now, having just finished my sophomore year in high school, my only aspiration is to write a best-selling fantasy novel.

My sister goes to beauty school, which is a huge disappointment to my pediatrician mother. Simone can't bear to tell people that my father distills sewer water for a living. Even though I love them, I sincerely believe my parents to be narrow-minded religious fanatics, and as for Simone, I think beauty school might be an intellectual stretch. As far as I can tell, our family is nothing more than a bunch of people living in the same house who are disappointed in each other.

But we all love Buckeye. He's the only thing we agree on. The fact that Simone and my parents would go for someone like him is surprising when you consider the coarse look he has about him, the kind of look you see on people in bus stations and in the backs of fruit trucks. Maybe it's his fine set of teeth that salvages him from looking like an out-and-out redneck.

Tonight Buckeye is taking me on a drive. Since we first met, Buckeye has spent more time with me than he has with Simone. My parents think this is a good idea; I don't have many friends and they think he will have a positive effect on their agnostic, asocial son. We are in his rust-cratered vehicle that might have been an Oldsmobile at one time. Buckeye has just finished a day's work as a pantyhose salesman and smells like the perfume of the women he talks to on porches and doorsteps. He sells revolutionary no-run stockings that carry a lifetime guarantee. He's got stacks of them in the back seat. At eighteen dollars a pair, he assured these women, they are certainly a bargain. He is happy and loose and driving all over the road. He has just brought me up to date on his teenage years, his father's death, the thirteen states he's lived in and the twenty-two jobs he's held since then.

"Got it all up here," he says, tapping his forehead. "Don't let a day slide by without detailed documentation." Over the past few days I've noticed Buckeye has a way of speaking that makes people pause. One minute he sounds like a West Texas oil grunt, the next like a semi-educated Midwesterner. Buckeye is a constant surprise.

"Why move around so much?" I wonder. "And why come to Texas?"

He says, "I just move, no reason that I can think of. For one thing, I'm here looking for my older brother Bud. He loves the Cowboys and fine women. He could very well be in the vicinity."

"How'd your father die?" I say.

"His heart attacked him. Then his liver committed suicide and the rest of his organs just gave up after that. Too much drinking. That's when I left Wisconsin for good."

We are passing smelters and gas stations and trailers that sit back off the road. This is a part of Tyler I've never seen before. He pulls the old car into the parking lot of a huge wooden structure with a sign that says THE RANCH in big matchstick letters. The sun is just going down but the place is lit up like Las Vegas. There is a fleet of dirty pickups overrunning the parking lot.

We find a space in the back and Buckeye leads me through a loading dock and into the kitchen, where a trio of Hispanic ladies is doing dishes. He stops and chatters at them in a mixture of bad Spanish and hand gestures. "Come on," he says to me. "I'm going to show you the man I once was."

We go out into the main part, which is as big as a ballroom. There are two round bars out in the middle of it and a few raised platforms where some half-dressed women are dancing. Chairs and tables are scattered all along the edges. The music is so loud I can feel it bouncing off my chest. Buckeye nods and wags his finger and smiles at everybody we pass and they respond like old friends. Buckeye, who's been in Tyler less than a month, does this everywhere we go and if you didn't know any better you'd think he was acquainted with every citizen in town.

We find an empty table against the wall right next to one of the dancers. She has on lacy black panties and a cutoff T-shirt that is barely sufficient to hold in all her equipment. Buckeye politely says hello, but she doesn't even look our way.

This is the first bar I've ever been in and I like the feel of it. Buckeye orders Cokes and buffalo wings for us both and surveys the place, once in a while raising a hand to acknowledge someone he sees. Even though I've lived in Texas since I was born, I've never seen so many oversized belt buckles in one place.

"This is the first time I've been back here since my baptism," he says. "I used to spend most of my nonworking hours in this barn."

While he has told me about a lot of things, he's never said anything about his conversion. The only reason I even know about it is that I overheard my parents discussing Buckeye's worthiness to date my sister.

"Why did you get baptized?" I say.

Buckeye squints through the smoke and his voice takes on an unusual amount of gravity. "This used to be me, sitting right here and drinking till my teeth fell out. I was one of these people—not good, not bad, sincerely trying to make things as easy as possible. A place like this draws you in, pulls at you."

I watch the girl in the panties gyrating above us and I think I can see what he's getting at.

He continues: "But this ain't all there is. Simply is not. There's more to it than this. You've got to figure out what's right and what's wrong and then you've got to make a stand. Most people don't want to put out the effort. I'm telling you, I know it's not easy. Goodness has a call that's hard to hear."

I nod, not to indicate that I understand what he's saying, but as a signal for him to keep going. Even though I've had my fair share of experience with them, I've never understood religious people.

"Do you know what life's about? The *why* of the whole thing?" Buckeye asks.

"No more than anybody else," I say.

"Do you think you'll ever know?"

"Maybe someday."

Buckeye holds up a half-eaten chicken wing for emphasis. "Exactly," he says through a full mouth. "I could scratch my balls forever if I had the time." He finishes off the rest of his chicken and shrugs. "To know, you have to do. You have to get out there and take action, put your beliefs to the test. Sitting around on your duff will get you nothing better than a case of the hemorrhoids."

"If you're such a believer, why don't you go around like my parents do, spouting scripture and all that?" I reason that if I just keep asking questions I will eventually get Buckeye figured out.

"For one thing," Buckeye says flatly, "and you don't need to go telling this to anybody else, but I'm not much of a reader."

I raise my eyebrows.

"Look here," he says, taking the menu from between the ketchup and sugar bottles. He points at something on it and says, "This is 'a,' this is a 't,' and here's a 'g.' This says 'hamburger'—I know that one. Oh, and this is 'beer.' I learned that early on." He looks up at me. "Nope, I can't read, not really. I never stayed put long enough to get an education. But I'm smart enough to fool anybody."

If this were a movie and not real life I would feel terrible for Buckeye—maybe I would vow to teach him to read, give him self-worth, help him become a complete human being. For the climax he would win the national spelling bee or something. But this is reality and as I look across the table at Buckeye, I can see his illiteracy doesn't bother him a bit. In fact, he looks rather pleased with himself.

"Like I've been telling you, it's not the reading, it's not the saying. It's only the doing I'm interested in. Do it, do it, do it," Buckeye says, hammering each "do it" into the table with his Coke bottle. He leans into his chair, a wide grin overtaking his face. "But sometimes it certainly is nice to kick back and listen to the music."

We sit there quiet for awhile, me doing my best not to stare at the dancer and Buckeye with his head back and eyes closed, sniffing the air with the deep concentration of a wine judge. A pretty woman in jeans and a flannel shirt comes up behind Buckeye and asks him to dance. There are only a few couples out on the floor. Most everybody else is sitting at their tables, drinking and yelling at each other over the music.

"Thanks but no thanks," Buckeye says.

"What about you?" she says.

I panic. My face gets hot and I begin to fidget. "No, no," I say. "No, thank you."

The woman seems amused by us and our Cokes. She takes a long look at both of us with her hands on the back of an empty chair.

"Go ahead," Buckeye says. "I'll hold down the fort."

I shake my head and look down into my lap. "That's quite all right," I say. I don't know how to dance and the brace I'm wearing makes me look like I've got arthritis.

Buckeye sighs, smiles, gets up and leads the woman out onto the floor. She puts her head on his chest and I watch them drift away, swaying to the beat of a song about good love gone bad.

When the song is over Buckeye comes back with a flushed face and a look of exasperation. He says, "You see what I mean? That girl wanted things and for me to do them to her. She wanted these things done as soon as possible. She asked me if I didn't want to load her bases." He plops down in his chair and drains his Coke with one huge swallow. It doesn't even make him blink.

On our way home he pulls into the deserted front of a drive-in movie theater and floors the accelerator, yanking the steering wheel all the way over to the left and holding it there. He yells, "Carnival ride!" and the car goes round and round, pinning me to the passenger door, spitting up geysers of dust and creaking and groaning as if it might fly into pieces at any second. When he finally throws on the brakes, we sit there, the great cloud of dust we made settling down on the car, making ticking noises on the roof. The world continues to hurtle around me and I can feel my stomach throbbing like a heart.

Buckeye looks over at me, his head swaying back and forth a little, and says, "Now doesn't that make you feel like you've had too much to drink?"

Simone and I are on the roof. It's somewhere around midnight and there are bats zooming around our heads. We can hear the *swish* as they pass. I have only a pair of shorts on and Simone is wearing an oversized T-shirt. The warm grainy tar paper holds us against the steep incline of the roof like Velcro. Old pipes have forced us out here. Right now these pipes, the ones that run through the north walls of our turn-of-the-century house, are engaged in their semiannual vibrational moaning. According to the plumber, this condition has to do with drastic changes in temperature; either we could pay thousands of dollars to have the pipes replaced or we could put up with a little annoying moaning once in awhile.

With my sister's windows closed it sounds like someone crying in the hallway at the top of the stairs. My parents, with extra years of practice under their belts, have learned to sleep through it.

Simone and I are actually engaged in something that resembles conversation. Naturally, we are talking about Buckeye. If Buckeye has done nothing else, he has given us something to talk about.

For the first time in her life Simone seems to be seriously in love. She's had boyfriends before, but Simone is the type of girl who will break up with a guy because she doesn't like the way his clothes match. She's known Buckeye for all of three weeks and is already talking about names for their children. All of this without anything close to sexual contact. "Do you think he really likes me?"

This is a question I've been asked before. "Difficult to say," I tell her. In my young life I've learned the advantages of ambivalence.

Actually, I've asked Buckeye directly how he felt for my sister and this is the response I got: "I have feelings for her, feelings that could make an Eskimo sweat, but as far as feelings go, these simply aren't the right kind. There's a control problem I'm worried about."

"He truly loves the Lord," Simone says into the night. My sister, who wouldn't know a Bible from the menu at Denny's, thinks this is beautiful.

Over the past couple of weeks I've begun to see the struggle that is going on with Buckeye, in which the Lord is surely involved. Buckeye never says anything about it, never lets on, but it's there. It's a battle that pits Buckeye the Badger against Buckeye the Mormon. Buckeye told me that in his old life as the Badger he never stole anything, never lied without first making sure he didn't have a choice, got drunk once in a while, fought some, cussed quite a bit and had only the women that wanted him. Now, as a Mormon, there is a whole list of things he has to avoid including coffee, tea, sex, tobacco, swearing, and as Buckeye puts it, "anything else unbecoming that smacks of the natural man."

To increase his strength and defenses, Buckeye has taken to denying himself, testing his willpower in various ways. I've seen him go without food for two full days. While he watches TV he holds his breath for as long as he can, doesn't use the bathroom until he's within seconds of making a mess. As part of his rugby training, he bought an old tractor tire, filled it with rocks, made a rope harness for it and every morning drags it through the streets from his neighborhood to ours, which is at least three miles. When he comes inside he is covered with sweat but will not accept liquid of any kind. Before taking a shower he goes out onto the driveway and does a hundred pushups on his knuckles.

Since they've met, Buckeye has not so much as touched my sister except for some innocent hand-holding. Considering that he practically lives at our house and already seems like a brother-in-law, I find this a little weird. Buckeye and his non-contact love is making Simone deranged and I must say I'm enjoying it. The funny things is, I think it's having the same effect on him. There are times when Buckeye, once perpetually casual as blue jeans, cannot stay in one spot for more than a few seconds. He moves around like someone worried about being picked off by a sniper. He will become suddenly emotional, worse than certain menstruating women I'm related to: pissed off one minute, joyful the next. All of this is not lost on Buckeye. In his calmer and more rational moments he has come to theorize that a bum gland somewhere in his brain is responsible.

I sit back and listen to the pipes moaning like mating animals behind the walls. Hummingbird Lane, the street I've lived on my entire life, stretches off both ways into darkness. The clouds are low and the lights of the city reflect off them, giving everything a green, murky glow. Next to me my sister is chatting with herself, talking about the intrigues of beauty school, some of the inane deeds of my parents, her feeling and plans for Buckeye.

"Do you think I should get baptized?" she says. "Do you think he'd want me to?"

I snort.

"What?" she says. "Just because you're an atheist or something."

"I'm not an atheist," I tell her. "I'm just not looking for any more burdens than I already have."

The next morning, on Sunday, Buckeye comes to our house a newly ordained elder. I come upstairs just in time to hear him explain to Simone and my parents that he has been endowed with the power to baptize, to preach the gospel, to lay on the administering of hands, to heal. It's the first time I've seen him in his Sunday clothes: striped shirt, blaring polyester tie and shoes that glitter so brightly you'd think they'd been shined by a Marine. He's wearing some kind of potent cologne that makes my eyes tear up if I get too close. Damn me if the phrase doesn't apply: Buckeye looks born again. As if he'd just been pulled from the womb and scrubbed a glowing pink.

"Gosh dang," Buckeye says, "do I feel nice."

I can handle Buckeye the Badger and Buckeye the Mormon, but Buckeye the Elder? When I think of elders I imagine bent, bearded men who are old enough to have the right to speak mysterious nonsense.

I have to admit, however, that he looks almost holy. He's on a high, he's ready to raise the dead. He puts up his dukes and performs some intricate Muhammad Ali footwork—something he does when he's feeling particularly successful. We all watch him in wonder. My parents, just back from prayer meeting themselves, look particularly awed.

After lunch, once Buckeye has left, we settle down for our "Sabbath family conversation." Usually it's not so much a conversation as it is an excuse for us to yell at each other in a constructive format. As always, my father calls the meeting to order and then my mother, who is a diabetic, begins by sighing and apologizing for the mess the house has been in for the past few weeks; her insulin intake has been adjusted and she hasn't been feeling well. This is just her way of blaming us for not helping out more. Simone breaks in and tries to defend herself by reminding everyone she's done the dishes twice this week, my father snaps at her for not letting my mother finish, and things take their natural course from there. Simone whines, my mother rubs her temples, my father asks the Lord why we can't be a happy Christian family, and I smirk and finish off my pistachio ice cream. Whenever Buckeye is not around, it seems, we go right back to normal.

No only does Buckeye keep our household happy and lighthearted with his presence, but he has also avoided any religious confrontation with my folks. Buckeye is not naturally religious like my parents, and he doesn't say much at all, just goes about his business, quietly believing what the folks at the Mormon church teach him. This doesn't keep Mom and Dad from loving him more than anybody. I hope it doesn't sound too bitter of me to say he's the son they never had. Buckeye goes fishing with my father (I'm squeamish about putting live things on hooks) and is currently educating my mother on how to grow a successful vegetable garden. They believe a boy as well mannered and decent as Buckeye could not be fooled by "those Mormons" for long. They are just biding their time until Buckeye comes to his spiritual senses. Then they will dazzle him with the special brand of truth found only in the Holton Hills Reformed Baptist Church, the church where they were not only saved, but where they met and eventually got married. They've tried to get Pastor Wild and Buckeye in the house at the same time but so far it hasn't worked out. Up until now, though, I would have to say that Buckeye has done most of the dazzling.

One of my biggest worries is that I will be sterile. I don't know why I think about this; I am young and have never come close to having a girl. About a year ago I was perusing the public library and found a book all about sterility and the affliction it causes in people's lives. The book said that for some people, it is a tragedy that transcends all others. In what seems to be some sort of fateful coincidence I went home and turned on the TV and there was Phil Donahue discussing this very topic with four very downtrodden-looking men and their unfulfilled wives. I didn't sleep that night and I worried about it for weeks. I even thought about secretly going to the doctor and having myself checked. I guess I believe my life has been just a little too tragedy free for my own comfort.

This is what I'm thinking about with a rifle in my hands and Buckeye at my side. We are in a swamp looking for something to shoot. One of the big attractions of the Mormon church for Buckeye was that they don't have any outright prohibitions against shooting things. Buckeye has two rifles and a handgun he keeps under the front seat of his Oldsmobile. I've got a .22 (something larger might aggravate my shoulder) and Buckeye is toting some kind of high-caliber hunting rifle that he says could take the head off a rhino. My parents took Simone to a fashion show in Dallas, so today it's just me and Buckeye, out for a little manly fun.

I'm not sure, but it doesn't seem as if we're actually hunting anything special. The afternoon is sticky full of bugs, and the chirping of birds tumbles down out of old moss-laden trees. A few squirrels whiz by and a thick black snake crosses our path, but Buckeye doesn't even notice. I guess if something worthwhile comes along, we'll shoot it.

I tell Buckeye about my sterility worries. He and I share secrets. I suppose this is something women do all the time, but I've never tried it with any of the few friends I have. This sterility thing is my last big one and probably the one that embarrasses me the most. When I get through the entire explanation Buckeye looks at me twice and laughs.

"You've never popped your cork with a girl?" he says. The expression on his face would lead me to believe that he finds this idea pretty incredible. I am really embarrassed now. I walk faster, tripping through the underbrush so Buckeye can't see all the blood rushing into my face. Buckeye picks up his pace and stays right with me. He says, "Being sterile would have been a blessing for me at your age. I used to lay pipe all over the place, and while nobody can be sure, there's a good chance I'm somebody's papa."

I stop and look at him. With Buckeye, it's more and more secrets all the time. A few days ago he told me that on a few nights of the year he can see the ghost of his mother.

"What do you mean, 'nobody can be sure?' " I say.

"With the kind of girls I used to do things with, nothing was certain. The only way you could get even a vague idea was to wait and see what color the kid came out to be."

There's a good chance Buckeye's the father of children he doesn't even know and I've got baseless worries about being sterile. Buckeye points his gun at a crow passing overhead. He follows it across the sky and says, "Don't get upset about that anyway. This is the modern world. You could have the most worthless sperm on record and there'd be a way to get around it. They've got drugs and lasers that can do just about anything. Like I say, a guy your age should only have worries about getting his cork popped. Your problem is you read too much."

I must have a confused look on my face because Buckeye stops so he can explain himself. With a blunt finger he diagrams the path of his argument on my chest. "Now there's having fun when you're young and aren't supposed to know better, and then there's the time when you've got to come to terms with things, line your ducks up in a row. You've got to have sins before there's repentance. I should know about that. Get it all out of you now. You're holding back for no good reason I can see. Some people hold it in until they're middle-aged and then explode. And frankly, I believe there's nothing quite as ugly as that."

We clamber through the brush for a while, me trying to reason through what I've just heard and Buckeye whistling bluegrass tunes and aiming at trees. I haven't seen him this relaxed in a long time. We come into a clearing where an old car sits on its axles in a patch of undergrowth. Remarkably, all its windows are still intact and we simply can't resist the temptation to fill the thing full of holes. We're blazing away at that sorry car, filled with the macho euphoria that comes with making loud noises and destroying things, when a Ford pickup barrels into the clearing on a dirt road just to the south of us. A skinny old geezer with a grease-caked hat pulled down over his eyes jumps out.

To get where we are, we had to crawl through a number of barbed wire fences and there is not a lot of doubt we're on somebody's land. The way the old man is walking toward us, holding his rifle out in front of him, would suggest that he is that somebody, and he's not happy that we're on his property. "You sons of bitches," he growls once he's within earshot.

"How do you do," Buckeye says back.

The man stops about twenty feet away from us, puts the gun up to his shoulder and points it first at Buckeye, then at me. I have never been on the business end of a firearm before and the experience is definitely edifying. You get weak in the knees and take account of all the deeds of your life.

"This is it," the man says. He's so mad he's shaking. My attention never wavers from the end of that gun.

"Is there some problem we don't know about?" Buckeye says, still holding his gun in the crook of his arm. I have already dropped my weapon and am debating on whether or not to put my hands up.

"You damn shits!" the man nearly screeches. It's obvious he doesn't like the tone of Buckeye's voice. I wish Buckeye would notice this also.

"You come in here and wreck my property and shoot up my things and then give me this polite talk. I'm either going to take you to jail right now or shoot you where you stand and throw you in the river. I'm trying to decide."

This guy appears absolutely serious. He is weathered and bent and has a face full of scars; he looks capable of a list of things worse than murder. I begin to compose what I know will be a short and futile speech, something about the merits of mercy, but before I can deliver it Buckeye sighs and points his rifle at the old man.

"This is the perfect example of what my Uncle Lester Lewis, re-tired lieutenant colonel, likes to call 'mutually assured destruction.' He loves the idea. We can both stay or we can both go. As for myself, this is as good a time as any. I'm in the process of putting things right with my Maker. What about you?"

I watch the fire go out of the old man's eyes and his face get slack and pasty. He keeps his gun up but doesn't answer.

"Shall we put down our guns or stand here all day?" Buckeye says happily.

The man slowly backs up, keeping his gun trained on Buckeye. By the time he makes it back to his pickup, Buckeye has already lowered his gun. "I'm calling the police right now!" the man yells, his voice cracking into a whole range of different octaves. "They're going to put you shits away for good!"

Buckeye swings his gun up and shoots once over the man's head. As the pickup scrambles away over gravel and clumps of weeds, Buckeye shoots three or four times into the dirt behind it, sending up small *poofs* of dust. We watch the truck disappear into the trees and I work on getting my lungs functional again. Buckeye retrieves my gun and hands it to me. "We better get," he says.

We thrash though the trees and underbrush until we find the car. Buckeye drives the thing like he's playing a video game, flipping the gearshift and spinning the steering wheel. He works the gas and brake pedals with both feet and shouts at the narrow dirt road when it doesn't curve the way he expects. We skid off the road once in awhile, ending the life of a young tree, maybe, or putting a wheel into a ditch, but Buckeye never lets up. By the time we make it back to the highway we hear sirens.

"I guess that old cooter wasn't pulling our short and curlies," Buckeye says. He is clearly enjoying all this—his eyes are bright and a little frenzied. I have my head out the window in case I vomit.

Once we get back to civilization Buckeye slows down and we meander along like we're out to buy a carton of milk at the grocery store. The sirens have faded away and I don't even have a theory as to where we might be until Buckeye takes a shortcut between two warehouses and we end up in the parking lot of The Ranch. The place is deserted except for a rusty VW bug.

"Never been here this early in the day, but it's got to be open," Buckeye says, still panting. I shrug, not yet feeling capable of forming words. It's three in the afternoon.

"When's the last time you had a nice cold beer?" Buckeye says a little wistfully.

"Never, really," I admit after a few seconds. What I don't admit to is that I've never even tasted any form of liquor in all my life. My parents have banned Simone and me from drinking alcohol until we reach the legal drinking age. Then, they say, we can decide for ourselves. Unlike Simone, I've never felt the need to defy my parents on this account. When I get together with my few friends we usually eat pizza and play Dungeons and Dragons. No one has ever suggested something like beer. Since I've known Buckeye, I've discovered what a sorry excuse for a teenager I am.

Buckeye shakes his head and whistles in disbelief. I guess we surprise each other. "Then let's go get you a beer," he says. "You're thirsty, aren't you? I'll settle for a Coke."

The front doors, big wooden affairs that swing both ways, are locked with a padlock and chain. Buckeye smiles at me and knocks on one of the doors. "There's got to be somebody in there. I know some of the people that work here. They'll get us set up."

Buckeye knocks for a while longer but doesn't get any results. He peers through a window, goes back to the doors and pounds on them with both fists, producing a hollow booming noise that sounds like cannons from a distance. He kicks at the door and punches it a few times, leaving bright red circle-shaped scrapes on the tops of his knuckles.

"What is this?" he yells. "What is this? Hey!"

He throws his shoulder into the place where the doors meet. The doors buckle inward, making a metallic crunching noise, but the chain doesn't give. I try to tell Buckeye that I'm really not that thirsty, but he doesn't hear me. He hurls his body into the doors again, then stalks around and picks up a three-foot-high wooden cowboy next to the cement path that leads to the entrance. This squat, goofy-looking guy was carved out of a single block of wood and holds up a sign that says, "Come on in!" Buckeye emits a tearing groan and pitches it underhand against the door and succeeds only in breaking the cowboy's handlebar mustache. Buckeye has a kind of possessed look on his face, his eyes vacant, the cords in his neck taut like ropes. He picks the cowboy up again, readies himself for another throw, then drops it at his feet. He stares at me for a few seconds, his features falling into a vaguely pained expression, and sits down on the top step. He sets the cowboy upright and his hands tremble as he fiddles with the mustache, trying to make the broken part stay. He is red all over and sweating.

"I guess I'll have to owe you that beer," he says.

• • •

Simone, my father and I are sitting around the dinner table and staring at the food on our plates. We're all distraught; we poke at our enchiladas and don't look at each other. The past forty-eight hours have been rough on us: first, my mother's diabetic episode, and now Buckeye has disappeared.

My mother is upstairs, resting. The doctors told her not to get out of bed for a week. Since yesterday morning old ladies from the church have been bringing over food, flowers and get-well cards in waves. In the kitchen we have casseroles stacked into pyramids.

As for Buckeye, nobody has seen him in two days. He hasn't called or answered his phone. My father has just returned from the boarding house where Buckeye rents a room and the owner told him that she hadn't seen Buckeye either, but it was against her policy to let strangers look in the rooms.

"One more day and we'll have to call the police," my father says. He's made this exact statement at least three times now.

Simone, distressed as she is, cannot get any food in her mouth. She looks down at the food on her plate as if it's something she can't fully comprehend. She gets a good forkful of enchiladas halfway to her mouth before she loses incentive and drops the fork back onto her plate. I think it's the first time in her twenty-one years that she's had to deal with real-life problems more serious than the loss of a contact lens.

It all started three days ago, one day after the incident with the guns. I spent that entire morning nursing an irrational fear that somehow the police were going to track us down and there would be a patrol car pulling up outside the house any minute. I was the only one home except for my mother, who had taken the day off sick from work and was sleeping upstairs.

I holed myself up in my basement bedroom to watch TV and read my books. At about four o'clock I heard a knock at the front door and nearly passed out from fright. I had read in magazines what happens in prisons to young clean people like me. I was sure that trespassing and destruction of property, not to mention shooting in the general direction of the owner, would get Buckeye and me some serious time in the pen.

The knocking came again and then someone opened the front

door. I pictured a police officer coming in our house with his pistol drawn. I turned off the light in my room, hid myself in the closet, and listened to the footsteps upstairs. It took me only a few seconds to realize the heavy shuffling gait of Buckeye.

Feeling relieved and a little ridiculous, I ran upstairs to find Buckeye going down the hall toward my parents' room.

"Hey, bubba," he said when he saw me. "Nobody answered the door so I let myself in. Simone told me your mother's sick. I've got something for her." He held up a mason jar filled with a dark-green substance.

"She's just tired," I said. "What is that?"

"It's got vitamins and minerals," he said. "Best thing in the world for sick and tired people. My grandpop taught me how to make it. All natural, no artificial flavors or colors although it could probably use some. It smells like what you might find in a baby's diaper and doesn't taste much better."

"Mom's sleeping," I said. "She told me not to wake her up unless there was an emergency."

"How long's she been asleep?" Buckeye said.

"Pretty much the whole day," I told him.

Buckeye looked at his watch. "That's not good. She needs to have something to eat. Nutrients and things."

I shrugged and Buckeye shrugged back. He looked worried and a little run-down himself. His hair flopped aimlessly around on his head. He rubbed the jar in his hands like it was a magic lamp.

"You could leave it and I'll give it to her. Or you can wait until she wakes up. Simone will be home pretty soon."

Buckeye looked at me and weighed his options. Then he turned on his heels, walked right up to my parents' bedroom door and rapped on it firmly. I deserted the hallway for the kitchen, not wanting to be implicated in this in any way. I was there only a few seconds when Buckeye appeared, short of breath and a peaked look on his face.

"Something's wrong," he said. "Your mother."

My mother was lying still on the bed, her eyes open, unblinking, staring at nothing. Her skin was pale and glossy and her swollen tongue was hanging out of her mouth and covered with white splotches. I stood in the doorway while Buckeye telephoned an ambulance. "Mama?" I called from where I was standing. For some reason I couldn't make myself go any closer.

I walked out into the front yard and nearly fell on my face.

Everything went black for a moment. I thought I'd gone blind. When my sight came back the world looked so sharp and real it hurt. I picked up a rock from the flower planter and chucked it at the Conleys' big bay window across the street. I guess I figured that if my mother was dead, no one could blame me for doing something like that. I had always felt a special distaste for Mr. Conley and his fat sweating wife. I missed the window and the rock made a hollow thump on the fiberglass siding of the house. I cursed my uncoordinated body. If I had played Little League like my father had wanted all those years ago, that window would have been history.

I reeled around in the front yard until my father and the ambulance showed up. My mind didn't want to approach the idea that my mother might be lying deceased in her bed, so I didn't go near the house to find out. I hung out in the corner of the yard and swung dangerously back and forth in the lilac bushes. I watched the ambulance pull up and the paramedics run into my house followed a few minutes later by my father, who didn't even look my way. Neighbors were beginning to appear. I noticed their bald and liver-spotted heads poking out of windows and screen doors.

After a little while my father came out and found me sitting in the gardenias. He told me that my mother was not dead, but that she had had a severe diabetic reaction. "Too much insulin, not enough food," he said, wiping his eyes. "Why doesn't she take care of herself?"

I'd seen my mother have minor reactions, when she would get numb all over and forget what her name was and we'd have to make her eat candy or drink soda until she became better, but nothing like this. My father put his hand on my back and guided me inside where the paramedics were strapping her onto a stretcher. She didn't look any better than before.

"She's not dead," I said. I was honestly having trouble believing my father. I thought he might be trying to pull a fast one on me, saving me from immediate grief and shock. To me, my mother looked as dead as anything I'd ever seen, as dead as my aunt Sally in her coffin a few years ago, dense and filmy, like a figure carved from wax.

My father looked at me, his eyes moist and drawn, and shook his head. "She's serious, Lord help her, but she'll make it," he said. "I'm going to the hospital with her. I'll call you when I get there. Go and pray for her. That's what she needs from you."

I watched them load her into the ambulance and then went upstairs to pray. I had never really prayed in all my life, though I'd mouthed the words in Sunday school. But my father said that was what my mother needed, and helpless and lost as I felt, I couldn't come up with anything better to do.

I found Buckeye in my sister's room kneeling at the side of the bed. My first irrational thought was that he might be doing something questionable in there, looking through her underwear, etc., but then he started speaking and there was no doubt that I was listening to a prayer. He had his face pushed into his hands but his voice came at me as if he were talking to me through a pipe. I can't remember a word he said, only that he pleaded for my mother's life and health in a way that made it impossible for me to move away from the door and leave him to his privacy. I forgot myself completely and stood dumbly above the stairs, my hand resting on the doorknob.

Buckeye rocked on his knees and talked to the Lord. If it is possible to be humble and demanding at the same time, Buckeye was pulling it off: he dug the heels of his hands into his forehead and called on the Almighty in a near shout. He asked questions and seemed to get answers. He pleaded for mercy. He chattered on for minutes, lost in something that seemed to range from elation to despair. I have never heard anything like that, never felt that way before. Light was going up and down my spine and hitting the backs of my eyes. I don't think it's stretching it to say that for a few moments, I was genuinely certain that God, who or whatever He may be, was in that room. Despite myself, I had to peek around the door to make sure there was really nobody in there except Buckeye.

After Buckeye finished, I stumbled into my parents' room and sat on their bed. I put my hand on the place where my mother's body had made an indentation in the sheets and picked the hairs off her pillow. Buckeye's prayer had been enough; I didn't think I could add much more. I sat there and mumbled aloud to no one in particular that I backed up everything Buckeye had said, one hundred percent.

We went to the hospital and after an eternity of reading women's magazines and listening to Simone's sobbing, a doctor came out and told us that it looked like my mother would be fine, that we were lucky we found her when we did because if we had let her sleep another half-hour she certainly wouldn't have made it. Simone began to sob even louder and I looked at Buckeye, but he didn't react to what the doctor had said. He slumped in his chair and looked terribly tired. Relief sucked everything out of me and left me so weak that I couldn't help but let loose a few stray tears myself.

While my father filled out insurance forms, Buckeye mumbled something about needing to get some sleep. He gave Simone a kiss on the forehead and patted my father and me on the back and wandered away into the dark halls of the hospital. That was the last any of us saw of him.

My mother's nearly buying the farm and the disappearance of Buckeye, the family hero, has thrown us all into a state. I poke at a mound of Jell-O with my fork and say, "I bet he's just had a good run of luck selling pantyhose. By now he's probably selling them to squaws in Oklahoma." I don't really know why I say things like this. I guess it's because I'm the baby of the family, a teenager, and making flippant, smart-ass remarks is part of my job.

My father shakes his head in resigned paternal disappointment and Simone bares her teeth and throws me a look of such hate that I'm unable to make another comment. My father asks me why I don't go to my room and do something worthwhile. I decide to take his advice. I thump down the stairs, turn up my stereo as loud as it will go, lie down on my bed and stare at the ceiling. Before I go to sleep I imagine sending words to heaven, having the clouds open up before me, revealing a light so brilliant I can't make out what's inside.

I'm awakened by a sound like a manhole cover being slid from its place. It's dark in my room, the music is off, and someone has put a blanket over me. Most likely my father, who occasionally acts quite motherly when my mother is not able to. There is a scrape and a thud and I twist around to see Buckeye stuffed into the small window well on the other side of the room, looking at me through the glass.

He has pushed away the wrought-iron gate that covers the well and is squatting in the dead leaves and spider webs that cover the bottom of it. Buckeye is just a big jumble of shadow and moonlight, but I can still make out his unmistakable smile. I get up and slide open the window.

"Good evening," Buckeye whispers, polite as ever. He presses his palms against the screen. "I didn't want to wake you up, but I brought you something. Do you want to come out here?"

I run upstairs, go out the front door and find Buckeye trying to lift himself out of the window well onto the grass. I help him up and say, "Where have you been?"

When Buckeye straightens up and faces me, I get a strong whiff of alcohol and old sweat. He acts like he didn't hear my question. He holds up a finger, indicating for me to wait a moment, and goes to his car, leaning to the right just a little. He comes back with a case of Stroh's and bestows it on me as if it's a red pillow with the crown jewels on top. "This is that beer I owe you," he says, his voice gritty and raw with drink. "I wanted to get you a keg of the good-tasting stuff, but I couldn't find any this late."

We stand in the wet grass and look at each other. His lower lip is split and swollen, his half-ear is a mottled purple and he's got what looks like lipstick smudged on his chin. His boots are muddy and he's wearing the same clothes he had on three days ago.

"Your mother okay?" he says.

"She's fine. They want her to stay in bed a week or so."

"Simone?"

"She's been crying a lot."

For a long time he just stands there, his face gone slack, and looks past me to the dark house. "Everybody asleep in there?"

I look at my watch. It's almost three-thirty in the morning. "I guess so," I say.

Buckeye says, "Hey, let's take a load off. Looks like you're about to drop that beer." We walk over to the porch and sit down on the front steps. I keep the case in my lap, not really knowing what to do with it. Buckeye pulls off two cans, pops them open, hands one to me.

I have the first beer of my life sitting on our front porch with Buckeye. It's warm and sour but not too bad. I feel strange, like I haven't completely come out of sleep. I have so many questions loop-

ing through my brain that I can't concentrate on one long enough
to ask it. Buckeye takes a big breath and looks down into his hands.
"What can I say?" he whispers. "I thought I was getting along fine
and the next thing I know I'm face down in the dirt, right back where
I started from. I can't remember much, but I just let loose. I lost my
strength for just a minute and that's all it takes. For a while there I
didn't even want to behave." He gets up, walks out to the willow tree
and touches its leaves with his fingers, comes back to sit down. "I think
I got ahead of myself. This time I've got to take things slower."

"Are you going somewhere?" I ask. It seems to be the only question that means anything right now.

"I don't know. I'll keep looking for Bud. He's the only brother
I've got that I'm aware of. I've just got to get away, start things over
again."

Not having anything to say, I nod. We have a couple more beers
together and stare into the distance. I want to tell Buckeye about hearing him pray for my mother, thinking it might change something, but I
can't coax out the words. Finally, Buckeye stands up and whacks some
imaginary dust from his pants. "I'd leave a note for Simone and your
folks . . ." he says.

"I'll tell them," I say.

"Lord," Buckeye says. "Damn."

He sticks his big hand out for a shake, a habit he picked up from
the Mormons, and gives me a knuckle-popping squeeze. As he walks
away on the cement path toward his car, the inside of my chest feels as
big as a room and I have an overpowering desire to tackle him, take his
legs out, pay him back for my collarbone, hold him down and tell him
what a goddamned bastard I think he is. This feeling stays with me for
all of five seconds, then bottoms out and leaves me as I was before,
the owner of one long list of emotions: sorry that it had to turn out
this way for everybody; relieved that Buckeye is back to his natural self;
pleased that he came to see me before he left; afraid of what life will be
like without having him around.

Buckeye starts up his battle wagon and instead of just driving
slowly away into the distance, which would probably be the appropriate thing to do under these circumstances, he gets his car going around
in a tight circle, four, five times around in the middle of the quiet street,

muffler rattling, tires squealing and bumping the curb, horn blowing, a hubcap flying into somebody's yard—all for my benefit.

I go into the house before the last rumbles of Buckeye's car die away. I take my case of beer and hide it under my bed, already planning the hell-raising beer party I'll have with some of my friends. I figure it's about time we did something like that. On the way down the stairs, I wobble a little and bump into things, feeling like the whole house is pitching beneath my feet. All at once it hits me that I'm officially roasted. Gratified, I go back upstairs and into my father's den where he keeps the typewriter I've never seen him use.

I feed some paper into the dusty old machine and begin typing. I've decided not to tell anyone about Buckeye's last visit; it will be the final secret between us. Instead, I go to work composing the letter Buckeye would certainly have left had he learned to write. I address it to Simone and just let things flow. I don't really try to imitate Buckeye's voice, but somehow I can feel it coming out in a crusty kind of eloquence. Even though I've always been someone who's highly aware of grammar and punctuation, I let sentence after sentence go by without employing so much as a comma. I tell Simone everything Buckeye could have felt and then some. I tell her how much she means to me and always will. I tell her what a peach she is. I'm shameless, really. I include my parents and thank them for everything, inform them that as far as I'm concerned, no two more Christian people ever walked the earth. I philosophize about goodness and badness and the sweet sorrow of parting. As I type, I imagine my family reading this at the breakfast table and the heartache compressing their faces, emotion rising in them so full that they are choked into speechlessness. This image spurs me on and I clack away on the keys like a single-minded idiot. When I'm finished, I've got two and a half pages and nothing left to say. A little stunned, I sit in my father's chair and strain in the dim light to see what I've just written. Until now, I've never been aware of what being drunk can do for one's writing ability.

I take the letter out on the front porch and tack it to our front door, feeling ridiculously like Martin Luther, charged with conviction and fear. I go back inside and try to go to sleep but I'm restless—the blood inside me is hammering against my ribs and the ends of my fingers, the house is too dark and cramped. Instead of going up the stairs,

I push out my window screen and climb out the well and begin to run around the house, the sun a little higher in the sky every time I come around into the front yard. I feel light-headed and weightless and I run until my lungs are raw, trying to get the alcohol out of my veins before my parents wake up.

CONTRIBUTORS

LEE ALLRED'S award-winning short fiction has appeared in *Asimov's Science Fiction Magazine* and several national-market science-fiction anthologies. He's also written for DC Comics and Image Comics. His most recent publication appeared in *Otherworldly Maine* alongside stories by Stephen King and other top science-fiction and horror authors. "Hymnal" was first published in the anthology *Bones of the World: Tales from Time's End* (SFF Net, 2001).

MATTHEW JAMES BABCOCK teaches writing and literature at BYU-Idaho in Rexburg. He is the recipient of the 2008 Dorothy Sargent Rosenberg Poetry Award and his novella, *Impressions*, was a semi-finalist in *Quarterly West*'s biennial novella contest. His writing has appeared in several literary magazines, including *Alehouse*, *Spillway*, and *Weber Studies*. "The Walker" first appeared in *Dialogue: A Journal of Mormon Thought* (Summer 2006).

PHYLLIS BARBER is the author of a novel, two story collections, two juvenile books, and two memoirs, the latest titled *Raw Edges*, a coming-of-age-in-middle-age memoir to be published by the University of Nevada Press in spring 2010. *How I Got Cultured: A Nevada Memoir* (University of Georgia Press) won the AWP Prize for Creative Nonfiction in 1991 as well as the Association for Mormon Letters Award in Autobiography in 1993. She has taught at the Vermont College of Fine Arts in the writing MFA program since 1991, was one of the cofounders of Utah's Writers at Work conference, and is the proud mother of four sons and grandmother of four grandchildren. Her website is www.phyllisbarber.com. "Bread for Gunnar" is from her collection *Parting the Veil: Stories from a Mormon Imagination* (Signature Books, 1999).

ORSON SCOTT CARD is the author of the novels *Ender's Game, Ender's Shadow,* and *Speaker for the Dead,* which are widely read by adults and younger readers and are increasingly used in schools. Besides these and other science fiction novels, Card writes contemporary fantasy, biblical novels, poetry, and plays and scripts. Card was born in Washington and grew up in California, Arizona, and Utah. He served a mission for the LDS Church in Brazil in the early 1970s. Besides his writing, he teaches occasional classes and workshops and directs plays. He recently began a long-term position as a professor of writing and literature at Southern Virginia University. Card currently lives in Greensboro, North Carolina, with his wife, Kristine Allen Card, and their youngest child, Zina Margaret. "Christmas at Helaman's House" is from his short fiction collection, *Keeper of Dreams* (Tor, 2008).

MARY CLYDE is the author of *Survival Rates* (University of Georgia Press, 1999, and Norton, 2001), a short-story collection that won the Flannery O'Connor Award for Short Fiction in 1997. Her stories have appeared in numerous publications, including the *Georgia Review, Quarterly West, Boulevard,* and *New Stories from the South.* She has taught on the faculty of the Spalding University Master in Fine Arts Writing Program and as a visiting professor in creative writing and literature at Arizona State University. She currently teaches at Grand Canyon University and lives in Phoenix. "Jumping" is from her collection *Survival Rates.*

ARIANNE COPE is author of *The Coming of Elijah* (Parables, 2006), winner of the 2006 Marilyn Brown Novel Award. She is a BYU graduate and former managing editor of *The Tremonton* [Utah] *Leader,* and she currently writes for the *Cedar City* [Utah] *Daily News.* Her short stories, essays, and articles have appeared in numerous regional and national publications, including the *Ensign, Literary Mama, Publisher's Auxiliary,* and *Irreantum.* "White Shell" first appeared in *Dialogue: A Journal of Mormon Thought* (Winter 2005), which gave her a New Voices award for this story.

DARIN COZZENS grew up in Ralston, Wyoming. He has published fiction in *Greensboro Review, Cimarron Review, Weber Studies,* and *Irreantum.* In his seventeen years of teaching, he has worked in Georgia,

Arizona, and, since 2002, at Surry Community College in Dobson, North Carolina. "Light of the New Day" won first place in the 2006 *Irreantum* fiction contest and was first published in that journal's Spring 2007 issue.

LISA TORCASSO DOWNING is an adjunct professor at Collin County Community College, where she teaches freshman composition to "some of the world's most amusing students." She is a graduate of Brigham Young University and received her M.A. in English literature from Texas A&M–Commerce. She presently serves as the fiction editor for both *Irreantum* and *Sunstone*. Her short fiction has appeared in each of these publications, as well as in *Dialogue*, the *New Era*, and the *Friend*. She has been named a winner in the Eugene England Memorial Essay Contest and the Brookie and D.K. Brown Short Fiction Contest. She resides in north Texas with her husband and their three children. "Clothing Esther" originally appeared in *Sunstone* (December 2007) and received the 2007 Association for Mormon Letters Award in Short Fiction.

BRIAN EVENSON is the author of nine books of fiction, most recently the novel *Last Days* and the story collection *Fugue State*. His novel *The Open Curtain* (Coffee House Press) was a finalist for an Edgar Award and an IHG Award and was one of *Time Out New York*'s top books of 2006. Other books include *The Wavering Knife* (which won the IHG Award for best story collection), *Dark Property*, and *The Brotherhood of Mutilation*. He has translated work by Christian Gailly, Jean Frémon, Claro, Jacques Jouet, and others. He has received an O. Henry Prize as well as an NEA fellowship. He lives and works in Providence, Rhode Island, where he directs Brown University's Literary Arts Program. "The Care of the State" was first published in *Irreantum* (Winter 2003/Spring 2004).

ANGELA HALLSTROM is the author of the novel-in-stories *Bound on Earth* (Parables, 2008), which received the Whitney Award for Best Novel by a New Author and the Association for Mormon Letters Award for the Novel in 2008. She received her MFA in fiction from Hamline University and teaches creative writing for Brigham Young University.

She also serves as editor of *Irreantum* magazine and on the editorial board of *Segullah*. She lives in South Jordan, Utah, with her husband and four children. "Thanksgiving" received second place in the Utah Arts Council's Forty-Eighth Annual Writing Competition (short fiction) and first appeared in *Dialogue: A Journal of Mormon Thought* (Spring 2005), where it received *Dialogue*'s Best of the Year Award: Fiction. The story later appeared as the first chapter of *Bound on Earth*.

JACK HARRELL teaches English and creative writing at Brigham Young University–Idaho. His novel *Vernal Promises* won the Marilyn Brown Novel Award in 2000. Jack and his wife, Cindy, live in Rexburg, ID. "Calling and Election" was first published in *Irreantum* (Fall 2007/Spring 2008) and received first place in the 2007 *Irreantum* fiction contest. The story will appear in his next book, a short-story collection forthcoming from Signature Books.

LEWIS HORNE was born and raised in Mesa, Arizona, and received his Ph.D. from the University of Michigan. He is the author of the short-story collections *What Do Ducks Do in Winter?* and *The House of James*, and his award-winning fiction has appeared in *Best American Short Stories* and *Prize Stories: The O. Henry Awards*. Before his retirement, he taught English at the University of Saskatchewan. He and his wife live in Eugene, Oregon. "Healthy Partners" first appeared in *Sunstone* (September 2006) and was the 2003 Brookie & D. K. Brown Fiction Contest's Sunstone (first place) winner.

HELEN WALKER JONES received the Association for Mormon Letters annual short-story award as well as first place in *Sunstone*'s annual fiction competition and *Dialogue*'s fiction prize. She has been first-prize winner in the Utah Arts Council fiction competition, a Pushcart Prize nominee, and a finalist in the Iowa Short Fiction Contest. Her work has appeared in *Harper's*, *Wisconsin Review*, *Gargoyle*, *Richmond Quarterly*, *Florida Review*, *Indiana Review*, *Chariton Review*, *Cimarron Review*, *Apalachee Quarterly*, *Nebraska Review*, and many other journals. She grew up in Alberta but now lives in Salt Lake City with her husband, Walter. "Voluptuous" was the 2005 Brookie & D. K. Brown Fiction Contest's Sunstone (first place) winner and first appeared in *Sunstone* (June 2007).

BRUCE JORGENSEN has taught literature and writing at BYU since 1975. He has published poetry, short fiction, personal essays, criticism, and literary interviews in venues ranging from *Carolina Quarterly*, *Modern Fiction Studies*, and *Western American Literature* to *This People*, *Wasatch Review*, *Ellipsis*, *Black Ridge Review*, *Hotel Amerika*, *New Ohio Review*, and *Irreantum*. His poetry, fiction, and criticism have won awards from the *Ensign*, *Dialogue*, *Sunstone*, the Utah Arts Council, and the Association for Mormon Letters, and he received a Pushcart Prize nomination from *High Plains Literary Review*. "Measures of Music" first appeared in *Dialogue: A Journal of Mormon Thought* (Fall 1999).

LAURA MCCUNE-POPLIN works as an instruction librarian for Emerson College in Boston, where she earned her MFA in creative writing. Additionally, she has taught composition and screenwriting classes for Emmanuel and Emerson Colleges. In her free time, Laura enjoys writing, biking, traveling, and eating good food. She currently lives in Jamaica Plain, Massachusetts, with her husband Dave. "Salvation" first appeared in *Dialogue: A Journal of Mormon Thought* (Winter 2004), which gave her a New Voices award for this story.

LARRY MENLOVE'S stories have appeared in *Weber Studies*, *42opus*, *Dialogue*, *Storyglossia*, and other publications. He is the 2008 winner of the *Irreantum* Fiction Contest. He lives in Spring Lake, Utah, with his "lovely wife, some smart kids, pets, and whatever fowl and critters drop by unannounced." "Who Brought Forth This Christmas Demon" first appeared in *Dialogue: A Journal of Mormon Thought* (Fall 2008).

COKE NEWELL, a convert to The Church of Jesus Christ of Latter-day Saints in his late teens, has published fiction and nonfiction work in newspapers, magazines, books, and film. Formally trained in journalism and public relations, he spent more than a decade as an LDS Church media relations officer in Salt Lake City and today teaches rhetorical communication at the University of Saint Francis in Ft. Wayne, Indiana. His autobiographical novel *On the Road to Heaven* (Zarahemla Books, 2007) won the Association for Mormon Letters Award for the Novel and the Whitney Award for Best Novel in 2007. "Trusting Lilly" originally appeared in *Dialogue: A Journal of Mormon Thought* (Fall 2004).

TODD ROBERT PETERSEN was born and raised in the Pacific Northwest. He studied film and English and now teaches creative writing and visual studies at Southern Utah University. *Long After Dark* (Zarahemla Books, 2007), his collection of short stories and a novella, received an ARTYS Award from *Salt Lake City Weekly*. His novel *Rift* (Zarahemla Books, 2009) was awarded the Marilyn Brown Novel Award. Petersen lives in Cedar City, Utah, with his wife and two children. "Quietly" was originally published under the title "The Sad Truth of His Desire" in *Sunstone* (July 2002) and later appeared in *Long After Dark*.

LEVI PETERSON is retired as a professor of English from Weber State University in Ogden, Utah. Among his publications are two collections of short stories, *The Canyons of Grace* and *Night Soil*, the novel *The Backslider*, and the autobiography *A Rascal by Nature, A Christian by Yearning*. He and his wife, Althea, presently live in Issaquah, Washington. "Brothers" was first published in *Dialogue: A Journal of Mormon Thought* (Summer 2003).

PAUL RAWLINS lives in Salt Lake City and presently works as the editor at large for *Ancestry* magazine. His short fiction has appeared in a number of journals and magazines, including *Epoch, Glimmer Train, Tampa Review, Irreantum*, and *Confrontation*. His story collection, *No Lie Like Love* (University of Georgia Press, 1997), won the Flannery O'Connor Award in 1996. "The Garden" originally appeared in *Image: Art, Faith, Mystery* (Spring 2008); reprinted by permission.

KAREN ROSENBAUM, a retired college English teacher, writes short fiction, personal essays, and articles, many of which have appeared in periodicals and anthologies. She and her husband (and bird watching companion), Ben McClinton, live in Kensington, California. "Out of the Woods" was first published in *Dialogue: A Journal of Mormon Thought* (Spring 2002).

LISA MADSEN RUBILAR'S fiction, essays, and poetry have appeared in several journals and magazines, including *Dialogue: A Journal of Mormon Thought, Exponent II, Wasatch Review International, Brick, Publisher's Weekly, Timber Creek Review*, and *The Carolina Quarterly*. She holds a bachelor's degree from Brigham Young University and an MFA from Vermont College of Fine Arts. Her work was selected by the Vermont College faculty to represent the school in the national Best New American Voices contest and the Association of Writers and Writing Programs (AWP) Intro Awards. She lives with her family in Niskayuna, New York, and is currently teaching and working on a novel. "Obbligato" was a finalist in the 2007 *Hunger Mountain* fiction contest judged by Wally Lamb (under the title "My Mother's Kitchen").

ERIC SAMUELSEN is a playwright, a theatre director, a college professor, and a sometime essayist and fiction writer. After graduating in playwriting from BYU, he earned a Ph.D. in dramatic literature and criticism from Indiana University and subsequently joined the faculty at the BYU Department of Theatre and Media Arts in 1992. His plays include *Gadianton, The Way We're Wired, Family*, and *A Love Affair with Electrons*. He served from 2007 to 2009 as president of the Association for Mormon Letters. Eric is married, with four children. "Miracle" first appeared in *Dialogue: A Journal of Mormon Thought* (Summer 2005).

DARRELL SPENCER teaches at Ohio University. He has published five books: four story collections and a novel. He lives with his wife, Kate, who is an artist and writer. "Blood Work" is from his collection *Caution: Men in Trees* (University of Georgia Press, 2000, and Norton, 2002), which won the Flannery O'Connor Award for Short Fiction and the Association for Mormon Letters Award for Short Fiction in 2000.

DOUGLAS THAYER is married to Donlu DeWitt. They have six children and an increasing number of grandchildren. Doug grew up in Provo during the thirties and forties. He dropped out of high school at seventeen to join the army, serving in Germany during the occupation, later returning there as a missionary. He did a B.A. at BYU, an M.A. at Stanford, and an MFA at the University of Iowa, and has taught in the BYU English Department since 1957. Doug writes primarily Mormon fiction. He has published three novels, two collections of short stories, one memoir, and stories and personal essays in literary journals. His prizes include the Karl G. Maeser Creative Arts Award, the Association for Mormon Letters Prize in the Novel, the *Dialogue* prize for the short story, the Utah Fine Arts Award for a Collection of Short Stories, and the Smith-Pettit Award for his contributions to Mormon literature. "Wolves" was first published in *Dialogue: A Journal of Mormon Thought* (Summer 2003).

STEPHEN TUTTLE'S short stories have appeared in many national literary journals, including *The Gettysburg Review, Hayden's Ferry Review, Black Warrior Review,* and *Crazyhorse.* A graduate of the creative writing program at the University of Utah, he currently teaches fiction writing at Brigham Young University. "The Weather Here" was originally published in *Indiana Review* (26.2) and was the winner of the 2003 *Indiana Review* fiction prize.

BRADY UDALL is the author of *Letting Loose the Hounds, The Miracle Life of Edgar Mint,* and *The Lonely Polygamist,* which is forthcoming from W. W. Norton. He lives with his family in Boise, Idaho. "Buckeye the Elder" is from his collection *Letting Loose the Hounds* (Norton, 1997).

MARGARET BLAIR YOUNG is the author of two short-story collections and six novels, three of the novels coauthored with Darius Gray. She has also written several plays, two of which have been produced. Within the past decade, she has specialized in writing about African-Americans in the West and has authored two encyclopedia entries as well as numerous scholarly articles. She and Darius Gray recently completed a documentary titled *Nobody Knows: The Untold Story of Black Mormons.* Ms. Young teaches creative writing at Brigham Young University. "Zoo Sounds" is from her collection *Love Chains* (Signature Books, 1997).

CPSIA information can be obtained at www.ICGtesting.com
Printed in the USA
BVOW03s1348101213

338679BV00006B/104/P